AN ANGEL PASSING OVER

By the same author

THE MOON IS MY WITNESS
MIDNIGHT'S SMILING
GREEN BAIZE ROAD

ALEXANDRA CONNOR

An Angel Passing Over

HarperCollins*Publishers*

This novel is a work of fiction. The names, characters and incidents portrayed in it are the work of the author's imagination. Any resemblance to actual persons, living or dead, is entirely coincidental.

HarperCollins*Publishers*
77–85 Fulham Palace Road,
Hammersmith, London W6 8JB

Published by HarperCollins*Publishers* 2000
1 3 5 7 9 8 6 4 2

A catalogue record for this book
is available from the British Library

ISBN 0 00 225935 4

Typeset in Sabon by Palimpsest Book Production Limited,
Polmont, Stirlingshire

Printed and bound in Great Britain by
Omnia Books Limited, Glasgow

This book is dedicated to Diana MacLellan –
an angel who has passed over many lives and
enriched them all . . .

PART ONE

Look in my face; my name is Might-have-been;

DANTE GABRIEL ROSSETTI
'The House of Life'

Prologue

Oldham, Lancashire – 1910

No one went down Miller Lane, except in twos. The police had long since tried to clean the place up; but poverty and crime had been living there too long to be enemies easily defeated. Of the twenty-two houses on the terrace – euphemistically referred to as a lane – only ten were still occupied, the others boarded up and empty. Number 15 was rumoured to be haunted by old Albert Harris; people had reported seeing a light in an upper window when there was no one there. But nobody went to look.

Dora had no choice but to go down Miller Lane. She'd even been born there. One of five offspring, she had helped her mother look after the smaller children since she was ten. They came fast; her father in the Navy, intermittently coming home for a few days with presents and rough hugs. He liked to play with the kids but got bored easily, catching hold of his wife and making whistling noises between his big teeth. Dora would watch her mother smile distantly, her father – accent thick from Glasgow parents – jerking his head to tell her to clear off for a while.

Dora knew there would be another baby nine months later. Another brother or sister, another mewling child sleeping with her mother, the others all piled into one old double bed in the partitioned off portion of the bedroom.

There was no privacy: she could hear her parents making love when her father was home, and she could also hear him relieving himself into the chamber pot, kept under the bed. The same one everyone used – except for the youngest children, who were still in nappies.

Awake early, Dora would roll over onto her back, daydreaming up at the ceiling, careful not to wake her siblings in the bed next to her. She would have a nice house one day – one with a separate room just for her. She would have a brush and comb all to herself, and clothes that no one else had worn before. Shoes too . . . Her eyes would fix on the window, covered over with an old blanket. Her mother said that they should be grateful that her father was working. Most of the men round here were unemployed, she said almost proudly, half of them thieves.

Dora didn't feel that she had to be grateful for anything. It was ridiculous, like saying that someone drowning should be glad they had something to drink. She hated Miller Lane, hated the reaction in people's eyes when she told them where she lived. *Miller Lane,* their expressions said. *Must be villains; the kid's probably a bastard. Aren't they all down there?*

It was true, the villains down Miller Lane far outnumbered the honest men, but her father wasn't a crook – just unlucky, feckless with the little money he made. Ill-educated. Ignorant.

So when, one spring morning when her father was home, Dora asked if she could stay on at school, there was hell to pay.

'You have to work and earn your keep,' her father said sharply, rolling a cigarette with cheap tobacco kept in a tin on the shelf over the kitchen range. 'I was out to work at fourteen and if it was good enough for me –'

4

'But I want to learn –'

He cut her off automatically. What the hell was she thinking of?

'Dora, you'll go to work like your mother did when she were your age. Our sort have to work.' His tone softened. He was trying to be kind, she realized incredulously. 'Look, you'll get married one day and have kids, then you'll stay at home, have your husband support you.'

Of course Dora knew she was beaten; there was no point trying to argue or reason. She had nothing to reason with. All she wanted was to learn, to use the brain she knew she had. But there was no chance of that. The mill called, didn't it? The mill with the mill girls – all poor, but none of the others coming from Miller Lane. She would set off in the mornings and bring home her wages on a Friday and her mother would keep house and buy food, and before long people would start asking Dora if she was courting. There would be a boy, perhaps kind, and he would come to walk her out, and before long Dora would marry him. They would live in one of the myriad two-up, two-downs and then in very little time she would start breeding.

The image shattered her, and she glanced away. Her ambitions had been ridiculous. She came from the poor and would stay within the poor. There was no way she would escape her fate. It seemed to Dora that it was also her duty. Such a tiny life, she thought resentfully, such a wasted tiny life.

'Come on,' her father said, trying to jolly her along, 'things could be worse.'

How? she wondered, glancing back over to the window as a boy ran past after a mongrel dog. On the pavement opposite a child, no more than three, sat on the cobbles in a soiled nappy. Dora's gaze moved over to old man Harris's house – number 15 – and she wondered if his ghost really did live there. She wondered too if life was any different after death; if a person got to choose. But who would *choose* to stay in Miller Lane, to spend eternity in a two-up, two-down, a place which had been riddled with rats one summer? The council men had come and baited traps. Trouble was, the traps hadn't always been humane, and some of the rats had escaped injured. There had been reports of three babies bitten in Miller Lane alone. Two had died.

Dora could feel her throat tighten. Would she choke to death on her disappointment? And how would she ever manage to live here as the only one who could see just how foul it all was? Her head drooped. Her life was mapped out.

Then suddenly she felt her temper flare. She *would* marry, that was true, and she *would* have children. But they wouldn't ever live in Miller Lane. *She* might have to lose, but her children wouldn't. Her children would be able to walk anywhere and talk to anyone. Ignorance was not going to down them; she would see to it that they were educated so that they could get out. Out of the terraces; out of the cheap streets; away from the rats and the filth and the sour humility of their class.

'Dora?' her father asked.

'What is it?'

'You're not minding too much 'bout leaving school? It's just the way life is, luv. You have to learn to live with it.'

She smiled as though she agreed. But in her heart she knew that living with it was the last thing she was going to do.

Chapter One

1915

Heavily Dora rose to her feet and moved over to the kitchen range. Nine months gone, she thought, the baby due any time.

With a resolution which had surprised everyone in Miller Lane. Dora had obediently gone to work in the mill. Whilst there, she had saved what little money she could, then refused the first man who asked her to marry him – and the second.

'Don't be so bloody choosy,' her father had told her. 'You might not keep being asked. You're hardly a catch, are you? Looks aren't everything, girl. A pretty face don't count when you haven't a pot to piss in.'

But Dora didn't see it that way. Whatever her father said, she *was* a catch – and she would prove it. Besides, she wasn't going to settle for any man who thought Miller Lane was all right. Len Billings might have all the girls running after him and be able to charm a clam out of its shell, but what was he? A rat-catcher, a man who went round with traps on his belt and gloves as thick as armour plating.

'Stops me getting bit,' he'd explained to her once. 'I were faced with a rat the size of a small dog the other day. Had it in a corner, and I should have known better. You never corner a rat. Well, it turned round when it knew it were down to me and him, he looked me right in the bloody eyes and then jumped.' Len had paused for effect. 'Right over my shoulder. Jesus, I thought it were going for m' throat.'

Dora knew that some of the other girls revelled in Len Billings' tales with a mixture of excitement and horror, but to her they represented everything she wanted to escape. A rat-catcher for a husband? No, not her. She might not have much to offer, but she was better than that.

However, it was a pity that she found herself thinking a little too much about Len's quick smile, and remembering a little too vividly the sharp blue of his eyes, and the curly hair. She might be logical about Len's lack of prospects, but he had been around a long time and had made his feelings all too plain to be easily ignored. Over the years he had repeatedly teased her, flirted with her – always ignoring the other girls when Dora was about. Her indifference had acted like a magnet, and sometimes – not that she would ever admit it – Len Billings had stamped into Dora's dreams and made her wake, damp with shame. But Dora was too smart to let herself be carried away. Her heart wasn't going to overrule *her* head. She knew only too well that sexual attraction wouldn't get her out of Miller Lane.

After Len Billings, Ernest Feathershaw followed, and then Ernest Feathershaw went. A year passed, Dora still working in the mill, and waiting for her husband to appear. In the meantime she continued to help her mother bring up the other children, but when her father gave up the sea and got the job down the gasworks the house became suddenly oppressively crowded. Her mother, worn down and worn out, didn't comment, but it was obvious what her parents were thinking –

8

Dora's a passenger. She should marry and get a home of her own.

'You should think a bit more about Ernest,' her mother told her one day, bashing washing in a dolly tub, her sleeves rolled up above the sturdy forearms. 'He's a good man.'

The pressure was on. Dora knew it, felt it, saw it in her mother's eyes. *Why would you want to stay here when you could be mistress of your own home?* But how could Dora explain? How could she say: Len Billings and Ernest Feathershaw aren't good enough? I'm waiting for someone better, someone who doesn't eat tripe, who doesn't spit in the street. Someone who never had to take in the doctor's washing to pay for a visit.

'I'll find the right man.'

'The town's full of old maids who said the same,' her mother mumbled, not unkindly. 'Dora, don't be too picky.'

There it was again – as if she had nothing to offer a decent man. Don't be choosy, don't be picky. Don't get big ideas.

Then that summer Arthur Ellis came calling. A widower, he lived in Diggle, Upper Mill, in one of the cottages which verged on the moors. A cottage with a little garden and, better than that, Arthur had a shop on the High Street. A proper shop with his name over the window: 'Arthur Ellis – Greengrocer'.

A few months before, Dora had caught a bus up to Diggle and, smoothing down her well-brushed but well-used dress, had walked around the village. She didn't know what had prompted her to go there; it had been a whim. But she had got on the bus and paid her fare and watched as they climbed out of Oldham and into the clean winding streets of Diggle.

9

Terraced cottages snuggled together for warmth against the hillside, a few farms pitched high above the slate roofs. There were some poorer streets, but they were tucked away out of sight, like senile relatives at a party. On view had been the nestle of donkey-stoned front steps and the lure of white lace curtains. In one or two windows Dora had even noted bunches of flowers, and in another, a child had watched her pass, a blonde child with a bow in her hair. Well fed, well kept, not the rough-arsed kids from Miller Lane.

What would it be like to live here? Dora had wondered. A person would really think she had arrived. Living here, a person could write her address without shame, could hold her head up . . . When she got off the bus she'd found herself fascinated by the cobbles. They had been clean and swept, no slimy skirting of rubbish or spittle marking the walls. Then she had made her way up to the Heights and, taking in a breath, she'd looked down over Oldham, stretched out before her.

The Diggle air had been cold and clean, without smog, the sky rid of the sullen overhang in the streets below. Breathing in deeply again, Dora had marked out the boundaries of the town before her, recognizing church spires and the numerous mill chimneys. A mill for every day of the year. A mill on every street, their chimneys throwing long shadows down the narrow terraces.

She had wanted to stay up there for ever, away and above Oldham, with the clean little village of Diggle around her. But finally Dora had walked back to the High Street to wait for the bus to take her home. Then, tempted by the fruit in Arthur Ellis's shop, she had wandered over to his window and looked in.

The produce was far too expensive for her. Any fruit

Dora's family ate was brought off Tommy Field's market. For as long as Dora could remember there had been a Tommy Field's. It used to be called Curzon Ground, then became – how, no one was sure – Tommy Fields. Fairs had been held there and many a riotous public meeting, until the market stalls took over the place in the 1830s.

Since then, there hadn't been a poor family in the district who hadn't got food or clothing off the paraffin-lit stalls. The men stood for long hours, calling out prices and chatting up the housewives, the nickname 'barkers' describing the hoarse calls they made.

'Who'll give me a penny? A ha'penny? Come on, ladies, the old man will never know.'

Others favoured a more aggressive approach.

'What am I asking for this dolly tub? Sixpence? No! Thruppence? No! I'm feeling good-hearted today. Like this lady down the front – looks like she's got no complaints at home! What about tuppence? Yes, tuppence!'

There would be a rush for the tubs, but more often than not those they took home weren't quite like the tub the barker had been banging his hand on. They leaked. Some of the clothes stalls were the same. You bought a shirt and when you washed it one sleeve came out longer than the other. You couldn't complain, though.

When you went back the stall had gone, or someone else was there.

Dora had sighed to herself, looking into Arthur Ellis's shop window. It was so inviting, each little red apple in its own tissue pocket, the grapes moist and glowing with juice. Her fingers had tingled with a desire to reach out and touch the fruit, wondering how someone could have enough money to pile it high in a bowl.

If she could afford to do that she would never eat it, just look at it, like a bouquet of flowers.

'Can I help you?'

Dora had jumped, startled by the man beside her in his clean white apron.

'I was just looking,' she'd heard herself say with as much composure as she could muster.

But it didn't fool him – Dora had known that at once. He had seen that she was poor, just *looking*. Always looking, without being able to join in. Taking in a deep breath Dora had then walked into the shop, the man following her. She had some money – if she walked home and saved the bus fare she could afford it. So Dora had spent the last of her money on two glowing red apples, wrapped in blue tissue paper, Arthur Ellis putting them into a bag for her and wondering just who the striking young woman was.

They had talked that afternoon, Dora trying to sound intelligent and wondering repeatedly if Mr Ellis had noticed just how shabby her dress was. Pulling her shawl over her shoulders to cover a darn on the sleeve, Dora had smiled, flattered by the attention of this respectable man. Oh, Arthur Ellis might not have Len Billings' looks, but he was a cut above the rest, and a couple of notches up from Miller Lane.

Further visits had followed. Dora was invited to tea and she had accepted, knowing instinctively that Arthur Ellis was a gentleman. A slight man, wearing glasses and always dressed neatly, Arthur had been alone for ten years. He had no family, no children, and, although he knew many people, he had no intimate friends. He was a reclusive, solitary man who found Dora a good listener.

At first, he had simply liked the look of her, the frank

intelligence in her face and her straightforward manner – but he had been put off by her background – until he got to know her a little better and realized that she was nobody's fool. Not one of the usual slatternly women off Miller Lane.

Diffidently, over the weeks which followed, Arthur had begun to talk to her about politics and about the war, which seemed imminent, and Dora had listened to him, admiring the well-to-do voice and his well-worn but smart clothes. Soon he had asked her if they could go out for a walk and before long they saw each other most days. Her interest had flattered him. He wasn't that young and had never been good-looking, yet she seemed to like him.

She had a good brain too, and was a quick learner. Questions came easily to Dora and answers came even easier to Arthur. Having had little to do with anyone for a decade, he'd found himself starting to look forward to seeing her, and then after a couple of months, he'd been unable to imagine living without her. He would have liked to explain his feelings, but he was shy and Dora had to coax emotion from him.

Their first kiss had been a disaster – but what did that matter really? Dora asked herself. She didn't need passion that much, she needed someone to admire, someone who didn't look down on her. *Someone who needed her*. So before much longer, Arthur had put aside his reservations, Dora had suppressed her desires, and when he'd proposed she had accepted.

She said *I will* to him, and to his house and his shop. *I will*, to the step up in the world. *I will*, to the way out of deprivation and defeat. If Dora had ever wondered what the future held for her she had suppressed any doubts. Arthur Ellis would make a good husband and a good father. He had savings and she had ambition. How could they fail?

Now Dora sighed at the memory. She was exhausted by her pregnancy. She should bank up the fire, but she was too tired to go out to the coal hole in the back yard. Arthur would do it when he came home. Closing her eyes, Dora leaned back in her chair, her hands spread over her distended stomach.

Well, living with Arthur had turned out to be quite a lot more than she'd bargained for. After their marriage, he had continued to be kind, thoughtful, caring, not exactly passionate – but that was more for the likes of Len Billings than Arthur Ellis. Yet there was also a huge change in Arthur. It was as though something had shifted in him: his heart as thoroughly sprung as one of Len's traps. A decade of loneliness had terrified Arthur, but it was only when he'd married Dora, when she was finally ensconced in his home, that he'd been able to express his relief. He was devoted to her – unusually – from the beginning, proud of her, never once mentioning Miller Lane and her background.

He'd even visited home with her in the first months they were married. But Dora's father had been awkward with him and her mother always busy with the other children, too busy to talk. At first Dora had resented their coldness, and then she'd realized that they were awed by Arthur. He was their superior, someone they would never normally talk to. Arthur's shop was too expensive for Dora's mother, and his accent – well-modulated and precise – made theirs sound ill bred.

So before long Dora had visited Oldham alone and gradually – after she had asked her parents repeatedly to visit her in Diggle – they had drifted apart. There had been no animosity from her parents; she had done well and they were proud of her. But she was a stranger now, confounding their predictions. Dora had got above herself – and way above them.

When Dora became pregnant, she'd hoped the news might restore some warmth between her and her parents, but it was only partially successful. They'd congratulated her, of course, but still felt their daughter was too good for them and kept their distance.

The only trouble was that many other people kept their distance too. If Arthur could forget where his wife came from, his acquaintances couldn't. Diggle was very contained, the families upright, respectable. No one – except for the Highleys and the Strattons – was rich, but no one was dirt poor either.

Perched high up, Diggle was a crisp little enclave looking down its nose at its industrial neighbour, its rigid little back to the moors. All strangers were frowned upon, and strangers from Miller Lane were regarded with discreet suspicion. There were no slums in Diggle, no workhouses had ever existed there. It might be only a bus ride from Oldham, but its inhabitants had little to do with the rough life down in the valley.

They were – quite literally – a cut above the slum-dwellers, clawing their genteel way up the landscape to the bleak cold Heights, just above the stench of the chimneys below. There were no pubs throwing out drunks late at night, no kids sent to ask for their fathers and standing, cold in the doorway, until he finally emerged. There were no uninvestigated screams in the early hours, or quarrels, or fist fights. There wasn't that much room in the Diggle houses, but people didn't sleep six to a bed and in the summer the streets didn't stew with the stench from the glue works, tempers flaring amongst the odour of bodies and booze and dirt.

Dora had never wondered what life would be like away from Oldham; certainly had never realized that her neighbours would see her as an upstart. And yet what could she expect? She had loathed Miller Lane herself; now away from it she viewed it with horror – just as everyone else did. Except that they hadn't been born there.

There was nothing to be done about it, Dora thought calmly, sitting straighter to ease her back. No one could change their past and when the baby was born it would be born in Diggle. The child wouldn't have to shoulder what she had to; it would begin life with a head start. If it had her ambitions it might end up in a detached house on the coast somewhere . . . Dora smiled to herself. What wasn't possible? If you could dream it, you could live it. She had.

A sudden sharp pain made her grip her stomach and lurch forwards. Another followed as Dora staggered to the door to call for help, her waters breaking as she did so. Unexpectedly afraid, she pulled open the front door and tried to scream, but instead the world turned over before her eyes and she plummeted heavily to earth.

Chapter Two

Nine years later

It was very cold, ice on the outside of the window, the only fire burning downstairs in the kitchen. Dressing hurriedly, Grace pulled her coat over her clothes and paused on the little square landing. She could hear her father's breathing, sonorous and uneven, the occasional mumbled cough barking into the sharp air. She knew full well that her mother would have kept him warm, banked up the bed with blankets and put a stone bottle on his feet. Carefully she would turn him and then later, when she had come back from the shop, she would sit by the bedside and tell him about the customers.

Arthur had had a stroke seven months ago. The doctor had told her mother that in time, he might well recover, but he would never be strong. Speech would be the last to return – speech, the one thing which had glued her parents together. Memory, acid and shocking, came back to Grace in a rush. The shouting of her mother, the calling for the doctor in the early hours of a summer day. Birds had been singing outside his window, but Arthur had been on his back, unspeaking, unmoving, rigid as a felled tree.

Fear had left Grace shaking at the bedroom door, the doctor leaning down to talk to her.

'You'll have to help your mother out now, my dear. You'll be a tower of strength, I know you will.'

She had looked up at him. 'Is Father going to die?'

'No, no,' he reassured her. 'He's not well, but he'll get better in time.'

He hadn't said how much time. Just time. And time, Grace knew, was different for everyone. Before her father had had his stroke, time was plentiful for her. The indulged child of a father who adored her, the daughter of a mother who was always strict. Times without number Dora had corrected Grace's speech, pushing out the flat Northern vowels, and reminding her that she was going to be a lady someday.

The shop had provided just enough money for Grace to be sent to the best school in the area, and every morning her mother walked her there, and every afternoon, Dora was at the gate to see her home. No child was ever listened to more avidly, praised more thoroughly, reprimanded more readily.

For as long as she could remember, Grace had been told she was special, she had a future to prepare for. If she lapsed, she was rebuked by her mother. If she triumphed, she was praised. If she was ever lazy, she was taught a lesson. One of those lessons Grace would never forget . . .

One day – without explanation or preparation – Dora took her daughter on a trip. They climbed on a bus and slowly wound down the Heights, leaving Diggle and going down, down into the soot streets. Finally they got off when they entered the backstreets of Oldham.

Surprised, Grace looked around her. Automatically she hung back as she watched the shabby children playing in the streets, hopscotch printed on the flagstones, a man smoking a pipe at an open door. Voices, raucous and high-pitched, came out into the fetid air, the cobbles smeared with dog muck, a blocked drain pooling dirty water in the acrid August heat.

Her head held high, Dora took her child's hand and walked on, ignoring comments and passing everyone as though they weren't there. Finally, she stopped when they reached Miller Lane.

Its grim terrace was dirtier than Dora remembered, the roof of number 15 finally fallen in, old man Harris's ghost exposed to the elements.

Dora's parents no longer lived in Miller Lane. Her mother had died and her father now lived with his youngest daughter in Salford. The other children had married or moved, one brother killed in the war, another serving time in Strangeways for theft.

Grace continued to hang back behind her mother as Dora walked towards her old home, calling Grace after her.

'See this house?'

Grace nodded, sun on her back, a group of jeering children watching the strangers.

'This was where I was born,' Dora said simply.

Thoughtfully the little girl regarded the grim doorway, pigeon droppings smearing the upper windowsill. She was thinking of her home. It was small – even to a child's eyes – but cosy, the kitchen window looking out over the tended garden to the moors beyond. Seasons changed under her window, snows coming early, and then spring warmth chasing the blossom into hurried bloom.

Her home smelled of fresh air, clean linen, soap. Food was nourishing, on time, served in simple but matching crockery. Before eating Arthur would always say grace, his head bowed, his scalp showing through the thin hair, his eyes closed behind glasses. They had books too, not that many but some *National Geographic* issues and a *Family Doctor*. Grace had stolen a look inside when her parents weren't around and then slammed the book shut, startled by the photograph of a burned child.

The man coughed from the doorway to their right, then spat out into the street. The spittle landed only a yard from Dora's feet, but she seemed impervious to it, holding onto her daughter's hand as she bent down to her.

'Look, sweetheart.' Grace was surprised by the term of endearment. Her mother was not indulgent. 'I want you to remember this place because I won't bring you here again – and I don't ever want you to come here of your own choice. Or be *forced* here.' Her voice had a persuasive tone. 'I dreamed of getting out of here and I did. I wanted more than this, and I got it. But it cost me, Grace. It cost me.'

Dora straightened up for a moment and looked about her. Grace stared at her mother, not knowing what to say. For the first time in her life she saw Dora vulnerable. She might talk calmly, but her mother's hand was gripping hers with real force, and Grace could see her mother swallow repeatedly.

What was the matter, Grace wondered, alarmed. Was she ill? Or frightened? It certainly was a place to be frightened of, Grace decided, wondering with horror if they had to stay. She wanted to run away back to Diggle and her father, but then her mother leaned down to her again, her voice low.

'Remember,' she commanded the child, 'this is what life is for some people. It was my life for a while, but it's not yours, Grace. Your father and I both want a good life for you. And you can do it. You've got a quick brain and a pretty face.' She touched her child's cheek, uncharacteristically demonstrative. 'I want you to think of Miller Lane as the place you run from. It's your nightmare, Grace, the last street on earth you want to be. Remember it – but never return.'

With that, Dora straightened up again and turned. Automatically Grace fell into step with her, the boys jeering loudly from the end of the street.

But Grace wasn't listening to them, all she could hear was the phrases repeated over and over in her mind like a drum roll. *Miller Lane is the place you run from. It's your nightmare . . . Remember it – but never return.*

Shivering, Grace's thoughts came back to the present as she moved downstairs. Her mother had made the porridge the previous night. Something Arthur could easily swallow for breakfast. Something he wouldn't gag on, or throw back.

Although her father had made some progress since his stroke, it was achingly slow. Speech was coming back, but it was intermittent, conversation as staccato as Morse code.

Grace missed him. Missed the way he used to read to her when she came home from school. Missed the wave from the top of the street, or through the greengrocer's window when she passed. Every Sunday her father had cleaned the windows of the shop, ready for the coming week, starting out early every morning to get the best vegetables from the market.

People came to her father's shop from all round; even the nobs on Queen's Road. He had been proud of his little kingdom, and fiercely protective of it. Too old to fight in the war, Arthur had given all his spare time to the war effort, growing what he could in the back garden, helping his elderly neighbours with theirs, and just eking a living on what supplies he could muster.

Both Dora and Arthur thought that Grace didn't know, but whilst she'd been at school her mother had gone down to one of the posh houses to do sewing and washing for them. The money she'd earned had been put with her husband's and hidden in an old tin behind a loose brick in the coal hole outside.

But the hard times had stopped after the war and things had settled down again. The shop had soon reverted to its old prominence, Arthur setting aside some money as soon as he could and forbidding Dora ever to work again. Everything had been set fair – and then Arthur had his stroke.

The shop was run by Dora now. Every day, early, she would make Arthur his breakfast and settle him for the morning. Then she would go to work and check the food stuff for the day, delivered by a wholesaler from Manchester. At lunchtime, she would call home, feed and – at the beginning – wash her husband. Then she would return to the shop and stay until closing time. After that, she would repeat the same routine and late, very late, fall into bed and sleep like an old horse.

In the first sodden weeks after the stroke, Arthur had been almost totally incapacitated, unable to relieve himself or wash. Dora had done everything for him then, without complaint, as though it was just something that happened to everyone. One other thing to take in her impressive stride. But although she never said anything, before long it was obvious that Dora was exhausted. The broken nights, early risings and the eternal washing – not to mention the running of the shop – would have taxed an Amazon. And Dora had no help – at home *or* in the shop.

Although she was only a child Grace was very susceptible to her mother's feelings. The bond between them was not one of open affection, but something deeper. So as Dora grew wearier Grace knew instinctively that her mother would rather drop in her tracks than look for aid from anyone. Anyone outside the family, that is. But *inside* . . .

Grace had made her plan the night before and now she had woken and got up – for the first time rising before her mother. From the other side of the door she could hear her parents breathing, and glanced at the clock as she lit the gas. Six o'clock.

Grace filled the old kettle and set it on the range, putting on the porridge to heat up. Then she cut some clumsy pieces of bread and poured a little milk into two cups. Finally she took down a large towel from the clothes rail over the kitchen range and laid it on the tray set out in front of her – just as she had seen her mother do.

'Morning.'

She jumped at the sound of her mother's voice.

Dora walked into the kitchen and looked at the laid-out tray. Words wouldn't come, instead she felt an unexpected desire to cry. Her child had done this; her Grace. Without being asked, she had assumed responsibility; seen that she was needed. It wasn't difficult for Dora to remember how she had helped her own mother but that had been Miller Lane, and the dependants had been her own brothers and sisters. Not a fifty-year-old man.

Slowly she walked over to the tray. What could she say to her daughter? Dora pretended to check the objects set out. Grace was so young, only nine years old. Dora hadn't wanted her to grow up so soon; had wanted her to have the childhood Dora had never enjoyed. But circumstances were going to force Grace into adulthood. Nothing her mother could do could stop it.

'You did a good job,' she said at last, and Grace flushed with pleasure.

Dora wanted to take hold of her child and hug her, to stroke her hair and praise her. But she couldn't. Life was hard; she would do her child no favours if she made her soft. Her father could do that. It was Dora's job to make her daughter resilient. A fighter. A person who could cope with whatever happened in life.

Carefully Dora picked up the tray and moved to the door. Then she paused and, turning back to Grace, said simply, 'Why?'

'I wanted to help you.'

Dora nodded. 'Your father will get better, you know.'

'I know.'

'He'll get well, in time.'

A moment stretched out its arms between them.

'In the meantime, we need each other,' Dora said evenly. 'I need your help. Can you help me?'

My mother is asking me for help! Grace thought proudly. She needed her. Her mother – the handsome, strong, fearless Dora Ellis – *needed her*.

Pride filled Grace and made her almost giddy. There and then, her future character was made.

Chapter Three

Five years passed, taking Grace to the age of fourteen. She had inherited little from her father, but was – everyone agreed – unmistakably Dora's child. Her figure was erect, as she had been taught, and her diction was accentless. Soft chestnut hair surrounded an intelligent oval face, her eyes deep set, smoky grey. She was tall for her age, her figure already showing signs of her mother's statuesque curves. Looking at Grace Ellis it was difficult to see her as a child; she appeared mature, mentally and physically.

Some said it was because of being brought up so strictly by her mother. 'Stuck up bitch,' the Miller Lane residents referred to Dora bitterly. 'Besides, that Len Billings has been bragging about how he went up to see Dora only the other week. He could be lying, but then again . . . The older Diggle inhabitants were no less scathing, if less crude – You can take a girl out of the slums, but you can't take the slums out of the girl.'

In the past Arthur had had his misgivings about the way Dora was bringing up Grace too, but he had never mentioned them. Instead he realized that Dora had the last say on everything. And after he had his stroke there was nothing he *could* say. He could just watch as Dora took over their child completely. Nothing was too good for Grace. She was to have the best they could afford, and Dora's constant mantra was: 'If you believe it, you can live it.'

Their daughter was not going to help out in the

greengrocery shop, biding her time until she married. No, Grace was going to make her mark in the world – whether she liked it or not. It wasn't to be her choice, Arthur realized uncomfortably; Dora was going to sort it all out in advance.

The pity of it was that Arthur had planned to talk to his wife about her pushing Grace but, silenced by his sudden illness, he had never achieved the conversation. Instead he saw – not long after his stroke – his daughter assume some of the responsibility for looking after him. Speech was difficult, leapfrogging back into normality, Grace patient, waiting to understand. He wanted to say, 'Get out and play with your friends. Act your age, Grace. Be a child whilst you still can.' But the words – accurate in his head – came out like a lunatic's and made him burn with frustration. He was dependent, and worse than that, he was dependent on his wife *and child*. God, Arthur thought helplessly, who would have believed it?

He had thought himself so lucky to meet Dora, had loved her, always taking her side, never mentioning where she came from. Anyway, why did it matter? She looked and acted like a lady, better than some that were born to it.

He never considered that he had married beneath him. Never! It almost seemed like the other way round. The oddest thing was, Arthur thought – because thinking was one of the things he *could* still do – that Dora wasn't a snob. It wasn't as though she looked down on others, just that she wanted to get as high as she could. And she wanted the same for her child.

In the first three long years following his stroke, Arthur had recovered in snatches, his walking, his speaking, his movements all coming back as though someone had finally noticed and rewound an old clock. Dora had run the greengrocer's, Grace had been at school

26

or helping her father. Two years further on, Arthur was well enough to help in the shop. To *help* in his own shop.

His wife had done a good job, he had to grant her that, feeling ashamed of his resentment. What else could she do? Let the business fail? It was a credit to her that she had coped so well. But even as he thought it, Arthur watched his wife serve a customer and was fascinated by her. There was a bloom on her as luminous as on the fruit; she was confident, sure in her own kingdom. He realized then that she had usurped him.

She could hardly help it. He had been ill. 'What a shame,' people had said at first. 'He'll recover, don't worry.' Then gradually they'd asked about Arthur a little less often, and after three years he was ghosted up into the back bedroom in Diggle, his memory a vague presence amongst the fruit and veg.

His old customers still asked how he was, but there were new people coming into the shop and they knew nothing about Arthur. They thought the shop belonged to the tall, rather autocratic Dora, and would have been surprised to know that she had a slight, bespectacled husband, many years her senior.

So when Arthur finally began to visit the shop again, people greeted him either with surprised recognition, or they didn't know him at all. Shuffling from the shop to the back room he noticed objects that had been moved: his overall taken down from the hook behind the door; All his mementoes put away for safekeeping in a drawer. The produce books laid out over the desk were in Dora's handwriting, not his.

Then one morning Arthur came to the shop to find Dora remonstrating with a delivery man.

'That is not the quality I want. I said *large* apples.'

The man was sullen. 'Them's the biggest I've got.'

'Then I don't want them –'

He interrupted her. 'Oi, you ordered 'em, you 'ave to take 'em.'

Arthur walked over to them, smiling genially at the delivery man.

'I'm sure we can work this out –'

Dora cut across him immediately, even physically moving in front of him to address the indignant man.

'Take them away and bring me some better apples. Please. Before nine o'clock.'

Embarrassed by his wife's dismissal of him, Arthur turned away as the man left the shop, but, not concentrating, he lost his balance and tipped forward into the stacked shelving. At once, Dora was beside him, helping him to his feet without a word of reproach.

'Are you all right?' she asked anxiously. 'Arthur, are you all right?'

He wanted to say – *No, but not because I fell over. Because you made me feel small, impotent, because you've taken over the shop and made me redundant.* Shame made Arthur brush aside his wife's hand and move to the back room where he sat down on a crate and leaned his chin on the head of his walking cane.

Age had got the better of him, age and thick blood and time. He might fool himself, but he was a stranger in the shop he had inherited from his own father. The dark green paint he had chosen for the outside and his name written proudly on the window said that it was Arthur Ellis who owned the premises – but he knew different. His was just a shell of a life, all that is left when a snail is turned over, its innards plucked out by birds.

It was then that Arthur knew that his wife didn't want him around. He was clumsy, a burden to her.

Alone, Dora could move about quickly, go to market, do the books, serve. Make money, make profit. Make progress. Everything about her was quick, quick, quick. Always running, always hurrying towards something.

He had been wrong, Arthur finally realized. Marrying Dora, he had hoped he would give her enough security to settle in herself, to stop the jammering in her head and rest. Instead *he* had stopped. There was no jammering of ambition in him, and there was nothing else he could give her. Dora was his wife, she had his name and his business. She hadn't meant this takeover to happen, but it had. His sickness had been her fecundity; his demotion, her promotion in life. She had learned everything he knew – picked his brain clean and mastered his business.

And – worse of all – none of that had been done in malice, or for spite. It was all in the name of love.

Chapter Four

Frowning, Miss Holden walked over to Grace's school desk and looked down.

'Are you all right?'

Grace jumped, then nodded. 'Sorry, I was daydreaming.'

Surprised, the teacher looked at her star pupil. For two years she had taught Grace Ellis; two years in which she had come to learn how quick the girl's mind really was. It was obvious that Grace was well beyond her peers. Something about her, some quality, made her thinking overtly mature. She could discuss without emotion, and was patently eager to learn.

Her intelligence had not gone unnoticed by the Spencers either. The two stiff-backed spinster sisters had seen in Grace Ellis someone who could put their little school on the map. 'Why,' they said to each other, 'she could even go to university. That would be a feather in our cap, and no mistake.' So the Spencer sisters encouraged Grace and they encouraged Coral Holden's interest in the girl. 'Talk to her,' they said. 'Gain her confidence.'

Yet it took a while for Coral to win Grace over, and only gradually did she learn about the family, about the sick father. So that was it! That was why Grace had had to be moved from the expensive private school. Well, well, well, Coral thought, so Grace Ellis was one of those children who had been forced to grow up before their time. Information about the mother followed on slowly – but not from Grace. The other teachers told Coral

Holden about Dora Ellis, and where she came from.

Miller Lane ... it hardly seemed possible, Coral thought. How could a girl like Grace Ellis come from a mother with a background like that? Encouraged by the Spencer sisters, Coral had gone to visit Dora only a fortnight ago. Standing on the pavement outside the greengrocer's Coral had looked in and seen a tall woman serving. Dora was dressed in black like a widow, a white apron over her skirt. Then, as Coral had walked in, a pair of alert grey eyes had met hers calmly.

'Good morning. Can I help you?'

'Good morning. Are you Mrs Ellis?' Coral had asked.

Dora had nodded. 'And you are?'

'Coral Holden – your daughter's teacher.'

Immediately Dora had walked to the door and turned the sign to read 'Closed' from the outside. Then she had ushered Coral Holden into the back room, setting a kettle to boil.

'Forgive the paperwork,' Dora had said evenly. 'Please, take a seat.'

To her astonishment, Coral had found herself faintly awed by the greengrocer's wife. There was something so naturally gracious about her, a presence which was almost palpable.

'I came to talk about your daughter.'

Dora had smiled, pouring boiling water into the teapot. 'Is she doing well?'

That was a surprise, Coral had thought. Most parents immediately assumed that their child was doing badly when confronted with the teacher.

Smiling, she had accepted the offered cup of tea. 'She is doing well, yes. Grace is a fine girl.'

Dora had nodded. 'And clever.'

'And clever,' Coral had agreed, studying the woman in

front of her with fascination. 'She could do really well.'

'I intend that she should. She has my full backing.'

What is it? Coral had wondered as she had sat sipping her tea. Fruit scents had come headily from the shop, a scuffle of footsteps had passed by, a horse whinnying at the end of the street. Normal scents, normal sounds, and yet somehow out of place. Or was it Dora Ellis that was misaligned?

Yet the woman before her had seemed poised, contented. But still Coral had sensed an aura about her, a hurrying, an urgency which she'd been unable to disguise. Dora Ellis was in a rush, but to *where*? There was a strange animal quality about her too, a sensuality which had nothing to do with her clothes or her manner. Coral had seen it as a woman so she'd guessed it must be obvious to men. That dark sultriness; hardly apt in a greengrocer's wife.

'More tea?'

Coral had blinked. The room had been small and very warm. Afternoon sunlight had poured through the back window, whilst dust motes rode the soft air.

'No, thank you . . . I came here because I want to talk to you about your daughter's future.'

Dora had stopped drinking and put down her cup. Her eyes had settled on the teacher and Coral had seen her breathe in deeply as though she had been waiting for the words for a long time.

'My daughter's future,' Dora had said slowly, 'must be protected at all costs. She is a clever child – you said that yourself – we have to make sure she makes the most of herself.' Dora had paused, smoothing the black cotton of her skirt. 'I'm proud of my daughter, but with good reason. I'm not a fool, I know Grace could go far. With the right tuition. She has the will to learn, to succeed . . . I did what I could with my opportunities. From my beginnings, I came a long way.' Dora's eyes had returned to the teacher. 'In this life a handicap has to become an advantage.'

Coral had frowned. 'I don't understand.'

'If you're born with nothing, you work to get something – *anything* you can call your own. Grace wasn't born destitute, but obviously we're not well off. We get by. But I want to see my daughter at the top. She has to be guided there. Coached.'

Without thinking, Coral had asked: 'Will you be proud of her then?'

Dora's eyes had flickered with disbelief. 'Proud? What on earth has pride to do with anything?' Her voice had relaxed. 'Oh, I see. You think I'm just a snobbish mother, trying to live through my child, but you're wrong. Grace must succeed for herself, not for me. I don't need to lean on my child. I can survive on my own.'

Coral had had no doubt about that when she'd left the greengrocer's wife that day. She had also realized that – by some verbal sleight of hand – a pact had been made between them, one which Coral understood instinctively. Dora Ellis had actually been saying: *I've done all I can for my child with my limited knowledge. You're educated, you have to take her over now. Together we can make sure that Grace gets on in life. That she fulfils her promise.* It was a pact that Coral Holden had been eager to enter in to.

Which was why she was so surprised to find Grace day dreaming now. It simply wasn't like her.

'Are you feeling all right?'

'I'm fine,' Grace replied, turning back to her books. 'Just fine.'

A little way off, a bell rang. For the juniors, Grace thought, to call them out into the playground.

33

Grace missed her old school. She had fitted in there and made friends, but money had been tight after her father's stroke and in the end – to Dora's chagrin – Grace had *had* to be moved. It wasn't what they'd planned, Dora said, but it would do for the meantime. After all, it could have been worse. It wasn't one of the council schools where no one came out with an education.

But Dora would not have liked Joan Cleaver, the one and only friend Grace had made at her new school. Grace was academically clever, but Joan was smart, quick, and common. Grace could imagine her mother thinking her daughter could find a more suitable friend. But Joan was a good listener, and funny. Only Joan knew all about the Ellis household – about Arthur's stroke, about the way Dora was always pushing Grace. She confided in her in a way she had never confided in anyone, and in return Joan told Grace about her sisters and her parents running The Bell and Monkey pub. She laughed about the fights on Saturday nights, and mocked her sisters' boyfriends, giving Grace an insight into a life outside sickrooms and Dora's hot-house control.

Shorter than Grace, and thinner, Joan's boyish shape. had been little changed by puberty. Always flippant, she was fearless and unfazed by anyone. Tough, they called her, and tough she was, probably because her background was rough. Not as bad as Miller Lane, but close. The Cleavers didn't live in Diggle, but over the pub in Oldham's Fencross Street. Joan saw in Grace something she liked. Something she hadn't got herself. *Class*. But she'd also felt pity for her the moment Grace had come to the school; her uniform pressed, her hair neatly tied back with a ribbon. Others had mocked her and called her a prig – 'Who does she think she is? She's only a greengrocer's daughter.' Later they'd found out about Dora's background and then they'd been exquisitely cruel in the way only children can be.

Joan had moved in at that point. Grace's dignified silence had looked good, but Joan was astute enough to know what the cool exterior hid. And so, within days of Grace's arrival at the school, they had become inseparable, Joan telling Grace about her elder brother, who was working down the pit, and about the pub. Hell of a place, Joan told her. Even the rats go round in pairs.

From the start, Grace knew that her mother would be enraged to know who her best friend was. *How could you mix with a girl like that?* Dora would say. *People are judged by the company they keep, and Joan Cleaver is bad company* ... But for once Grace ducked her mother's standards, keeping Joan a secret and relishing her defiance.

She was tired of being mature, responsible. Her childhood had been too short, the responsibility of her mother's ambition and her sick father setting Grace apart from her peers. Only one of them didn't judge – and that was Joan.

Which was why Grace was shattered now that Joan had left school. She had failed her last exams and her parents had decided that education was a waste of time for her. Joan hadn't fought to stay on – quite the opposite – and had told Grace only days before that she was off 'into the real world'.

'I'm leaving,' Joan said blithely, 'and not before time.'

Grace winced. 'Why?'

'I failed every exam –'

'But you wouldn't if you worked harder.'

Joan pulled a face. 'Hark at you! What a swot. Maybe I don't *want* to work hard.'

Poor buttoned-up Grace, Joan thought. So good-looking, so clever, but so unhappy.

'I didn't mean –' Grace began, but Joan cut her off at once. 'Forget it, it doesn't matter. Did you see those clothes in the magazine –'

'Joan! What about school? You *can't* leave.'

Joan shrugged and slipped her arm through Grace's. 'I have to. But we'll stay friends. We'll always stay friends . . . So, *did* you read the magazine?' Her eyes looked dreamily into the distance. 'Someone called *Chanel* designed them.' Joan said the name carefully, uncertain if she had it right. 'Long dropped waists – good for someone with my shape, or rather, no shape. And the women were wearing make-up too. Lipstick and something to make their eyelashes dark.' Joan touched her own fair lashes. 'I could look like a movie star if I had make-up.'

Grace regarded her, exasperated. 'A movie star!'

'Well, why not?' Joan replied heatedly.

'It's hard work.'

'Making films?' Joan countered, picking up her satchel. 'I'd just have to say some lines and then work my fingers to the bone spending my fortune. I think even *I* could work that hard.'

'But you're clever, Joan. You could do most things if you set your mind to it. Most normal things, anyway.'

'What? Like be a secretary? Or what about something really thrilling – a book-keeper?'

Grace dropped her voice. 'People from Oldham don't go to Hollywood. It's stupid.'

Immediately Joan flushed. She had been to the cinema repeatedly and seen Mary Pickford – and from then on her life had changed. The actress was cute, not that beautiful, but she made films – and money. Joan

36

daydreamed about making a fortune too, and marrying a millionaire. Just like Mary Pickford.

So what did it matter if she never learned about physics and mathematics? Actresses didn't have to sit exams – and besides, she wanted out of the North, out of England, to California, where they grew oranges outdoors and where the sun shone sixteen hours a day. She just hadn't worked out how she would do it.

Joan's face was red-hot with embarrassment.

'Oh, you may laugh, but I never laugh about your ambitions, do I? In fact, I'm the only one round here who doesn't.' Joan paused, ashamed of her words. 'I didn't mean it, Grace! You know I believe in you. I know you'll go far . . . You have to, anyway, or your mother will kill you.'

Grace smiled despite herself.

'You could have a business,' Joan went on. 'You could do anything. But me, I'll have to go another way to get where I want. Besides, I'm lazy; I don't want to work hard.'

Joan had inherited her lethargy from her father, Duncan. He was a marvellous landlord and could talk anyone into buying a round, but he suffered, as his wife, Sal, said repeatedly, from *idle-bloody-itis*. Joan carried the same trait. Her daydream of Hollywood was her way of pretending that she wasn't going to end up in Oldham, but Joan knew she was only fooling herself and had already fixed up a job as an undermaid in one of the biggest houses in Diggle, owned by the Strattons.

'I'm going to be the undermaid, well, the *under-undermaid*. I walk *under* the door, not through it,' she laughed wickedly. 'Still, I get a black uniform and Saturday mornings off. I've also got a little job helping out in a chemist's shop in Union Street.'

Grace raised her eyebrows. 'For someone who doesn't like hard work, you've taken a lot on.'

'Oh, it's only for pocket money. To buy make-up . . .'

Grace stared at her school books, aware that Coral Holden was watching her. She would miss Joan so much; miss the laughs, the arguments, the way she could say what she thought. Which she never could at home. There she was always on her best behaviour, always aware that everything she did was watched and judged.

Only with Joan could Grace be herself – a fourteen-year-old girl who liked practical jokes and shouting at the top of her voice. They had often gone out of town on to the moors beyond Diggle. There they had laboured up the hillsides, screaming as they ran back down again, their arms flailing above their heads. Once they had even gone fishing with Joan's brother, Geoffrey, in the greasy little stream by the cotton mill. Trying to impress Grace, he had been clumsy, getting his line caught up in the waterweeds and reeling in an old kettle, Joan laughing giddily on the bank.

Idly Grace doodled in the margin of her school book and thought of Joan, the clock ticking round on the wall at the head of the class as Coral Holden watched her prize pupil. Never for a moment did the teacher connect the empty desk at the back of the class with Grace's disquiet. In fact, if the truth be known, Coral would have been hard pushed even to remember the girl who had sat there only days before.

Chapter Five

Panicked, Dora rushed from the back room of the shop and then turned the front door sign to 'Closed'. Glancing around, she checked to see if there was anyone in the street, but it was empty and so she stepped out. She should be opening up for the market boy to deliver now, but for once he would find the shop closed. It was unavoidable.

Walking hurriedly, she went to catch the trolley bus to Oldham. She couldn't think what to do – she of all people, who *always* knew what to do. Dora stared out of the bus window, thinking hard. A stout woman with an empty basket climbed into the seat next to her. The wicker pressed against Dora's arm, making ridges in the soft flesh.

Where in God's name was she going? Dora wondered suddenly. Why go back to Oldham? There was nothing there for her, no family, no close ties. Only Miller Lane . . . She knew *why* then. The answer was obvious. After what she had done, she belonged there. Oh, she might pretend to herself that she had moved up in the world, but at heart she knew better. As did everyone else.

She was slum offspring. And they always reverted to type . . . Dora eyes fixed on the streets passing outside. The clean little Diggle roads had gone; now the streets were longer and dirtier, shops huddled in rows, others left abandoned or burned out. On one street there was an old sign – 'Royal Vinolia Vanishing Cream', the woman on the tin poster looking the worst for wear, her complexion soot-spotted and grey.

Other advertisement followed, beer signs, 'The Grade A Virginia' making a brief flurry amongst the more pragmatic signs for Capstan. Then gradually the advertisements thinned out as the bus approached the borders of the slums, only the pubs standing to attention on the corner of every other street.

There were fewer people on board now, Dora noticed. People had got off to shop, the men to bet, the employed having already left for work long since. Dora rested her forehead against the cold glass of the window, her eyes closed.

What in God's name had she done? She had been so sensible before. When she was younger she had been controlled, had mapped out her life and what she had planned had happened. How often had she said, 'If you can dream it, you can do it'? Well she *had* dreamed it and she *had* done it – and now she had thrown it all away. It wasn't Arthur's fault. He couldn't help being ill, being confined to bed. He didn't want to be half a man. She had thought at first that it wouldn't matter, had fought against the dreariness of her life . . . But she was still young, Dora had heard her inner voice whisper, she had a right to be happy, fulfilled.

She had a right. But what about *Arthur's* rights? He had loved her, given her a home, defended her by marrying her. And he had given her their daughter. Oh God, what had she done? She was no good, no good at all.

Her nature had beaten her. Not life, not hardship, her own nature.

'Hill Down,' the conductor called out suddenly.

Dora turned in her seat. 'Where are we?'

'Hill Down,' he replied, taking in Dora's respectable clothes and wondering what a woman like her was doing there. 'I think you've missed your stop, luv.'

'No,' she replied, rising to her feet and passing him. 'This *is* my stop.'

She would do what other women of her ilk did. Hurriedly Dora fumbled for the address in her handbag and then walked to the street. Her eyes fixed on the broken number on the door. Number 129. *Ask for Mrs Williams, she'll help out . . .* How many times had Dora heard Mrs Williams's name over the years? The local abortionist, the scourge of the local doctor. Someone who asked no questions, just ridded women of their unwanted and unplanned pregnancies.

Dora swallowed. She would have to go in and get it done, there was no choice. Not if she wanted to go home. Back to Diggle. No one would know, she told herself. She would just have the abortion and go back to Arthur and Grace. After that she would work for them for the rest of her life, be a good wife and good mother, never think of what she was missing.

Never think of Len Billings.

She closed her eyes against the name. She didn't love him, didn't really want him. All he offered was sex, a hurried, hot-breathed fumble in the park, culminating in a few moments of blind longing. And a child . . . Dora raised her hand to knock on the door, then dropped it and turned her head away as a couple passed.

God, if anyone saw her they would know what she was there for. Gossip would follow. But there would be more gossip if she carried on with the pregnancy, Dora thought. After all, it would be obvious to everyone that it wasn't Arthur Ellis's child. Just a bastard, born out of adultery. The kind of thing that never happened in

Diggle – but something that often happened in Miller Lane.

There was no excuse, Dora thought. It wasn't enough to say that she had been so tired, so weary of the work . . . Len had passed her on the street – not by chance, she now realized – and they had stopped and talked. And soon Dora had felt young again, and all thought of Arthur and bedpans and the vegetable shop had faded. She'd been able to think only of Len's hands, his smile, the crinkly hair, his smell and his talk – and she'd wanted it all. Just for a moment, she'd wanted it all.

No one would find out, she had told herself at the time, shocked to the core but responding when he'd touched her. No one would ever know. She had pulled away the first time and the second, but when she'd seen him again her heart had hammered in her chest and she'd been moist with longing. Soon it had become a compulsion. She'd wait for the sound of his voice, or for a sight of him in the street, a stranger in Diggle. She wouldn't acknowledge him in public, but when they met later she would cling to him as she had never clung to Arthur.

It had stimulated him, she knew that – the secrecy, the ever-present danger that they might be discovered. But they hadn't been. She'd got pregnant in secret and was now about to abort her child, in secret.

Dora turned back to the door and then suddenly ran, exhaling, her breath warm on the air. Panic made her breathless. Hurrying down the street she moved back into the heart of Oldham and was soon part of an unseeing crowd. Only then did she pause, her throat dry with confusion and fear. She was an adulteress who had betrayed her husband and child, but she was no murderess. The child she carried had a right to live.

There *had* to be another way out of the mess, Dora told herself desperately. *There had to be another way.*

Grace came down very early, long before she normally would. As usual, she paused on the top stair to listen for her parents' breathing and then moved on, her mind filled with the tests she had that day at school. Had she learned enough about King John? And where exactly was the Ivory Coast? Miss Holden was expecting great results, she had told Grace only yesterday.

Grace was so absorbed that she didn't notice them until it was almost too late. Two people talking by the coal hole outside in the small garden. She thought suddenly of the loose brick behind which Dora hid their money, but then realized that one of the people was her mother.

For a moment she nearly called out, but the look on Dora's face was too intense to welcome interruption. She looked furtive too, her skin flushed, the pale yellow of her dress making her body seem fuller, like some exotic swell of bloom. Grace stared at the dress, sure she had never seen it before. Then suddenly Dora's hair temporarily lost its darkness – lightened and transformed by the overhead sun – and made a stranger out of her.

Grace stared, mesmerized. The morning was becoming very hot very quickly, the light intense. The sounds of pigeons cooing and a child's cry seemed to ride the still air, the noises shimmering in the heat.

Cautiously Grace drew back behind the pantry door and listened to the conversation outside.

'Len, what are you talking about? This has to stop. You know that and so do I.'

There was a rustle, as though the man had reached out and taken hold of her mother.

43

'Dora, come on, you've done your best here. He's as well as he's ever going to be.'

He was talking about her father, Grace realized. Talking about him as though he was something to be pushed aside.

'He needs me,' Dora replied, her tone sharp.

'I need you.'

'Not like Arthur does!' She dropped her voice. 'Sshh, he'll wake and hear us; our bedroom's window just up there.'

'I can't live like this,' the man replied, his voice lowered, 'creeping around. It's not fair.'

'Fair!' Dora hissed under her breath. 'What's fair about anything in life? I chose to marry Arthur, not you –'

'You married him to get away from Miller Lane.'

'And who could blame me for that?'

'But I would have taken you away.'

'Would you?' she countered. 'Would you really? Where would a rat-catcher's wife fit in? Only places like the one I came from. Don't lie to me, Len. I think you'd just keep making promises and nothing would come of them. I think we'd grow old and stay poor.'

'What about passion?'

'What about *position*?' Dora retorted. 'I might not have been in love with my husband when I married him, but I've been a good wife and I've looked after Arthur Ellis better than any other woman could have done.'

'Until lately.'

Grace could hear her mother take in her breath.

'Lower your voice!' Dora ordered him. 'I'm ashamed of what happened, but it won't happen again, you can be sure of that.'

44

'Oh, come on, we can't do without each other. You know that as well as I do.'

Grace could hear her mother's footsteps coming closer, and she ducked further behind the pantry door.

'I'm not sure I do.' Dora replied, but her tone was uncertain, unlike her. 'I have responsibilities, a husband, a shop – and a daughter to care for.'

'She's grown up! How old is she now? Fifteen, sixteen?'

'Fourteen.'

'She's looks older,' the man replied, surprised. 'Anyway, your girl is plenty old enough to accept change. She isn't a baby any more.'

'She is to me!' Dora snapped. 'I'll do nothing to harm my daughter. I want Grace to have the best and I'll see to it that she does. Nothing must trouble her and put her off her studying – do you hear me? Nothing.'

But Grace could sense something in her mother's voice, something she had never heard before. Panic. What in God's name was happening? She pressed her body back against the wall as she heard her mother speak again.

'Len, it's over.'

His voice was even when he answered her.

'I don't think so.'

Looking through the crack in the door, Grace could see the man lean towards her mother and Dora back away. She moved hurriedly onto the little patch of lawn. Behind her, on the washing line, two white bed sheets were blowing in the summer wind under that white-hot sky. Still moving away, Dora's hands went up in front of her as though she was warding off something evil, the sheets suddenly whipping round both of them as the man caught hold of her and kissed her.

Horrified, Grace moved and knocked over the bread board on the pantry shelf. Dora heard her and turned, hurrying towards the house and pulling open the back door. She stood for a long moment looking at her daughter, her face alternately embarrassed and outraged.

Then Dora's hand went out to her daughter – but Grace moved away and ran, bolting for the front door and the unforgiving day outside.

Summer had made the garden parched, grass dry underfoot, branches hanging down against the side of Lodge House as Grace sneaked up to the drawing-room window. Mrs Stratton – pigeon-breasted and serious – was holding court to three browbeaten women dressed in dark clothes. Although Grace couldn't hear exactly what she was saying, she could tell that the pitch of Mrs Stratton's voice never once faltered.

Silently Grace moved round to the back of the house, peeking in at another window: obviously Mr Stratton's study. It was piled with books and leaflets, an old dog bed by the side of his desk. In it snored an large terrier – but no Mr Stratton. Relieved, Grace moved further round to the back door, next to the kitchen.

The cook was reaching up to get something from a high shelf, Joan standing watching her with a look of total boredom. When the cook moved out of the kitchen, Grace tapped on the window.

At once Joan looked up, then smiled and jerked her head towards the stables round the back. In a moment she had joined Grace there.

'How do?' Joan's overall was too large for her, her thin arms poking out of the rolled-up sleeves.

'Can you get away for a bit?'

She pulled a face. 'I'm supposed to be helping Cook

make lunch. Well, not cooking, just dogsbodying. Anyway, why aren't you at school? You won't half catch it if your mother finds out.'

Grace's face coloured. 'Can you get away or not?'

'Hey! Don't snap at me. I have to get the cook to let me off.' She looked towards the house and then back to Grace. 'Give me five minutes.'

True to her word, Joan reappeared shortly after. Grace took her arm and pulled her into one of the stables. A large grey gelding snorted and kicked its leg against the stable door.

'What did you say to her?'

'I said my parents were fighting again and that someone had sent for the police. I said I wouldn't be long, but I had to go home.'

'Joan, that was a lie!'

She looked at Grace impatiently. 'Oh, for God's sake, it's only a matter of time. It'll probably be true tonight.'

The horse whinnied next to them, blowing warm breath against Grace's shoulder.

Joan was the first to speak. 'So, what is it?'

'I can't tell you.'

'Then why drag me out of work?' Joan snapped, 'Jesus, that was a waste of a good excuse.'

'It's my mother.'

'Is she ill?'

'No.' Grace looked about her, as though frightened that she might be overheard.

'Has she left home?'

'No.'

'Because if she has, that wouldn't be as bad as it seemed. My mother's left home a couple of times, but she always comes back.' Joan waited for Grace to continue. 'So, what is it?'

Resigned, Grace leaned against the wooden partition in the stable and stared at her regulation school shoes.

'Why do people marry?'

'For love,' Joan said, rolling her eyes heavenwards. 'Or money. But that's only if you're the Queen or some other rich sod.'

'So if people marry for love, do they *always* love each other?'

'Haven't you met my parents?'

Despite herself, Grace smiled. She wanted to tell Joan outright, but she was finding it a lot harder than she had anticipated. If she confided, she was betraying her mother's trust – and yet wasn't that what her mother had already done to her and her father? Betrayed their trust?

'What if someone married and still loved someone else?' Grace hurried on. 'They never mentioned it, and no one had ever known the secret.' She paused. 'And just say that everything went along fine for a long time. That the person stayed married and seemed happy – but then one day the person they *really* loved came back. Then what?'

Joan had caught the drift some while back. Although she was only fourteen, she had two elder sisters and had heard plenty about men and love affairs. She had also grown up watching the intermittent viciousness between her parents, the malice of their bitterness and resentment of each other. Love – Joan believed – was only real on the films. Or if you were Mary Pickford married to Douglas Fairbanks.

'Are you saying that your mother's in love with someone else?'

'I saw her kissing some man.'

'Oh God!' Joan said, goggle-eyed. 'What did you do?'

48

Grace didn't seem to hear her. '*Len*, she called him. Len . . .'

'Len who?'

'How do I know?' Grace snapped. Then her tone dropped to a whisper. 'Maybe she'll run away with him.'

'But –'

'I don't know what to do, Joan,' Grace replied, panicked. 'I can't go home.'

'You have to sometime.'

'And what do I say to her? *My mother*.' Grace paused. 'And what do I say to my father? What will he do when he knows?'

Quickly, Joan caught her friend's arm. 'Oh, come on, why should he ever find out? If you don't tell him, he won't ever know.'

'But that doesn't make it all right, does it?' Grace countered. 'My mother has a boyfriend and as long as my father doesn't know is that supposed to make it all right?

'I didn't say that!'

'It sounded as though that was exactly what you were saying,' Grace replied, biting the edge of her thumbnail.

'I meant – what's to be gained by making a lot of noise about it? You don't know if your mother loves this man. She might just have been . . . you know, carried away.' Joan frowned, struggling to remember what her sisters and the cheap novellas had said. 'It was just the passion of the moment, Grace. Nothing serious. Things like this happen all the time.'

'Not to my parents they don't.'

'That's just the point, isn't it?' Joan countered impatiently. 'It couldn't happen to you, could it? Not Miss Perfect with her Perfect family. Not the golden girl . . .'

She trailed off, surprised by her own venom. 'I didn't mean that.'

'Yes, you did,' Grace replied fiercely. 'And you're right: I *don't* want it to happen to me. And not just for myself. I don't want everything my mother's worked for to be ruined. I don't want people to find out and say that it was only to be expected from *a woman like her*.' Grace hesitated. 'I've grown up with the shadow of Miller Lane hanging over my life, with the terror of "losing face" – I can't let it happen.'

'So pretend that you never saw it.'

'But I did,' Grace said sadly. 'You can't *unsee* something.'

'You could try. People do it all the time.'

Grace shook her head. 'Not me. I saw what happened – and I'll remember it until I die.'

Chapter Six

It was still dark at four in the morning, even in August. Sliding out of bed, Dora rose without disturbing Arthur, and dressed in the dark. Carrying her shoes in her hands, she then crept downstairs and moved into the kitchen, closing the door noiselessly behind her. There was no sound from Grace's room above.

Her discarded school books were on the kitchen table where she had left them the previous night. Dora stared at them, touching the covers with her fingers, allowing herself for once to revel in pride. She had done a good job, raised a fine girl, someone who would be a success. Grace would never knew how her mother had kept her baby clothes and rested her cheek against them, smelling the infant scent. Grace would never believe that her mother had watched her in the school playground, Dora hiding behind a tree, keeping an eye out for her extraordinary child. How could Grace ever imagine that her stern mother had wept – alone – when she had passed her entrance exam to the fine school she had once attended? Who, Dora Ellis? No, never, she was too cold, too harsh.

Oh, but you're wrong, Dora thought, and then realized that she was glad her daughter knew nothing of her soft side. Better that Grace should hate her mother than feel sorry for her. This way Grace would remain untouched by her mother's actions. People would side with her automatically – and with Arthur, the wronged husband.

What could you expect? they would tell each other.

A Miller Lane woman through and through. In time they would hear about the pregnancy too, because Dora would have the child – even if later it was put up for adoption. It had a right to a life, Dora had decided. As for her, she had no choice. She *had* to run away, pregnant with Len Billings' baby. She would sneak off in the night so that her daughter could despise her. But Grace would be free of her. And that was all Dora could do for her now. If she stayed she would drag poor Arthur down and ruin Grace's chances.

Better that they believe she had gone off with Len Billings. No one knew about the baby yet, but they would, and news would reach Grace and push her even further away from her mother. But she would survive, she *had* to, Dora thought.

She knew how much the Spencer sisters admired her child, knew that Coral Holden would encourage Grace. If the truth be told, Grace didn't really need her mother any more. Not now, anyway, not disgraced. She had done the best she could, Dora thought, for as long as she could. In the end something feral inside her had sabotaged her own success. But it wouldn't spoil Grace's . . .

Sighing, Dora drew on her shoes and then went into the larder, pulling out the small suitcase from behind the door. Arthur could cope again; he wasn't an invalid any more. Better to run off than stay to explain.

Dora paused. She had seen Len Billings and that had been it. Years of repressed emotions, years of living the life of someone else had turned Dora inside out. There was nothing of her left: she had brought up her child and nursed her sick husband but the life, the sexuality, the animal wants and needs, had gone.

Until she felt Len Billings hold her. Then, suddenly,

she was back in Miller Lane. Back to the hated stinking streets and the crowded rooms. Len Billings, the rat-catcher, back from the war with his medal. A shabby hero with big hands that touched her and felt her breasts, and a mouth that moved over hers and made her skin burn.

And in the end Dora had given in. Lost the control of a lifetime because she had *wanted* to feel again. Wanted the hot bed and the sex, the smell of crowding, the memories of her childhood that repulsed her and yet drew her. Miller Lane *was* her reality, after all. The place she most feared, and had so longed to leave, was the dark side of her. And there was no antidote for it.

Miller Lane was in her blood, Len Billings was in her blood, madness was in her blood, and in the end she had given in. She had failed and she despised herself for it. How could she expect her husband and child to forgive her when she could never forgive herself? Dora's heart closed down inside her. She had made her bed and she would stew in it.

People would rally round Grace, and Dora was aware she had instilled enough grit into her child to know that Grace would survive, even though it would be hard. It would strengthen her to face up to what her mother had done. Dora had fought against Miller Lane, now Grace would have to fight against the shadow of her mother.

No one would know where to look for her, Dora decided. She would not write or be in touch. She would simply slink off like an animal in the dark, letting people think that she was going to Len Billings. But she wasn't: Dora was going off alone. Go now, a voice said, and let your daughter hate you. Go now.

Slowly Dora picked up her case and then let herself out of the back door, walking down the High Street and taking the steep road down towards Oldham. The dawn was beginning, making the hedges light-tipped, the summer full trees heavy with leaf. No one passed her and twice she paused, swapping the case from one hand to the other.

Len Billings would be waiting for her at the tram station. He would be smoking a cigarette, hot with desire, his hands rough. He didn't know about the baby she was carrying. He never would, from her . . . Impatiently he would wait, aware of how long it took Dora to walk from Diggle down to the town. From the sweet high air to the choking streets of Oldham. He would wait for the sound of her footsteps coming down from Mumps station and then hurry out to greet his woman. The rat-catcher from Oldham with his grimy prize.

Minutes would pass, the clock on St Mark's church tolling the half hour. Six, six thirty. Len would be warmed by the soft August air and turn down the collar of his jacket, lighting up another cheap cigarette as he waited. He would remember how he had bragged of getting Dora Ellis away from Diggle and her old man, of how she was mad for him. His cronies in the pub had watched him, licking their lips with envy at the thought of Dora Ellis brought so low.

He would wait to feel her and touch her and enjoy her. To relish his triumph . . . Walking grimly, Dora thought of his face and the way it would change when he realized the truth. It would take him a while. Then, gradually, as the church clock pealed on the hours, Len Billings would know that she wasn't coming. He would know then that Dora had used him as a decoy, an excuse. She was leaving her family all right, but not for him or Miller Lane.

She had sworn never to go back, and she never would.

Chapter Seven

'Are you all right?' Grace asked her father as she came in from school. December had ended bitterly, snow on the streets, the buses throwing long ochre lights as they struggled up the steep incline.

Arthur looked up at his daughter with dull eyes. 'I'm fine, love, just fine.'

Her mother had killed him, Grace thought. If Dora had poisoned him she could not have done a more thorough job.

The news of Dora's departure had spread across Diggle within hours, then slid down into Oldham, her name, coupled with that of Len Billings, on everyone's lips. They had run away together, people said. Billings had been bragging about it in the pub, but no one had thought he was serious.

Nobody knew the truth of the matter: that Len Billings had waited for hours for Dora and then had realized, with violent embarrassment, that she wasn't coming. She had stood him up. Jesus, he'd look a right fool if anyone found out. After all he'd said . . . So Len had done alone what he'd thought he would be doing with Dora – he'd left Oldham for Salford. And everyone had jumped to the conclusion he knew they would – that Len Billings and Dora Ellis had run off together.

This was what Grace and her father believed. At first the shock of the news had winded Grace, but she'd been more prepared for it than her father was. When Arthur was told he'd rocked on his feet in the shop and then sat down heavily, ageing in an instant. His eyes had clouded, his back bent, his right hand automatically reaching out for the stick he had relied on after his stroke. He'd clung to it, his knuckles white, his mouth moving without words.

Grace had expected that he would have another stroke, but in that she'd been spared. Instead Arthur Ellis had been suddenly reduced to a shadow pattern on the wall, a cut-out, nothing more substantial. His wife, his adored, accepted, admired Dora, had betrayed him. Why? he asked his daughter repeatedly. Why had she stayed with him when he was ill, only to go now? Who had she gone with?

Grace knew the answer only too well, but she couldn't tell her father. Because if she did, he would want to know how she knew, and then she would have to explain about the washing, the high wide white sheets and the couple embracing amongst them.

So she said nothing and had let the gossips tell him. And she'd waited for the inevitable teasing and finger-pointing which would come. But it never had. Dora had anticipated the reaction to perfection: she had been the outsider, not Arthur or their child. Dora had been the slum cuckoo coming into the sweet Diggle nest. People would never forgive her, but they pitied her family. They rallied round Grace now. Poor Grace, such a pretty, intelligent girl, what a shock for her. It wasn't the child's fault, the do-gooders said.

Mrs Stratton smiled at Grace in the street; the vicar came to call regularly. Choosing his words carefully, he talked about sin and damnation and Grace wondered how much she could possibly hate her mother and still manage to breathe. The image of the washing and the embrace played in her dreams at night and dogged her thoughts in the daytime.

Her mother had rejected her and her father and chosen another man. How could she? Grace thought. It was so out of character. Dora had been so severe, so controlled, so determined never to let herself down, and yet she – of all people – had thrown everything away. Her family, her status, *her reputation* – the one thing Grace had thought her mother valued above everything. Something Grace couldn't understand, some force, had compelled her mother to fall from grace. Something that man Len Billings had offered had made her mother into a tramp.

So Grace hated both her mother and Billings, imagining how they would whisper together and be forever folded in white sheets ... Sleep didn't come soundly to Grace for weeks after her mother left. At two and three in the morning she would rise and walk downstairs and look at the kitchen, fingering the dishes her mother had touched, and washed, and chosen. Sometimes little memories rendered her mute with distress: the sight of Dora's basket hanging on the back of the larder door, or the scent bottle with its last vestiges of perfume on the dressing table. Dora had been too large a personality to leave when her body left; her voice was still half heard, her footfall still sounding on the step outside the back door. Many times Grace turned at a sound, expecting the door to open and her mother to walk in, take off her coat and make porridge for Arthur's breakfast. She was everywhere and nowhere. Within reach and yet always out of it.

Arthur felt her presence too; and missed her. Never once did Grace hear him criticize Dora, but at night she would catch him crying softly in the darkness and had seen him touch her mother's clothes when he thought she wasn't looking. Their wedding photograph, usually

57

in the front room, found its way to his side of the bed and Dora's nightdress lay on the pillow next to him every night.

And so for six months Grace laboured under her own and her father's loss, Christmas coming and going without word from Dora, Coral Holden anxious at Grace's indifferent school results. How much did Grace know, she wondered, having heard a rumour that Dora Ellis was pregnant. Oh God, Coral thought, how would Grace react when she knew? Or did she know already?

'Grace, you have to try to concentrate,'

She looked at her teacher. 'I do try.'

'I know, but you've fallen behind.' Coral sat down on the seat next to Grace in the empty classroom. Outside the window they could hear the younger children playing. 'I know how difficult things have been for you.'

Grace looked at her teacher. 'My father's not well again. He's finding it difficult to run the shop alone. I said I'd run it with him.'

This was bad news, and left Coral gasping. Grace Ellis was the best pupil she had come across, a girl who could achieve a great deal in life. But not working in a greengrocer's shop. It would be a waste, a ludicrous waste. She would tell the Spencer sisters; it couldn't happen. It just couldn't.

'Grace, let me talk to your father –'

'It would do no good,' she replied. 'He can't help it. He's not able to manage on his own.'

'But . . .'

Grace looked away. It was as though she had lost all interest in her schooling, in anything. 'It'll only be for a while, Miss Holden. Things will get better.'

'No, they won't!' she snapped, suddenly impatient.

'If you lose out now, you've lost for ever. You won't come back to school if you leave, Grace. We both know that.'

'My father needs me.'

'I understand,' Coral replied, 'but you can't sacrifice yourself for your father.'

Grace's eyes flashed. 'And if I don't, who will?'

Coral looked away. What could she say? There was no one else to help with Arthur Ellis. A silence fell between them, Coral thinking back to the time she had gone to see Dora at the shop. It had never seemed believable to her that Dora Ellis had run off with a man. Not that determined, controlled woman. Something had happened, obviously, but nothing so simple as adultery. Dora Ellis had had too much control for that, too much respect for herself. So when Coral heard about the pregnancy she thought it explained a lot. Dora would leave knowing that the scandal would be too much for Arthur and Grace to live down if she stayed.

Coral could see Dora as though it was only yesterday, the two of them talking at the back of the greengrocer's shop, Dora passing her daughter over to Coral. Almost making her pledge that she would lead Grace to the gilded future Dora could envisage for her. The two women had been in perfect agreement, both of them wanting the same thing. And both of them still wanted the same thing – of that Coral Holden was sure.

But what had happened to their hopes? Grace Ellis was falling behind, doomed to working in a shop, supporting her father emotionally and financially. It was stupid, cruel – it was wrong.

'Your mother wouldn't want this for you.'

Grace stared at her teacher with fury in her eyes. 'My mother didn't care what happened to me!'

'That's not true,' Coral replied. 'Your mother loved you and believed in you –'

'She left me,' Grace said, her voice faltering. 'She left both of us.'

'I don't know why she did what she did,' Coral continued, 'I only know that she was a remarkable woman and that she wanted you to succeed.'

Silence fell down, complete and untouched as Grace sat still, nonplussed by her teacher's words. Miss Holden had been the only person not to criticize her mother, the only one who had a good word to say about Dora Ellis. For a moment Grace didn't know whether to admire or hate her for it.

'My mother's gone,' Grace said at last. 'I have to do the best I can for my father now.'

'And for yourself.'

Grace faltered. She had been so angry at her mother that she had seen the one way she could repay Dora for her rejection – she would reject her mother's ambitions for her. She would be a nobody, waste her brain, her talent, submit to whatever domestic martyrdom was coming her way. So what if the shop was failing due to Arthur's disinterest? What did it matter any more if they ended up penniless?

She thought of the windows grown dirty, the fruit sometimes left overnight in the stalls. Flies – something her father would never have tolerated before – had hummed around the stricken apples that autumn and now that winter was here the fruit looked solemn, undressed, out of its seasonal finery. There were no blue-tissue-papered apples now, no shiny nuts, no oranges seducing the passers-by with their heady scent.

Customers had begun to look elsewhere, Arthur morose and silent, unwelcoming. His thin hair was often uncombed, his suit dusty, his apron left hanging on the back of the door. Even the OPEN sign looked faded. The shop was lying down to die like its owner. And it would take Grace down too – if she let it.

'I don't want to give up school,' she murmured, suddenly realizing just how much it mattered to her. 'But I have to help out in the shop.'

Coral saw her chance and snatched it. 'I'll give you private tuition –'

'We could never afford it!' Grace countered.

Her teacher put up her hands to stop the interruption. 'There will be no charge, Grace. No fee for you to pay. I'll even have a word with the Misses Spencer . . . All I ask is that you study and make a career for yourself.' She paused to allow Grace to consider her words. 'I won't see you waste yourself. Help your father in the shop, but in the evenings we'll work together.'

It was on the following Saturday that Joan came into the greengrocer's and looked around for Grace. Arthur saw her enter, but looked away, as though he couldn't face her.

'How do, Mr Ellis?'

He turned, smiled wanly and then moved very slowly into the back room, away from the shop. A second later Grace walked out. She was wearing her mother's white apron, and for an instant, with her back to the light, Joan thought she was seeing Dora Ellis standing there.

'How's your dad?' Joan asked, rolling her eyes.

'Not well,' Grace replied, taking her friend's arm and walking her over to the window, out of earshot. 'I heard him crying again this morning. He couldn't stop – even though there were people in the shop. D'you think I should call the doctor?'

The shop was musty, sad; Grace no longer young. God, Joan thought, she's changing.

'Maybe you should get the doctor to look at him.'

'It would cost too much,' Grace replied, suddenly remembering the parlous state of their finances. 'I don't know what to do for him. I can't talk to him, or make him listen to me. I just can't seem to reach him.'

'You need a change,' Joan said hurriedly. 'You have to get out of here. It's spooky.'

'I can't go yet –'

'Oh, come on!' Joan interrupted. 'You've got no customers and from the look of that window you won't be having any more today. Or any other day.' She stared at the window display. 'Grace, you have to do something about that, it's awful. I heard Mrs Stratton talking about it the other day. She said that the shop had gone downhill and that it looked as though it might close.'

Grace stared at her friend. She knew that people were talking and that what they said was right, but how could *she* change it? The little money they made hardly covered their bills and if they lost the shop, then what? She would have to go to work at the mill. Her father couldn't do anything. Arthur could hardly string together two words any more.

'I know what they say,' she said coldly, 'but perhaps Mrs Stratton would find it hard to manage on next to nothing.'

Joan stuck her hands in the pockets of her uniform coat and shuffled her feet.

'Look, I could let you have a couple of bob to tide you over.'

'Thanks, but I'll manage.'

How had it happened? Grace wondered. Only months earlier Joan had been the down-at-heel one and Grace

62

had been the one set for a fair future. And now the positions were reversed: Joan, a scullery maid for the Strattons, was offering to help Grace.

Her hand went out to Joan and rested for a moment on her arm. 'I'll manage. But thanks, thanks for the offer.'

Joan brushed the matter aside, changing the subject. 'I thought we'd go for a walk, up to Greenfield.'

Grace glanced over to the window. 'It'll be dark soon. I have to stay until we close.'

'Your father doesn't know the difference,' Joan said bluntly. 'Who's going to come now, Grace? Close up and let's get out of here.'

Only hesitating for another moment, Grace turned the sign on the door to 'Closed' and then went into the back room for her father. Arthur was docile as his daughter helped him into his coat and led him to the door. She walked him up the hill to the cottage, Joan following behind, scuffing the slushy snow with her button-up boots.

Inside the cottage, Grace laid the fire and cut some bread for her father, setting it on a tray for him next to a steaming pot of tea, some hard-boiled eggs and a wedge of Lancashire cheese. Arthur watched her, but remained by the door, unmoving, until Grace took his coat off and settled him in the chair in front of the fire.

'Now you eat that, Dad, and I'll be back soon.' She smoothed back the long strands of his hair from his forehead, watching his hands break the bread and shake as his lifted it to his mouth. Pity, strong as a pain, made her glance away and put the guard up before the fire. 'You stay here now, won't you, Dad? Just eat your meal and I'll be back in a little while.'

His eyes moved to her face, but his expression was blank.

'Dad, d'you hear what I say?'

He nodded, twice, then went back to his food.

The snow began falling again as the girls climbed the steep incline to the hill above Diggle. Deep in thought, Grace wrapped her shawl around her shoulders, her hands in rough mittens, her fingers numb.

Beside her walked Joan, a stick figure in her over-long uniform, her hair resting in a long plait down her back.

'Our Geoffrey got me a picture the other day – of Mary Pickford.'

Grace was oddly comforted by the banality of the conversation. 'Oh Joan, you're not still thinking about going to America, are you?'

Joan pulled a face, turning round in the snow and making a little blank hole with her feet. 'You want to know something?' she asked conspiratorially. 'They've got some lipsticks down at the chemist –'

'Lipsticks!'

'Yeah, lipsticks,' Joan repeated. 'I asked Mrs Proctor if I could buy one with half my wage this morning. She looked right put out – until I said it was for my mother.' Joan paused, digging into her pocket and bringing out a little tube. Slowly she pulled off the top and then rolled up a column of bright vermilion.

Grace was transfixed. 'God, what a colour!'

'It makes you look like a *vamp*,' Joan replied, repeating a word she had heard her sisters use.

Self-consciously she dug into her pocket again and pulled out a mirror. Then, slowly, with intense concentration, she applied the lipstick. When she had finished she looked round, then ran to stand under the gaslamp which lighted the drive entrance to the last house before the moors.

Smiling, Grace approached her and then stared. Joan's lips seemed huge for her tiny white face, making a cartoon out of her, the snow falling softly onto the black uniform coat.

'It looks dreadful!'

'You're just jealous!' Joan replied, mortified, and looking into the mirror again. 'All the actresses wear make-up now.'

'But it's too bright,' Grace countered, taking the lipstick out of Joan's hand and looking at it, suddenly interested. 'No one's lips are that colour.'

Irritated, Joan snatched the lipstick back and put it in her pocket, her tongue running over her shiny lips as she fell into step with Grace.

'I'm not staying here all my life,' she said simply. 'It's freezing and I'm not being a maid for ever. That Mrs Stratton's a right stuck-up cow. She talks about people behind their backs although she's always going on about the poor and how she helps people.' Joan kicked the snow under her feet. 'Her husband's never home and when he is he never says a word to her . . . When I get married I'll have a handsome man who'll want to be with me all the time.'

'I'm not getting married,' Grace said evenly.

'Of course you are!' Joan replied. 'Everyone gets married.'

'I'm going to have a career instead.'

'And I'm going to be a film star –'

'No, Joan, I *mean* it. I'm not daydreaming. I'm going to have a career and I'm going to make money.' Grace pulled her shawl around her tightly. 'I'm going to have enough money to never have to worry again about rent . . . Dad and I are going to lose the shop – you know that, don't you?'

65

Joan was stunned. 'No! Not really?'

'I think we are. I don't see how we can help it,' Grace replied, staring ahead at the darkening sky. 'There's hardly any money coming in from customers any more. It's a struggle to meet the rent.'

'I thought your father owned the shop?'

'I thought so too,' Grace said, 'but the landlord came round the other day and my father wasn't up to seeing him, so I did. He told me that we had to pay the rent weekly – and that we are already behind.'

'What about the cottage?' Joan asked, her eyes wide.

'That's ours, Dad owns that,' Grace assured her, 'but there's nothing else . . . I don't know how to run the shop, Joan. My father always ran it before, and then my mother did after Dad had his stroke.' She stopped, her voice faltering. 'I keep thinking that I should *know* how to buy things and where to go. Which markets and who to talk to. I should know about what to buy and how much to pay. But I don't! And now the landlord's saying that unless we can pay the rent next week, together with what we already owe by the end of the month, he wants us out.'

Joan stared at her in disbelief. These kinds of things happened to her sort, to the rough families, not to the likes of Arthur and Grace Ellis.

'He can't do that!'

'He can,' Grace replied shortly. 'It's his shop, after all. The worst thing was that he hinted that he already had someone else interested in running the place. Then he said that my father was no good to anyone and that the shop was a mess now and getting worse every day. He said people in the village had started to complain.'

Joan knew that what the man said was true, not that she would have told Grace. In fact, she had overheard

Mrs Stratton complaining about the greengrocer's only yesterday and saying that it let down the tone of the place: 'I can't think what's come over the man. Arthur Ellis was always so respectable before. Everything went wrong when he married that woman. We all said at the time that it would end badly. But why he's gone off his head now I can't imagine. He should be glad that she left him. Should count his blessings and pull himself together.'

Joan also knew that the Ellises' landlord visited Mrs Stratton a week earlier. No doubt Mrs Stratton had told the man what she thought – and she was a woman to be listened to, a person who could make or break a humble landlord.

'If you did have to leave the shop, how would you manage then?'

'I'd have to go to work in the mill. Or in service, like you.'

'What about your father?'

Grace gave her a slow look. 'Oh, Joan, come on. You know as well as I do that my father's not capable of work any more. He couldn't understand anything that anyone said to him, let alone follow orders. He doesn't know what time of day it is.' She paused, temper rising. 'It's all my mother's fault. If she hadn't left, he wouldn't be like this and we'd never be losing the shop.'

Joan touched her friend's arm gently. 'You could ask for help –'

Grace's eyes blazed. 'From the likes of your Mrs Stratton! I don't think so. Oh no, I'm not asking for charity. I'll manage, you'll see. I'll get a job and more than that, I'll keep up my studies and finish my education too.' Grace's voice hardened. 'I'll get through this and show them all. I'm going to the top. Right to the top. I'm not meant to be anyone's maid or mill hand. You watch me, Joan, because as God's my judge, I'll do it.'

Chapter Eight

By spring of the following year, at the age of fifteen, Grace had finally gone to work in the ELK mill down in Oldham. Viciously teased for her accent and aloofness, she learned to arrive on time, work all morning and then leave at dinnertime without saying a word to anyone. Walking briskly, she would then catch a bus to Diggle at noon and call on her father, repeating the duty her mother had done years before.

Arthur, silent and prone to fits of weeping, waited in his seat for her. Grace knew that a widowed neighbour looked in periodically to check on him, but the duty of feeding her father was hers and hers alone. In silence. Grace would make his food, feed it to him, kiss him and leave. Then the long trip back to the mill began, and the longer afternoon followed.

When the hooter finally sounded at six, Grace left first, hurrying past the other mill girls and making her way to Cheviot Avenue, just outside the centre of town. It was a small street with houses which bore the pride of their owners – teachers and accountants, people who were going somewhere. Like Coral Holden.

Now working part time as a supply teacher at the Spencer School, Coral had married Frank Higgins, a portly, cheerful clerk from the town hall who – on seeing Grace arrive – would always go through the same ritual. He would open the door and smile, bowing slightly.

'Your tutor awaits,' he would say, standing back for

Grace to walk in. 'Lucky be the learned.'

Since her mother had gone the change in Grace Ellis had been remarkable. There was no child left, just some severe woman temporarily parked in a youthful body. Grown even taller and abnormally serious, Grace had tried to run the greengrocer's shop but had finally been evicted by the landlord. The sight of her and her father being escorted from the shop had been the talk of Diggle for weeks, the news filtering down to Oldham, to the spiteful little slums – and finally to Miller Lane.

Ashamed and anxious for her father, Grace withdrew into herself and before long the two of them had cut themselves off from the world. There were only a couple of people allowed to impinge on their enforced exile – Joan and Coral. Otherwise Grace walked about looking straight ahead, as though she neither saw nor heard anyone. And to all intents and purposes, she didn't. Her attention was fixed somewhere that no one else could see – on her future. On the way ahead, the career which would end the nightmare for ever.

For outsiders, it was impossible to guess how much Grace was affected by her family's degradation. Certainly she confided in no one, and when Mrs Stratton came calling Grace was politely cold when she offered charity. *No, they didn't need help*, she told the woman, *they could cope. But what about your father? Doesn't he need medical attention?* Mrs Stratton pushed. *No,* Grace had replied, *my father isn't ill.*

Just dead inside.

To her credit, Coral never asked after Grace's father, knowing that the girl would think she was checking up on her. So instead Coral called round at the little house every week and had a look at Arthur Ellis for herself.

His chair was always in the same place, before the fire,

coal smouldering dimly because they couldn't afford the good stuff and used slack instead. His hands shook constantly, his mouth turned down and slightly opened – as though he was just about to say something vital. Something which would change everything.

But he never did. His bodily functions Arthur could control and was thankfully not incontinent, but his eyes were flat as the lead roof of the Mission Hall and though his heart was still beating, it was doing it out of habit, not desire.

The cottage itself was immaculately tidy – Grace made sure of that. She hadn't known how to run a shop, but she knew how to run a house. Outside – unless it was raining or freezing – washing hung on the line. Bed sheets, white and wide as ships' sails, clapping their hands in the wind. But inside, whatever the weather, a sense of sorrow permeated.

No girl her age should be alone, left to cope with a mentally disturbed father, Coral thought. She had said so to her husband often, implying that Arthur might end up in an institution – and perhaps it would be better for his daughter if he did. The girl needed help. Fast.

The idea of tuition had been Coral's when Grace had had to leave school. She had spoken to the other teachers at the Spencer School, asking if they would volunteer to help Grace Ellis. There had been a murmur of sympathy – *yes, she was a very intelligent child, but she wasn't the only one around those parts to miss out. Some children just fell by the wayside.*

Coral's small round face had coloured, her voice rising. 'But Grace could do so well –'

The maths teacher had cut across Coral immediately. 'She's not that gifted in mathematics.'

'Mathematics isn't her subject, Mr Anderson, English

71

is, so are art and chemistry. She's a good mix. She also has a fine intelligence: she can reason and she can communicate. Her diction is excellent,' Coral had gone on. 'Her mother taught her well.'

The old teacher had looked surprised. 'I imagine that the things Dora Ellis taught her daughter were those a girl should never know about.'

Coral had thrown her hands up in despair.

'I don't see why we all have to act so priggishly! We've all heard about worse families than Grace's. There are plenty that have more to be ashamed of in this town. She isn't responsible for her mother's actions – and, as far as I know, poverty doesn't make someone immoral. What *we're* doing is immoral, if we don't help her.'

But the supplication had fallen on deaf ears. Coral could give her time freely, but the other teachers had more than enough work to get on with already. It was sad about Grace Ellis, but it was life. However, the Spencer sisters were fully on Coral's side.

'I believe you want to coach Grace Ellis in your own time?' Violet Spencer had said, glancing over to her sister.

They were both of indeterminate age, with short, suspiciously dark hair and oddly plastic complexions, which had led to their nickname, the Waxworks. The only difference between Violet and Charlotte were their voices: Violet sounded like a woman, Charlotte like an old man.

Coral had nodded. 'I think she has too much potential to waste.'

'I agree,' Charlotte had rasped. 'Keep us in touch with her progress, will you? We might help out.'

'We might,' Violet had agreed.

'If it was necessary.'

Violet had nodded. 'If it was necessary, yes.'

So for months Coral coached Grace and slowly she

saw the girl become more and more tired. Arriving late, Grace would hurry in with apologies and offer up her work, settling down to read whilst Coral looked over it. But time and time again, Coral would look up to find Grace's eyes closed, her head nodding, white flecks of cotton dust in her dark hair, her work apron still on. In a matter of months, Grace's hands had coarsened, her skin becoming pale, her grey eyes huge in the colourless face.

It was late April, when the weather was turning mild, that Grace began coughing.

'How long have you had that cough?' Coral demanded.

'It's just started,' Grace replied, turning back to her books. Coral followed her gaze and picked up the nearest volume.

'What's this? It isn't one of mine.'

'I got it from the library.'

Slowly, Coral laid down the book and looked at Grace. 'You're doing too much. You'll break down if you go on like this.'

'I *have* to go on,' she replied calmly. Her voice was without expression, as was her face.

She was turning into an automaton, Coral thought bleakly.

'No one can do all the things you're doing, Grace, and keep going. You're not well. If you get sick, who'll look after you? Who'll look after your father?'

'My father's fine!' Grace replied, her voice dropping immediately. 'He's fine. I just want to learn, that's all. Surely you understand that? I want an education. I want to work.'

'But why do you need to go to the library now and add to your load?'

'Because it stops me thinking!' she snapped suddenly,

getting to her feet in the neat front room and facing her teacher. Her eyes were dark with anger, her hands clenched. 'When I read I don't think, I don't remember. When I look after my father, wash the clothes, wash the dishes, I don't think. When I go to the library and come here and write and read I DON'T THINK.' She put her hands up to her head as though it hurt her to talk. 'I don't want to think about what's happening. About the house, the mill, my life.'

Startled, Coral got to her feet and reached out to her, but Grace backed away.

'I would rather die trying to better myself than accept my lot.'

Just as quickly as she had lost her temper, Grace became calm. Watching her in rigid surprise, Coral wondered what she would do next. Would she break down? Apologize? Or leave?

But Grace did none of those things. Instead she sat down, picked up the book in front of her, and – taking a deep breath – began to read.

Chapter Nine

It was three weeks later that Coral found a formal, imposing letter on her doormat. Making herself some tea, she opened it. It was from a firm of solicitors in Leeds.

> Dear Mrs Higgins,
>   We have been instructed by our client – charitable benefactors who wish to remain anonymous – that we are to advance you a sum of money every month to ensure the education of one Miss Grace Ellis, aged fifteen, who resides at 17 Wide Hill Lane, Diggle.
>   If you would be kind enough to make an appointment with this office, we can then arrange matters to our mutual convenience.
>   We trust we will hear from you as soon as possible.
>   Yours sincerely,
>   Malcolm Seagrave

'Look at this,' Coral said to her husband as he followed her into the kitchen. 'Would you believe it?'

Frank, huge in a pair of striped pyjamas, read the letter and grinned.

'Well, well, well. Perhaps someone heard about your tutoring Grace in your own time, and decided to give you a helping hand.' He studied the letterhead. 'It sounds like a big firm. I don't suppose it's a joke.'

'A *joke*!' Coral said, snatching the letter from her husband's hand. 'It had better not be or, God knows, someone'll swing for it.'

'I don't believe it!' Joan said when she went over to her friend's the following day and Grace told her the news. 'You're rich!'

'The money's not for me, it's for my education,' Grace replied, 'enough to send me to the High School.' Her face was shining, animated. 'I always wanted to go there. There's money enough for my uniform too. And just enough to keep the house going. I can leave the mill.'

'I wish I had a rich benefactor,' Joan said idly. 'I could leave that bitch Stratton and go to America.'

Grace was staring ahead, lost in thought. 'I wonder who it is.'

'Does it matter?'

'Course it does!' Grace replied, catching Joan's sleeve. 'Actually, I think I know.'

'Go on! Who?'

'The Spencer sisters.'

'*The Waxworks!*' Joan hooted. 'Oh, come on, why would they help you?'

'Because it would help them indirectly.'

'How do you make that out?'

'They could say that I had been educated at their school, that they had done well for me. Besides,' Grace added, 'Mrs Higgins was hinting at it the other day, saying how nice they were. How they had no children of their own and wanted to help young people do well academically.'

'Well,' Joan replied drily, 'it's easy when you're loaded. After all, they were supposed to have inherited some money from their parents, weren't they?'

Grace raised her eyebrows. 'I didn't know that.'

Joan nodded. 'Oh yes, Dad said that old man Spencer was some hot-shot factory owner over in Derbyshire.'

'I don't suppose I could ask, could I?'

'Who? The Waxworks?'

'No, the solicitor.'

Joan shook her head emphatically. 'If I was you I would ask no questions, just take the money and run.'

'But –'

Joan slapped the table between them. 'Come on, enough of this. Let's go to the pictures tonight. You can pay, seeing as how you've come into money. It's a Chaplin film.'

'I thought you liked Mary Pickford?'

'I do,' Joan replied, 'I like everyone in the films.' She linked arms with Grace. 'Did you ever show Miss Holden –'

'She's Mrs Higgins now.'

Joan grimaced. 'When I get married, I'll pick a better name than Higgins . . . Anyway, did you ever show her your sketches?'

Embarrassed, Grace shook her head. 'Oh no, they weren't good enough.'

'They were!' Joan replied. 'If I had any kind of talent I'd be bragging about it all over town. You *should* show her, let her see everything you can do. Let her know how clever you are. She'll tell the Waxworks –'

'Let it drop, Joan.'

Joan shrugged and then reached into her pocket to draw out a crumpled photograph.

'I torn it out of one of Old Ma Stratton's magazines. Skirts are getting short now and all the fashionable women are having their hair cut too.'

Looking over her shoulder, Grace studied the picture. She had had no time for fashion before – Dora would have thought that it was frivolous to talk about make-up and clothes – but Dora wasn't around any more.

'It says,' Joan went on, 'that the Pope has complained about the new fashions and won't have the women wearing short skirts in church!'

Grace frowned. 'It would be too cold up here to try it.'

'Oh, I don't know,' Joan replied, hitching her skirt up to knee level. 'How do I look?'

'Like a chicken,' Grace replied, unusually light-hearted. 'Like a very *thin* chicken.'

A weight had been lifted off her shoulders and suddenly Grace could feel alive again. Her dream was coming closer. She could forget the mill, the girls, the humiliation. Even walking past the old shop wouldn't hurt so much, seeing her father's name painted out, 'DUNCAN McCLOUD – Haberdasher' in its place.

The High School, Grace thought, glowing with pride. She was going to the High School. She had made it at last. No one could stop her now. This was the beginning – and who had made it happen? People she hardly knew. They were the ones who had committed themselves to providing for her. They had rescued her. Not her family, not her poor sick father nor her mother. *Her mother . . .*

Grace bit her lip hard. A feeling she didn't expect suddenly welled up inside her. If only she could tell her mother that she was going to the High School. She could imagine Dora's face, the pleasure in those fearless eyes. The triumph . . . In that moment that Grace realized that she missed her mother. Always had, and probably always would.

An old memory came back: Dora taking her to Miller Lane, to her nemesis, to the past which haunted her and made her run. And now Grace was going to run away from her own version of Miller Lane. She was going to leave the mill and start the steady climb upwards. Her mother had done it, but in the end her past had grabbed her back. Grace wouldn't let that happen to her.

And then she realized that her mother had actually given her what she needed above all. Not affection, indulgence, material wealth or comfort. But courage.

For an instant she loved her for it.

PART TWO

There's no art
To find the mind's construction in the face;

SHAKESPEARE, Macbeth

Chapter Ten

Alexandra Park, Oldham – 1933

Grace was watching the people go by. A nanny pushed her charge in a large carriage-built pram. From one of the big millowners' houses, Grace thought, watching the woman as she passed. In a dark uniform the nanny walked in regimented fashion, the wheels of the pram making long shadows on the gravel path.

Grace had attended the High School and had finally found herself stretched. Her personal history had segregated her, as did her reserve, but the teachers had seen in her what Coral had and had cultivated Grace Ellis's clever mind.

Everything had fascinated her: the arts and the sciences. She had been, for a time, unable to learn and read enough, but gradually she had relaxed. She'd also kept in touch with Coral, who had come to think of Grace as her own daughter and who saw in her charge's success a validation of her own judgement. She was always careful not to mention Grace's benefactors – but the occasional reference to philanthropists kept the Spencer sisters to the forefront of both their minds.

Malcolm Seagrave had proved to be an efficient solicitor and the arrangements made with Coral had soon been put in place. The anonymous sponsor had laid down few rules, only that the money was to be used to support Arthur and educate Grace.

'Of course,' Coral's husband had said one morning, 'it could be the Spencer sisters – or it could be Dora Ellis.'

Coral had nearly dropped the teapot.

'*Dora Ellis!* How on earth could she earn that kind of money? Dora Ellis wasn't even educated.'

'Maybe she's living with someone,' he'd replied, catching the shocked look on his wife's face.

'Frank!'

'Oh, come on,' he'd chided her. 'Things like that do happen, you know. Dora was a striking woman; I dare say she has plenty of admirers to chose from.'

'It's immoral.'

Frank had shrugged. He'd heard of too many incest and cruelty cases to be shocked by anyone's lapse in grace.

'Mind you,' Coral had said thoughtfully, 'it *would* be like Dora to do something like this, to try to make amends. I could never believe she ran off with someone like Len Billings. She had too much class.'

'She had a baby by him –'

'That's just rumour, Frank!'

He'd nodded his head seriously. 'No, it's fact. I heard that Dora Ellis gave birth to a son in Huddersfield and that the baby was adopted.'

'You didn't tell me.'

'I thought it might upset you. You know, you might think you had to tell Grace.'

Gently, Coral had kissed the top of her husband's head. 'God, she must be struggling. Having a baby and giving it up.' She had pressed her lips against Frank's hair. 'You know, Dora Ellis *was* tough, but she was caring too. I wouldn't like to be in her shoes now. She's suffered enough for what she's done.'

Frank had looked at the latest payment lying on the

84

table in front of them. 'However you look at it, it's a lot of money. A lot to keep finding month in, month out.'

'Could Dora Ellis do it?'

Frank had bitten into a piece of toast and raised his eyebrows. 'If she's earning it the way I think, it won't be that hard.'

'It would for someone like her,' Coral had replied sadly.

Then, four months after the first payment had been made, the shattering news had come that Dora Ellis was dead. Coral had overheard the gossip on Union Street and – horrified – had stopped one of the women talking to ask her what she knew. The gossiper had been curt. Dora Ellis had been killed in Salford. Knocked down by a trolley bus. That was all there was to it. There was no kindness, even toward's Dora's memory.

In shock, Coral had walked to the High School and waited until the pupils finished for the day. The first snow of the winter had started falling, and her hair was whitened by the time Grace had emerged. Running out, she'd seen her old mentor and waved, then stopped.

It had seemed to take her an hour just to walk the few yards towards Coral.

'What is it?'

The snow had been ruffled by the wind, catching against Coral's cheeks and eyelashes. Her hand had reached out towards Grace's, her fingers closing over the girl's palm.

'I'm so sorry, my dear, but your mother's been killed.'

Grace had heard the words, reading Coral's lips at the same time. Then she'd frowned and shaken her head.

'No, she's fine, she's with Len Billings.'

Coral's mouth had dried, the snow still falling on the two of them, the playground emptied.

'Come on, Grace. Come home with me for a while.'

Hanging back, Grace had shaken her head again. 'My mother isn't dead,' she'd said emphatically. 'She's just gone away, that's all.'

Suddenly Coral had wondered if Grace had actually expected her mother to return one day. Her throat had tightened with sadness.

'Grace, I'm so sorry, but it's true – your mother's dead.'

'No!' the girl had replied helplessly. 'No! NO!' Grace had been breathing rapidly, her face paling. 'Where is she?'

'Grace, calm down –'

She'd shaken Coral's hand off her arm.

'Where is she? I want to see her.'

Coral had tried to catch hold of Grace's hands, but the girl had pulled away, running towards the school gates. When she reached them she'd turned, her face raw with cold.

'I want to see her!'

Coral had shaken her head. How could she explain that Dora's body was mutilated? That she was so horribly disfigured that she had only been identified by her clothes?

'Grace, she's dead. Let her be.'

'I thought . . .' Grace's voice had faltered. 'I thought I'd see her again, you know. One day, I thought I'd see her again.'

But she'd been wrong. Her mother was dead, there was to be no happy ending, no trying to make up for the past. Dora Ellis had done what everyone thought. Upped and left. This world for the next.

What was left of Dora Ellis had been buried up at Leesfield the following Tuesday. Grace had gone with

Joan and seen Coral by the graveside. For a moment Grace had hesitated and then walked over and stood by her teacher, looking at the dark bank of earth over the grave, a marker with the name DORA ELLIS written in black lettering identifying the plot.

'I haven't told my father,' Grace had said softly.

Coral had glanced at her profile. 'Why not?'

'Because I have to keep him alive. That's why.'

Now Grace shook her head, her thoughts returning to the present. Time had moved on since that bleak day and she had taken her examinations and succeeded.

'University beckons, Coral had said brightly. 'It's possible for you. Anything is possible for you now.'

But Grace thought otherwise.

To attend university would require money, much more than her benefactors – whoever they were – were supplying. But even if her sponsors were generous enough to extend her education still further, Grace had no desire to accept another penny. It was time to earn her own living – to stand on her own two feet.

Besides, she knew that she could get a job anywhere now. She had qualifications and her future as a teacher was predicted by Coral . . . But Grace didn't want to be a teacher. She wanted to do something very few women did. She wanted to run her own business.

It had been Joan who had given her the idea. Joan, with all her talk of the movies and Hollywood. Joan, besotted by fashion and make-up, her hair shingled, her skirt raised, the boys standing at the top of Waterloo Street and whistling as she passed. Grace had been gradually sucked into Joan's fantasy, the films a welcome relief from the pressures of school work and home.

The Riviera was their favourite cinema – not that they hadn't frequented every cinema in Oldham over the years. But the Riviera, with its flashy opulence and queasy glamour, was their second home. Here they had watched Garbo, and Frederic March, and here Joan had kissed her first boyfriend, running back to Diggle to tell Grace all about it.

Under the Riviera's auditorium chandelier Grace would sit with her scarf round her neck and her gloves on when the heating broke down, Joan pulling her collar up under her eyes. They would shiver and moan, but then the music started, the lights dimmed, the gaudy ruched curtains swished back to reveal the film's opening sequence, they were away. Two girls in a cold Northern town, walking with the stars.

Joan – mouth open, eyes agog – would stare up at the vision of Marlene Dietrich and then rush home to pluck her eyebrows to thin arches. Whereas Grace would study the films and look at the effect the make-up was having on the actresses' faces. She found herself getting more and more interested in the different moods make-up could achieve, the actresses' features as perfectly painted as old masters. It was odd, Grace thought, but here she was, the blue stocking, finding herself consumed with the movies.

'No one has eyelashes that long naturally!' Grace hissed one evening as they sat together in the Riviera.

Joan sighed besides her. 'They're wearing false lashes.'

False lashes . . . Well, Grace had heard about such things, but she didn't know where you got them, or how they were made. And as for make-up, apart from the thick, foul-tasting lipsticks at the local chemists, there was little else. Oh, she knew that some women wore dark shadow around their eyes – from wiping their finger down the back of the fire grate and smearing the soot dust over their lids. And powder had been going for years. But mascara – which gave that heavy, black-lidded look – no nice girls used it. That was only for the fast ones, or women on the game.

Once Grace had tried talcum powder on her nose to give it a matt look. But it only made her nose white and faintly ludicrous. Her knowledge of make-up was virtually nil; Dora had never used any, and Grace had no sisters to ask for guidance. And, for all her enthusiasm, Joan's budget didn't run to much experimentation.

Grace looked back at the screen, digging Joan in the ribs as she sighed over Greta Garbo.

'Ouch!'

'Sssshhhhh' a fat woman said behind them.

Grace dropped her voice. 'I wonder who does her make-up.'

'What?'

'Greta Garbo – I wonder who does her make-up.'

Joan kept her eyes on the screen. 'She looks like that naturally.'

'In a pig's eye!'

'Sssshhhhh!' the fat woman repeated angrily, poking Grace in the shoulder with the handle of her umbrella. 'Some of us are trying to watch the film.'

'Then stop talking or you'll miss it,' Joan replied smartly, hunkering down in her seat.

When they came out of the auditorium thirty minutes later, Grace was distant, preoccupied. In the foyer the manager was dressed in a shiny dinner jacket, his narrow face a study of bland irritation.

'What's on next week?' Joan asked him.

'Gary Cooper.'

'That's means it's a boys' film,' Joan replied, disappointed. 'When's the next romance?'

'Watch the paper for details,' the manager replied curtly.

'Can't *you* tell me?'

'It'll be in the paper.'

Joan couldn't resist provoking him, knowing all too well that he had the reputation of being the rudest man in Oldham.

'What paper?'

'What paper d'you think? The bloody *Hong Kong Times*?'

Grace tugged at Joan's sleeve, but she resisted.

'Don't they tell you what's coming on?'

The manager's eyes narrowed, his fingers clenching the door handle of the entrance.

'Of course they tell me! I'm the manager.'

'So tell me.'

'It'll be in the paper.'

Joan turned to Grace and pulled a face. 'He doesn't know.'

'A romance! It'll be a bloody romance next week!' the manager shouted, exasperated.

'A romance?'

'You got cloth ears?' he asked her meanly.

'Who's in it?'

Hurriedly, Grace tugged Joan to the door and out to the street just as the manager slammed the door behind them.

'I don't know why you have to rile him. We'll get banned.'

'Nah! We're his best customers,' Joan replied phlegmatically.

For a moment Grace walked on in silence and then turned.

'That lipstick you wear, what is it?'

Joan looked at her, faintly triumphant. 'I was wondering when you'd ask,' she said smartly, digging into her bag and bringing out two cheap gold tubes. 'This is "Tangee" and the other one's "Evening in Paris".'

Grace wound the lipsticks up in the tubes and then stared at them thoughtfully.

'They're horrible colours, don't they make better ones?'

Annoyed, Joan snatched the lipsticks from her and dropped them back into her bag.

'You needn't be such a snob,' she said. 'I can't afford better ones. If I had the money I'd use the posh ones, but they're too dear.'

'So where did you buy those from?'

'The chemist, where I work Saturdays. We have a deal. I work cheap, and he sells make-up to me cost.'

'But he doesn't sell the expensive makes?'

'Oh, come on,' Joan replied, 'who could afford those around here?'

Grace stared at her friend. 'What do your sisters use?'

'Same stuff as me.'

'And your mother?'

'Oh, my mother's like Old Ma Stratton, neither of them has ever used make-up. My mother spends all her money on corn plasters and arch supports; she's got feet like a bleeding camel.' Joan paused, puzzled. 'Why the interest all of a sudden? I thought you were above all this stuff.'

'If someone could make good, inexpensive make-up for the ordinary women, there would be a demand, wouldn't there?' Grace asked, ignoring the remark.

'Course there would.'

'So why hasn't anyone done it?'

Joan shrugged. 'I dunno. Why?'

Grace turned to her and smiled. 'Because I'm going to do it,' she said, her tone certain. 'I'm going to learn everything there is to learn about make–up and set up a business.'

'You can't!'

'I can and I will,' Grace replied, 'and you're going to help me.'

Chapter Eleven

If the decision had come as a surprise to Joan, it had shaken Grace. It was as though she had put into words something she had not consciously decided, but longed for with all her heart. *This* was what she wanted to do, Grace realized. She had been starved of glamour all her life, her existence fixed on domestic and academic work. But now she was older and the images at the Riviera cinema seemed to represent what she wanted to be. glamorous, wealthy, powerful.

She, Grace Ellis, the swot! Who would have believed it? But why not? Grace thought. She had never had a burning desire to be a teacher. That had been everyone else's plan. She knew how much she owed to her benefactors. It wasn't that Grace was ungrateful, but the career she chose was her choice surely? She had been controlled all her life, now she wanted to build something of her own. Her own business, her own responsibility. God, Grace thought with real pleasure, it felt good. She was going to be someone to be reckoned with – on her own terms and no one else's.

From then onwards, Grace spent every free moment she had reading up what she could find about make-up – which was very little. For once, the library was of limited help and – having no one nearby to ask – Grace was forced to find information elsewhere. Conversations with Joan's sisters, Myra and Kate, supplied her with some insight, although Kate, twenty-one and courting, was disinclined to waste time on one of her little sister's friends.

Myra, moon-faced and stocky, was more willing. Woolworths was the main place they bought their cosmetics, she told Grace, lipsticks like 'Snow Fire', selling at sixpence each. Here they also bought their face cream by Potter and Moore, and powder. If they could afford it, they sometimes splashed out and treated themselves to some rouge by Bourgeois, in a round blue cardboard tub.

'What does that do?' Grace asked Myra.

Myra ran her plump forefinger along the garish red and applied it to her full cheeks.

'It makes me look healthy,' she said.

It makes you look like you have a fever, Grace thought. 'What are these?' she asked, pointing to what looked like a miniature book.

'Powder leaves,' Myra said smugly, flattered by the attention of Joan's snobbish friend. Carefully she opened the book and pulled out what looked like a fine cream leaf, tapping it onto her nose to powder it.

'But I thought powder came in pots?' Grace said, fascinated.

'It does,' Myra replied, her tone superior, 'but this is for when you're out and about and want to stop your face from looking shiny.'

'They don't work then,' Joan said cuttingly. 'Your face is always shiny.'

'Hark who's talking! If I looked like you I'd take all the help I could get,' Myra replied, turning back to Grace. 'We use Vaseline on our eyelids.'

'What for?'

'To make them look glamorous,' Myra went on, 'Like the film stars do.'

Grace couldn't hear enough. 'What about your eyebrows?'

94

'We pluck them.'

'Pluck them? What with?'

Joan grinned to herself as Myra reached for the tweezers and turned back to Grace.

'You have good eyebrows,' she said knowledgeably, 'but they could do with some shaping. Now relax, and I'll do it for you.'

Carefully Myra closed the tweezers over a hair in one of Grace's dark eyebrows and yanked.

'Och!' Grace shouted, her hand going up to her eye. 'That hurt!'

'Oh, come on, stop being such a baby. Every woman has to suffer to be beautiful.'

'You haven't suffered enough then,' Joan said smartly.

Myra ignored her and turned back to Grace. 'Let me do it properly.'

'But it hurts.'

'I know, you have to stretch the skin first,' Myra went on, taking Grace's forefinger and making her pull the skin tautly above her eye. 'Now, hold it there.'

Twenty agonizing minutes later Grace looked into the mirror and then stared, stupefied, at the image facing her. Her face had altered, the brows arched finely, her eyes huge and luminous. She was suddenly older, even sophisticated. She was also, from that moment onwards, completely hooked.

'God,' Joan said admiringly, 'you look amazing. Like a film star.'

Thoughtfully, Myra regarded her handiwork. It was quite a transformation, she had to admit. Why didn't *she* look like that after plucking her eyebrows, she wondered, suddenly envious.

'Well, that's the general idea, anyway . . .'

'Hey, Myra, make up Grace's face, will you? Go on,' Joan encouraged her sister. 'You can do it.'

Myra wasn't too sure if she wanted to, suddenly suspecting that her sister's scholarly friend might turn out to be quite a stunner. Yet, with a little more coaxing from Joan, Myra's chance to show off overcame her reluctance and, tipping out the contents of her make-up bag onto the bed, she studied Grace's upturned face.

For the next thirty minutes Myra worked, slapping away her sister's hand when Joan's tried to rummage through the pots and tubes, and standing back frequently to check her handiwork. With her back to Joan, Grace closed her eyes, giving herself up to the sensuous experience. Nothing like this had ever happened to her before; for as long as Grace could remember she had been attending to her studies, or her father. The effect was mesmeric, Grace feeling herself falling under the spell of Myra's attention. Soft perfume scents tickling her nose, the sensation of her skin being covered with cooling powder, the skill of Myra's podgy fingers running over her cheeks and along her eyelids – Grace didn't want the time to end, the sheer joy of being spoiled.

'That's it,' Myra said finally, stepping back.

Heaving herself up from her supine position on the bed, Joan stared at the back of Grace's head.

'Turn round then, and let's have a look.'

Slowly, Grace open her eyes and glanced up at Myra, surprised by her odd expression. Uneasy, Grace then turned and looked at Joan, whose mouth was hanging open.

'What is it?' Grace asked, her hands going up to her cheeks. 'Do I look a mess?'

'You look . . . God, Myra, what did you do?' Joan

asked, getting off the bed and reaching for a mirror. 'Here, Grace, have a look for yourself.'

Alarmed, she took the mirror and glanced into it. A woman looked back at her with arched eyebrows, a full dark mouth and matt skin. A woman from off the screen at the Riviera, Oldham's answer to Marlene Dietrich. The make-up was obvious, too crude for words, but Grace could see beyond it, past the caricature and knew that *she could be beautiful.*

She, an attractive girl of eighteen, could – with make-up – become a beauty. The thrill of the discovery was more for what Grace could do, than for how she could appear. This was the inspiration she had been looking for! This was what she wanted to do with her life. She would turn women – ordinary women – into goddesses.

Suddenly, Grace snatched up a cloth and then wiped off most of the powder.

Myra reached out to her in surprise. 'Hey! You'll spoil it!'

Joan was also trying to stop her. 'Grace, leave it alone, it looks good.'

'It could look better,' she replied, working on her face and blotting off the excesses, then wiping off half of the lipstick colour and adding Vaseline to soften the image. 'Now look,' she said to Myra. 'What d'you think now?'

Her eyes, which had narrowed in irritation, took in Grace's alterations for a few seconds before she shrugged.

'Yeah, you're right, it's better.'

Joan stared at Grace's face from every angle. 'Well, I liked it before.'

'So did I,' Grace replied tactfully, 'but this is more natural.'

Myra folded her arms, miffed. Grace wasn't dummy after all; she knew that the make-up was too much and had altered it to suit her. Smart girl, Myra thought admiringly, smart *and* beautiful.

'It's better, Grace,' she said again, turning to her sister. 'Come on, you know it is.'

'Well, she couldn't have done it without you,' Joan replied, on the defensive.

Grace nodded. 'You're right, I couldn't and I know that.' She turned back to Myra. 'Will you show me what you did, please? I would be so grateful.'

'I bet you would,' Joan said, turning to her sister. 'Grace is going to have a business. She's going to be a businesswoman.'

Myra stared at her. '*What?*'

'I want to have a business, yes,' Grace replied, embarrassed that her ambition should have been so grudgingly exposed. 'I want to make cosmetics available for ordinary women, up here in the North.'

Myra kept staring at her. What the hell was Grace talking about? Women in Oldham didn't have businesses – unless they had to. Grace Ellis was good-looking and smart; she could get herself married any time and then never have to work.

It isn't so easy for me, Myra thought. She knew she wasn't any great shakes in the looks department, and was pushing twenty-five. It was typical, she thought: Grace Ellis could probably get a man just like that, but she wanted a career instead. Silly cow.

'Why the bloody hell would you want to work?'

'I want a career, I always have.'

'I thought you were going to be a teacher,' Joan said, lying back down on her sister's bed. 'I bet that Coral Higgins thinks you are.'

Grace was surprised to find herself under attack.

'It's my choice what career I pick.'

'Is it?' Joan countered, rolling over onto her stomach. 'Maybe your benefactors might have something to say about it. I mean, if they're supplying the money, they might want to make the choice for you. You know, see that their money's well spent.'

Grace's tone was cold: 'That's why I'm not going into further education. I want to earn a living.'

'Oh yeah, just go out and set yourself up in business now –'

Grace spun round on Joan. 'What's the matter with you? I never make light of your ambitions.'

'Because mine aren't real, are they?' Joan countered, her tiny face pinched with anger. 'Mine are just dreams. How could I go to Hollywood? I'll never go there, I'll never get out of Oldham! They're just *dreams*, Grace, daydreams to stop me going mad.'

Shaken, Grace sat down beside Joan on the bed, Myra hurriedly collecting together her make-up and walking out.

'You could *try* to get to America,' Grace said quietly.

'How? I couldn't even afford the fare! I'll never be a film star, and I know it. You know it too, if you're honest. I'm just some common backstreet kid who'll have to think herself lucky to work for the likes of Old Ma Stratton.' Her eyes fixed on Grace. 'I'm being a mean cow, that's all. Ignore me.'

'But I don't *understand*.'

'Oh, for God's sake!' Joan snapped, sitting upright. 'Look at yourself, Grace. Look in the mirror. All right, if you won't, I'll tell you what you'd see. A beautiful woman. A lady, someone with class. And more than class, a brain. You've been talking about having your own business for a while now and I let you ramble on because I thought it was a dumb idea. Like me going to Hollywood, the kind of thing I know is stupid – just like I know I'll end up in Oldham marrying some snotty-nosed oik from the pit. Well, that's what I thought until now – that your big ideas were daydreams too. But now I look at you and I know you can do it. And that really makes me sick.'

'Oh, Joan –'

'Don't "Oh, Joan" me! You'll do it, you'll get your business and you'll get out of here. But don't ask me to be pleased about it, Grace, because *I* won't be going anywhere.'

'Joan, I've told you,' Grace replied. 'I've said that I want you to work with me.'

'For how long? I don't want to be in your shadow, Grace. It's my fault, I know, I'm a selfish bitch. But you see, I don't like work much and I certainly don't have the ambition to set the world on fire. I know what my life will be, Grace, and I can come to terms with it. It's just that, at the moment, I can't come to terms with *you*.' She studied Grace's face for a long moment. 'God, you look like your mother now, and she was terrifying.'

Smiling, Grace took Joan's hand and squeezed it.

'We'll stay friends.'

'Yeah, we'll stay friends and I'll help you with your dumb business. But the day will come, Grace, when you'll move on.' She stood up. 'You're meant for better things. As for me, who knows?'

Coral Higgins was sitting opposite her husband, her foot tapping irritably against the leg of the table. It was so stupid she could hardly believe it. How could Grace be so wilful, so ungrateful?

'I think –'

'Oh, not again!' Frank groaned, laying down his knife and fork.

'Hear me out,' Coral replied, leaning over the table towards him. 'After all the help she's had, after people have pulled out all the stops for her –'

Frank cut his wife off.

'Grace Ellis hasn't become a murderess, she's just got her own ideas about what she wants to do with her life.'

'Set up a cosmetics business!' Coral screeched. 'That's a worthwhile career? Paint for women's faces! There's so much unemployment now, what makes her think that such products would sell? How could she be so naïve? That girl could make a fine teacher.'

'But she doesn't want to be a teacher, does she?' Frank replied, toying with his steak and kidney pudding. 'She wants to do something different.'

'I'll say it's different!' Coral snapped, turning away.

Annoyed, Coral tapped her foot even quicker against the side of the table.

Frank paused with a forkful of kidney in front of his mouth. 'Why don't you encourage her?'

'*Encourage her!*' Coral exploded. 'No, I'm not going to encourage her. I've spoken to Malcolm Seagrave and told him what Grace said. He seemed to think that the benefactors might not look too kindly on Grace's decision. That they might stop the money.'

'They want their own way too.'

'Frank!' Coral snapped, slamming her hand down on the table and sending the kidney flying off her husband's fork. 'It's not a question of our getting our own way.'

'Yes, it is,' Frank replied, eyeing the fallen kidney with patience. 'If you all really trusted in Grace Ellis you would support her. Think about it – if she does make a success of this business, she will have rewarded everyone's belief in her.'

'She is eighteen years old.'

'Yes, she is. And at eighteen many women round these parts are married and some already have kids. She's not asking for anything, Coral, just emotional support. She's already said that she'll work whilst she learns what she needs to know – how can you think she's not dedicated?'

'I never said she wasn't dedicated, I'm just afraid she's going to waste her life.'

Frank stabbed at the cooling piece of kidney, then eyed his wife thoughtfully. 'There's more grit in that girl than there is in any four men I know. What you taught her won't go amiss, Coral. All that education and studying will stand Grace Ellis in good stead – but she has to use it *her* way, not yours.'

But Coral couldn't accept what had happened and finally sent for Grace. She came round that afternoon and told Coral that she would not be applying for teacher training or university. She wanted to start earning a living instead.

'How?' Coral replied. 'Why not get all the qualifications you can, whilst you can?'

'I don't want to go on,' Grace continued patiently, 'I want to set up a business. I need practical experience now. I'm so grateful for what you've done for me, Mrs Higgins, but I have to do this now. I'll work to support myself and my father while I learn my new trade.'

'Work!' Coral snapped. 'Where? Back at the mill? You should be careful, my girl. The mills are closing: there's a depression on.' Her voice softened. 'Oh, do think about it, Grace. You hated work like that, you couldn't wait to get out of the mill before.'

'I know, but I didn't have a plan then,' she replied carefully. 'Now, I do.'

'What kind of plan?'

'I need to learn about cosmetics, like how they're made. There's no good make-up around for women in the North. In London, it's different – they have more money and so they have more choice. There's some choice up here, but the better quality make-up is far too expensive for ordinary women. Round here, no one can afford Elizabeth Arden, so they use any cheap stuff they can lay their hands on.'

'You seem to know a lot about it,' Coral replied, 'but unless my memory fails me, you never seemed to show much interest in such things before. All the other girls at school were full of it, talking about clothes, make-up, boys. But you were different –'

'That's just the point!' Grace responded. 'I *wasn't*. I wanted what they wanted, but it wasn't possible for me. I was the clever one, the one who was destined for higher things. Everyone was so busy making me fulfil their dreams they forgot I was human like everyone else.'

'I'm sorry it seemed that way to you,' Coral said, her tone frigid. 'I suppose you thought I was living through you as well?'

'I didn't mean that,' Grace replied. 'You helped me and I wanted that help . . .'

But it was obvious that Coral was wounded, cut to the quick. 'You always seemed keen to learn.' She shook her head, exasperated. 'I'm sorry, Grace, but I'm totally confused. You studied constantly, you seemed dead set on an academic career. You never showed an interest in anything else – and now you come here and tell me that you want to make cosmetics. What *are* you talking about?'

'It's not something that came to me overnight –'

'It seems that way,' Coral replied bitterly.

'I've dreamed about it for a while, but I was scared of saying anything. I knew how people would react.'

Coral turned on her. 'How are we *supposed* to react, Grace? Are you surprised that I'm disappointed in you? It's a waste. And it's ungrateful of you to behave this way.' Her voice hardened. 'You talk about setting up a business. How? You're hardly more than a girl. Grow up!'

Grace could feel her face flush, but she wouldn't back down.

'I've been talking to all kinds of people. Women who use make-up, asking them where they get it, and what they use. I've been to the local chemists – and I went over to Manchester the other day to talk to the staff at Kendal Milne. It's the best shop in Deansgate.'

'I know what it is! But talking to people isn't running a business,' Coral retorted hotly. 'Just think about what you're saying, Grace. Make-up is superficial, frivolous stuff. With your brain you could teach children, inspire them. Do something worthwhile with your life.'

'But *this* is worthwhile,' Grace countered. 'I don't want to teach; I haven't the patience or the skill. I don't even like children that much. But I could run a business, I know I could – and I could make a success of it. I could also make money.'

'Or lose it,' Coral replied.

All those hours working, all that studying, poring over books, toiling every free minute. And for what? To use that good brain to make cosmetics? God, Coral thought angrily, she couldn't be serious. There had never been anything to suggest that Grace Ellis would want to dedicate her life to something as superficial as beauty. And now – when she had the chance to make a career in teaching, to do something respectable – now she was going into business for herself. Hadn't life been difficult enough for her already?

'Women don't do that kind of thing,' Coral said at last. 'What do you know about business?'

'I can learn,' Grace countered, feeling alternately apologetic and defensive. 'I know about colour, I have a feel for what looks good and expensive. I can keep the books – and I can cost things. I ran a shop before, when I was only fourteen.'

'And it failed,' Coral said, the words out of her mouth before she had time to stop them.

Stung, Grace took in a breath and moved to the door.

Coral called after her. 'I didn't mean it! Oh, come here, Grace, we'll talk about this further. I don't want you to throw your life away.'

'But I *won't* be throwing it away,' Grace called back, 'I'll be making something of it.'

Chapter Twelve

Times, which had never been easy in Oldham, became even tougher. The depression of the thirties crucified the town and some had the sour experience of losing their income and their savings when share prices collapsed, loans were defaulted and there followed a passing of dividends.

Wage cuts, unemployment and short time followed as many of the mills closed or ran on three-day weeks. The likes of Elmer Shaw, who ran Ark Mill, managed to keep his head above water, but he was one of the few. As for the ordinary men, the unemployed got dole money – 17 shillings weekly, 8 shillings for his wife and 2 shillings for a child. It was worse for those who didn't qualify for dole. Then they went on poor relief. Then, if they didn't find work after a period of time, they were means tested. This was the most feared measure. Everything was scrutinized for the Means test; savings and any assets, furniture included. It was humiliating, and forced many into outright dishonesty.

Living conditions deteriorated as a result of poverty. Children roamed the streets and unemployed men hung round corners. Boredom and hunger were the enemies in the worst affected areas. Cheap cuts of meat and bruised vegetables were bought late on Saturday, after trading, up at Tommy Field's. Malnutrition took its toll too, children surviving on jam and bread, and the pawn shop doing a lively business. On Friday nights the debt collectors called and many men, disillusioned and cold, stayed hidden in bed, ignoring the knock. The bailiffs always followed.

The only luxury was the cinema, where the unemployed queued for cheap tickets in order to get a few hours of escapism. Film stars became idols, *Anna Karenina* offering some welcome fantasy, Laurence Olivier in all the papers. And in amongst all this hardship, Grace dreamed of a making beauty a reality. Affordable glamour, something to aspire to.

The chemistry of the products proved hard to master. Grace set up a tiny laboratory in the pantry, to the left of the kitchen. All the pots and pans had been removed and a small worktable put in, a shelf fixed above for Grace's notebooks. There was no window, but if she kept the door open behind her there was enough light in the daytime. At night, she took in a lamp.

Joan's brother, the gentle Geoffrey, had become devoted to Grace and was more than willing to help her out. Joan had often teased him about his devotion, but Geoffrey – although embarrassed – refused to be put off. Grace Ellis was, he knew only too well, far beyond his reach. But a cat could look at a king, couldn't it? And whatever anyone said about her, Grace was the most unusual woman in those parts. She might not think of him as a boyfriend but he would do anything just to be around her.

Arthur Ellis, now finally bedridden, had changed beyond recognition, had become more melancholic and more violent. Although able to cope with her father's moods most of the time, Grace began to rely on Geoffrey's visits, knowing that he would sit with Arthur and talk to the old man. At other times Joan would visit, but she was too excitable and bored easily, Arthur becoming fretful when she was around him.

The doctor said that Arthur's condition could only deteriorate, that his heart was weak and that his depression had turned into senility. The suggestion of hospitalization was quickly vetoed by Grace and never mentioned again.

Meanwhile, Grace laboured on with her dream. Yet there were times when she wondered if she really had done the right thing: her investigations were time-consuming and incomplete, her visits to Manchester stores to see what was available a waste of time when so few women had money to spend. Her one and only visit to London was a disaster too. Grace didn't get past the door of a Bond Street salon, when she tried to pose as a customer, and she caught the train home in crushed silence.

At times she wondered why she kept going. But she did; experiments done on the kitchen table and in the sink. Before long, the smell of lanolin seemed to permeate the house, lemon scents and eau de cologne mixing oddly with the odours of cooking.

Always skilful at drawing, Grace had designed an image, her name scrolled across a line sketch of a woman's elegant profile – 'Grace cosmetics, to give you grace.' She had studied the advertisements in *Vogue* for Chanel, Cyclax, Madame Gris and Coty, noticed how they selected a type of woman to promote their products. Grace realized the kind of female she was aiming at – a woman with limited money who wanted elegance, rather different from the Chanel market, though hoping to achieve the same look.

But as the months passed, Grace found it difficult to avoid her own doubts. There had to be a way to make the dream reality, there *had* to be. It was so difficult, knowing that people wondered how she could have thrown away her chance of being a teacher, someone important.

As Coral had predicted, the anonymous benefactors withdrew their financial support. Malcolm Seagrave confided to Coral that he expected Grace to relent – but she didn't. Although her sponsors no longer supported her, some of the money they had given for her education and Arthur's support, Grace had set aside. Without telling anyone, over the years she had accumulated a nest egg. Having been poor and humiliated once, she was determined never to find herself in that position again.

No one at the mill knew what Grace was up to. The girls there were only aware that they had a stranger in their midst, a young good-looking woman of some confidence. The reason for that confidence caused much amusement. *What the hell was she so pleased about? She was a mill girl again.* Other wondered what she was doing there. Word was that Grace Ellis had been educated, had come into money – so why was she back slumming it at the mill?

Yet something in Grace's demeanour did not invite bullying. Instead the other mill girls kept their distance, never including her in their activities and seldom in their conversation. To them she was just the tall dark woman at the end of the loom. Always thinking, always quiet.

She was quiet because she was always preoccupied. Whilst Grace moved back the little shuttles and saw the cotton threads twirl round on their pulleys, she dreamed of cosmetics recipes, colours, consistencies. Whilst the cotton dust settled on her hair and the weaving shed clattered around her, Grace glanced at the mill girls and tried to imagine how they would look with make-up.

Several of them already wore it: garish lipsticks and rouge, looking like cheap dolls. Others – the younger ones – emulated the film stars, their hair pinned away from their faces, their nails painted blood red. Their look was hard and smart, their lips a damning crimson. These were the girls who went to the Roxy every Friday night and swapped magazines after work. Avidly they read the one precious, well-thumbed copy of Vogue for inspiration, and hung about the dance hall in their home-made swagger coats draped over pinched waists and thin skirts.

But most of the mill girls didn't bother to wear make-up to work, and many of the older women never wore any at all. Money was too tight to spend on frivolities when there was a family to feed and a man coughing his guts up down the mine. So it fell to the younger, single girls to follow the trends.

One woman in particular fascinated Grace. Moving between the looms with quick elegance, Elsa James wore her fair hair tied up in a scarf, her white skin emphasizing the blue of her eyes. Her make-up was so subtle that it took Grace a while to realize that she was wearing any, until one day she had opportunity to observe Elsa as she stopped several times, to supervise the workers.

When Elsa had moved off to the back of the mill, Grace slowly threaded the cotton onto the shuttle and set the machine off again, her thoughts wandering. She had found out how to make powder and colour it – the chemist had helped with the dyes and perfumes – but the texture wasn't right – too coarse.

Grace frowned. She had made little real progress. It was true that she knew more about cosmetics and how they were manufactured, but it had also become obvious to her that she hadn't the ability or the funds to make her own line of make-up. Or the premises. Her vision of a cosmetics business was beginning to look rather foolish.

True to her word, Joan had been an ally, coming over to Diggle when she had finished at the Strattons. She had even begun to believe in Grace's dream, and talked about how they would make a fortune. She would give up working for Old Ma Stratton, and save up for that trip to America . . .

Grace sighed, suddenly disillusioned. Who was she kidding? Herself – and worse, Joan. She couldn't set the business up on her own, she needed backing. Financing. It was no good otherwise, she thought, slamming down the shuttle she was holding and making the girl next to her jump in surprise.

She had to find someone who could make the cosmetics for her. She had the ideas, the style, and she knew she could sell herself – but she didn't have the equipment. And who, in the middle of a depression, would invest in her? Irritated, Grace bit down hard on her lip and stared at the white cotton cloth in front of her – a memory coming back with a nauseous jolt.

White cloth, white sheets – a couple embracing, falling into the white sheets under the wind and the summer sky.

'Watch it!'

Grace jumped.

'Watch what yer doing, will ya?' the woman next to her shouted.

'I'm sorry, I wasn't thinking.'

'That's all you bloody do, think,' the woman went on, red-faced and irritated. 'Toffee-nosed bitch. You ain't pulling your weight. Yer bloody lucky to 'ave a job. Our Lilian came for same job, but you gorrit. It ain't fair. I've bin watching you and you're slow.'

Grace turned away, but the woman caught hold of her arm. 'Hey! I'm talking to you.'

Angrily, Grace shook her off. 'I work as hard as you and anyone else here.'

'It don't look that way from where I'm standing,' the woman replied, her narrow face shadowed under the eyes. 'You think yer too good for us, don't you? Well, we don't like havin' you around either. The place hasn't bin the same since you came 'ere.'

Suddenly she shoved Grace hard with her elbow, Grace stumbling against the loom. She was just regaining her feet when the supervisor, Elsa James, emerged at the woman's elbow.

'What's going on here?'

The woman winced. Elsa was a hard taskmaster, and there was nothing she disliked more than fighting amongst the women. It was a reason for dismissal. Oh God, the woman thought, if she was fired there would be no money coming in, and then what would she do with her man on the dole and three kids to feed?

Helplessly, she stared at Elsa. It was common knowledge that the stunning Miss James was *seeing* the owner. Mr Elmer Shaw. Ruthless, middle-aged Mr Shaw, with a wife and two kids at home, and a lot of late meetings to go to. Fearful of Elsa's power and terrified of losing her job, the woman glanced down at her feet.

'Nuthin' 'appened.'

Sighing, Elsa turned her attention to Grace. 'What's been going on?'

'Nothing,' Grace replied. 'I stood on her foot, that was all. It was an accident.'

Elsa's serene eyes studied the pale woman standing next to Grace. She had seen the exchange, and seen Grace being pushed.

'Is that true?'

'Sure it is,' the woman said, rubbing her toes convincingly. 'Like she said, she stood on m' foot. It bleedin' hurt too.'

'I see,' Elsa replied evenly, moving away and then turning back to face Grace. 'You should be more careful. Always avoid stepping on people's toes.'

'Thanks,' the woman said under her breath as Elsa walked away. 'That were right good of you. You could 'ave shopped me there – and I'd 'ave asked fer it.'

Grace didn't reply. Her thoughts were already wandering. She was thinking about Elsa James and about her relationship with the wealthy Elmer Shaw, and, as she watched the tall blonde enter the office at the top of the mill steps, a plan began to form in Grace's head.

It was a long shot, but it might just work.

Chapter Thirteen

'Bloody hell!' Ernie Cox said, throwing down his paper. 'What the hell's the matter now?'

His eyes moved to the partition wall between the houses, his eldest son, Tom, wincing as the shouting increased from next door.

'Daft old bugger should be in a home,' Ernie said, rising to his feet and standing bow-legged in front of the fireplace. 'I said SHUT UP!' he shouted suddenly, banging on the wall.

Silence fell unexpectedly. Tom looked at his father. Ernie looked back – and then the shouting began again.

'Sweet Jesus!' Ernie exploded. 'Go round and see what's going on, will you? I'd go myself but my leg's bad.'

And besides, Tom thought, he was bigger . . . Pulling on his coat, Tom walked over to next door and knocked. A light was on upstairs, the sound of shouting clearly audible in the street. Then he heard footsteps hurrying downstairs.

When Grace opened the door she was faced with a tall young man with thick blond hair the colour of hot sand. She looked at him and felt a sudden surprised interest. As did he.

'Oh, hello,' he stammered. 'Are you all right?'

Grace blinked, then replied hurriedly, 'Oh, yes. I'm fine. Fine.'

Above them, the shouting softened, Arthur mewling instead.

'We've just moved in next door . . . We heard shouting and wondered if . . .'

Grace smiled wanly. 'That was my father. He's not well. Sorry if he disturbed you and your family.'

'He sounded very angry.'

'He doesn't mean it,' Grace replied, trying to smooth her hair. She was embarrassed, not about Arthur's shouting, but about her own harassed appearance in front of this handsome man. 'He's confused.'

'He sounded *violent*.'

She stammered, unusually ill at ease. 'It's his condition. He doesn't mean it, really he doesn't.'

'Does he hit you?'

Grace paused. At times Arthur did swing out. Luckily, being bedridden, he couldn't reach her, but on occasions he had hit Grace when she was leaning over, or feeding him.

'No,' she lied, 'he never hits me.'

Tom didn't believe her and was intrigued. Not wanting to finish the conversation, he suddenly put out his hand.

'My name's Tom Cox. I work at the town hall, in Oldham.'

He paused, to let the information sink in and impress her. He wasn't unemployed, he was working – and even better, he was a clerical worker.

Grace smiled, but offered no information in return.

'I think he'll be quiet now,' she said finally, glancing up the stairwell behind her. 'I'm sorry he disturbed you.'

'Well,' Tom said, departing reluctantly. 'If you need me, just knock on the wall. Anytime, day or night.'

Ernie put down his paper when Tom walked back in. His head went on one side, his eyes narrowed under his heavy lids.

'It's gone quiet,' Ernie said, impressed. 'What did you do? Strangle the old bugger?'

'I spoke to his daughter,' Tom said, turning away and avoiding his father's eyes. 'She's very . . . brave.'

Ernie let out a long sigh.

'And very pretty?'

'I didn't notice.'

'I did,' his father replied, looking up at him and winking. 'She's got a pretty face all right – and a mad father. Watch your step, Tom.'

It was March, the snows ending early, the weaving shed warming up with the first hesitant spring days. With the unseasonable mildness, the mill girls sat around outside in their breaks, talking, some of the younger ones discussing their boyfriends.

From where she was sitting in the sun, Grace could see Elsa at the office window in the building opposite the weaving. Obviously animated, her tall figure was moving backwards and forwards. She was talking to someone, Grace thought, glancing over to the courtyard outside and seeing Shaw's Daimler parked there, his chauffeur taking off his hat and wiping his brow.

Over the past few weeks Grace had found out everything she could about Elsa James and Elmer Shaw. Elsa, set up in a little flat near Oldham Park, had been seeing Shaw for some time. Apparently, within two months of her coming to work at the mill, Shaw had promoted her to supervisor and more. She was Shaw's mistress, with all the cool control such power gave her.

As for Shaw, he was fifty-two years of age and married to a woman who had her own fortune in mining. A financial match, no more. If Mrs Shaw cared about Elsa James she didn't make it public knowledge, and besides, judging from the way Shaw looked at Elsa, his wife would never succeed in eradicating her rival.

Shaw's own fortune had been made in cotton. A fortune large enough to build an impressive house by the park and another, smaller, in Southport. It was to that residence that Mrs Shaw took the children for most of the year, leaving the way clear for Elsa. Shaw, rich and powerful, had bought himself into the council and local politics. His money oiled many deals and, rumour had it, he was always looking for new investments, even in the depression . . . But he was no fool, and neither was he partial to throwing his money about.

Grace stared up at the window. Elsa was still talking, her bright blonde hair catching the unexpected sunlight. A few moments later, she came out with Shaw and walked with him to his car. There was no embrace, only a touch on his arm and then she walked away.

Grace caught up with Elsa outside the office door.

'Can I have a word with you?'

Surprised, Elsa nodded and showed her in. The room was low-ceilinged and cool, the floor bare. On the desk by the window was a telephone, some books and an expensive handbag.

'Is there a problem?' Elsa asked coolly.

The sunlight caught her face, Grace noticing the choice skin and the clear eyes.

'No, no problem,' she replied. 'I wanted to talk to you about something, that was all.'

Raising her eyebrows, Elsa motioned for Grace to take a seat. She was intrigued, and studied the woman in front of her. It had been a surprise to find Grace Ellis coming for a job, especially as Elsa had heard some rumours about her background. What in God's name was a woman like her doing working in a mill?

But Elsa wasn't given to worrying about other people. Her ambitions were only for herself and her advancement, nothing more. So although she had been interested in Grace at first, the interest had soon waned.

'I have a proposition to make to you.'

Elsa's still face betrayed no emotion as Grace continued, 'I've been working on something for a while now, an idea which could be a great success. I want to start up a business in cosmetics. I know about the subject and I know how to make women look good. But I don't have any funds. I need a backer.'

Elsa frowned. 'I can't back you.'

'But you know someone who could,' Grace replied, hurrying on. 'Mr Shaw has funds; he might well be interested in investing in new products. Make-up is in demand. Women want it now, all kinds of women –'

'There's make-up already available.'

Grace nodded. 'Yes, there is. But most of it's too expensive for ordinary people. I want to make it available for everyone.'

'When there's a depression on?'

'That's the point. It's at times like these that women want their spirits lifted. Things are so hard, their lives are grim – but that doesn't stop them feeling like women. They want to look like the film stars they see. They look at the magazines and see the new clothes and hair, and they want that. They want to be beautiful. They're working hard, standing by their men, bringing up their children – they need something as a reward, something to make them feel special.'

Elsa was listening, surprised by how eloquently Grace Ellis put her case.

'There are cosmetics houses in London –'

'I know,' Grace interrupted her, 'but that's the point –

118

they're *in London*. There aren't any up here. That's why a Northern manufacturer could do so well. And make a lot of money.'

'Why do you think Mr Shaw would be interested in this?' Elsa asked smoothly. 'You're a mill girl, with no experience. He only works with businessmen.'

'I can do it,' Grace said with perfect conviction. 'I don't need anything, just a patron. I would pay back any investment Mr Shaw chose to loan me.'

'You would have to,' Elsa replied. 'He doesn't like to lose money.'

Taking a deep breath, Grace stared at the woman opposite. 'You could convince him.'

Elsa met Grace's gaze, her eyes steely.

'Don't try and use me.'

'I'm not,' Grace replied, 'but you like to have power, and so do I. If you go to Mr Shaw with an idea and it works, you'll impress him. He won't forget that you made him money.' Grace could see Elsa's eyes flicker with interest. 'It's one thing working for Mr Shaw but quite another having your own interest – an interest which could benefit him. It would be another string to your bow.'

Elsa regarded the woman sitting opposite her for a long, silent moment. She was clever, this Grace Ellis, clever and ambitious. What she said was true: it *would* be good to have another hold over Elmer, and where could she get a better grasp than on his wallet? Love faded, Elsa knew, but money stayed fresh for ever.

There was only one problem – Grace Ellis was altogether too handsome. Elmer might find himself attracted to the dark eyes and the clever brain. Oh, it was tempting, Elsa thought, but she would have to think about it very carefully, very carefully indeed.

*　　*　　*

Tom had to admit to himself that he was in love. Well, it had to be that, didn't it? Nothing else had ever put him off his food for long ... Looking down from the bedroom window, he stared into the garden next door, hoping that Grace might come out and hang up some more washing. But she didn't, and instead Tom sat silently, straining to hear any movement through the partition wall.

His attempts at furthering their acquaintance had failed. Grace never knocked for him to come over and the next time Arthur had shouted she never even answered the door when he came round. Instead she pretended not to hear and a few minutes later Tom saw the light go out in Arthur Ellis's window above the front door.

Several times Tom had waited outside the mill to see her. But on the one occasion he was successful, Grace came out alone and was immediately greeted by a thin girl in a maid's uniform. The same girl who came over to Diggle so often. The girl he thought was called Joan.

Tom sighed. Grace Ellis hadn't got a boyfriend, he knew that much. Oh yes, he had seen a hulking young man come and go, but it was obvious to anyone looking that Grace wasn't interested in the devoted Geoffrey Cleaver. So the way was clear for him – if only he could get to her.

'Hey, come away from that window, you'll wear out the glass,' his father called upstairs.

Reluctantly Tom went down into the cramped kitchen, his mother sewing by the black-leaded range, his younger brother polishing his boots with a well-worn brush.

'What the hell's so interesting in the view up there?'

'Oh, Father,' Sylvie Cox replied, smiling at her husband, 'the lad's in love.'

Sniggering, Joe looked up to his elder brother. 'In love! You must be mad.'

By this time Tom's face was on fire, his voice unconvincing. 'I don't know what you're talking about.'

'Your mother's talking about that lass next door,' Ernie replied, looking impatiently at his son. He didn't want to see his eldest boy mixed up with a woman who had problems. No, Ernie had bigger ambitions for Tom. 'She's bonny, no mistake, and she cares for her father, but you have to think carefully, lad. Mr Ellis – now what's exactly's wrong with him?'

'He's sick,' Tom said, not seeing where the conversation was leading.

'Sick or tapped?' Ernie replied, knocking his temple with his forefinger. 'There's sick and there's barmy – and unless I miss my guess, Arthur Ellis comes into the barking category.'

'Oh, Ernie,' Sylvie said, her tone sympathetic, 'you don't know that for sure.'

But her husband was in full flow. He worked in the local hospital as a clerk and sometimes – when he had time on his hands – Ernie liked to read the patients' medical records. There was little he didn't know about anyone who had been a patient at Boundary Park hospital, and he fancied himself as a natural diagnostician. Unfortunately, although he had searched thoroughly, there were no notes on Arthur Ellis so he had to guess at his neighbour's condition.

'Mr Ellis,' Ernie said authoritatively, 'could have a brain tumour.'

'Oh, never!' Sylvie said, startled and accidentally pricking her finger with the needle she was using.

'Or,' Ernie went on, pushing his round glasses up his snub nose, 'he could be criminally insane.' He liked the sound of that. Sylvie looked at him in dismay, but Joe stared at his father with ill-concealed joy.

'*Criminally insane!*' he said gleefully. 'Does that mean he could kill someone?'

Annoyed, Tom interrupted, 'Mr Ellis is bedridden –'

'A good thing, keep him safe. Keep everyone safe,' Ernie went on, warming to his theme and beginning to believe that only incapacitation kept Arthur Ellis from multiple murder.

'He's a sick old man,' Tom went on, towering over his stocky father. 'And I like his daughter, she's very caring.'

'Of course she could be a murderer too,' Joe offered from the floor.

Ernie nodded sagely. 'The lad has a point; criminal tendencies do get passed down in the family.'

Exasperated, Tom moved to the door and grabbed his coat.

'I'm going out.'

'If we don't see you for a while, we'll call the police,' Joe said, smirking and throwing a boot after his older brother as he left.

Mrs Stratton was in her drawing room, her full lips pursed, her hands resting on a copy of *Oliver Twist*. She liked to be seen reading improving books; they added to her reputation as a humanitarian. After all, hadn't she colluded with Eisha Bardsley, the Mayor, and organized a soup kitchen a few years earlier?

Her husband was travelling again, she thought with relief. How lucky that Mr Stratton was so busy. It left her free to lord it at home, calling in her do-gooding friends and the redoubtable Misses Spencer. Many a time she and her companions had gone down to the likes of Miller Lane and Bow Street, visiting the poor.

She had to admit that she thought they could have been less sullen, more grateful for her attentions. But there you were: what could you expect from a pig, but a grunt? It was true that times were hard, but the hospitals had improved and the rate of child mortality was considerably lower than it had been before the war. Pity of it was that religion had suffered. People were embittered and only the Catholics kept the faith.

Mrs Stratton sighed to herself, inordinately bored. It was difficult to help some people; they wouldn't help themselves. The only good thing anyone could say about the depression was that there was so little money about it was rare to see a drunk on the streets of Oldham any more.

Suddenly her attention was caught by a small figure walking out onto the lawn. It was her undermaid, Joan, one of the few who didn't mind staying in service. Others thought it beneath them. Not like before the war, Mrs Stratton thought nostalgically, then every decent girl was grateful for a position in a good house.

Her eyes fixed on Joan's small frame and then moved up to her face. Was the girl wearing make-up? Mrs Stratton picked up her glasses and peered through them. She was! Her maid was wearing make-up! That would have to stop, she thought, ringing the bell and waiting for Joan to appear.

She did within moments, standing in front of her employer, her face bland.

'Are you wearing make-up?'

Joan thought about lying and then decided against it.

'A little.'

'I don't care about the amount, I don't want anyone in my employ painted up like a trollop,' Mrs Stratton said, suddenly warming to the conversation. 'I should warn you, Joan, that young ladies do *not* wear cosmetics. Only the fast ones do.'

'All the women my age wear make-up –'

Mrs Stratton silenced her at once. 'The women you know do not work for me. I don't approve of cosmetics.'

You should, Joan thought to herself, you could use some.

'I'm sorry, Mrs Stratton, it won't happen again.'

But the subject wasn't going to be dropped. Vera Stratton was bored and had been looking for someone to preach to for a while. Joan, in her employment and unable to answer back, would do nicely.

'You don't want to get a reputation, do you?'

Secretly amused, Joan stared at the heavy woman in front of her, Vera Stratton grossly overdressed in unfashionable clothes. She looked like a relic from the past. Hadn't Old Ma Stratton heard that they were cutting their hair and raising their skirts now? Didn't she know about the films? Hadn't she heard Gracie Fields singing, or George Formby?

For a moment Joan pitied her employer in her big house, with her absent husband. Vera Stratton was a dinosaur. She'd never been dancing with the lads at the Hill Stores, or walked on the 'monkey parades' down Union Street on a Sunday night. Poor old soul had never been kissed in the back row of the La Scala cinema or had a beau who cuddled her by the park lake.

'Joan, are you listening to me?' Mrs Stratton asked, her tone imperious. 'You should think about your future.

I imagine you would like to marry some nice young man with prospects one day.'

Like your husband? Joan thought, no thanks. I don't care if my fella's got money or not, I just want him home with me.

'Sorry if I've offended you, Mrs Stratton,' Joan said automatically.

She would placate the old fool and keep her job, until something better came along. Like Grace's business. But she didn't have to be in awe of Old Ma Stratton any longer. Those days were gone.

'You're a good girl at heart,' Mrs Stratton said generously. 'I know that you understand my concerns, and that I won't have to mention this matter again.'

It was just past seven when, on her way to visit Grace, Joan felt someone catch hold of her arm. Startled she jumped and pulled away.

'What the hell . . . ?'

'It's only me,' Tom said quietly, drawing her under the lamplight.

'Hey, I know you. You live next door to Grace.'

Tom nodded. 'That's right. That's what I want to talk to you about.'

Joan studied his face, suddenly interested. A flush of warm pleasure started around her cheeks and then ran down her neck. God, she thought to herself, I don't believe it, I'm blushing!

'Joan,' Tom said cheerfully, 'will you take a message to Grace?'

Her disappointment was obvious. 'Why don't you talk to her yourself?'

'I can't just go and knock on her door, can I?' Tom replied, looking into Joan's upturned face. She was prettier than he expected, her hazel eyes bright with mischief. 'I've written her a letter.'

Joan took it from his hand, allowing her fingers to brush against his.

Embarrassed, Tom smiled and backed off. 'You will give it to her, won't you?'

'Oh yes,' Joan replied, 'I'll give it to her all right.'

A loud crash echoed down the stairwell as Joan walked into Grace's house, Arthur's voice raised and angry. Running up the stairs Joan hurried into the front bedroom to find Arthur swearing and swinging his arms uselessly at his daughter.

'What's up?'

Grace glanced over to her friend. 'Dad's not too good tonight –'

'I'm bloody well fine, you stupid bitch! Bloody well fine!'

Her hair falling around her shoulders, Grace tried to settle her father and then, exasperated, left the room, Joan following her downstairs. In silence, she made them some tea and then let down the rack over the range, folding the dried clothes.

Aware that Grace was upset, Joan stayed silent and automatically began to help her with the washing, both of them folding sheets and pillowcases. Finally Grace dropped into a chair and laid her head on her arms.

Alarmed, Joan sat down beside her.

'Hey, what is it?'

'He's getting worse,' Grace said brokenly. 'I thought he'd settled down, but he's more and more angry. When I go to work he broods and then lets rip when I get back.' She lifted her face. 'I get tired. So tired.'

Suddenly remembering the letter in her pocket, Joan passed it to her friend, hoping it would cheer her up.

Blinking, Grace read her name on the envelope and then opened it. She read it and then passed it over to Joan.

Dear Miss Ellis

I hope you won't think that I am being too forward, but I wondered if you would like to come to the pictures with me on Saturday night? I could call for you at seven fifteen.

Yours,

Tom Cox, (your neighbour)

'So?' Joan asked. 'What d'you think?'

'I don't want to go.'

'Course you do!' Joan replied hotly. 'He's good-looking, very good-looking.'

'Then you go with him.'

'I can't do that!' Joan retorted. 'He asked you.'

'And I don't want to go with him on my own. It would look like we're courting.' Grace rubbed her eyes and then turned to Joan. 'You could come with us, couldn't you?'

Now this was more like it! Joan thought. If Grace wasn't interested in the charming Mr Cox, she might well be. Besides, she had seen it happen all too often to her sister Myra. Beaux that Kate had considered and then dismissed were often picked up by her less appealing sister. So why shouldn't Joan be the one to console Mr Cox if Grace refused him?

'Oh, wait a minute,' Grace said. 'I can't go, there's no one to look after Dad.'

The thought of not seeing Tom Cox was too terrible to consider, Joan coming up with an immediate solution.

'Geoffrey will baby-sit.'

'On a Saturday night?'

'Why not? He's not going anywhere.'

Grace frowned. 'He should have a girlfriend –'

'Hark at you!' Joan replied, laughing. 'You're not exactly living it up, are you?'

'I'm busy.'

'You should never be too busy for boys.'

'I have other things on my mind,' Grace replied, somewhat shortly. 'I might have thought of someone to invest in the business.'

Joan narrowed her eyes.

'Like who?'

'Elmer Shaw.'

'*Elmer Shaw!* He'll want more of an investment than you'd be willing to offer. That man's always trying to get into someone's knickers.'

'I spoke to Elsa James,' Grace went on, ignoring the comment. 'She's his mistress. I thought she might like to get an even stronger hold on Shaw – so I offered her a way to get it.'

Joan frowned. 'Shaw's a rough diamond, a real hard case. Why couldn't you go back to your old benefactors?'

Grace rolled her eyes. 'Are you joking?'

'No, why not?'

'Because to go back would be to admit failure, and besides, they withdrew their support when I didn't carry on with my education. 'They did enough for me, I have to do the rest myself.'

'But you can't,' Joan replied practically. 'I was just thinking that they might be interested to know what you're doing.'

'Look, I don't know who they are, so how can I get hold of them? When I asked Malcolm Seagrave ages ago he said he couldn't tell me and never would. Besides, I think I've let them down.'

Surprised, Joan stopped drinking her tea. 'What! That's not like you. You're the one who's always so certain of what you're doing.'

'Maybe I was too certain,' Grace replied. 'I'm wondering now if I just went rushing in without thinking it through enough. I was so determined to start making my own way that maybe I cast aside an opportunity which might never come again. Perhaps I did something I could come to regret.'

'D'you mean that we're not going to be rich any more?' Joan asked.

Arthur suddenly banged on the floor above their heads.

Slowly Grace looked upwards. The ceiling paint had cracked from years of Arthur hammering with his stick, the cream discoloured to a dull porridge. Swearing loudly, Arthur cursed his daughter and his wife, Dora's name repeated over and over again.

'God,' Joan said, aghast, 'what's come over him?'

'I don't know. He's remembered my mother suddenly and nothing I can do seems to calm him.'

Together they listened to the hammering and shouting, Grace finally covering her ears with her hands. Thump, thump, went the stick on the floor above, curses and obscenities following. She couldn't manage for much longer like this, Grace thought; her life was closing in around her. Where was the brilliant future she had craved? She was alone, working in a place she hated with a mad father making constant demands.

The frustration of the years settled on her at that moment, Arthur calling for Dora and slamming his stick down every time he said her name. The syllables sounded around the neat house, echoing in Grace's head, becoming louder and more pressing.

Finally, in one quick movement, she pushed back her chair and ran to the bottom of the stairs, shouting up to her father, 'She's dead! Dora's dead!'

At once, the stick stopped hammering on the floor. The curses stopped too. Arthur's voice seemed to be cut off in mid-breath. Then, silence, heavy and oppressive, fell over the house and the crying figure at the bottom of the stairs.

Chapter Fourteen

What he liked most about the Daimler was the smell of the leather interior. Its aroma was dark, musty, expensive. He liked it, and he liked the way people looked at him as he passed. There goes Elmer Shaw, they said, men with hollow eyes seeing the sleek car and the sleeker occupant driving by.

He liked to be envied, even feared. It gave him a stimulus very little else could. Even sex. Not that women bored him – in small doses they were a tonic, as long as they didn't become demanding. And Elsa was never demanding. Just compliant and affectionate.

And clever. Oh yes, Elmer thought, he had her measure. She wanted to be Mrs Shaw, but she had no chance of that. Not that he would ever tell her so. Best to travel in hope, than arrive in despair. No, Elsa was beautiful and skilful in the bedroom, but not woman enough to make him divorce his wife's fortune.

'Stop here,' Elmer said to the driver, then wound down the window on his side.

Smiling, he looked over his property, the Gaiety cinema, one of many picture houses in Oldham. It was a match for the Odeon now, with its comfortable seats and special sound and lighting. He had bought the best organ too, and had good looking, uniformed usherettes to keep himself ahead of the rest.

Oh, there was a Depression on all right, but that didn't stop people going to the flicks. If anything, it made them more eager. Elmer's cinemas weren't the cheap flea pits in town; they had class – and graded seats. Something for everyone. He knew that at least half the population of Oldham went to the cinema every week, others more often. So he kept the majority of his seat prices at sixpence, less for those with a bad view of the screen. People could always find sixpence to escape their desperate lives.

Elmer was one of the few who was doing well in the depression. He lived off others people's misery, some said, but he disagreed. He offered the audience hope and escapism. He offered them release from their own private hell. How could they criticize him for it? He was doing society a service.

Slowly Elmer got out of the car and walked up to the front door. There was to be a show that night – Clark Gable – sure to bring in the women. And on Saturday there would be a matinée for the kids. Elmer liked to see the queues of raggedly children pushing and shoving outside the Gaiety, waiting for the doors to open. He was even thinking of putting on a special show for them on New Year's Eve – please the parents and get more custom at the same time. Satisfied, Elmer slid back into his seat and motioned for the driver to continue.

He had been interested in what Elsa had told him the previous night. Some woman wanted him to invest in her dream of a cosmetic empire. His eyes had betrayed nothing as he'd listened to Elsa. The woman's name was Grace Ellis, and she worked part time in the mill.

What the hell was she doing in the mill? Elmer wondered. He didn't want anything to do with some snot-nosed tart who couldn't string together two words of English. He wasn't in business to finance pipe dreams.

'She's very capable,' Elsa had gone on serenely, 'very

presentable too, and a good worker.'

'How old is she?'

'About twenty, I think.'

Elmer's dark eyes flickered. Twenty and very presentable . . . So why was Elsa introducing them? She knew he bore her no loyalty; theirs was an affair of little love. There had to be some ulterior motive; his mistress was too astute to pursue anything without gain for herself.

'Why are you interested?' he'd asked her, his hand reaching out and touching her knee, then sliding up her skirt.

'I thought it was a good idea. Grace Ellis is right, women do want to look good.'

His fingers had caught at the lace around the leg of her panties.

'You look good to me,' he'd said huskily.

Elsa had smiled, sliding onto the seat of his chair. She hadn't been able to tell if he was interested in the cosmetics business or not. So she'd kissed him when his mouth moved over hers and let him pull up her skirt and unfasten the buttons on her blouse. Feigning excitement, Elsa had arched her back against the desk, Elmer's lips fastening around her right nipple.

'I like the idea,' he'd said, his mouth moving away and settling against her neck. 'Maybe I should have a meeting with this Ellis woman.'

Elsa had pretended not to hear, her arousal too intense. But she'd made a mental note to call in Grace Ellis the following week – and then she'd laid back against the desk and watched Elmer struggle to unfasten his flies.

Tom knocked on Grace's door punctually, Joan answering and grinning at him.

'Lo there.'

He smiled dimly. 'I thought – did you give Grace my note?'

'Oh yes, she's invited me to come along with you,' Joan replied lightly. 'Is that OK?'

What else could he do but nod? Walking into the kitchen, Tom winced as the scent of lanolin and lemon assaulted his nostrils. The aroma was cloying but at the same time faintly acidic. Grace came out of the larder, wiping her hands on a cloth.

She had dressed herself up for the evening out and had carefully applied make-up, making her eyes darker and – Tom realized with a jolt – sensual. But her manner wasn't in the least flirtatious.

'Hello there, Tom. How's your family?'

Bloody furious that I'm seeing you, he thought, but said calmly, 'They're all well. How's your father?'

She flinched. It was the tiniest movement, but he caught it.

'Not too good at the moment,' Grace said at last. 'He's very quiet.'

She had called out the doctor to see Arthur the night she had told him that Dora was dead. Fear had at first left her immobile at the foot of the stairs, Joan running up to Arthur's room and checking on the old man. She had found him staring ahead, his eyes unfocused. Had he understood what Grace had shouted to him in a rare fit of temper? How could he have understood, when he understood so little?

But his daughter knew all too well that Arthur had understood. The name Dora had cut through the suet of his madness and the news of her death had stamped into the tiny lucid part of his brain which remained. And when it had found its mark, there'd been a moment of complete and terrifying understanding – and after that, nothing.

The doctor had told Grace that her father had had another stroke.

'Has he had a shock lately? Something to cause it?'

Joan interrupted before Grace had chance to speak. 'He was ranting and raving all evening,' she lied. 'He just went crazy.'

The doctor nodded. 'Keep him warm and nurse him as you've always done.' He touched Grace's shoulder, noticing her eyes were puffy from crying. 'You've been a good daughter.'

But when he'd gone Grace had stood for the long time in the kitchen, her arms wrapped tightly around her. Oh no, Joan had thought, you're not going to carry the guilt for this all your life. You've done enough.

'He doesn't know what's going on any more. It's a blessing, really it is.'

Grace's eyes had bored into hers with vehemence.

'A *blessing*? I caused my father's stroke! I caused it. I should never have told him about my mother's death. I'll look at him from now on and wonder how much he understands. If he remembers what I did. But he'll never be able to tell me, will he? He'll never speak again.'

'Good thing,' Joan had said bluntly. 'Oh, don't look at me like that, Grace! You've been a martyr to your father for years. Your mother ran off and you were left holding the baby. No one could have done more for him than you.' She paused, her voice dropping. 'Your father could die tomorrow or he could hang on for years. What are you going to do about it? Let it kill you? Give up your own ambitions, your own life? Oh, for God's sake!' she'd added sharply, exasperated. 'Snap out of it, Grace! Life goes on. Everyone's always known you were special,

135

someone who would succeed, and now look at you. Are you going to give up because of your father? Are you going to let a sick old man bugger up your life?'

Stung, Grace had glanced away. 'I still say that I should never have told him –'

'But you did! It's done – over. You can't change it. Your father's been ill for years. You didn't start it; he had his first stroke ages ago. It was bound to happen again one day. Besides, if anyone made your father into the monster he became it was your mother.'

'I don't want to talk about it!' Grace had snapped, moving away.

'She was twice the woman you are.'

'How can you say that?'

'Because she had *guts*. And you've got guts, you just get bogged down with looking after people. Always putting them first. Put yourself first, Grace, for a change. There's a bloke next door who's crazy about you and you don't even see it. If you give your life for your father he'll never know it – and you'd make a lousy spinster.'

The argument between the two friends had resulted in Grace agreeing to go out with Tom Cox – albeit with Joan in tow.

Now that her neighbour was standing in front of her, Grace had to admit that she was pleased to see him. He was a good-looking young man, with an easy manner. And it was obvious he liked her.

'Who's looking after your father tonight?'

'Geoffrey, Joan's brother,' Grace replied, picking up her coat and closing the front door behind them.

The film was a gangster story with James Cagney, several kids at the front mimicking the actor's voice, Tom sitting between Joan and Grace and wondering if he should talk or stay silent. If he talked would Grace think he had no manners? If he didn't, would she think he was dull?

Beside him, Joan munched happily on an apple, her thin legs jiggling to the background music, Grace staring calmly at the screen. Tom could feel the warmth of her body next to him and once accidentally brushed his knee against hers, blushing automatically.

But Grace hadn't even noticed, she was too busy looking at the actress on the film, the woman's face blown up to thirty feet on the screen in front of them.

'Look at that,' she said to Joan suddenly, 'look at her eye make-up.'

Tom leaned back in his seat to let the two women talk across him.

'She looks awful,' Joan said.

A man behind ssshhhed them angrily. Silence fell. A few minutes passed and then Grace leaned to Joan again.

'The film next week is in colour.'

'*Colour?*' Joan echoed. 'I want to see that.'

Tom was still sandwiched between them.

'Me too,' Grace agreed. 'I want to see the make-up.'

'We could come here next week,' Tom offered suddenly, the two women looking at him. 'I mean, if you want to . . . You said there was another film you wanted to see . . .'

'That would be nice,' Grace said, smiling and leaning back in her seat. 'That would be very nice.'

Chapter Fifteen

In the Ark Mill, Hannah nudged the woman next to her on the loom and jerked her head. Old Annie glanced behind her and then winked. Elsa James was walking up the steps to Elmer Shaw's office. A moment later, the blind was drawn.

'Do you think they're developing photographs?' Hannah said, laughing softly under her breath.

Annie glanced at the clock on the wall at the far end of the mill.

'Five minutes and she'll be out.'

Hannah grimaced. 'I say ten.'

'Nah,' Annie replied, sucking on her teeth. 'That bugger never keeps going longer than five.'

Another woman leaned over to them across the loom.

'He did once. Eight minutes was the longest we timed it.'

'You never!' Annie replied. 'When were that?'

'After he came back from holiday,' the woman said, chortling. 'The sea air must have done him good.'

Hannah glanced at the clock. 'Three minutes and rising.'

'I bet it is,' Annie replied, all the women laughing.

Three pairs of eyes fixed on the mill clock, Hannah counting the minutes as they passed.

'Four . . . four and a half . . . five . . .'

'She'll be out any time,' Annie said firmly.

Hannah was leaning against the loom, the woman opposite watching the clock too. They knew that as soon as Elsa reappeared they would have to look busy, but for the moment that could relax. *She* was working, but for once, they weren't.

'Six minutes!'

'Bugger,' Annie said ruefully.

The woman opposite smiled smugly. 'I say he'll do nine.'

'Nine! Never!' Hannah replied. 'I say eight.'

'If my Doug had been here we would have had a bet on it.'

Hannah turned to her. 'If your Doug had been here he would have taken Shaw's place.'

'And been out in three minutes,' Annie added, throwing back her head and laughing.

They stopped immediately as the blind was lifted on the count of seven minutes. Turning back to their looms, the women began working. Elsa walked back down into the mill and glided between the rows of looms. Her face was still, expressionless. Old Annie sucked noisily on her teeth as Elsa passed by.

Standing at the office window, Elmer Shaw studied Grace Ellis as she left the weaving shed and crossed the mill yard, mounting the steps one at a time. It was raining, the sky dismal, dark streaks flecking the blocks of cloud.

'Come in,' he said when she knocked, watching her as she took a seat.

Elsa wasn't present; Elmer had made sure of that by sending his mistress on an errand to keep her out of the way. He was unexpectedly impressed with the young woman in front of him. She was good-looking all right, and seemed very mature for her age. Her dark eyes held his without fear or intimidation.

'So, Miss Ellis, you wanted to put a proposition to me?'

She nodded. 'I want to set up in business making cosmetics. I've been in touch with several people who could make the products and I know I could market them. This is a list of the charges.' She passed it across the desk to him. Elmer flicked on a lamp to read the page.

Although he didn't know it, he intimidated Grace. His looks, sleek and prosperous, were unlike those of any other man she had ever met. His voice too was different – no broad accent there – and his clothes were obviously hand-made and expensive. On his silk tie he had a diamond pin and as he read her figures he fingered it slowly.

Finally he glanced up. 'It looks fine – as far as it goes. But it's amateur. I don't invest in amateurs.'

Grace could feel her colour rising, but kept her voice calm.

'I need money to rent some premises and employ a few members of staff. I could recoup the money when I sell the products –'

'*If* you sell them,' Elmer replied, glancing out at the heavy rainfall and frowning. 'What makes you think that anyone will buy make-up? There's a depression on.'

'People pay to go to your cinemas,' Grace said bluntly. 'That could be classed as a luxury, but they still go. People *need* some luxury in their life. Where you were clever was making sure that your prices weren't too high. I aim to do the same – make products that are good, but affordable.'

He smiled distantly. 'I've never invested in a woman.'

'Perhaps it's time you did,' Grace replied, astonished by her own cheek.

Something she didn't quite understand was happening

in the room. The man in front of her was interested, his attention caught. And then she realized what it was – *he was intrigued by her*. Grace took in a deep breath. She had seen the same look before on Tom's face and on Geoffrey's – but this was different. Elmer Shaw's face betrayed attraction and challenge – none of their open devotion; this was sexual.

The thought alarmed her, but she kept her nerve. This man was a bully, who would browbeat anyone who didn't stand up to him.

'So, Mr Shaw, what do you think?'

'How much?'

Grace blinked.

'I'm not saying I'm going to invest in you, Miss Ellis. I just want to know how much you're looking for. So I can think about it.'

'Two hundred pounds.'

He laughed in her face. 'Oh come on, what would a little girl like you do with all that money?'

'Double it,' Grace said emphatically, seeing Elmer's eyes narrow.

'You've got nerve, I'll give you that,' he said at last. 'But I don't like to lose money.'

'You like to make it, though.'

'Yes,' he said coolly, 'I like to make it. Maybe we should have dinner and talk about it.'

The gauntlet was thrown down with all the assurance of a man who was not used to being refused. Elmer Shaw knew that Grace would have to accept if she wanted him to loan her money. If she didn't agree, she would lose her chance. On the other hand, if she *did* accept, he would lose respect for her instantly. He would also know that getting her to a restaurant was the first step to getting her into bed.

'I can't go out to dinner with you,' Grace said after a long moment had passed. 'You're a married man; it wouldn't look right.'

'It would be a business dinner,' Elmer replied quietly.

'But it wouldn't look like that.'

He was suddenly piqued. Who the hell was she to ask him for money and give nothing in return? He should just throw her out on her ear. Slowly he studied her again. She looked classy and she was obviously intelligent. She sounded good too, no Northern trollop. But who was she? No mill hand he had ever come across had spoken with such confidence or had such grit.

'Are you sure about dinner?' he pressed her.

Grace hesitated. She had failed. But to dine with Elmer Shaw wasn't worth two hundred pounds.

'I can't. I'm sorry.'

'You should be,' he replied, getting to his feet and showing her the door. 'Goodbye, Miss Ellis.'

Breathing quickly, Grace descended the steps just as Elsa James came back into the mill. Raising her eyebrows, Elsa looked over to Grace and then glanced up at the office window where Elmer was standing. The blind was up. But when he saw her he didn't wave, merely dipped back into the dim room, as Grace hurried away under the thunderous sky.

Chapter Sixteen

'You can't be surprised!' Joan said, painting her finger-nails a bright red and holding up her hand to admire the effect. 'I told you about Shaw; everyone knows what he is.'

'I thought Mrs Stratton didn't like you wearing make-up,' Grace said, a mite peevishly.

'She can't do anything about it on my day off. And don't change the subject – we were talking about Elmer Shaw.'

'What else do you want me to say?' Grace replied flatly. 'He asked me out and I refused. That seems to be the end of the story.'

'You could have gone.'

Grace's eyes widened. 'No I couldn't! We all know what he was suggesting – and it wasn't a business meeting.'

His attention suddenly caught, Tom glanced up from the evening paper he was reading. He had called round to see Grace and had found the two women talking in the kitchen and, loathe to interrupt, he'd disappeared behind a copy of the *Oldham Evening Chronicle*.

'*What* did you say about Elmer Shaw?'

Grace glanced over to him. 'Nothing important.'

'Did he insult you?' Tom said protectively, the paper put to one side. 'You said he asked you out – he's a married man.'

'King Arthur's dead,' Joan said smartly. 'That's old news.'

Tom was struggling to comprehend what they were

talking about. He knew that Grace worked at Shaw's Ark Mill, but why had Shaw picked her out for particular attention? His jealously slid into place in an instant, his stomach tied into a queasy knot.

'What happened?' he demanded suddenly, his tone serious.

'Grace wanted him to invest in her.' The words were out of Joan's mouth before Grace had time to stop her.

Sighing, Grace glanced warningly at her friend and then at the astonished Tom.

'I want to start a business.'

'A *business*?'

'Is there an echo in here?' Joan asked.

'What's so incredible about it?'

'Women don't run businesses,' Tom said, his voice firm. 'That's a man's job.'

Grace's expression was a study. 'Oh, really? Well, if my mother had thought like that who would have run the greengrocer's shop when my father had his stroke?'

It was the first time Tom had heard Grace mention her dead mother directly. What gossip had told him about Dora Ellis had not been flattering: a woman from the slums, who had married well and then run off with a rough. Had his child too, and then been killed. Good thing, Ernie Cox had said. What kind of woman could live that down? Ernie also said that Dora must have been unstable; obviously a mental condition had affected her brain.

'Well, that was a different kind of situation,' Tom replied, not quite so sure of his ground.

'I don't see how,' Grace replied. 'She ran a greengrocery business and I want to set up a cosmetic business.'

Now Tom was really nonplussed. His mother had very little truck with make-up and his own opinion was that it was not quite respectable for ordinary women. And yet he had noticed the make-up Grace had worn and liked it. As for Joan, hers was a little too blatant for his taste.

'Women like to look good. They always have and they always will. Make-up makes them feel confident, glamorous.'

'And you went to ask Elmer Shaw for a loan?' Tom asked. '*Elmer Shaw?*'

'He's not the devil incarnate.'

'Not yet,' Joan replied, rolling her eyes heavenwards. 'Although they do say that he doesn't throw a shadow.'

Tom ignored her. He was struggling to understand this new and startling information. Grace Ellis wanted to set up her own business and she was asking Shaw to invest in her. It's incredible! he thought, choking on the idea, and on the overwhelming smell of acetone from Joan's nail varnish.

'But . . . but . . . it's asking for trouble.'

Grace nodded. 'I know that now. Don't worry, I won't be going out to dinner with Elmer Shaw.'

'*Dinner!*' Tom exploded. 'He wanted to take you out to dinner. Alone?'

'No, they were going to take a brass band with them,' Joan replied. 'Oh, don't be so daft, Tom! He couldn't seduce her if there was anyone else around, could he?'

Tom eyes were starting out of his head as he turned from Joan to Grace.

'It's improper!'

'It's not going to happen,' Grace assured him. 'Why all the fuss? I just have to look for someone else to invest in me now.'

'You're going around selling yourself?' Tom asked, incredulous.

The choice of word needled Grace.

'No – I'm not *selling myself*, I'm selling an idea for a business which could succeed. If you don't like it, Tom, I'm sorry, but that's the way it is. I want to do this and I will.'

He saw then the steel in her and it unsettled him. Tom had known from the first that Grace Ellis was different; he had also found out something of the hardships she had endured. But he had never considered that she might be ambitious. Somewhere in the back of his mind he had hoped that marriage might rescue her from the tedium of Ark Mill. And why not marriage to him? He had never considered that she might be capable of improving her lot by her own efforts.

The thought rattled him. He had fallen in love with Grace, he knew that, and also knew that he had built up a fantasy around her. Within weeks of first seeing her he was besotted. Every thought seemed to centre around the colour of her eyes, every woman on the street reminded him – yet never matched – the one he idolized.

His devotion accelerated like a runaway car. The future was getting planned in his mind. He would marry Grace and help her support her father. She would stay at home, leave the mill, become the respectable wife of a town hall clerical worker.

There was no room in Tom's plans for his wife going into business.

Totally unaware of what he was thinking, Grace could feel only slightly annoyed at his reaction. To her, Tom was a friend. Oh, she knew that he was becoming devoted to her, but she didn't have the same feelings for him. There was nothing wrong with Tom Cox; he would make a fine man for most women, but not for Grace. She had no plans to marry for a long time –

and when she did she wanted someone with as much ambition as she had.

She knew that she would be unlikely to find such a man in Diggle. But the memory of her mother – overcome with attraction for Len Billings – the thought of such a formidable woman brought low by longing . . . Grace shook her head. No, she wasn't going to fall in love and be tied to Diggle for ever. And she wasn't going to let any man undermine her or belittle her either. Dora might have taught her many things, but her fall from grace had shown Grace how quickly a person could lose everything. And she had no intention of following Dora's example.

'What makes you think you can run a business?' Tom asked at last.

'I believe I can,' Grace replied, wearied at having to explain herself. Why couldn't he just accept it? Or support her?

'Well, why don't you set your sights a bit lower? You could work in a shop selling make-up. That would be something.'

He had damned himself in that moment. Disappointed, Grace turned away. Joan stared down at her nails. She wanted to share her friend's regret, but couldn't. Shame made her itchy with discomfort. She had suspected all along that Tom Cox wasn't man enough for Grace, and now he had proved it. Her relief was so intense that she was sure Grace would read it on her face, so she kept her head down. If Tom couldn't live up to Grace's expectations, he could certainly live up to hers.

'Are we still going to the flicks on Saturday?' Joan asked finally.

Tom's eyes were still fixed on Grace. It seemed for a

moment that he hesitated and then he nodded. 'Yes, if you still want to go. Grace?'

She turned; a slat of sunlight had cut through the clouds and fell on her dark hair. Standing erect in a navy skirt and white blouse she looked suddenly unobtainable, remote.

'Why don't you two go? I'm in Manchester in the afternoon. If I get back early I'll join you.'

All three of them knew it was a lie.

It had been a while since Elmer Shaw had had a challenge. Work was always interesting, but nothing had given him quite the thrill that the encounter with Grace Ellis had done. Only moments after she left, Elsa had walked into the office, the contrast between the two women – one blonde, cool, the other fiery, dark – was emphasized.

Calmly, Elsa sat down. 'So how did the interview go?'

She was anxious suddenly, though careful her manner didn't betray it.

Perhaps Grace Ellis was a little too tasty a morsel for Elmer to resist. Oh yes, she had offered Elsa a way to get more control over her lover, but at what cost? Maybe Grace Ellis had her eye on Elmer herself.

'She can certainly stand up for what she wants,' Elmer replied, determined to keep Elsa on a string for as long as he could.

'What did you think of her proposal?'

'Interesting.' He leaned forward in his seat and stared at the papers in front of him.

'Something you might be interested in?' Elsa prodded gently.

'I asked her out to dinner to talk about it.'

148

He had the satisfaction of watching Elsa's serene face tighten. The reaction was infinitesimal, but he saw it because he was waiting for it. She was worried now, worried that she had overplayed her hand. But what had been her motive anyway? Was she trying to set up his next conquest? Choosing Grace herself to lessen the damage? A woman she knew instead of a stranger?

Smiling, he kept his head down. No, it couldn't be that. It was obvious that Grace Ellis wasn't out to make her fortune horizontally. So maybe Elsa had been interested in the Ellis woman's proposition for herself? If Elmer put up the money, would it be for Grace Ellis or, indirectly, for his mistress? Perhaps the lovely Elsa fancied herself as a businesswoman and had been too wary to approach him herself.

Either way, he wasn't going to let her off the hook easily.

'You asked Grace Ellis out to dinner?' Elsa said, finally able to find her voice.

'A business meeting.'

'Of course.'

'She refused.'

Elsa was relieved and then disappointed. What did her refusal mean to Elmer now? That he would no longer want to invest in Grace Ellis's scheme? Or had her refusal aroused his interest? . . . Suddenly Elsa didn't care about the project any more. She didn't want her lover going out to dine with Grace Ellis, because although she had refused him once, would she refuse him a second time? Elsa knew Elmer was persistent and didn't like to take no for an answer. Grace Ellis's refusal had made Elsa's position not more secure, but less.

Elsa wondered then why she had been so stupid. Elmer was sly, much smarter than she was, and she was no fool.

He had been piqued and that could prove fatal for her. It was obvious from the start that she couldn't trust Elmer, but what about Grace Ellis?

'Well, it was just a vague business idea,' Elsa said with all the calm she could muster. 'I don't suppose it would have worked anyway.'

'With Grace Ellis behind it, it could have done.'

'But you said –'

He cut her off. 'I said that I had asked her out to dinner and she had refused. I didn't say that I had decided against making an investment in her business.'

It was all that Elsa could do not to scream at him, but she knew that losing control would be counterproductive. Anyway, she had no one to blame but herself. She had tried to secure her position and undermined it instead. But she could repair the damage; no one knew Elmer Shaw as well as she did.

Smiling, she rose to her feet. 'Will I see you tonight?'

Elmer paused. 'No, I'm at home tonight,' he replied, knowing how she would worry, that bland face hiding a thousand nagging doubts. 'We'll meet up later in the week.'

Chapter Seventeen

Malcolm Seagrave was oiling the hinge of his office door when his clerk came over to him. The door had been creaking for a while, irritating him every time someone walked in. He could have asked the handyman to repair it, but Malcolm was a man who liked to do things his own way. *Always.*

'Yes?'

The clerk passed him a letter. 'This was just hand delivered.'

Malcolm put down the oil can and wiped his fingers on a rag before taking the missive.

'Any message?'

'No, only that I was to deliver it to you in person.'

Nodding, Malcolm walked over to his desk. The clerk closed the door behind him when he left. It didn't creak.

By rights, at sixty-seven Malcolm Seagrave should have been retired, but he had no wish to stay at home all day. He had no family, no hobbies and his friends – the few there were – bored him. The firm was everything to him, the name of Seagrave and Paulton established by his father, the late Mr Paulton dying young and leaving Malcolm in sole charge.

Which was what he thrived on. The firm of solicitors had grown a little, gradually taking on several other new solicitors, and burying a couple of old ones, but Malcolm was always the head partner – and intended to remain so. He liked to imagine that people felt reassured by the continuity. His clients knew that he was always in his office, from nine to five, every week, apart from two days off at Christmas and one at the New Year.

Efforts to buy him out had failed; Malcolm didn't want a larger practice and was comfortably well off. Anything more, he reasoned, would be superfluous to his needs. Flashy attention-grabbing cases did not appeal to him; he liked the ossuary of long-term briefs, liked the detail, the minutiae.

To his credit, his small-mindedness served his clients well. Malcolm – slight in tight clothes – looked as controlled as his intellect, his rapidly blinking eyes darting from case note to case note, searching for discrepancies like a pig roots for truffles. Nothing got past Malcolm Seagrave.

Pulling on his reading glasses, he sat down and opened the envelope, taking out the letter and smoothing it flat on the desk in front of him.

> Dear Mr Seagrave,
>
> It has come to our attention that Miss Grace Ellis – in whom we were interested previously – is now working at Ark Mill part time. Her insistence at curtailing her education – which could have lead to university and a promising career – was entirely her choice, but we do however feel that she is now wasting her talents.
>
> We understand that Miss Ellis has an interest in starting her own business and that she has approached someone to invest in her –

This was news to Malcolm Seagrave and he wondered how the writer knew about it.

> – a certain Mr Elmer Shaw.

Good God! Malcolm thought, blowing his dry nose and staring hard at the wall opposite. Elmer Shaw was only one step up from a crook, and a known womanizer. Whatever was the girl playing at?

He is not the kind of person we would like Miss Ellis to associate with. Either professionally or privately.

Therefore we would be willing to offer a single donation of £150 (one hundred and fifty pounds sterling) to Miss Grace Ellis for the furtherance of her venture.

We would also like to donate £2/11s (two pounds sterling and eleven shillings) weekly to enable Miss Ellis to leave her part-time job at Ark Mill (owned by Mr Elmer Shaw).

This money should cover the living costs for Miss Ellis and her father, Mr Arthur Ellis, and make up for any lost income.

This is an offer made on behalf of my clients and cannot be negotiated. It is our first and last offer. There will be no more money forthcoming for Miss Ellis's business – unless she can make it a viable concern within two years of the date of this offer, i.e., by 13 July 1938.

As ever, Miss Ellis's benefactors wish to remain anonymous. Any queries you may have should be addressed to myself, acting as the agent on their behalf. We would also like to establish the fact that we will deal directly with Miss Ellis through your offices. Mrs Higgins's considerable assistance is no longer required in this matter.

Yours sincerely,
Frederick Conrad
Blomfield and Rosen, Solicitors

Well, well, well, Malcolm thought, rereading the letter and then placing it to one side. His curiosity had always been limited, but he found himself intrigued by Messrs Blomfield and Rosen's letterhead.

He had always been always fascinated by Frederick Conrad, one of Oldham's luminaries, with a house in Delph and a bevy of admiring female clients. Malcolm Seagrave didn't like Frederick Conrad; he was jealous of him, as were most of the solicitors in that area. Conrad may have been married to the gargoyle-faced Emmeline but he was altogether too handsome to stomach. And now he was dealing with Grace Ellis's benefactors ... Hah! Malcolm thought peevishly, in that case the sponsors *had* to be women.

Probably some do-gooders, Malcolm thought. Possibly the Spencer sisters, grinding on into old age as stern as Huguenots. Whoever they were, they had rescued Grace Ellis just in time. Mixing with the likes of Elmer Shaw could do nothing for a woman's reputation. And Grace Ellis should be steered away from the same kind of temptation that had ruined her mother. But, Malcolm thought suddenly, how did *they* know about Elmer Shaw when he didn't?

Still, the letter from Frederick Conrad at Messrs Blomfield and Rosen was welcome. The arrangement meant a good, steady job, with a regular fee – and if it ran for as long as the previous arrangement had, there was a tidy sum to be made out of it. Oh yes, Malcolm thought piously, he was glad that someone was looking out for a young woman who could so easily have gone wrong.

Miss Grace Ellis's success was going benefit everyone.

It was approaching midnight when Grace heard a knock at the front door. Afraid that it would disturb her father, she hurriedly pulled on her dressing gown and ran down into the small tiled hallway.

'Who is it?'

Silence from the other day of the door.

'Who is it?' she repeated, then opened the door a crack to look out.

Immediately Elmer Shaw smiled and walked in, pushing past Grace. Startled, she pulled her gown around her tightly.

'What do you want?'

'I was just coming back from a dinner out, and I was passing so I thought I would call on you. Have a talk about your business.' He was looking round the kitchen, flicking on the lights and moving into the larder beyond, his dinner jacket incongruous in such a setting. 'Your little empire is rather cramped, isn't it?'

Still hovering in the doorway, Grace wondered what to do. Should she knock on the wall and hope to summon Tom? Or would that be overreacting? Besides, there was her father to think about. If he heard, Arthur would be alarmed, and God only knew what fright could do to a man in his condition.

Stay calm, Grace told herself. After all, perhaps Shaw did just want to talk. But then which man came calling at midnight to discuss business?

'Mr Shaw, I think we should talk about this tomorrow.'

He turned, blithely unconcerned. 'I'm in London tomorrow. I thought you'd want a final answer.'

'I thought you'd already made up your mind,' Grace replied coolly. 'You didn't seem interested in my proposal.'

'All women are alike,' he said, his voice relaxed. 'They jump to conclusions. I admit I wasn't that impressed to begin with, but the more I thought it over the more the idea appealed to me.' He sat down, uninvited. 'You were right about luxury, Grace: everyone wants some. They live for it, dream of it. They want to get out of their hovels and live in big houses, with fine clothes. They want to live like their heroes do in the films.' He paused, smiling. 'I trade on that dream – I have done for a long time – and oddly enough the depression helped me – because people wanted to escape even more.'

'Mr Shaw –'

He cut her off. 'I'm bored with my other businesses, the mill and the cinemas. I want a change. I thought about owning nightclubs, but that didn't really interest me. Better to visit them than to run them.'

Grace didn't know what to say. She had never been to a night club and all she wanted at that moment was to get Elmer Shaw out of the house. She had been stupid to ask him for help; she was out of her league with people like Elsa James and Shaw. They were worldly, Machiavellian. She felt suddenly naïve, foolish – and threatened.

'I've had some second thoughts myself. I don't want to do it any more,' she said, her voice remarkably composed. 'I've thought it over and it wasn't such a good idea after all.'

He didn't believe her for one moment.

'That's a shame, a real shame. Personally I think it could be a winner – with the right amount of backing and support.'

'I don't think so.' Grace said lightly, as though the matter was closed. 'Thank you anyway for your interest, Mr Shaw. I'm sorry if I've wasted your time.'

He was getting annoyed; the game wasn't moving the way he had planned. In his imagination he had seen

Grace cornered into accepting his loan and then he could bring pressure to bear slowly. But she was either being very smart – stringing him along – or very childish.

Smiling politely, Grace moved into the hallway and opened the front door. All she knew for certain was that she had to get him out of the house as quickly as she could.

'Thank you for calling, Mr Shaw.'

He stood up, suddenly feeling foolish himself. Who was this bloody chit of a girl to give him the run-around? She had come to him for money and he was offering it. Against his better judgement. Of course he knew the bloody business would fail, an idiot could see that, but he wanted Grace Ellis. And he was more than prepared to buy her.

'I don't think you really want to drop it,' Elmer said, rising to his feet as Grace remained by the door. 'You know as well as I do that you're ambitious.' He touched her shoulder. Grace flinched. 'Oh, come on, we're both adults. You knew about me before you came to ask for help. You must have known I would try it on. It's all part of the game, part of business.'

Suddenly his hand moved down her shoulder and slid into the front of her dressing gown, tightening on her breast. Gasping with shock, Grace knocked his hand away, but as she did so, Shaw slammed the door shut with his foot and turned on her.

'Don't bugger me about!'

'Get out!' she shouted, slapping his face as hard as she could. 'Get out!'

His cheek stung from the unexpected blow, and Shaw's temper snapped. With considerable force, he hit Grace, sending her sprawling against the door of the front room. Winded, she felt under her the cold tiles, her dressing gown falling open and exposing her bare legs. Her focus was blurred, her head ringing as she saw Shaw bend down over her.

Instinct made her strike out repeatedly, Shaw trying to lift her nightdress and then fumbling between her legs. Feeling blood run down her cheek, Grace – with all the strength she could find – lifted her knee and caught him straight in the stomach. Shaw winced and caught his breath.

What followed seemed to Grace to happen in staccato bursts, like watching a black-and-white film, frame by frame. One, she watched his arm go back. Two, she saw his hand balling into a fist, and then, three – frame by agonizing frame – she saw the fist come closer and closer until it struck her face.

Blood rushed in her ears, the tiled floor cold and hard against her cheek as she lay beaten where he left her. All Grace remembered after that was the bitter night air blowing in from the front door, left wide open – after Elmer Shaw walked out.

PART THREE

The black and merciless things which are behind the great possessions.

HENRY JAMES, *The Ivory Tower*

Why do I love thee?
Why do I breathe?

ANON

Chapter Eighteen

Grace's ambition of running a cosmetic empire was finally achieved in the cramped conditions of St Andrew's Place, an old workshop next to a derelict church at the end of an alley in Oldham's town centre. After eighteen gruelling months of endless work and limited sleep, the little factory was doing two shifts to produce and pack the cosmetics. The sponsors' money had been used well. Knowing that the deadline of 13 July 1938 was imminent, Grace was determined to make a profit, however small. She would show her benefactors that she could succeed.

Grace chose the Auden Line as the name for her cosmetic range, because it reminded her of an actress, Lily Auden, whom she had seen in a magazine. A woman whose cool beauty and elegance epitomized the image Grace wanted for her cosmetic line.

Side by side with Joan and the two day shift women – Tilly Sugden and Mary Wells – Grace sifted powder into blue drums and screwed on round gold lids. She checked every lipstick for quality and colour, and named every shade, avoiding the obvious, crass labelling. Chic was the word. Nothing had to look like it was produced in a workshop next to a derelict church. Class and elegance was paramount – the make-up had to look and feel like the best – but at a reasonable price.

Neighbours and friends of the workers were pressed into testing innumerable products. What did this rouge look like when it was on fair skin? What did it look like on a sallow complexion? How did it feel? How did it wear? Did it stain or was it easy to remove? How did it make you feel when you wore it? What did you think of the price?

Long sheets of questions were drawn up and typed out by Grace and Joan, then handed out to everyone who tried any of the Auden Line products. Then the answers were scrutinized. If any product caused irritation it was passed over for Aaron, the chemist Grace employed, to check out. If it didn't last, the composition was changed. If it was drying, more lanolin was added. Petroleum jelly made the lips soft, but too much made the lipstick bleed. Too much dye kept the colour on, but stained the lips. The detail was scrupulous and never ending, Grace often working past ten at night, in the company of the night shift, and Joan, yawning on a stool.

St Andrew's Place had been a dismal, dirty area when Grace had first rented it. Joan had stared at the workshop and rolled her eyes.

'Tell me it's a joke. *Please.*'

But Grace had seen that it provided enough space for what she needed and so she set to, cleaning it. Joan, after finishing work at the Strattons in the evening, had helped her, her brother, Geoffrey, doing the donkey-work. He had fixed new electric lighting overhead, cleaned the high windows and distempered the ceiling and walls. The floor had then been scrubbed and varnished, every surface pristine. Finally the tables had been brought in and subjected to boiling water and disinfectant before any scrap of make-up touched their surfaces.

Likewise every woman who worked at the Auden Line was spotlessly clean. Wearing white overalls and head-scarfs, they had to wash their hands before work and after every break. Glad to have a job, the women were willing and quick workers, their wages not extravagant, but fair. Besides, they enjoyed the work, trying out the cosmetics and often emerging from St Andrew's Place in full *maquillage*.

Before long the local lads called the alleyway 'The Bachelor Trap', and stood whistling when the day shift came off, Tilly and Mary both pretty and unmarried, Joan as quick-witted as ever.

'What you hanging around here for?' she'd asked them chirpily on one occasion. 'Haven't you ever seen film stars before?'

Immediately, one of the lads had fallen to his knees on the cobbles, his hands clasped.

'Whoever it is under all the war paint, marry me!'

The night workers were different. Enid Taylor and Ivy Morris were older and married. Enid's husband, Patrick, was on the sick, and Ivy's Alf was a known gambler. Both women needed their wages for food and rental. Unlike the day shift, they worked without the radio on, talking in muted voices in the back yard when they had a break.

'I'll swing for that bugger when he gets back,' Ivy said flatly one cool summer evening, her face creased with worry. With Grace's determination to be in profit by July, the women were working extra hard, but Alf had lost the rent money for the previous week and with it the little Ivy had put aside for their eldest daughter's wedding. She rubbed her rough hands together for warmth.

'You should get rid of that man of yours,' Enid said bluntly.

'Oh aye? And who would I get instead?' Ivy countered, staring into Enid's plump face. Her eyes were prominent, a goitre at the base of her throat. Derbyshire neck they called it, even in Oldham. 'Your Patrick's not bringing in a wage either.'

Enid shrugged her heavy shoulders. 'He can't, he's on the sick.'

'Again?'

Enid tapped her breast bone. 'It's his heart.'

'Broken?'

Enid grinned at her friend. 'Doctor says it's too fast. Says one day it'll kill him.' She sighed and tucked some loose grey hair under her cap. 'He was a good-looking bloke when I met him.'

'They all are – when you meet them,' Ivy replied phlegmatically. 'Alf had a full head of hair and a job when we wed. Both disappeared with the years.'

They laughed, Ivy wiping her mouth with a handkerchief.

'Better get back,' Ivy said suddenly. 'Work to do and money to earn.' She walked to the back door of St Andrew's Place, and, grim as it was, was fleetingly grateful to have escaped her own dismal house.

As Grace had expected, soon after she opened St Andrew's Place Joan left the Strattons and came to work for her – proving herself astute and surprisingly industrious. Although Grace had already calculated every pound of her sponsored money in wages, materials, rent, postage and delivery, Joan could always find some little corner to cut, or someone who knew someone who could get their hands on the very thing they were looking for.

No detail escaped Grace, and when it came to hiring staff she found more than enough people looking for jobs. Having been made redundant, Geoffrey was the first to be employed and was keen to act as delivery man. Borrowing long term an old van from a friend, he painted it a dark blue – as requested by Grace – and a sign writer friend wrote 'The Auden Line' on it in gold.

The winter and spring of 1938 had been cold, then summer – long overdue – started in earnest on 3 July. After extended months of snow, followed by relentless winds, the temperature lifted, the moors behind Diggle losing their dark humped foreboding. Grass began to grow again, although the peaks of the hills were always bare and slaked with stones. Wild flowers, thirsty for warmth, chattered between paving stones and at the base of St Anne's, the church up on the Heights, they clustered in congregations of colour.

Aaron Bloom looked over the landscape from the Heights above Diggle where he was walking that summer day. The day was clear, the road winding down to the river and the packed streets of Oldham visible below. Mill chimneys caught the light of the sun, though many of the mills were now closed, the weaving sheds busy only on part-time shifts. Others remained locked up, the looms a ghostly sight through the tall windows, old cotton dust masking the floor, the roof beams and the stone window ledges.

Aaron sighed, pulling his knees up to his chest and resting his chin on them. His keen brown eyes looked over the town below as he thought of the smuggled letter in his pocket. He had hoped that his brother, Solomon, would have escaped Germany by now, and the next letter he received would contain news of his imminent arrival, but he was still there.

I'm leaving soon. Things are bad here and getting worse. There is a feeling of terror, something I have never known before, and rumours that Hitler is talking of ridding Germany of Jews.

There are some arrangements I have to make and then we will leave. Your talk of Oldham hardly conjures up the image of a new Eden, but it does sound safe and we long to join you there. My dear brother, don't worry for me. I have good friends and will leave soon with Rosa.

Your loving brother,
Solomon

Disturbed, Aaron wondered why his brother had to stay another day in Berlin. Surely there was no business important enough to make him stay? But he knew that Solomon, as the older brother would feel responsible and would do everything he could to safeguard what they had. Their father had been a prosperous businessman, their mother a socialite. Both had died in a freak sailing accident. The money the two brothers had inherited Solomon had managed, expanding the jewellery business and paying for Aaron's university education. His faith was rewarded, Aaron graduating with Honours in Chemistry.

Then Solomon had started privately to worry, and after a while he'd talked about the rumours he had heard. At first Hitler, made Chancellor of Germany in 1933, had been intent on remaking the German economy, but as his power and dream of an idealized race had begun to obsess him, anti-Semitic propaganda had followed. There was no part in the xenophobic new Germany for Jewish businesses.

To show off German athleticism, the Olympic Games of 1936 had been supposed to underline the superiority of the Master race, but when the American Jesse Owens had won gold, Hitler had refused to shake his hand. A black man was no victor in his eyes.

Aaron, by then working as a projects chemist in one of the largest firms in Berlin, had been asked to call in to see his brother one evening soon after. Solomon had been sitting in the office their father had built, the lights of the street outside shining through the window and making yellow smears on the rainy road.

'I want you to get out of Germany,' Solomon had begun.

'What?'

'You have to get out. Aaron we're Jewish, before long things will be intolerable. You've seen for yourself how we've been undermined. Our colleagues are suspicious of us and our neighbours watch our every move.' He paused. 'Well it's going to get far worse, I'm certain. Go to England; I have some friends in Manchester who will help you out.'

'But I want to stay here.'

'You can't,' Solomon had said emphatically. He'd known he must keep himself in control, allow Aaron no chance to argue. He had to get his brother out of Germany, though he would miss him terribly. This was no time for sentiment. 'You have to go now.'

Stunned, Aaron had stared at his adored brother. Astute and serious, Solomon had managed everything since their parents' deaths, looking after Aaron and running the business, a young man of twenty-six acting like a middle-aged patriarch. So Aaron had known that if his brother was telling him to get out of Germany, the situation was becoming serious.

'I can't leave yet, Aaron. I have to help Rosa's family leave first. But as soon as I've done that, we'll follow.'

'But –'

Solomon had turned to his brother in the dim evening light, his hand resting on Aaron's shoulder.

'Do as I say. Go to England and let me know that

you're safe. You'll help me more by doing that than anything else. I *will* follow with Rosa, honestly I will.'

In the end Aaron had had no choice, and within the week Solomon had arranged for him to go to England, to stay with old friends of their parents, the Abolsoms, in Manchester. It had been as perfectly planned as all of Solomon's operations, but Aaron had not been able to settle with the light-hearted Abolsoms.

His worry for his brother and sister in law had hung heavily on him. 'I'm sure there's nothing to worry about really.' Mrs Abolsom told him, when he'd confided his anxieties. 'It'll all blow over in a while. People just get carried away with gossip, that's all.'

No, Mrs, Abolsom, he had wanted to say, there's something terrible about to happen, don't fool yourself. There's gossip about there being concentration camps for the Jews; camps that were set up three years ago. It can't all be rumour.

But he knew it was useless to try to explain, so instead Aaron had looked for a way to leave Manchester and had heard of a job going for a chemist in Oldham.

As soon as he had secured the post, which he'd done by letter, without even seeing his future employer, he'd left – to everyone's relief. So Aaron had followed the instructions he'd been given to Oldham – and had found himself in a small alley which ran down the side of a shabby deserted church, St Andrew's Place.

At that moment Aaron had wondered what on earth he had done. The place was depressed and the rain made it look worse, a few recalcitrant weeds hanging grimly to the edge of the cobblestones. The church windows, smashed and patched up with boards, had looked blindly down on him as he'd stood, nervously twiddling his hat in his hands and staring at number 19, St Andrew's Place.

Footsteps had made him turn, a woman approaching. Seeing him, she'd smiled.

'You Mr Bloom?'

Aaron had nodded, staring into the alert little face.

'I'm Joan. Welcome to sunny Oldham.' She'd shaken his hand. 'You don't know what you've let yourself in for.'

As she said the words, Joan had opened the side door of 19 St Andrew's Place – and the noise had hit Aaron forcibly. A radio had been playing, two women humming to a big band tune. In front of him had been various assorted tables and the smell – heavy, perfumed, yet faintly acrid – was momentarily over-whelming. There had appeared to be several women working on the tables, labelling and packing. And at the far end of the room Aaron had seen a heavy-set man with a bald head, talking to a tall woman.

She had had her back to Aaron and had only turned round when Joan had nudged her.

Curious, Grace had glanced at the stranger and then walked over to him.

'Good to meet you, Mr Bloom,' she'd said pleasantly. 'Come into the office.'

Aware of the scrutiny of the workers, Aaron had fol-lowed her into a side room made elegantly comfortable. He had looked round, surprised, and then studied the woman he had come to meet.

He had decided that she was probably in her mid-twenties and very handsome – but had a cool, remote quality about her. She was perfectly groomed, her make-up subtle and flattering. As she talked Aaron noticed a fine scar by the side of her left eye. Oddly, the first impression Aaron had had of Grace Ellis was that she was someone who knew all about suffering. The thought calmed him unexpectedly.

In the following months, Aaron had found himself an ally. He had no interest in Grace as a woman, but as a friend, finding her ambitions stimulating and worth pursuing. He'd grown fond of St Andrew's Place, the noisy, crowded workshop, and found to his intense pleasure that he was allowed to express himself and put his own ideas forward. The work was absorbing and kept his mind fully occupied during the day, but the evenings dragged in the rented room round the corner, and Aaron found himself keeping longer and longer hours to avoid the anxiety of lonely thought.

Make-up had not been an area he had ever investigated before, virgin territory. Having had only a couple of girlfriends – both blue stockings and uninterested in glamour – Aaron had had no idea what cosmetics were made of or how they were produced. But he had soon learned, and research and Aaron's own tests had backed up the scores of notes Grace had accumulated.

Although Grace had tried another chemist before Aaron, he had been lazy and disinterested. By contrast – and to her intense relief – Aaron was committed from the first. He was in early and left late, his narrow shoulders hunched over his worktable in the laboratory off the workshop. At night, through the glass window at the top of his door, Grace would look up and see Aaron absorbed, relieved by the thought that she wasn't alone.

Aaron had written to Solomon, telling his brother about his job, and Solomon had written back that he was amazed to find his brilliant little brother in the glamour trade and that he wished him well. Oh, and he'd added that he was leaving Germany. *Soon* . . .

Aaron sighed and stretched out his legs before him, his thoughts coming back to the present and the letter he had received that morning. So much time had passed, so many letters signed off *I'm leaving soon. Soon . . .* But soon had become the past, and stretched into the future and now Aaron's anxiety was turning into a deep, uncontrollable dread.

'I thought I'd find you here,' Grace said, sitting down on the grass next to him and looking out over the view. 'Summer at last.'

Aaron nodded, glad of her company. Gradually he had learned a little of her past, had visited her father, and Joan had hinted something about Elmer Shaw. 'That was how she got the scar by her left eye, where the bastard hit her . . .' But Aaron had never asked Grace anything directly. And she had returned the compliment.

'Geoffrey said that we could deliver the next batch of lipsticks and rouge to Dudley and Proctor's by Thursday, after the van's repaired.' Grace chewed on a blade of grass. 'I wish we had more reliable transport, but it'll come in time.'

Aaron was still looking out over the landscape, his voice distant. 'That's good, that's really good.'

Grace glanced over to him, curious for once. 'What's the matter?'

'I was thinking about my brother. He's still in Berlin. He should have left by now. He says he has things to see to, but I don't think he'll ever leave, however bad the Nazi threat.'

'How serious is it?'

'Very,' Aaron replied. 'I know most of what we learn here is called rumour, but from Solomon's letters, reading between the lines, it sounds bad. I want him out of Germany.'

Surprised by the unexpected confidence, Grace took a moment to reply.

'Your brother's an intelligent man, you've always told me that. He'll know what he's doing.'

Aaron shook his head. 'Rosa's parents won't leave Berlin and that means that Rosa won't either. Don't tell me that Solomon will leave his wife. He *couldn't*, and he *wouldn't* leave her . . . I feel so guilty for running away. I should have stayed with him.'

Grace's voice was low when she answered him: 'How would that have helped, Aaron?'

'It would have helped me.'

'But not your brother,' Grace countered. 'He would have someone else he loved to worry about if you'd stayed. He's happy to know that you're safe. That matters if you love someone. Believe me, you're helping him most by being here.'

'It doesn't feel that way. I feel like a coward.'

'I feel like a coward too sometimes.'

He was surprised. 'Why?'

'Because of my father, because I sometimes wish he was dead. Isn't that a hell of an admission to make? To wish your own father dead.'

'It's understandable, he's ill –'

She cut Aaron off. 'No, I don't wish it just because he's ill . . . I feel so guilty for the past, for what I said that caused his stroke. My father lost his voice then, and I'll never know what he's thinking – if he heard what I said; if he understood. So I keep looking after him and wonder, always wonder, what he's thinking, and if he hates me.'

It was the first time Grace had ever talked about her father in such terms and for a moment Aaron didn't know how to respond. He had heard about Arthur from Joan, but had no idea of the depth of feeling and resentment which lingered. He was also slightly confused. Why was Grace confiding in him? Because he had confided in her, or because she wanted his advice? And in what capacity – as a friend, or something more? He suddenly hated his naïvety with women.

'When I think back to my childhood, all my parents wanted was for me to be a success,' Grace continued. 'My mother lived for that – but now she'd dead and my father doesn't understand anything.' She smiled bitterly. 'The two people I loved most will never see what I've done.'

Aaron felt suddenly hot, her body close to his. Who was this woman he had thought of as just a friend?

'But your benefactors will know what you've achieved.'

Grace nodded. 'But they're not flesh and blood, Aaron. What do strangers' opinions mean? They aren't close to me. They don't know me or love me. There's no one at home I can talk to or confide in.'

What *was* she saying to him? Aaron thought blindly.

'Don't you talk to your boyfriend?'

Grace winced. 'What boyfriend?'

'Tom Cox. I thought you two were going out together.'

'Tom's a good friend,' Grace replied evenly. 'He's a kind man, but he's not the man for me.'

Aaron struggled to work out if there was a hint in her words. 'He seems to think otherwise.'

'I can't help that. I've tried to tell him many times over the years, but he won't have it. Tom should go out with Joan. She loves him.'

'*Really?* Joan and Tom Cox? That would be an odd pairing.'

'Why? Tom needs a strong woman with ambition,

and Joan has that. He's also a bit naïve – and that's the last thing you could say about Joan.'

'But he's not interested in her,' Aaron said tentatively. 'I've watched him, Grace. When you're around he doesn't see anyone else.'

She turned to look at him and he held her gaze for a long instant.

'He will,' Grace assured him. 'In time, Tom will know how much Joan loves him. She would die for him. No one on earth could ask for more from anyone.'

Chapter Nineteen

The Bell and Monkey was busy at night, Joan making some dinner in the back whilst her father argued with her mother over a spill of beer. Nothing changes, Joan thought, tossing a cloth to her mother and watching her mop up the mess, her husband's feet only inches away from her fingers. Lazy sod.

Yet Joan couldn't tolerate staying another moment in Grace's company. If she heard about 13 July once more she would scream. It was important, she knew that, the very day Grace's benefactors had set to judge her achievement. OK, Joan thought, so it was possible that any future funds depended on Grace's success, but there was nothing more anyone could do. To all intents and purposes, Grace Ellis had done well. She had even made a profit. Only a small one, granted, but then how many businesses made any profit at all in the first few years? And how many small concerns went bust in the depression?

But it was no good, Grace couldn't stop worrying. So, exasperated, Joan had decided to take an evening off. Now, at her parents' pub, she was wondering if she had done the right thing. Idly, Joan laid out the food on the table and chewed at the crust cut from a loaf. She had seen Tom earlier, after he had called at St Andrew's Place to visit Grace. He seemed irritable, ill at ease – as he always was now, after seeing Grace.

The dope, Joan thought, hadn't he given up hope yet? Grace wasn't interested in him; he should give up and realize that Joan herself was in love with him . . . Joan watched her mother pass by, her feet splayed in their wide-fit sandals . . . Just how long was Tom going to keep pining? He was changing, getting more and more frustrated by the minute.

Just as she was. But he never showed any interest in her. To Tom, she was just a mate, a friend, someone he could talk to; but nothing more. Joan had the unpleasant sensation that she could have taken off all her clothes in front of him and he wouldn't have batted an eyelash. It was enough to make a girl choke.

'What are you mooning about for?' Myra asked, walking in and looking at her sister. 'You want to forget that Cox fella and set your cap at someone else.'

'I wasn't mooning about him.'

'You're *always* mooning about him,' Myra replied, checking her appearance in the mirror.

She had put on weight, but then she was courting Stan Oldman, who was fat and unlikely to complain about her spreading hips. Smug at her success, Myra had crowed repeatedly to her single sister about her impending engagement, and was smiling at that moment, flashing her ring.

'You want to watch it,' Joan said. 'Don't wear it too often or your finger'll go green.'

'Huh!' Myra replied. 'You're just jealous.'

Kate had married the previous year and moved to Stockport, a baby on the way. But Joan remained stubbornly unattached.

'Tom Cox is crazy about Grace Ellis,' Myra went on, stamping all over her sister's feelings. 'Anyway, he's not the only fish in the sea. He's not that handsome. You want to give up and get someone else.'

'Like Stan? *Wobble arse?*'

Stung, Myra threw a tea towel at her sister.

'You can make all the smart remarks you like, but you won't be laughing when you're still on the shelf at thirty.'

'I'm twenty-three years old!' Joan snapped. 'You just *want* me to be a spinster.'

'Suit yourself,' Myra replied, breathing on her engagement ring and then polishing it against her sleeve. 'But if you take my advice you'll forget Tom Cox and look elsewhere. What about that chemist bloke?'

'*Aaron?* Are you mad?'

'He's all right,' Myra replied, 'quiet, but clever.'

Throwing down the remainder of her chewed crust, Joan put her feet up on the fender.

'He can't talk about anything but Germany and the war.'

'What war?'

'The one he says is coming. He says England and Germany will be at war before the end of the year.'

Myra rolled her eyes. 'Never! There'll never be another war.'

'I'm not so sure. Some people think it's on the cards. You want to stand at the bar and listen to what the customers say.'

'They're all drunks,' Myra replied dismissively. 'What would they know?'

'Aaron says that there are rumours about the Germans mistreating the Jews.'

'Lucky he got out then,' Myra replied sourly. 'But he shouldn't come over here with tales of woe.'

'He's got family in Germany still. Don't be so bloody hard-hearted.'

Shrugging, Myra turned back to the mirror. She didn't want to talk about war. Everyone seemed to be fretting about it – not that anyone believed it would come to a fight. After all, it wasn't that long since the Great War. She didn't want to think about it, would rather daydream about her wedding instead, planned for the following September.

'Stan says there won't be a war.'

'Oh, that's a comfort,' Joan replied drily. 'I'll stop worrying now.'

'There's no talking to you any more! You've got worse lately. I've told you, Joan, you want to get that man off your mind. Tom Cox will never give your a second's thought whilst Grace Ellis is around.'

Pulling a face at her sister, Joan watch Myra leave and then walked back to the doorway. The pub was busy, men making a pint last, a few women there with their husbands, children hanging about outside, waiting for their parents to come out at closing time. The smell of warm beer and cheap cigarettes hung on her mother's clothes as she passed by, the buckles on her father's braces catching the light as he bent over the taps.

What a bloody life, Joan thought suddenly. A rough pub in a rough part of town. Slumping against the door jamb, she continued to look out, smoke rising from behind the snug partition glass, an old man in a muffler leaning against the bar.

'Hey, Joan,' her father called. 'Get some more onions from the back, will you?'

She eyed her father, the long anteater face, his arms leaning on the bar as he talked to his cronies. Why can't he get the bloody onions? she thought meanly.

'I don't know where they are.'

He looked at her, peeved. 'Ask your mother.'

'*You* ask her.'

His eyes narrowed. 'Get the onions, you lazy sod.'

'*Lazy!*' Joan snapped back. 'Who does all the work round here?'

'Well, not you!' he retorted, aware that everyone in the bar was listening. 'You mind who you're talking to, girl. I'm your father and don't you forget it. Now, get the sodding onions.'

Sullenly, Joan walked into the back room. There was a pantry off the kitchen, filled with cheap food, a bottle of white onions on the top shelf.

Peevishly, she pushed them to the back and called out. 'There aren't any onions. They've all been used.'

The place smelled of damp, and of the old dog sitting by the back door, chewing its lead. Suddenly Joan's frustration threatened to overwhelm her. She wanted out, and remembered her old dreams.

Hollywood – God, who was she kidding? She knew it had always been an illusion, but sometimes – just sometimes – she thought she might get away. Might make it, whatever that meant. Once she had even gone to Manchester to see a theatrical agent.

What d'you do? he'd asked ... *Huh?* she'd replied. *What d'you do? Oh, I act ... In what?* he'd pressed her. *Films ... Films, my arse,* he'd said. *The only film you've ever seen is the one you get over your eye.*

Well, he's been right, hadn't he? But she had always thought she would get away from the pub smells and Oldham; Had no idea of a career, but she wanted *something* more. She was smart, quick; surely she didn't have to be buried alive here? Ruefully, Joan glanced through the door. Her father was still talking, laughing now and then as he leaned on the bar. A lazy man leading a lazy life. She didn't want that.

Bugger it! Joan thought suddenly. It was all right for Grace, she had people who believed in her. Who the hell believed in Joan? Not her parents. They thought she should have remained with the Strattons and they moaned about her giving up a secure job. *That Grace Ellis might flop*, they'd said, *and then what would you do? Jobs don't grow on trees and from the way you're going on you're a bit behind the wall finding a husband to carry you.*

Joan's mother suddenly walked into the hallway. She was in a cheap print dress, her feet flat, bunions pushing against the straps of her scandals. You got flat feet from being on them all day, serving behind a bar with a toerag of a husband that never pulled his weight . . .

Tom Cox wouldn't be like that, Joan thought, staring gloomily at her father, his thin, slicked-down hair resting on the back of his collar, a tattoo on his right forearm. Men like Tom Cox didn't have tattoos, or beer bellies.

'Are you going to stand there all night?' her mother asked her suddenly.

'I was just going out.'

'Where?' she asked, pulling a beer crate down the hall along the faded linoleum.

'I'm going dancing. The Hill Stores.'

'Jesus, moving that creases me,' her mother said, stretching up and rubbing her back.

'Get Dad to help.'

Mrs Cleaver raised her eyes in exasperation, then folded her arms as she looked at her daughter.

'You know, I used to go dancing a long time ago.'

'Really?'

'Yeah, when I were young.' Her mother paused, then unexpectedly took her daughter's hand and swept her into a clumsy waltz. 'It were before I married your father. I was happy in those days.' She stopped suddenly, dropping her daughter's hands. 'You want to get a move on, get out.'

'I told you, I'm going to the Hill Stores.'

'Not just dancing,' her mother replied, 'but out of all of this.' An worn-out woman in a cheap dress she glanced at her husband regretfully. 'Don't miss any chances, Joan – or you'll end up like me.'

Malcolm Seagrave was tidying out his desk drawer when his clerk announced a visitor. Impatient, Malcolm looked up.

'She hasn't got an appointment.'

'Miss Ellis says that she appreciates that she has come unannounced, but that she would like to see you, if you would give her the time.'

Really, Malcolm thought, that was what everyone wanted, *time*. He had never met Grace Ellis and wasn't excited at the prospect. He liked all his relationships to be by post, once removed. People could be so demanding.

'Show her in.'

A moment later Grace Ellis stood in the doorway of Malcolm Seagrave's office, dressed in a navy suit and a cream hat, the brim turned away from her face. Steady grey eyes regarded him and for a moment he was almost intimidated by her.

'Mr Seagrave, thank you seeing me,' she said, smiling to put him at his ease.

'I don't usually see people without appointments,' Malcolm said, gesturing her to a seat. 'Is there a problem?'

'The deadline the thirteenth of July, is the day after tomorrow.'

'I know.'

'Well, it's just that my benefactors won't know how their investment has done. I mean, no one has contacted me to ask for documents or records. Have you heard from them?'

'No.' Malcolm replied, thinking of Blomfield and Rosen and wondering idly why the smug Frederick Conrad hadn't been in touch. 'I haven't heard from anyone.'

Grace nodded, unfastened her bag and took out a large envelope. She slid it across the desk towards him.

'Those are the figures. The Auden Line is a going concern. In fact, it has made a small profit. But that's nothing to what we could do in the future. Business is –'

'Not my concern,' Malcolm interrupted her. He had no wish to get involved, and had one of his tempers coming on. His could feel it start, like a growl in the chest. 'I'm always of the opinion that one should never volunteer anything. Especially information. If they want it, they'll ask for it.'

'But any future monies rely on their opinion,' Grace countered. 'What my benefactors have been generous enough to provide has set up my business and supported my father for two years. With due respect, Mr Seagrave, I have to know where I stand – if they want to continue to sponsor me, or not.'

'I think we should wait until your benefactors' solicitors contact us.'

'Who are they?' Grace asked, aware that she was being fobbed off.

'I hardly think that that is a concern of yours,' Malcom replied, needled.

'But if I understand correctly, only the name of my benefactors is to be withheld. *Not* the name of the agents acting for them.'

Malcolm didn't like the way the conversation was going. He had made a tidy sum from handling Grace Ellis's affairs and had no desire to let her go directly to Blomfield and Rosen, cutting him – and his income – out of the picture.

'I'll contact them.'

Grace studied him for a long moment and then rose to her feet.

'If you would, Mr Seagrave, I would be grateful.'

On her way out she paused by the clerk's desk and smiled at him. The man smiled back and nodded consolingly as she explained how she had forgotten the name of the solicitors working for her benefactors. Mr Seagrave *had* told her, but she had forgotten and didn't dare to disturb him again.

Aware of Mr Seagrave's tempers, the clerk nodded sympathetically and wrote down Mr Frederick Conrad, of Messrs Blomfield and Rosen, followed by the address. Then he passed it over to Grace with a knowing look.

Taking the bull by the horns, Joan had arranged to bump into Tom as he left his office at the town hall. She was dressed in her best clothes and had spent a long time on her make-up. Not too much though; Tom wasn't keen on make-up.

Her eyes scanned every man who left. Finally Tom emerged. Swallowing drily, Joan brushed his sleeve.

'Sorry! Oh, Tom, it's *you*.'

He looked at her and smiled. Her stomach flipped like a landed fish.

''Lo there, Joan.'

'Are you finished for the day?' she asked, then rushed on recklessly, 'I was just going off to the cinema. Like to come?'

He hesitated. 'Well . . .'

Oh God, she thought, don't let him humiliate me. God, why could the appalling Myra land someone and she couldn't? It wasn't fair, none of it was.

'Oh, come on, Tom,' she urged him. 'It's a musical. You like musicals.'

He glanced round. Joan was sure she would faint with shame if he refused.

'Well, OK,' he said at last. 'Why not? I'd nothing else planned for tonight.'

Jesus, Joan thought wryly, would she be able to cope with the passion? Still, they were going to the pictures. It was a start.

For the past eighteen months Grace had known that she needed someone to sit with her father whilst she was at work. She was away too long to leave him unattended and was frightened that he might be taken ill, or fall out of bed when she wasn't there. Someone had to sit with him, spoonfeed him and change him. But such assistance cost money and Grace was struggling with the limited finances she had. Then unexpectedly, Don Clegg, her father's old friend, called to see her one morning early.

'Mr Clegg, how are you?' Grace asked. 'I haven't seen you for ages.'

It had actually been years, since her childhood. For a long time, Arthur and Don had been friends, but an argument had caused a rift in their friendship, and when Don moved to Salford they hadn't kept in touch.

But here he was on the doorstep again – a heavy-set man, short, his face mottled with broken veins from working outdoors in all weathers.

'You've changed, Grace.' He paused. 'And I heard

about your father. That were sad. My Clara died a month back. It's quiet now in the house with her gone.'

Grace offered her condolences and then waited, wondering what Don wanted.

'Time hangs heavy on my hands now. Clara was ill for a long time. I nursed her.'

'That's hard work,' Grace said sympathetically.

He nodded. 'It is. You know, me and your father were good mates in the past. We went back years – and then we had a stupid argument and fell out . . .' He hesitated. 'I suppose you're wondering why I haven't been round for such a long time. I've no excuse; I was just fully occupied with Clara.'

'It's all right, Mr Clegg. My father doesn't understand much of what's going on any more. I doubt if he would know his old friends.'

'That bad, is he?'

'Yes, and getting worse.'

'Not much company for you then?'

'I'm not much company for him either. I work long hours now with the business,' Grace replied. 'If the truth be known, I feel that I should be around my father more, but I can't spare the time.'

'It must be hard for you,' Don said, adding quickly, 'I could help out.'

Surprised, Grace stared at him. 'I don't understand.'

'Like I said before, I knew your father a long time ago and I feel bad about our argument. It were about your mother, Grace, I won't lie to you. I said some cruel things and if you want me to clear off now, I'd understand. But I'm sorry, really I am. And I want to make amends.'

'You don't have to –'

'I want to,' Don persisted. 'I've nothing to do all day now. If you let me, I could help with your father.'

She was shaken by the suggestion.

'Mr Clegg, you don't know what he's like. I'm very grateful for the offer, but it would be a thankless task. My father's not the man you remember.'

Don puffed out his chest. 'I'm probably not the man he remembers either, but I'd still be glad to help. Listen to me, love. I need to get out of the house. I can't sit around thinking about Clara all day. It's not healthy. I hope you'll forgive me saying, but I've been hearing about Arthur for a while. The Coxes mentioned that you were struggling and there was talk of your dad's . . . your dad's *difficult* ways.'

Embarrassed, Grace glanced down at her feet.

'I could do with the help. But I couldn't pay you much, Mr Clegg.'

He shrugged. 'I'm not fussed. Give me what you can.'

'But my father needs feeding during the day. And changing.' She paused. 'He's incontinent.'

'So was Clara.'

'But Clara was your wife. Why would you want to do something so difficult for someone who isn't family?'

Shaking his head, Don tucked his hands deep into his pockets.

'Arthur Ellis was a friend of mine when we were lads. He was better off and better educated, but he never made me feel inferior. I was the runt of the litter round these parts and I was bullied for it. Your father stood up for me, stood my corner more than once – and yet I let him down when your mother left. So I reckon I owe him something, now he needs help.' He hurried on, 'My Clara was ill a long time. You have to do things you never thought you could: cook and clean and all those things I thought were women's work. I got used to looking after someone. I miss it now.' His ruddy face was serious. 'Let me help you, Miss Ellis. You'd be doing me and your father a favour.'

Chapter Twenty

Mr Frederick Conrad sneezed noisily into his handkerchief. Then sneezed again. A summer cold, would you believe it? he thought, his eyes prickling, his nose blocked. It had been a freezing winter and he hadn't coughed once. Now summer had finally come his head was on fire.

That morning he had received a letter from Malcolm Seagrave – the wiry little toad – saying that Miss Grace Ellis was showing some interest in the deadline of 13 July, and had the benefactors been in touch with him? Miss Ellis had accounts and figures for them to look at, and it appeared that she had had some modest success. What did Mr Conrad think the next step should be?

Frederick Conrad sneezed again, his impressive head of white hair jerking with the motion. A handsome man, he had been something of a Lothario in his youth and could never resist flirting. Dark eyes and heavy brows gave him an autocratic look, and his studied, mellifluous voice added to the impression. He never went any further than flirting – his wife would have maimed him if he had – but he could appreciate women and knew that often the appreciation was mutual.

Not that Conrad was looking his best that morning when he awaited the arrival of Miss Grace Ellis. Her phone call had come only half an hour before the second post had brought Seagrave's letter, so she had pipped her solicitor to the post. Good, thought Conrad, he had never taken to Seagrave. Mouldering old fart.

The calendar on his desk said 12 July – one day before the deadline set by the benefactors. God knows why Seagrave should seem surprised; naturally the woman was concerned. It was bloody obvious to anyone with half a brain that she would want to know where she stood. Coughing again, Conrad buzzed his secretary to show Grace in.

He rose as the door opened, giving her the benefit of his perfect teeth as he smiled at her. She was a good-looking woman, Conrad thought, quite the lady.

'Sit down, please,' he said, his manners exquisite. 'Can I get you a cup of tea?'

'That would be nice. Thank you,' Grace replied, looking round at an office surprisingly stuffed with antiques.

Ornately carved bookcases rubbed shoulders with several polished tables, two high-backed chairs in front of a massive stone fireplace. Behind Conrad's chair was a church lectern, a stuffed eagle crouching on the top, and by the window a cabinet full of stuffed foxes caught the light, their glass eyes flickering malevolently.

'It's a hobby of mine,' Conrad said, following her gaze.

'What? Taxidermy?'

'No, collecting things,' Conrad replied, baffled. Fiercely he rubbed his nose with his handkerchief. 'Summer cold.'

Aware of the eagle's unblinking stare, Grace passed a sheaf of papers across the desk.

'I don't know if you've already heard from Mr Seagrave, but I wanted to deliver this to you personally. Two years ago I was told that my progress would be assessed today.' She still wondered about Mr Seagrave's advice that she should ignore the deadline and wait to see if anyone contacted her. But she knew she couldn't do that; she had to know what was proposed for her future. 'Have you heard from my benefactors?'

Conrad nodded. His eyes were beginning to stream. It looked like he was bloody crying, for God's Sake!

'I heard from my client first thing this morning.'

'And?'

'I was instructed to extend your financial assistance for the next twelve months.'

'But no one's seen the books,' Grace said, surprised.

Conrad laughed. 'I've never seen anyone so keen to have their business examined,' he said, his voice rasping with his cold. He needed an lozenge, a hot bath, a whisky, a bullet. Anything to stop the way he was feeling. 'My clients seem satisfied and that's what matters.'

'Who are they?'

Conrad blinked, unsure he had heard correctly through the fug of his cold.

'Pardon?'

'I'm wondering who my benefactors are. I mean, they've done a great deal to help me and my father. I'd like to thank them.'

'They don't need thanks,' Conrad replied. 'They're just pleased to see you make a success. You've done well too, Miss Ellis. These aren't the easiest times and cosmetics are a new business. Frankly, up here I'm surprised you've managed to find customers.'

'Women like to look good. They need to feel special and they need to be able to afford to take care of themselves. That's what I set out to do – offer them make-up they can afford.'

Conrad's interest was waning. He wanted to go home and get back into bed. He could even stand the thought of his wife fussing over him, coaxing him with junket and milk pudding.

'My benefactors –' Grace persisted – 'will they always want to remain anonymous?'

'They usually do –'

'So they've helped other people?'

Conrad blinked, wrong-footed and unable to think clearly. 'No, I meant that if anonymity is requested, it is usually maintained.'

'But you could ask them if I could be told, couldn't you?' Grace pressed him. 'I've always wanted to know why they picked me.'

'They believed in you.'

'In a *child*?' Grace queried. 'How could they know what I was like then? How I would grow up?'

Conrad coughed again, rattled now. 'I don't know how or why they picked you, Miss Ellis, they just did. They will have done their homework thoroughly before committing themselves. No one gives money away lightly.'

Her curiosity wasn't to be quelled so easily.

'Are they in this area?'

'I can't say.'

'Do I know them?'

'Really, Miss Ellis, I can't tell you anything further.' Conrad stood up to signal that the interview was over. 'They wanted to help you, and they have. They want you to succeed and you appear to be doing quite well. They also wanted to help you when it looked as though you were falling into the wrong company.'

Stunned, Grace stared at him. 'What?'

Had he said too much? Conrad couldn't think straight and he didn't like being cross-examined, even when he didn't have a cold.

'You had some dealings with Elmer Shaw,' he said. 'The man is notorious, altogether the kind of person a young lady should avoid. The police should have been brought in, Miss Ellis, but it was decided that it would be better for everyone if you were *rescued* and not reliant on his financial help. Personally, I would have liked to see the man gaoled for what he did, and any gentleman would say the same.' He paused. 'Are you all right?'

Feeling her legs weaken, Grace suddenly leaned against the chair arm, her head bowed. She had told no one but Joan about Elmer Shaw attacking her, and Joan had been sworn to secrecy. No one knew what had happened that night – so how did her benefactors find out about Elmer Shaw? Who had been there apart from her and Shaw?

There had been no one on the street and the Coxes had overheard nothing, of that Grace was certain. The following day Tom had asked her about the cut and bruising on her face, but Grace had explained it away by saying that she had tripped on the tiled floor, and he had shown no inclination to disbelieve her.

She had told the same story to everyone. Cold compresses and vinegar had taken down the swelling, the cut healing quickly, though leaving a scar which had never gone. Joan had been so angry that she had wanted to call in the police, but Grace had stopped her.

'If I tell the police there will be questions and people will talk,' she had said firmly. 'I would have to give evidence and it would be my word against Shaw's. He has the money to get the best legal representation. Do you really think they'll believe that I didn't encourage him?'

She had wanted to add that she feared they would actually say: *So she turned out like her mother after all. A real tart. Going cap in hand to Elmer Shaw. I wonder what else she offered him apart from a business idea.* They would sneer and point at her, marking her out. Giving her a bad name which would stick for ever. What chance would her business have had then?

No, she insisted, she had got away relatively lightly. She had been frightened and hurt, but it was over. Elmer Shaw wasn't going to risk coming near her again. She had to forget it and get on with her life.

Time had passed and she had gradually managed to put Elmer Shaw to the back of her mind. And only Joan had known what had happened. Joan, who could always keep a secret. No one else *could* have known.

But her benefactors had.

'Are you sure you're all right, Miss Ellis?' Conrad asked again, helping Grace to her feet.

Confused, she nodded, but her heart was beating hard and her mouth was dry. *Someone was watching her*, someone knew everything that happened to her. Someone – whoever they were – had known about Shaw. That was why they had so conveniently come forward again with financial support. The people who had watched over her as a girl were watching over her as a woman. But who were they?

'Will you do something for me, Mr Conrad?' she asked when she found her voice again.

'Of course.'

'Will you thank my benefactors for me? Tell them . . . tell them I'm grateful. Will you also tell them that I would like to say thank you in person one day?'

'Be sure I'll pass on the message.'

Grace walked to the door and then turned.

'Do you believe in guardian angels, Mr Conrad?'

'It's a nice thought, Miss Ellis, but I'm a solicitor. We only believe in what we can see.'

Chapter Twenty-One

By November Solomon Bloom's smuggled letters came to Oldham imbued with a sense of hesitant calm. Things seemed quieter, he wrote. He *would* have to get out soon, but Rosa would still not leave her parents. Solomon had suggested that they take her parents with them, but they were old school and could not believe that their neighbours and country would turn against them. They wanted to wait and see how things went, Solomon told his brother. It might blow over.

In her office Grace could see Aaron reading his letter, his shoulder hunched over his laboratory bench. In Lancashire he had suffered no discrimination but she knew that he was suffering daily, wondering if his brother would get out of Germany in time.

> Just leave, *Aaron had written the previous week.* Forget the business, the money, just get yourself, Rosa and her parents over here. We can manage, you can start again, just get out. The situation is bad, Solomon. There is a good deal of gossip about camps and rumours which beggar belief. It could be hearsay, but who knows for sure?
> Get out. Please.

St Andrew's Place was full of fog, greeny yellow and smelling of soot as it came into the factory following Enid Taylor. She had a scarf round her head and over her mouth, coughing hoarsely. Ivy had arrived only a minute before, hanging around at the entrance and catching Enid's coat as she came in.

'God!' Enid said, startled. 'Oh, it's *you*, Ivy.'

Ivy looked round furtively. 'Enid, I need some help, luv.'

Enid coughed and then nodded. 'What's up?'

'Can I take your shift tomorrow?'

'But, Ivy, I need that shift. Patrick's had the doctor out again and that costs.' She stared into Ivy's pinched faced. 'I'd help you if I could, but I can't.'

So Alf had been up to his tricks again, Enid thought. It wasn't news. There had obviously been a fight at the Morris house the previous night, for Ivy's left eye was bloodshot. That bugger Alf was a right bastard, and no mistake. He was running up bills at the dogs and God knew where else. If he was owing to the bookies now, Enid thought, then he was really in trouble. Alf Morris had no job and the only wages coming in were his daughter's, from the mill, and Ivy's. Hardly enough to pay off the rent and get food – certainly not enough to pay off debts and keep the toughs off the doorstep.

Enid had seen too many men bring down their families through gambling. Once you were in deep, there was no way out. She knew it – and so did Ivy.

'Please, let me have your shift,' Ivy pleaded. Her eyes were wide with desperation. 'Just this once. Just to let me get some money in fast.'

'I can't, luv,' Enid replied, her hand touching Ivy's shoulder. 'I can't, I would if I could, but I need every penny.'

Ivy stared into her face. 'Please, please . . .'

Enid glanced away miserably. Why was she asking her? She knew that she had no money spare, not with Patrick being ill. God Almighty, Enid thought, I'd help you if I could, but it's all I can do to keep my own family afloat.

Then suddenly Ivy straightened up, her voice losing its pleading tone.

'I shouldn't have asked you, luv. I should have known better. No matter,' she said bravely. 'Something'll turn up.'

Yes, Enid thought, I just hope it isn't the bailiffs.

'Shut the bloody door!' Joan called, watching Ivy and Enid huddled together in the corner. For once she wasn't curious to know what the gossip was; her thoughts were elsewhere. She was getting irritated with Grace. She was becoming a tyrant, Joan thought unjustly. Working everyone to the bone to get the make-up made, packaged and sent off. God Almighty, the way she went on, you'd think it was blood, not lipstick.

Rubbing her hands with some of the beeswax used in the lipsticks, Joan looked round the workshop. The smell was hardly noticeable to her, she had worked in it for so long, but she guessed that it would be stronger in the laboratory where Aaron was. The laboratory now had an extended workroom next to it where six people – four men and two women – worked. The demand for Auden Line products had grown to the extent that Aaron had had to hire more help. First came the bald-headed Czech, Solar Giversky, and then followed five locals. Some were chemists in their own right; others were apprentices, learning their trade not under a pharmacist in a chemist's shop, but at the workshop in St Andrew's Place.

Still massaging her hands, Joan thought about Solar and Aaron, and wondered why they hadn't become fast friends. After all, they had so much in common, being foreigners and all. The others she hardly saw – there was a separate entrance and exit for them – and they had little to do with the packing or administration of the Auden Line.

The latter was Grace's responsibility, although from the first Joan had helped her out. The wages were only reasonable, but then anything was better than working for Old Ma Stratton. Besides, Grace was her oldest friend, and the idea of their working together had seemed more a pleasure than a hardship.

But now Joan wasn't so sure. Grace had been given another year's sponsorship. Now, wouldn't you think that she would relax? Not a chance, Joan thought; she was driving herself even harder. No time for going out to the pictures, no times for her friends, no time for her father hardly, not since Cleggie came so helpfully on to the scene.

Grace had no time for anything but the Auden Line. Life beyond that didn't exist for her. The usual worries about husbands, having a family – that meant nothing to Grace. Joan bit her lip. Perhaps she didn't *have* to worry, what with Tom in love with her and the besotted Geoffrey around all the time, driving the Auden Line van about like he was delivering diamonds to the Aga Khan. Joan realized that Grace could do anything to Geoffrey and he would accept it.

She wondered if the same was true about Tom Cox ... Sighing, Joan nodded to Aaron as he passed the workshop door. Her sister Myra had wondered if *he* could be a possible suitor and Joan looked at him in that light for the first time. Then decided against it. Oh no, Joan thought, grimacing – Aaron was a kind man, but not the sort she was looking for. The sort she wanted was Tom Cox.

It was too bloody unfair! Grace didn't want Tom, so

why couldn't she – Joan – have him? It was obvious that Grace – if she ever married – would pick someone influential and rich. She wouldn't look twice at the likes of Tom; she didn't want a clerk at the town hall, a man who thought that Diggle was the best place on earth. Grace wanted someone who could show her things she had never seen – places, people, culture. She wanted someone better than herself in order *to* better herself.

Still chewing her lip, Joan wondered just how long she would have to wait until Tom realized he was getting nowhere, or Grace met someone else. Time was getting on; Grace might have no fears about not getting married, but Joan did. Still, Joan consoled herself, she was making some progress. She and Tom had been to the park together and although Tom had hardly acted like a suitor, he had been friendly.

What he needed, Joan decided, was a good kick in the pants. She would have to *make* him fall in love with her. Hell's bells, it couldn't be that difficult, could it? She would talk to her sister Kate – not Myra – and read up on her romantic novels; perhaps pretend that she was interested in someone else . . . Joan's eyes drifted over to Aaron again. *That* was an idea, she thought. Men always got more interested when they thought they had a rival . . .

Joan frowned, she *had* to know once and for all if she stood a chance with Tom. She looked through the glazed top half of the Grace's office door. There she was, her dark head bent over some drawings, sketching out an advertisement. The Auden Line was her first, middle and last thought. Nothing else mattered.

It was all so irritating. Where had the old Grace gone? The one Joan could have a laugh with? Even when she'd first started the business there had been times they could chat and Joan could tell her about the films; times they sneaked out for a matinee to the Riviera; times they exchanged confidences. It seemed so long ago since Joan used to call round at the house in Diggle, looking in on Arthur.

Grace had had a lot to put up with, no one could argue with that, Joan thought. But it had changed her. In the two years since the business was founded, Joan and Grace had had fewer and fewer talks. The exchanged looks, that shorthand of friendship, became less frequent, and now Joan wondered if Grace saw her as just one more employee. The thought needled her – and made her quarrelsome.

'Got a minute?' Joan asked, tapping on the office door and walking in.

Grace looked up and smiled. 'Course I have.'

A moment tingled between them. Surely we never had awkward moments before, Joan wondered.

'I was thinking it would be fun to get out and see the new Joan Crawford film. It's on at the Riviera, Thursday night.'

'I don't know,' Grace said, gesturing to the papers on her desk. 'I have a lot to do.'

'You always have a lot to do. It wouldn't kill you to take some time off.'

'But –'

'Oh, forget it!' Joan snapped. 'It was just an idea, but I suppose you don't want to be seen out with one of the workers now.'

At once Grace was on her feet, closing the office door and staring hard into Joan's face.

'What the hell is that supposed to mean?'

'You know.'

'No, I don't. Enlighten me.'

Joan turned away, pointing to one of the advertisements Grace had been working on. It was propped up against the wall, a sketch of an elegant woman perfectly made up, her hat tipped over to one side to make the best of her profile.

'That's all you care about now,' she said, pointing to the picture. 'You don't have time for anything unless it has "Auden Line" written across it.'

Stung, Grace took in a sharp breath.

'I have to make this a success, Joan, you know that. I have people who've invested in me.'

'Oh, don't come it! You're neglecting some of the people who've invested in you the longest.'

'Like who?'

'Like me!' Joan snapped, her temper finally shorted. 'I was the one who listened to you when all this was just a pipe dream. I encouraged you and believed in you – helped you out.'

'I know you did, I'm grateful –'

'I don't want bloody gratitude!' Joan snapped. 'I just want things to be like they were. You don't see anything any more, Grace. You don't understand what's going on. It's like anything outside these walls doesn't matter. Well, it does to me. I want more than being your handmaiden. I want a normal life, even if you don't.'

'I don't know what you mean,' Grace countered, bewildered by the attack. 'I want a normal life too –'

'No, you don't, or you'd have got married by now. Tom's been hanging around you for years and you've never given him a second look. You know he's crazy about you, but you don't care. You just use him – *good old Tom, someone to go out with if and when I choose, someone who'll help out in the business if I get pushed. Someone who'll always be there.* It's not fair!' Joan shouted suddenly. 'He's being used and for what? Nothing. You don't want him and you don't care if someone else does.'

Inflamed by the accusation that she was using Tom, Grace rounded on her friend.

'You're just jealous!'

'Yes, I am! I want him. And I should have him, because I care about him. You should let him go and give me a chance.'

'BUT I'M NOT HOLDING ON TO HIM!'

Their raised voices had alerted the women in the workshop outside and Tilly was looking over, seeing the two woman going hammer and tongs in the office.

'You *are* holding on to him!' Joan retorted. 'By not telling him he's wasting his time.'

'I've never encouraged him –'

'You've never discouraged him either!' Joan shouted, even Aaron now walking to the door of the laboratory to see what all the commotion was about. 'He still thinks he's got a chance. And he always will think that until you tell him otherwise.'

'Why should I?' Grace said suddenly.

Outraged, Joan yelled, 'You bitch! You just want to hedge your bets, don't you? Hold on to Tom in case no one else comes along? Just like you hold on to Geoffrey, my poor stupid brother, who thinks you're an angel. But you're no angel, Grace, are you? You're hard underneath. Hard through and through. Oh yes, you've had it rough, but you don't really care about anything except this bloody place!'

Furious, Grace caught at her friend's arm. 'This place gives you a job. A chance to save some money for your own ambitions –'

Angrily, Joan shook her off. 'I don't *have* any ambitions! I don't want anything more than to get married –'

'To Tom?'

Thinking that Grace was mocking her, Joan struck out and caught her on the shoulder.

Enraged, Grace hit back, slapping Joan roundly on the cheek.

'You cow!' Joan said, backing away and moving to the door.

'Oh, come on, Joan, I didn't mean to hurt you. You hit me first,' Grace said, trying to placate her.

But Joan was long past placating. She felt humiliated, as though Grace was lording it over her, triumphing in Tom's devotion.

'Joan, please, calm down,' Grace continued trying to soothe the situation. But she had no chance.

It had been obvious to Grace when they first met that Tom was in love with her, but, after years of devotion, over the past six months it had seemed as though he was becoming more distant. Grace had hoped that it was because he had finally become interested in Joan; indeed, she knew that they had gone out walking together.

'I care about Tom, Joan, but not how you think. He's not in love with me any more.'

But Joan was past reason. She was angry and frustrated, and at that moment she found – in the argument – a reason to fall out with Grace. If they were enemies, how much easier it would be for her to try to win Tom over. After all, she would no longer be betraying a friend.

'Joan,' Grace said, pleadingly, 'I'm sorry. Don't let's fight. It's stupid. Let's talk this out.'

'Talk it out?' Joan countered. 'I don't want to talk any more, Grace. I've done all the talking out I'm going to do.'

* * *

Don Clegg was sitting by Arthur's bedside and talking to him, although he had no idea if his old friend understood a word. Stories of the old days mixed with the news of the present. Did he think there would be another war, he asked the silent figure in the bed. It looked bad. If there was a war all the young men would be called up again. Men like Geoffrey Cleaver and Tom Cox.

He wiped the side of Arthur's mouth gently and then settled his rotund form back into the bedside chair. A cold wind was blowing and making the bedroom draughty, although Grace had had heavy curtains put up, and the fire had been banked high in the grate opposite the bed. He wondered how she managed to lay the fires, make the food and change her father before she left for St Andrew's Place in the mornings. And she often worked until ten at night. It was a hard grind – hard for a man, let alone a young woman.

But sitting with Arthur was no hardship to Don. He had the radio upstairs, and when it was quiet he sometimes dozed to the sound of the Palm Court orchestra. Arthur was no trouble; he was like baby-sitting a corpse really. The only sounds came from next door when the Cox brothers squabbled. Still boys will be boys. But then Tom's brother was eighteen now, hardly a boy any longer, old enough to be called up.

Don was suddenly relieved that he didn't have to fight again. The last time had been enough for him. He had come home gassed but recovered slowly over time. Others had not been so lucky – like Billy Hinkley up on Waterloo Street, shell-shocked and still jerking every time he heard a dog so much as bark. It seemed so pointless, Don thought, after all the hardship of the depression, all the men laid off, the families struggling on nothing. For what? To have another war? What the hell was going on?

The cotton trade was all but done with, the wealth of Oldham crushed. People who had enjoyed a good standard of living before now lived off the dole, and men who had come home to a land fit for heroes found that they had fought for nothing. And now it was going to happen again?

Don thought back to the previous night when Grace had come home with Aaron Bloom. Don hadn't known any Jews before, but he liked Bloom and found himself listening avidly to the young man's stories of Germany. He had a brother there who wouldn't, or couldn't, leave. If there was a war he might be killed, Aaron had said. Don thought of his own brother, killed at the Somme. Nothing changed. It was always down to the politicians, not the common man. Always the ordinary Joe who suffered.

He thought of all the young people he had met in Arthur's house. Joan, Tom, Aaron, Geoffrey – what would their lives be like? He wondered then if Grace would marry the devoted Tom and be left a widow. Which was worse? Staying unwed or risking the loss of your man?

Then Don remembered that it was the thought of Clara that had kept him going. He had had someone to come home to, someone waiting for him. But things seemed different now. Poverty had made people reluctant to marry and the women were working as hard as the men. Like Grace, running her own business. It's all such change from Arthur's greengrocer's shop, Don thought, and that's a fact.

Sighing, he glanced over to the window, where night was coming down fast. The radio played a jazz tune, dark and melancholic. Looking at the still figure of Arthur in the bed, Don wondered if anyone ever knew what was going to happen to them, and, if they did, would they know how to prepare for it?

He doubted it, and felt suddenly a long cold shadow move over the room and wedged itself hard against his heart.

Chapter Twenty-Two

Huddled in the cramped air-raid shelter, Solar Giversky kept his head bowed. Aaron was next to Grace, and the women from the night shift huddled opposite. Ivy was silent, Enid, beside her, a blanket round them both. Coats had been thrown hurriedly over work clothes, Grace's hair falling around her face as she glanced up to the sound of the planes passing overhead.

Manchester had been struck heavily, the German bombers going for the River Irwell and the munitions factories, Oldham receiving some of the fallout, being only seven miles away. It seemed that since war had been declared, twelve months earlier, posters had sprung up everywhere like dismal flowers. 'DIG FOR VICTORY', 'BUY WAR BONDS', 'CARELESS TALK COSTS LIVES'.

Too sick to move, Arthur remained in his bed in Diggle, Grace staying with him if she was home. If she wasn't and Don was there when the sirens sounded, Don would ease his bulk under the bed and wait for the all clear. He was too old to make a run for the shelter in the garden, he said. Besides, if it was his time to go, so be it. Arthur – unmoving and unresponsive – was the only one who didn't seem to realize that war had broken out again. Wherever he was, it wasn't touched by the air raids or by the repeated shouts of 'Put that light out!' when the wardens went on their nightly patrols.

Grace had kept the business going, but not long after war was declared, many of the staff had gone to work at munitions factories, and Aaron had been called up for war work. Unable to fight because of poor eyesight, he nevertheless kept working part time with Grace at St Andrew's Place, although the output of the Auden Line was much reduced. The output – but not the demand. It seemed that even in wartime women wanted glamour.

The benefactors had extended their sponsorship of Grace indefinitely. The war changed nothing. But all Grace's requests to know who her benefactors were met with refusal. The previous year Malcolm Seagrave had died from a heart attack and now Grace dealt directly with Frederick Conrad, the money coming regularly by cheque, to be paid into the bank in Oldham.

A plane passed close overhead. Silence, then the far-off shattering sound of a bomb exploding and buildings falling. Solar prayed silently; a pale Aaron glanced over to Grace.

His brother had never left Berlin. The smuggled letters had continued for a long time, the news of horrors escalating. Even in 1938 Solomon had written:

German children are being recruited for the Nazis' anti-Jewish campaign. I have seen boys of fourteen and younger marching along the Friedrichstrasse and smearing the Star of David on Jewish shops. Pupils are forbidden to talk to, or play with, Jewish children. The Nazis are even going into schools now and asking the pupils where their uniforms were bought. If they say that their uniforms come from Jewish shops they are told to stand in a corner for punishment. What are they doing? What is going to happen here?

I walk around now thinking that I am being

watched, judged. There is a terrible sense of impending disaster here. Hitler is making us into scapegoats. This is no longer my home.

Gradually, the intensity of the bigotry had escalated – secretly and publicly – until anti-Semiticism had become overt. Good Germans did not tolerate inferior races, they were told. Then had come the infamous pogrom on 9 November 1938. Josef Goebbels had said that the violence against the Jews had been as a direct result of the murder of a German diplomat by a Polish Jew. Jewish shops and businesses had been wrecked, Jews beaten by Storm Troopers and even by middle-class people. As the shops had burned, women had taken their children to see Jews being beaten senseless and, Solomon had written to Aaron, there was viciousness everywhere.

The event was referred to a *Kristallnacht* – Crystal Night – a name meant to underline the amount of glass windows which had been smashed. Jews were openly hated and victimized by the government and the people. No one had even been shocked when Goering commented, 'They should have killed more Jews and broken less glass.'

Hatred – Solomon wrote – is everywhere, fear like a smell in the air. By December of that year, the German authorities were measuring suspects' noses to see if they were Semitic. Jews were suddenly being forbidden to deal in jewellery or precious metals. They were not allowed to invest in property or operate bank accounts. Finally it was declared that all Jewish businesses would be closed down by executors appointed by the Government.

Then suddenly, in 1940, the letters from Solomon had ceased, the only news of him coming from a friend who had made it over to Manchester in time. Yes, they *had* seen Solomon, they told Aaron. He was fine, and Rosa was pregnant. He had told them he was following soon, but although arrangements had been made somehow Solomon never managed to leave Berlin. The brothers' company had been taken over by Germans and their family house had been repossessed. The last anyone had seen of Solomon and Rosa Bloom had been a sighting one day on the street. After that, nothing.

'Bloody Krauts,' Ivy murmured sourly as the planes hummed over head. Alf had done a bunk, leaving her. Now Ivy paid his debts off herself, knowing that she would have to work for the rest of her life. Her head down, she stared at the floor of the bunker. What did it matter if the bombs hit? she thought. If they did, it would all be over for her and good riddance.

Opposite her, Aaron smiled listlessly at Enid. What was he doing in a bomb shelter in the middle of Oldham? he wondered. Hiding away, saving his skin. He was good at that. He felt like a coward, ashamed of his own fear. Beside him, Grace sat watching Solar Giversky. The man's ruddy face was unreadable. If he was afraid, he didn't show it. His family had long since died. Now over fifty, he was alone but safe. He, like Aaron, had escaped the Nazis. Yet it seemed that the although two men had so much in common their history estranged rather than united them.

Grace's heart was thumping fast, giving away her fear. I don't want to die, she thought, not here, not in a damp tin bunker. It's not what I've worked for, and I've so much to do . . .

'God!' Aaron said suddenly. 'That was close!'

Grace felt his hand close over hers. He was under no

illusions any more; they were friends, but nothing more. Romance had never been on the cards.

'It's going on too long,' Grace said quickly, her voice wavering. 'I want to get out.'

At once Aaron gripped her arm. 'Ssshh, it'll be over soon,' he assured her.

Ruefully, Grace nodded, hung her head, thought about her family.

As they all did.

Another plane passed over low as Grace closed her eyes and thought of Joan. She missed the humour, the friendship. Since their argument they had not spoken again. Joan had left St Andrew's Place and gone to work first in a shop and then in a munitions factory on Thorn Leigh Road. Occasionally Grace saw her pass on the street, but they never exchanged so much as a direct look. All that friendship, all those dreams and confidences, gone. And I could do with her now, Grace thought. God, Joan, where are you?

She had expected the argument to blow over, but time passed and neither of them made the first move. Instead, Grace found herself alone. In wartime. Her father was no comfort and although Aaron was a good ally, he was weary with anxiety. Only the other day as she walked by the Roxy, Grace remembered the times she had sat with Joan watching the films and talking about the actresses' make-up. And then she remembered Tom.

Tom, who had gone off to fight. Tom, not married, not engaged to anyone. Not even Joan. Perhaps that was the real reason for her anger, Grace thought. Joan had truly believed that she could get Tom and she had failed. He might to longer be hanging around Grace, but he wasn't hanging around Joan either. Rumour had it that he had been seeing a girl in Upper Mill. Gossip even suggested that it might be serious, but who knew for sure?

One thing was certain: Tom had visited Grace less and less, and when he did he never mentioned his girlfriend. Finally he stopped coming.

Yet strangely, when Grace had heard about Tom's new love *she*'d felt something shift inside her. Something unexpected. But how could she be jealous? Hadn't her feelings been perfectly plain over the years? She wasn't in love with Tom, she wasn't in love with anyone and she wasn't the marrying kind. Now it seemed that he loved some else. All the affection had taken for granted was turned off. Rightly so, Grace thought. But it hurt more than she expected. A lot more.

Damn it, she thought suddenly, why hadn't Tom fallen in love with Joan? They could all have stayed friends then; things would have been like they were in the old days. Grace knew Joan had tried every trick in the book, even attempting to make Tom jealous of Aaron, but nothing had happened. Even her own intervention hadn't helped.

Grace had been talking to Tom one day and she had thought to mention Joan.

'What about Joan?'

'*What* about her?' Tom had replied.

'I thought that you two might . . . like each other.'

He'd nodded. 'She's great fun.'

'But nothing else?'

'Like what?'

Grace had sighed. 'Oh God, Tom, you can be dense. Don't you know that Joan thinks the world of you?'

He'd been baffled. 'What *are* you talking about?'

'Joan. She loves you. You must have noticed.'

'*Joan?*' he'd replied, laughing. 'But she's . . . she's . . . You are joking, aren't you?'

'No,' Grace had answered him. 'She's a good person and a very loving one. Joan's cared about you for years.'

He looked into her face steadily. 'I cared about *you* for years,' he had replied. 'Looks like both of us are going to be disappointed, doesn't it?'

Nudging her, Solar brought Grace's thoughts back to the present with a jolt. Jerking his head he gestured upwards the planes rumbling overheard, the bombs still falling. Phlegmatic as ever, Tilly was reading a copy of *Picture Post* and Mary Wells was knitting for her sister's new baby. Both women were now married, both husbands called up, letters and news exchanged in the tearoom at St Andrew's Place.

'Sssh! Listen,' Aaron said suddenly. 'I can hear someone shouting and moving about outside.'

Solar listened. 'They're probably running for shelter.'

'I hope they find it. The Davies children were killed in the last raid. Up on Abbey Hills Road. Direct hit on their house.'

Grace shivered. Jesus, no deaths, please no deaths. She could hear Mary counting the stitches on her needle and then watched her tuck the ball of wool under her arm. Why was she so calm? Grace thought, panic rising in her throat. She should be at home, out of the shelter. Her breathing accelerated again.

'I wonder if my father's all right.'

Aaron looked over to her. 'Don's with him. He'll be fine.'

She nodded, but her breathing still intensified. I'm a coward, she thought. Not brave at all. Her gaze took in the others in the cramped space. Ivy, Tilly, Mary and

Aaron – everyone was calm. Only *she* was fighting panic, her palms sweaty, her head buzzing.

Overhead the planes still came low, a bomb falling a long way off, although the explosion reverberated faintly under their feet. Calm yourself, Grace thought, think of work. That's it! Think of work ... The make-up was selling well. Everything they could produce was in demand. It seemed that women were desperate to hold on to any femininity they could. Working in factories, their lives in turmoil, they clung to the little reminders of normality, a lipstick as imperative to morale as a Spitfire. Rumour had it that there had been a queue outside Lewis's in Manchester only the previous week, women jostling to buy the limited stock of Max Factor's pancake.

Grace thought of advertising, how she would expand it after the war ... A bomber passed overhead, everyone automatically ducking ... Oh God, we're going to be hit, she thought, her fists clenching. What good is make-up now? It's all pointless, stupid.

No, she told herself, stop it! Think about work ... She would extend the range, bring in more colours. Aaron could help with that ... Her thoughts lodged suddenly. What *was* she thinking about? What good were cosmetics when men were dying? What kind of woman was she who had only lipsticks to worry about?

Who did she care about? Depression fell like a smothering blanket over Grace. Mary and Tilly were talking quietly, both had husbands – but not her. Grace had no one to call her own. Oh yes, there was her father, but she looked after him because it was her duty. There was little love in it now.

If her mother had lived, Grace thought, if Dora had stayed with them, things would have been so different. Grace could imagine her mother working at St Andrew's

Place with her. Dora would have been so proud, and good at the marketing. She had had such style, such a sense of taste. God knows where it had come from, certainly not Miller Lane.

For a minute Grace allowed herself to imagine her mother working beside her. She wouldn't have missed Joan so much, wouldn't have felt so alone if Dora had been there ... The image lifted as suddenly as it had arrived. Her mother wasn't there. Never would be. She had lost her mother to Len Billings and later to the road accident which killed her. Nothing remained, not even a clear image of Dora at her handsome best; the accident had damaged her face beyond recognition. In the end she had lost everything, dying robbed of her reputation *and* her beauty.

Was that why she herself had been so unwilling to make attachments, Grace thought suddenly. No man had moved her, her memory of Elmer Shaw making her all the more wary. It had been a shock, but it had been a long time ago. Why hadn't she fallen in love since? Why hadn't she looked forward to seeing a man? To being held, comforted, courted? Why was that? Was it that by putting her whole self into the business she had sought to control her life? To make certain that no messy emotions took her off course as they had wrong-footed her mother?

For the first time Grace saw herself as Joan had the night of their argument. Yes, she *was* selfish, self-absorbed, cold. Love offered had been rejected – not out of any finer feelings, but because she was *afraid*. Frightened to love, to give herself. To risk losing control. The thought was unpalatable and left her breathless. Tom had been a good man and she had let him go. She hadn't seen his qualities until it was too late.

Grace's nails were pressing into her palms. It was no good lying to herself any more, she thought. When she had heard about Tom seeing the girl in Upper Mill she *had* been jealous. She had wanted him then. Maybe she had felt safe, knowing that Joan loved him because she knew instinctively that they would never be lovers. But this unknown woman – who was she? She was a real threat. She had taken him away; she had offered love and he had taken it.

Suddenly, in that dank little air-raid shelter, Grace felt an overwhelming sense of loss. She would seek him out again, when he came home on leave, get to know him again. After all, they were neighbours, it would be easy.

She would win him over, make him fall in love with her again because she realized that she had loved him all along, but never admitted it. Memories came back in droves: the times he had made her laugh, the many occasions he had mended things at her home. Time and affection given so willingly. *Knock on the wall if you need me*, he'd said. *If you ever need me, just knock and I'll be there.*

And he would have been, if she had ever knocked. His faults were minimal, his virtues obvious to everyone but her. It was too late to lie to herself, Grace realized. She hadn't given up on Tom to leave the way clear for Joan, she had rejected him because she was afraid to love him.

Well, she would change all that. When she got out of this godforsaken shelter – *if* she got out of it – she would change everything. She would earn his love . . . It wasn't too late. She would speak to him, see if he still loved her. After all, Tom hadn't married the girl in Upper Mill. If he loved her, he would have married her, surely?

215

He was abroad fighting, Ernie Cox had told Grace only the other day. He would be home next week. *Tom was coming home*, Grace thought to herself, a sensation of excitement catching her out. For a moment she imagined his face, and felt herself blush. Confused, she kept her head down. Was this love? Was this feeling love? She had never allowed herself to think of him as a man before, but now that she did, she wanted him.

But she wouldn't rush it. She would show him her feelings gradually, build up trust between them. Otherwise it would look too hurried, too silly. She had rejected him before, now she had to make him feel secure with her . . . Another bomb landed, shaking the shelter, dirt falling from the corrugated roof on to the bowed heads. Let me live, Grace thought, *please* let me live and I'll make it up to him. Just let me get out of here.

'That's the all clear.'

'Grace,' Mary said, tapping her shoulder, 'that's the all clear sounded.'

She lifted her head and felt suddenly embarrassed, sure that everyone would read her face and see the fear there. Hurriedly she rose to her feet, ducking under the doorway as she moved out into the yard of St Andrew's Place. A full moon was shining over the deserted church, marking out the cross on the top of the spire.

Please God, let Tom be all right, Grace prayed. Please bring him home to me. I promise I'll make him happy if you give me the chance. Please, bring him home.

Chapter Twenty-Three

Ernie Cox was standing by his front door smoking his pipe as Grace came home, the sound of a dog barking coming from the kitchen beyond. He saw her and nodded politely.

'How do?'

'I'm fine, Mr Cox, how are you?'

He studied her under the moonlight, her dark hair lightened, her face a pale oval, her eyes deep-set. She was good-looking, and no mistake, but he was glad his son had taken up with some other girl. He'd wasted too much time pining over Grace Ellis.

'Is Tom still coming home at the weekend?' she asked, trying to keep her tone light.

Ernie nodded warily. Now, why did she want to know that? Just an idle question from a neighbour, or more?

'Yes, he's back on Friday night,' he replied, sucking on his pipe. 'How's yer father?'

'Not too good. His condition doesn't change much.'

'Don Clegg's a real help,' Ernie went on. 'Takes a weight off your shoulders.'

She wondered why they had to talk about Don when she wanted to know about Tom. In the moonlight Ernie's round face was bland, his glasses blinking.

'Put that light out!' came a sudden shout from the darkness.

Immediately Ernie pulled the front door closed behind him, wanting to finish his smoke before going in. He expected Grace to move away as she normally did, but for once she hung around awkwardly on the street.

'Did you hear the raid?'

'The dead heard that raid,' Ernie replied. 'Bloody Germans. If you ask me they're all touched in the head.'

Smiling faintly, Grace looked for her key.

'So Tom's home on Friday?'

'That's what I said.'

'You'll be looking forward to seeing him.'

'That we will. Our youngest is still in France. Poor Joe, no leave for him just yet.'

He was talking about Joe now, Grace thought. Why couldn't they stay on the subject of Tom? Then she realized how oddly she was behaving. Why was everything so imperative *now*?

'How long's he's staying home?'

'He's not got his leave yet.'

'No, not Joe,' Grace replied patiently, 'I meant Tom.'

Well, this was a turn-up and no mistake, Ernie thought. Why the interest in Tom all of a sudden? He didn't like it; it had taken him and his missus too long to break the tie with Grace Ellis, and he didn't want to see Tom besotted again. He had to be careful, very careful.

'I'm not sure how long he'll be home,' Ernie replied at last. 'I think it would be a good idea if he didn't see you, though.'

Grace reeled from the remark. '*What?*'

'Miss Ellis, I've nothing personal against you, but Tom's not here so I can say my piece. He damn near broke his heart over you. You don't know how he was, pining like a kid. You made a right fool of him –'

'I never meant to!'

'What you meant doesn't really matter. It's what it did to him that matters.' Ernie took a last long smoke and then banged the remaining tobacco from his pipe onto the street. 'Well, it took time, but he's sorted himself out now and found a new lass. Let him be, there's a good girl.'

'Mr Cox –'

He gave her a warning glance. 'Just let it be, Miss Ellis. I don't want to have to pick up the pieces again. Our Tom fighting in the war; he's got enough to put up with. He can't take any more upset. I don't want him seeing you and getting all stirred up again. He's settled now – I don't want him going off to war again not caring if he lives or dies.'

She was hurt by his words. It would take her a long time to win over Tom now – and even longer to win over his family.

'Mr Cox, I didn't mean to hurt Tom.'

'Be that as it may,' Ernie replied, 'this is the time to think about *him*, not how you feel. If you care about him at all, Miss Ellis, leave him alone. Please, leave him alone.'

That Friday there was another raid, but it was a fire that lit up Waterloo Street. Naturally people presumed that there had been a direct hit and there was panic, people running for the bunkers, but the fire was caused by a ruptured gas main, the flames flickering in the night sky as the fire brigade and gas workers tried hurriedly to put it out.

Oddly enough, as the siren sounded Grace stood still. Then, to avoid going down to the shelter with everyone else, she climbed under Aaron's laboratory table. Above her, the lights flickered on and off, then finally cut out, the laboratory plunged into darkness. Pulling her jacket around her shoulders, Grace waited for the all clear, but it didn't come.

To keep herself calm, Grace closed her eyes and tried to fight her fear. Then she thought about Tom. It was Friday, and he was coming home. She didn't care what Ernie Cox had said, she would see his son and try to build a relationship between them. She wouldn't rush it – after all, he had a girlfriend – but she hoped he would come to love her again and choose her. There would be no scene, no declarations of love. *She* had to bide her time now.

Behind her closed lids Grace conjured up a picture of Tom's face. How could she have lived next door to him and have seen him so seldom? How could she have heard him moving around and not knocked on the wall for him?

Worst of all – how could she have tried to throw him into Joan's arms? He didn't love Joan, he had said as much. He had seemed amazed to hear that she loved him. Unimpressed, almost annoyed. He had wanted Grace, not Joan. But perhaps he had fallen in love with the girl from Upper Mill. No, he had loved Grace once, he must *still* love her somewhere. But how did she know? Grace asked herself. Time had passed; he might have grown to hate her.

But she didn't think so. It might be slow, but gradually he would relax and then trust her again . . . They would make plans for after the war ended. He would know then he had her and she had him. Ernie Cox was wrong – knowing that Grace loved him would give Tom something to fight for.

Suddenly she felt the silence coming down. Terrible, complete silence. Shaking, Grace huddled under the laboratory table. She felt small and afraid. A moment passed. God, what was it? Was there no one else alive out there? The minute stretched into infinity. Then, just

as suddenly, the all clear sounded. Slowly Grace climbed
to her feet and brushed down her clothes. The workshop
was deserted, moonlight coming in cold, the stacks of
boxes looming ominously in the dark.

It was Friday night, Tom would be coming home, and
Grace knew what she must do.

Hurrying through the streets, she was soon climbing
the steep incline in the darkness, up to Diggle. Out of
breath, she reached the village street and almost ran
past the old greengrocer's shop which had once been
her father's. The place was quiet, everyone still in their
homes or shelters, the blackout complete.

She felt suddenly uneasy and quickened her step.
Somewhere a long way off, she heard a man calling
out, but the sound was otherworldly. It seemed to her
then that the streets she knew so well were unfamiliar,
eerie. No lights came from the windows, no chink of
illumination. Above her, the moor rose up stern and
dark, the sky above unremittingly black.

The danger had passed and yet she was still afraid,
aware of how alone she was. Every alleyway seemed to
be sinister, every dark doorway posing a threat. After
hurrying on for another few minutes Grace was just
coming to her own road when she saw a figure before
her, heading the same way, silhouetted against the night
sky. The full moon had waned, but there was still enough
light to make out the familiar shape.

It was Tom Cox. She stopped; bolted to the spot.
Tom was home, alive and well. Nerves paralysed her
suddenly. This wasn't the old Tom, her pseudo brother,
this was the man she had only just realized she loved.
Unable to trust her voice and call out, Grace moved
forward, following him, trying to catch up. She would
arrive at her front door at the same time as he arrived

at his. Their meeting would happen naturally, easily, nothing alarming to scare him off.

Tom was walking quickly, as though he was in a hurry to get home, his tall figure erect. He seemed like a man who was excited, eager to return. *Please God*, she prayed, *let him return to me*. Tom didn't know it yet, but this was the leave he would never forget. He would have what he had wanted so much, for so long.

Then, only a few houses away from his own, Tom paused. He whistled softly and waited. Then whistled again. Surprised, Grace slid against the wall and watched him from the darkness, wondering what he was doing. Again, he whistled, the sound soft and sweet on the night air.

The woman came out running, running down the alleyway and into his arms. Hurriedly Tom caught hold of her and lifted her up, her face illuminated under the moonlight as she laughed. It had taken her years, but Joan had finally got her man.

Loneliness opened like a chasm around Grace and swallowed her whole.

Chapter Twenty-Four

High up on the area called the Heights there were few dwellings, the countryside too exposed, the weather too inclement most of the year. Past the Highborrow Farm there was only the workhouse for the poor, the church – St Anne's – and an isolated manor house called The Lockgate. Why, no one fully understood; there were no locks nor canals for miles.

The story was that the residence had once been the old vicarage but had burned down over a hundred and fifty years earlier, the vicar perishing in the fire. It had been rebuilt, and the Goodman family had lived there for many years, the grandfather of the current heir building up a fortune from millinery in Failsworth. The term 'roughyheads' came from that period. The hats then were made of rough felt and when they got wet they went out of shape, giving a rough head appearance. The slang term had stuck and from then on anyone poor in Oldham was referred to as a roughyhead.

Not that the Goodmans ever mixed with the poor of Oldham. A noted philanthropist, old Gregor Goodman donated money to charity, but seldom left The Lockgate. Of his ten children, five died in infancy, the only son inheriting the millinery business. In due course, David extended the family interests and bought property, renting it out to mill workers in Oldham. Benches appeared in the parks with his name on a brass plate screwed on to them, but old Gregor Goodman was never seen in person, just print.

Like his father before him, David was reclusive and only the arrival of his wife seemed to bring him out of himself. The vivacious, and at times shocking, Lucy Goodman had been the much-loved daughter of rich parents in Cheshire. A lover of parties and attention, only the love she had for David had managed to convince her to live at The Lockgate.

Within months of her arrival the house was being used for meetings and parties. Before there had only been occasional lights in the windows; now the house was lit up frequently, a glowing beacon over the glowering Heights. If she was going to be forced into the wilderness, Lucy said, then she was going to take part of Cheshire with her.

Good-natured and naturally sociable, Lucy soon adjusted to the severity of the weather. With every snowfall staff were sent off to clear the drive, the cold high rooms warmed with fires, eiderdowns thrown over the beds. Her charm, many said, could warm the coldest room and the hardest heart, and by the time Lucy was forty years old she had become the town's effusive and admired matriarch.

Then, at forty-one, the child both she and David had longed for was born – an heir, coming in her later years.

'It's the old cat's kitten,' Lucy would say, looking at her healthy child. 'My miracle.'

Her husband saw it as a miracle too. At last he had the son to which he could hand over the business, someone to preserve the past. The businesses – property, millinery and now mining – were thriving. All David had hoped for was a continuance of his line. And that had finally happened.

A life which should have been perfect lasted for only

a short time. Only three years later, David became ill with cancer. His prognosis – from doctors as far apart as Manchester and London – had been the same: a year to live. Lucy, as ever by her husband's side, had remained cheerful at first.

'What do doctors know?' she asked many times. 'Ghouls, that's what they are. All ghouls.'

But no one was fooled and only the thought of her child kept Lucy going as she watched her husband's deterioration. Within weeks of the onset of David's decline, The Lockgate was deserted. Only the staff came up to the big house, visitors no longer invited and callers turned away. The gregarious Lucy was changing, closing down as The Lockgate did.

At first she made light of David's illness: he would recover. Then she fell into a quiet phase, and then finally she resented her husband. How could he leave her? He was giving in, he was a failure, a coward. With every day that passed, David weakened, and Lucy clung tighter to her son. As David lost weight, she monitored Daniel's growth. As David grew out of breath easily, she watched Daniel running around the quiet house.

As one died, the other learned to live. And in the eleven months that it took for David to lose his fight, Lucy changed from a society belle to a rigid domestic tyrant. Her husband was dying, she thought repeatedly. Why? Why her? Why David, when he was still relatively young?

All Lucy's good fortune seemed to sour within her. She had little contact with her sister and parents and became daily more protective of her son. The past in which she had flourished was as effectively expunged from her mind as chalk wiped off a blackboard.

When David Goodman died, his bedroom warmed by

a fire, the bed hung with velvet drapings, grew cold around him as Lucy sat by her dead husband until well into the night. None of the staff could raise her or reason with her.

'Get the child,' her maid told the nanny finally.

Immediately Daniel was brought to his mother, the nanny placing him on Lucy's lap. She looked at her son for a long moment, glanced back to her dead husband, then lifted Daniel into her arms.

'Do you see your father?'

The little boy nodded, scared of the white figure in the bed.

'I want you to say goodbye.'

'Goodbye.'

'No,' Lucy said patiently, 'you must kiss your father, Daniel. Kiss him goodbye.'

Laying the boy on the bed, Lucy pushed Daniel towards his father. But the boy resisted, afraid. Breathing in, Lucy pushed her son's head against his father's cheek, Daniel crying as his lips brushed against the dead skin.

'Good boy,' Lucy said, taking him up in her arms again and wiping his mouth with her handkerchief. 'That's how the dead taste, Daniel. Remember that taste. Your father has left us alone. We have to cope now, look after each other.' She smiled at her son. 'You love your mother, Daniel, don't you?'

He nodded obediently.

'And you will never leave your mother, will you?'

'No.'

'Say never.'

'I'll never leave you.'

'Good boy,' Lucy said, her smile grim. 'There's a good boy.'

For the next three days David's body lay in state in the

drawing room of The Lockgate. Through the first snows of the winter, a ragged stream of people came to pay their respects to a kind man. His doctor, solicitor and banker came too, the latter assuring Lucy that she had no financial worries. The business was flourishing, David had made sound financial investments and expanded his own interests with considerable skill.

'Dr Mornald,' Lucy said, her tone composed, her figure upright in a black mourning dress, 'I want you to look at Daniel for me.'

'Is he ill?'

'No. I just want you to give him an examination, that's all.'

'But if the child isn't ill –'

'Just do it, Doctor,' she replied, her tone weary as she turned to her solicitor. 'I know what was in my husband's will, Mr Melrose, and I want to make one of my own now.'

'But, Mrs Goodman, this is hardly the time,' he replied, his Edinburgh accent obvious.

'This is exactly the time, Mr Melrose. I want to secure my son's future now. My husband let me down, I have no wish to do the same to Daniel.'

'Your husband died,' Melrose said coldly. He had cared for David and was surprised by the change in his wife. Shock could make people behave oddly, he knew that. But this was simple injustice to the memory of a good man. 'David provided for you very well. He didn't want to leave you.'

Lucy waved him aside. 'What's done is done. We have the future to think about, and Daniel is my future.'

At that moment Stephen Melrose saw that future and flinched. So Lucy Goodman had already chosen her role – that of the martyred widow. Despite the previous years of happiness she was going to see David as the man who had failed her. All that would matter to her from now on was her son. Her heir. Her boy of four years old.

Aware of the anger his suggestion might provoke, Stephen Melrose looked at his client cautiously.

'Isn't it about time that Daniel went to school? It would do him good to mix with other children. It's too quiet for him up here on his own.'

Lucy's blue eyes had chilled to the colour of a winter lake.

'Mr Melrose, when I want your opinion I will ask for it.'

'I have sons of my own,' Melrose persisted, 'and I know only too well that boys need the company of other boys. We should look at Daniel's education.'

'Which will be at home!' Lucy snapped. 'He will have the best, Mr Melrose, you may rest assured of that. I have already hired a tutor who is highly recommended.'

Holding on to his own temper, Melrose rubbed his bearded chin.

'Mrs Goodman, education is one thing, enjoyment is another. A child has to have equal amounts of both to thrive. The Lockgate is remote, Daniel will see very few people, and fewer children, if you keep him up here with you.'

'I will do as I please!'

'And I will say what I think.'

'Not if you wish to remain my legal advisor, Mr Melrose,' Lucy replied coldly. 'I pay you to act on my wishes, not to advise me on child care.'

You stupid woman, Melrose wanted to shout at her, you can't live your life through your son. You'll lock him away up here and spoil him, and then what? In ten years he'll be unable to mix normally with anyone.

He'll be tied to you for life – a mother's boy, the butt of jokes. Or worse, a bully used to his own way.

The youngest of Melrose's sons was Daniel's age. Before David's death they had talked about getting the boys together, David keen for his son to mix. But now David was dead, and Lucy Goodman was going to sacrifice her son for her own ends.

Over my dead body, Melrose thought. I'll bite my tongue now, lady, but I'll do it for your son, not for you. You're not going to find any excuse to fire me because your son's is going to need me. Unless I'm much mistaken, I could well turn out to be the only ally he's got.

'Whatever you say, Mrs Goodman,' Melrose replied.

Stephen Melrose was as good as his word. He never gave Lucy any reason to argue with him or to criticize his work. Whilst Melrose watched his own sons grow up, he took it upon himself to find a way of breaking Lucy's stranglehold over Daniel. In the school holidays he would bring his youngest son, Sandy, up to The Lockgate whenever he called. Lucy was at first irritated, but later accepted the infrequent visits as Daniel enjoyed them so much.

Although a selfish tyrant, Lucy adored her son and Daniel was denied nothing. Apart from a normal life. When he was seven, a pony was bought for him, someone from nearby Delph being brought in to teach him how to ride. But within a matter of months the man was fired, Lucy resenting the bond which had grown up between the man and her son.

Later Daniel was offered piano lessons, the teacher old and short-sighted. He lasted three weeks; Daniel didn't care too much for music. Art lessons followed, which were also given up, and then Stephen Melrose started to bring Daniel football cards. Football was something Daniel knew little about, although the gardener and his son, Archie, had told him all about the local team, Oldham Athletic. They described the game to him, demonstrating behind the greenhouses how it was played – out of sight of the main house and their mistress. Before long, Daniel was captivated. He liked the excitement and the physical endurance it demanded.

As a boy who was tall and well-built he needed to exercise or he would run to fat, Melrose knew that. He was attractive too – sandy-haired, with large dark eyes under well-defined brows. Not like Lucy or his father. A one-off. A boy who could do well and one who had to be guided. One day Daniel would inherit all the Goodman fortune. He had to be able to communicate with people. He needed to know and get on with the world.

The solitary child up at The Lockgate was the subject of much interest. As solicitors in the same area, Stephen Melrose and Frederick Conrad knew each other well and Melrose tried to persuade Conrad to talk to Lucy Goodman. After all, Frederick had been an old friend of Lucy's and his charm was devastating. But Lucy wanted no advice from anyone, and Frederick found himself reporting a rare failure to Stephen when they next met.

By the time Daniel was eight the stubborn Melrose had decided that the boy needed company. He could bring Sandy occasionally, but that wasn't enough; what was needed was someone close by, whom Daniel could see on a daily basis. Which was where Archie came in.

For over twenty years his father had been head gardener up at The Lockgate, as had his father before him. There was very little Mr Doyle didn't know about trees and shrubs, planting the few types which could survive and flourish in the keen winds from The Heights. Snow damage killed most plants, but he knew which were hardy. The vast greenhouses behind the house were heated, and sporting heavy crops of peaches and several vines. Grapes only a mile from Oldham! Mr Doyle would say, there's not many who could have pulled that off.

By this time, Archie – his only child, and two years older than Daniel – was a bright boy of twelve. Yes, he would do nicely, Melrose thought, studying him over the wall when he arrived for his next visit. Archie was quick-witted and, if the locals were correct, of strong character. In fact, he was just what Daniel needed. It should work well – providing Lucy Goodman never found out.

Melrose knew that it was wrong of him to pit his client's employees against their employer, but he didn't care much about that. He cared more about Daniel's progress and he knew that Lucy's employees were canny enough to manage the situation. Besides, their good will towards Lucy had run out long ago, and no one agreed with the way she was rearing her son.

From then onwards, Daniel spent as much time as he could manage with Archie. On the pretext of Daniel's supposed growing interest in gardening – a hobby Lucy despised – he was allowed to spend time away from her. She never realized that her son was playing with a gardener's boy.

It was the making of Daniel, Melrose thought with satisfaction. After only a few months had passed, the slightly bloated look that had dogged the boy was gone. Football and fishing had pared him down, made muscles in his arms, and the sun had browned his face and lightened his hair to an ashy gold.

He had learned guile too, Melrose realized. Enjoying his life for the first time, Daniel had understood from the beginning that if his mother got wind of his activities he would be stopped and Archie sent away. The thought of being entombed in the suffocating house and parted from his only friend made Daniel cautious. His life was lived in two parts: one at The Lockgate, sitting reading with his mother; the other out over the fields with Archie.

He had even ventured down to the village and mixed with some of the other local lads. They had heard weird stories over the years about how Daniel Goodman was deformed and locked away, and were surprised to see a strapping boy. The villagers took to Daniel as well, getting to know him in the shops and on the lanes running down to Oldham.

'That's where yer old man built 'is mill,' Archie said one day, sitting on the stone wall which bordered the high fields of Diggle. 'And that,' he pointed at the horizon, 'over to Failsworth – yer 'atter's place is there.'

Daniel looked to the horizon. He knew nothing of the world in the valley and could only piece together knowledge of his family from what others told him. His father had been a good, but quiet man, Melrose said, and Archie talked about Daniel's mother when she had first come to The Lockgate.

'She were always throwin' parties, m' father said. Always laughin'.'

'*My mother?*' Daniel asked incredulously.

Archie nodded, his floppy dark hair falling over his forehead. He didn't mind hanging about with Daniel because he was grown up for his age, not some snot-nosed kid.

'She's an old bugger now.'

'Hey!' Daniel snapped. 'Watch your mouth! That's my mother you're talking about.'

'Rather yours than mine,' Archie replied, cuffing Daniel lightly on the chin.

Four years passed, Melrose coaching Daniel in the ways of business at whatever opportunity he could, and Archie providing the companionship. The strong boy of ten grew into an athletic lad of fourteen. Archie remained at The Lockgate to tend the gardens with his father.

Incredibly, Lucy had never doubted her son's word about how he spent his time gardening. Besides, she would never have believed that the heir to the Goodman fortune would consort willingly with a *roughyhead*. Then, one day in August, Lucy unexpectedly visited the greenhouses which her late husband had loved. She had thought that it was time to show an interest in them, although she loathed gardening. Besides, she wanted to see what her son had achieved.

She did see him – playing football with Archie, Daniel's sleeves rolled up, his laugh loud and unaffected. In her dark dress Lucy stood watching her son, the sense of betrayal welling up in her like bile.

'Daniel!' she shouted.

He stopped and turned. His face gave him away at once, guilt making him into a child again.

'What are you doing? Come into the house at once.'

He hesitated, a cloud passing over the sun, the day unexpectedly chilled, then slowly he followed his mother in.

The reward for Daniel's betrayal was exile. Within days Lucy had secured a place for him at a strict boarding school in Sussex. Stephen Melrose, alerted by an anxious Daniel, came to reason with her but she was immovable.

'My son defied me. He lied to me,' she said coldly. 'Mixing with the likes of that boy – what was he thinking of?'

'Living a normal life,' Melrose answered her.

'This is your fault!' Lucy replied. 'You filled his head with ideas. You always wanted my son to turn against me.'

Years of suppressed irritation made Melrose over-react.

'Your son never turned against you. He's always done what you asked, but he had to have a life of his own, surely even you can see that? You couldn't expect to lock a child away for ever. Daniel isn't your plaything.'

Her voice was flinty. 'How dare you speak to me like that? I gave him everything he wanted –'

'He wanted a friend!' Melrose snapped. 'If David had been alive today he would have understood. Your son is a person in his own right, not just your companion.'

Slowly Lucy rose to her feet. 'I've long wondered about you, Melrose. I've always suspected that you wanted to undermine me. If I'm not mistaken, *you* have played a hand in all of this.'

He didn't deny it. Instead, angry and square-shouldered, he faced her and said simply: 'I did what I thought was right.'

'And now I am doing what I think is right. Daniel needs controlling, he needs a good education –'

'He doesn't need to be sent away to school as though he were being punished.' Melrose said heatedly. 'How could you do that to him? How could you make him feel guilty and ashamed for acting like a normal boy?'

'My son,' Lucy said fiercely, 'is *not* a normal boy. He is the heir to a fortune, the only one to carry on the Goodman name. He has to remain apart from the common herd, to know that his place is not amongst the crowd. Discipline is not a vice, Mr Melrose, it is an asset.'

'Cruelty is a vice, and God forgive you for it,' he replied savagely, walking to the door. 'And before you say it, Mrs Goodman, I hereby resign. I want nothing more to do with you. The only reason I stayed in your employ for so long was for your son's sake. But I warn you now, be careful how you act. Don't make an enemy of the only person on earth who cares about you.'

So, feeling like a criminal, Daniel was sent away to school and only returned to The Lockgate for the holidays – stilted, long weeks in the old house with nothing to relieve the tedium. His mother chose never to relent: her son had let her down, as had his father before him. There was no closeness between them left, only the tie of blood and money.

It seemed to Melrose that Daniel Goodman became a man overnight that summer day so long ago. From then on, all the joy and light-heartedness Daniel had enjoyed was dimmed, his character quietened. He wasn't cowed, but wary. His mother's severity, followed by the humbling and distressing exile to school, had made him suppress his emotions. He believed – from that time onwards – that happiness would always be punished.

But somewhere underneath the new version, lay the old Daniel. Melrose glimpsed this a few times when he arrived, unannounced, at Daniel's school. He'd take Sandy with him and watch the difference between the two boys; his own so open, Daniel at first so closed down, though gradually becoming less reserved as the visitors prepared to leave.

Unfortunately, Lucy Goodman's spite did not stop at

Daniel. She also fired Archie and his father, and people talked of her as though she was some bitter old harpy up on the hill. She neither heard the comments, nor cared what people said. The vivacious young party girl and the happy mother had long gone; time and self-absorption had killed any hope of compassion, or any desire for happiness – hers or others.

So when Daniel visited home she extended a cool cheek to her son and he had a vague memory of kissing other dead skin, his father's. For much of the time The Lockgate was closed down except for her suite of rooms, and had all the cheer of a chapel of rest.

After university, Daniel went into the family business at the age of twenty-one. He had grown to six feet in height and was broad-chested. His looks were strong, his manner reserved.

It was therefore inevitable that when war broke out Daniel would volunteer. To his delight he was accepted for the Royal Air Force. His mother had no say in the matter: if he wanted to fight, he would.

Melrose, now over seventy – his beard grizzled, his voice grown even more curt – tackled him about signing up.

'You should have waited until you were conscripted, Daniel. It would have come soon enough.'

'I wanted to be one of the first,' he replied, smiling that far-off smile of his father's. 'It's for the best. Oh come on, Melrose, you know how things are. I couldn't have settled up at The Lockgate. It would never have worked out.'

It was easy to see why. Daniel had been away for years, his sudden return to the family house to run the business had come as a shock to both his mother and himself. Lucy, used to being alone, had resented his presence,

236

whilst craving it at the same time. And as for Daniel, every room, every corridor, every glance into the garden reminded him of a bitter past.

'I'll be honest with you, Daniel –'

'You always are,' he replied, smiling.

Melrose nodded. 'Whatever I might think about her, your mother does love you, you know.'

Daniel studied the elderly man. 'You're generous. She never has a good word to say for you.'

Melrose returned the smile, but his heart felt like lead in his chest.

'When do you leave?'

'Tomorrow.'

'Which station?'

'I'm being driven into Manchester and then I pick up the nine o'clock train at Victoria.'

Melrose nodded again. 'Be careful, I care about you as though you were one of my own.'

'I know,' Daniel replied, suddenly moved and uncertain how to respond. Then something of his old self returned for an instant and he reached out, taking Melrose's hand. 'You've been good to me. Stood up for me, even when it cost you dearly. No one had a better friend, a more loyal supporter. Thank you.'

'You turned out well, Daniel. Despite your mother.' Melrose paused. 'A word of advice. Yes, another one! Your mother's a sad woman; don't judge all women by her standards. Don't block off love, Daniel, or she's won. Listen to me, and remember.'

There was a long moment of silence between them, Melrose smiling to himself.

'Do you know what that is?' he asked eventually.

'What?'

'That silence between us. That comfortable silence

between friends. The French have a phrase for it – *an angel passing over.*'

Daniel mulled the words over in his head. 'I like that. It sounds sweet, but sad.'

'Like life,' Melrose said quietly, 'just like life.'

Chapter Twenty-Five

Geoffrey was very silent leaving his home, his Air Force cap in his hand, his kitbag over his shoulder. He had already said goodbye to his parents and siblings, Joan hanging on to him fiercely until he pulled himself away. He could have gone to bed, but he knew he wouldn't sleep, so instead he waited up. But the night wouldn't pass. Finally, at around one thirty, he walked over to Grace's house and knocked on the door.

She came down hurriedly, asking who it was through the door and then, surprised, she let him in. He was grey-faced, dull terror in his eyes. At that moment he looked even younger than his nineteen years.

'Geoffrey, come in.' she said, pulling a dressing gown around her. 'Are you all right?'

'I couldn't sleep,' he said simply. 'I was thinking, over and over again. 'Bout the past mainly. You know, when I was a kid. Me and Joan.' His head hung. 'I don't think I'm very brave, Grace. I don't want to go off to fight.'

She led him into the kitchen, and banked up the fire, and put the kettle on the range to boil. Then she sat down next to him.

'No one wants to leave home.'

'But I should want to go,' he replied. 'My mates are all laughing and talking about giving the Krauts a good kicking.'

She had heard them running down the streets after they had been conscripted, swinging round the lampposts and bragging about how the war would be over in no time now they were pitching in. Some had got drunk and one had slumped, passed out, against the wall of the alley, vomit down his shirt front.

In the morning he would wake and remember and feel the way Geoffrey was feeling now ... Gently, Grace touched his shoulder and passed him some hot tea. The kitchen was slow to warm up.

'Will you write?' he asked. 'I'd like to get a letter.'

'Of course I will.'

He nodded, sipped at the tea, his big hands round the cup. She could remember him coming to work for her at St Andrew's Place, proudly driving the old van all painted up. He had travelled all over the North making deliveries, and then come back and helped to pack the cosmetics, Joan teasing him about all the shop girls he visited. Blushing, Geoffrey had insisted he wasn't seeing anyone and his sister had pulled a face, knowing that he was too good-natured to get angry with her.

But the image faded as quickly as it had come. There was no more Joan, and St Andrew's Place was devoid of men, apart from Solar and Aaron. All the fun had stopped, the high-ceilinged workroom lonely, the echoes of the women's laughter and gossip hanging about the rafters like the talk of uneasy ghosts.

Always devoted to Grace, Geoffrey had stayed with her after his sister left, and it was through him that Grace had learned of Joan's engagement to Tom Cox. Soon after, he'd told her that they'd got a special licence and had married. Grace hadn't received an invitation. She no longer feared bumping into Tom on one of his leaves home because he and Joan had moved down into the valley, into Oldham. Not long after, Joe Cox had been called up and then there were no more sounds of the brothers scrapping, their voices coming through the adjoining wall. Only Ernie and Sylvie Cox remained at home, quiet as moles.

The loss of Joan had been compounded by the loss of Tom. Grace had never thought that the feud would last so long. Often she had thought about calling to see her old friend, but something always stopped her. Joan had her man; why would she be pleased to see Grace now?

It was only after she had lost them that Grace fully realized how much she missed her old comrades. Years of seeing them day in and day out had made her take them for granted. There had always been Joan to talk to, or Tom, hanging round devotedly. Always the security of knowing that he was on the other side of the adjoining wall, even if she'd never knocked.

Now only Geoffrey remained close to her. She knew only too well why he had chosen to spend his last hours in Lancashire with her. Having no girlfriend, Geoffrey had turned to her for comfort. There was no useless hope on his part; Geoffrey knew that Grace would never think of him as a suitor, but he knew that she cared for him. Everyone else in his family had partners, his three sisters all married now. Only he and Grace remained alone. It was the tie which bound them.

'Grace, will you cope on your own?'

She smiled, mocking him gently. 'Oh, don't worry about me. Just look after yourself.'

His voice fell, hardly audible. 'I don't want to go.'

Silently Grace slipped off her chair and put her arms round him, Geoffrey's head leaning against her stomach, his sobs deep in his throat. Then gently she took his hand and led him upstairs, guiding him over to her bed. He lay down, his eyes closed, his hand clasping hers.

Before long, she could hear his breathing change as

he fell asleep. He was fully dressed, his chest rising and falling as he dreamed. Her action – so out of character and unexpected – had been one of comfort, not desire.

Turning her head, Grace saw the dawn beginning and felt Geoffrey roll over and rest his head against her shoulder. The minutes ticked over, the clock by her bed making the hours pass quickly, marching towards his leaving. Suddenly he moved as though alarmed, then fell uneasily back to sleep.

There had been many casualties of the war already, only recently a young man of twenty-one brought home and buried up at Leesfield. The fighting was not going to end quickly. Carefully Grace turned her head, the beginnings of daylight illuminating Geoffrey's smooth cheeks and stubble. He was too young. But then, who was old enough?

Time ground on. She couldn't sleep and knew that it would be down to her to waken Geoffrey. Down to her to send him off to God knew what. Suddenly she leaned towards him and rested her lips against his forehead as though kissing a child.

'What?' he said, dazed and waking. She could see him try to understand what he was doing there and then she could see him remember.

'It's time to go, Geoffrey.'

He nodded, unable to trust his voice.

'Come on,' she said. 'I'll make you something to eat.'

He came downstairs to find a sandwich waiting for him and Grace fully dressed, her coat on.

'What are you doing?'

'Going with you to the station,' she said calmly.

'But . . .' he trailed off. He wanted to remonstrate with her, but couldn't.

Arm in arm they caught the bus from Diggle, down to Oldham, and there caught a tram over to Mumps. Without asking her, Geoffrey let Grace come on the train with him to Manchester, the day cold, the train growing busier and busier with enlisted men. Finally they arrived at Victoria Station, steam blowing from the trains, the sounds of voices echoing in the steel girders of the station roof.

'You'll write, won't you?'

She smiled. 'I promise.'

Suddenly there were many men arriving, some in Army uniform, some in Air Force gear. Like Geoffrey. He had bragged about becoming a pilot, but Grace knew full well that that ambition would remain firmly grounded. Around them, many of the men were silent, others boastful to hide their unease, a few grey-gilled and hung over. Gripping her hand, Geoffrey lead Grace towards Platform 10 and passed though the barrier with her.

She clung to his hand as tightly as he clung to hers, bodies pushing past them as they hurried down the platform, soldiers hanging out of the train windows to kiss their mothers and wives. Finally Geoffrey stopped outside coach 4, opening the door and throwing his kitbag in. Then he turned and faced her.

'Give her a kiss!' someone shouted as they passed.

He blushed, Grace smiling and stretching up to kiss his cheek.

'Take care of yourself,' she said softly, the whistle blowing and Geoffrey hurrying to jump on to the train.

His eyes, childlike with terror, never left her face as he opened the window and leaned out.

'Grace . . .'

She nodded, took his hand and squeezed it hard.

243

'I know, I know,' she said, walking down the platform as the train started to move.

Soon she was hurrying and then running as the train picked up speed, her hand still clinging to his as she came to the end of the platform. In that final instant she felt his fingers pulled from hers and then stood, watching in the cold morning light, as the train left the station and took Geoffrey away.

Tears stinging behind his eyes, Geoffrey coughed to compose himself and then dropped into a seat. Beside him there was a burly figure fast asleep, others playing cards, and one quiet fair man staring out of the window. As he took his seat, Geoffrey saw him look up and nodded, noticing the Royal Air Force uniform.

'Is that your wife?' the man asked, his voice well modulated.

Geoffrey shook his head. 'No, just a friend.'

'She must be a good friend if she came to see you off at this hour.'

'She is,' Geoffrey replied, wiping his hand on his trouser leg and then offering it to the stranger. 'I'm Geoffrey Cleaver. Pleased to meet you.'

Without hesitation, the man took his hand.

'I'm Daniel Goodman.'

'Did anyone see you off?'

'No,' Daniel said, 'no one.'

Nodding, Geoffrey sat back in his seat. Occasionally as they travelled he stole a quick glance at his companion and felt – for once – the bigger man. Daniel Goodman was obviously educated and well spoken, but he – Geoffrey – had had someone see him off. A beautiful woman had cared enough to stay with him through the night and wave him goodbye.

Thinking of Grace, he experienced a sense of unexpected warmth. Hanging on to her image as a child might cling to its mother, he let her memory soothe him as the train moved relentlessly on.

Chapter Twenty-Six

At St Andrew's Place Tilly was moving cautiously around one of the benches, her huge belly making her clumsy. Watching her, Mary laughed outright.

'You'll never go full term, Tilly. You must have got your dates wrong.'

Tilly was perspiring, wiping her forehead with the back of her hand. She was due to give birth that month, but had kept working to keep the money coming in. There was no choice; her husband was away fighting and the rent had to be paid.

'I thought about Leslie for a name,' she said suddenly.

'That's a girl's name.'

'No,' Tilly said, sitting down heavily, 'it can be a boy or a girl's name. Think of Leslie Howard.'

'Sounds soft to me,' Mary replied, packing away some lipsticks in a box and pushing it to the end of the bench. Solar would collect it later with all the others. 'What about George?'

Tilly pulled her face. 'Nah, sounds like an old man's name.'

'Gilbert then.'

Tilly eyebrows rose. '*Gilbert!* That's old-fashioned. We wanted to pick something special. Different, you know. A name no other kid has.'

Mary paused, counted her lipsticks, and then looked up.

'Give a kid an unusual name and the poor little sod will be teased mercilessly at school. My mother's cousin called her youngest Wesley. Well, he never had a moment's peace. My mother said that was what caused his stammer.'

Tilly chewed over the information, her face flushed with heat.

'What about William Conrad Sugden?'

'*William Conrad?*' Mary repeated. 'W.C. Sugden. That would be great – all the kids would call him Wee Wee.'

Tilly winced, her hand going over her stomach.

'Pains?' Mary asked anxiously.

'Nah, I think it was those radishes I had earlier.'

'My sister ate coal when she was having her last child,' Mary replied, adding one more lipstick to the box she was filling and closing the lid. 'Her husband used to joke that the baby'd come out with a Davy lamp strapped to his head.' She laughed. 'Funny thing was, he went down the pit.'

Tilly had grown quiet, her eyes misty as Mary glanced over to her.

'Hey now, what's the matter, luv?'

'I was thinking about Johnny,' she said quietly. 'He said he'd try and get back next month. Said he'd swim home if he had to.' She fingered the letter in her pocket. 'He's so looking forward to the baby being born.'

Mary could sense that there were tears coming and changed the subject. It was no good letting Tilly wallow; she had to get on with it. There was a war on.

'What about Henry for a name?'

Tilly looked up, suddenly animated as she repeated the name. 'Henry, not bad. Sounds posh, though.'

'Wilfred?'

'Old-fashioned.'

'Clement?'

'Oh, Mary!' Tilly said, exasperated, but laughing.

'I had an uncle called Clement and he ran a pub in Macclesfield. Made a fortune, he did.'

'What happened to him?'

'Died of drink.'

'You're putting me on! Was he a boozer?'

'Nah,' Mary replied mischievously, 'the drover's cart ran him over!' She winked at Tilly and pushed an empty box over for her to fill. 'Come on, luv, time lost, money lost.'

Geoffrey sent Grace letters as often as he could, and she wrote frequently to him. It seemed to her that he had become the brother she had never had, and she worried for him. Knowing that Geoffrey was easily led, she also prayed that he would not fall in with the wrong crowd and was pleased to hear of someone called Daniel Goodman who had taken Geoffrey under his wing.

It turned out that Geoffrey was stationed with Daniel. As she had suspected, Geoffrey wasn't made into a pilot and worked on the ground in the administration offices. Before long, it was obvious that Geoffrey hero-worshipped his new acquaintance, his letter filled with details about his glamorous friend.

> Daniel is a fighter pilot on the Spitfires, You should see him, Grace, he's not afraid of anything. He comes from around our parts too, although he doesn't say too much about it. I think he's fallen out with his family, at least he doesn't talk about them and he gets no letters. Shame that. I get letters from home all the time.
>
> I was wondering if you could write to him? I mean, I know he's a pilot and all of that, but he's

not a bit standoffish. A letter might cheer him up at bit. Your letters always make me laugh and I've told him all about you. He saw you at the station when you saw me off – so it's not like he would be hearing from a stranger, is it?

Dad wrote me that Kate's husband was wounded and sent back home. I wish the same would happen to me, but I'm not in much danger. The pilots go out every day. Sometimes they only get a couple of hours off before being called back into action. We lost two pilots last week, but everyone knows we'll win the war. Morale is high. Joan wrote to say that she's having a baby and that Tom's OK, in France somewhere. I thought you would like to know their news.

Joan having a baby . . . Grace glanced up from the letter, trying to imagine Joan pregnant. With Tom's child. It was all so unreal.

Write again soon – and if you wouldn't mind, drop a line to Daniel. I'll pass it on to him. You needn't be afraid of what to put, he's a nice bloke, with no side.

 All the best,
  Geoffrey

Now what, Grace thought, was she supposed to write to a stranger? Thoughtful, she tucked Geoffrey's letter into her pocket and then laid a tray for her father. She would feed Arthur and then jot a note to Geoffrey – and to this Daniel Goodman. Carefully she made the porridge for her father, just as her mother had done so many years before, and then poured it into a bowl and laid it on the old tin tray.

Soon she would hear the key turn in the lock and Don would arrive, bringing the morning paper with him. It no longer seemed strange to Grace that Don spent so much time with her father. He was lonely, and since the war began he loathed being alone. Not that he expected anything for nothing. His coupons were placed on the table in the kitchen for Grace to use when she bought the food, and any little scraps of meat he got from the butcher were willingly donated.

Grace realized now that Don Clegg needed his visits as much as she needed him to look after her father. Sometimes, if it was late, Don would stay rather than go home to an empty house, the kitchen couch providing a makeshift bed. And through it all, Arthur clung on to life like a barnacle to a rock.

Why, Grace couldn't imagine. He had nothing to live for. Or maybe he did. Maybe in his silence he had flashes of remembrance. Perhaps he visited his old life running the greengrocer's shop and met up with Dora again. Whatever he thought or dreamed about – if dream he did – the old photograph of Dora remained by his bedside, her nightdress under the pillow next to his.

Had she lived, Grace realized suddenly, her mother would have been nearing fifty. She couldn't image Dora with grey hair, her rapid staccato movements slowed down, her voice losing any of its authority. Still deep in thought, Grace walked up the stairs and into her father's bedroom. Arthur lay with his head turned slightly to the window, his glasses on the table next to him. He hadn't used them for years, Grace thought, laying down the tray and picking the spectacles up, her throat tightening. The lenses were smeared with dust so she breathed on them and polished them on her apron.

The action seemed to sum up all that was pointless and sad. The war was on and her father was unable to protect her. There was no one left to protect her, in fact. With a shaking hand, Grace laid down the cleaned glasses and then sat beside her father on the bed.

Gently she took his hand and rested it against her cheek. Arthur did not stir, his eyes closed, the Sunday street quiet outside. He had lost the woman he loved, as she had lost Tom. He was segregated by illness, as she felt cut off from others. In their tiny enclosed world they had only each other and she understood finally what love really meant.

He couldn't protect her, or support her. She was looking after him, as he would willingly have done for her had the situations been reversed. All the resentment lifted in an instant, Grace feeling her father's cool hand against her cheek and a bond which had never been there before.

Dear Daniel,

I was asked by my good friend Geoffrey to drop you a line when I wrote to him. I'm not sure what he wanted me to write but here goes! First, thank you for keeping an eye out for Geoffrey. He's a good man and I know he thinks the world of you.

I don't know what you look like, sound like, or what you are interested in – which should make for an interesting correspondence! Geoffrey did say that you were from around Diggle – but where? What is your occupation? Your hobbies?

I don't know the answers, so I will have to begin by volunteering information about myself. I have

a business in cosmetics – the Auden Line. Before
the war we were doing well, but even now women
want to look good. Which must sound strange to a
man – trivial even. Now things are hard, as I have
to run the business virtually single-handed.

My chemist, Aaron Bloom, left Europe to escape
the Nazi threat. His brother was not so lucky. We
hear so many terrible stories but we are not in the
thick of it, as you are. I admire your courage.

If you would like me to write again, I would be
glad to.

Kindest regards,
Grace Ellis

She read the letter several times and it seemed strained to
her, even superficial. What was she supposed to write to
a stranger? He would think she was a fool, no doubt . . .

But he didn't, and within a week of receiving her first
letter, Daniel wrote back.

Dear Grace,

It was a real pleasure to receive your letter. How
kind of you to think of me. You were right, I do
come from your part of the world – Lydgate, to be
precise.

Lydgate, Grace wondered, where in Lydgate?

Geoffrey talks about you nonstop. I think he has
a bad case of puppy love, which is hardly surprising. I remember seeing you the morning we
left Manchester, running down the platform, your
hair loose around your shoulders.

You run a business! Remarkable, not trivial at
all. Beauty is always important and lifts the heart.

Please write again.
Daniel

Gradually Grace found herself looking forward to his letters, reading them repeatedly and carrying them with her in her bag. Newspapers were avidly scanned and the radio listened to whenever possible so that she could monitor the war – and Daniel's part in it. Geoffrey – delighted by Grace's kindness – wrote that Daniel would like a photograph of her, but was reluctant to ask.

The following day, excited and nervous, Grace tried on several outfits before finally putting on a blue dress and walking into town to Mr Chadderton's. A few days later she had her photograph ready to send. Did she really look like that, she wondered. Would Daniel be disappointed? Her clothes seemed scruffy, old-fashioned: but then it *was* wartime, so surely he would make allowances?

When the picture arrived Daniel opened the envelope and looked into the dark grey eyes of the woman he remembered so vividly. She was smiling, but there was a sadness about her which turned his heart. It was, he thought, oddly like looking into a mirror.

His reply was shorter than usual, but enclosed within it was a photograph of himself. Grace stared at the image and felt the hairs rise on the back of her neck. *She knew this man.* Not literally, but she recognized him. There was about Daniel Goodman something she had never found elsewhere. His eyes were intelligent, his mouth full but not sensual.

Staring at the photograph Grace was suddenly frightened. She had loved Tom, but this jolt of attraction was way beyond anything she had felt for her next-door neighbour. She knew instinctively that it was more than just attraction. *Daniel Goodman was familiar to her.* From where, she didn't know. But that they had met before – in this world, or another – she didn't doubt. Dear God, she thought with nervous hope, this was man she had been looking for.

Melrose was the first to see the difference in Daniel when he came home for his next leave. He was reserved, but the lingering melancholia seemed to have lifted. And Melrose knew why. A month before, Daniel had written to him about a woman called Grace Ellis. She had her own cosmetic business in St Andrew's Place, Oldham. Did he know her?

No, Melrose had written back, he didn't, but he would find out about her. He was as good as his word, and the source of his information came from none other than his old friend Frederick Conrad. He made it quite clear from the start that he couldn't divulge any professional details about Grace Ellis, but he was quite willing to talk about her generally.

What Melrose discovered intrigued, but, at the same time, worried him. Frederick had told him that she was an admirable woman, but that her background was far removed from Daniel's . . .

'She's the daughter of a shopkeeper and a woman who disgraced her family,' Frederick divulged.

He had invited Melrose over for drinks in his house at Upper Mill, and every couple of minutes Melrose could hear Frederick's wife's voice coming from another room. She was talking, but to whom? The other person never answered.

'Oh, yes,' Frederick went on, immune to the singular conversation 'Dora Ellis was born in Miller Lane.'

'*You're a wonder, and no mistake* . . .' came the voice beyond.

'Miller Lane?' Melrose repeated, sipping the sherry Frederick had given him. It was as sweet as molasses. 'That's a bad area of town.'

'*I couldn't live without my boy*,' came the voice again.

What boy? Melrose wondered, knowing that the Conrads had no children. Besides, he was amazed by the lulling tones of the terrifying Mrs Conrad, a woman who had the looks and charm of an alligator.

'What did Dora Ellis do that was so bad?'

Frederick smoothed his glossy grey hair, his wife crooning outside the door, '*And I'm going to give you something lovely for your dinner, darling.*'

Frederick didn't seem to notice and replied evenly: 'She ran off with some rat-catcher and had his kid. Dora was killed not that long after. Grace Ellis has benefactors to support her business – which is common knowledge.' He paused, sipped at his sherry and smiled guilelessly. 'But I know you won't ask me any details.'

Melrose nodded. 'Of course not, Frederick, but you see I have to find out about Grace Ellis because of Daniel. He seems rather keen on her –'

The voice came from outside the room yet again. '*Daddy will come and say hello to you soon.*'

Melrose's patience snapped. 'What the hell is that?' he asked, turning round in his chair.

'What?' Frederick replied, looking a little taken aback.

'Your wife. Who *is* she talking to?'

'Little Nelson.'

'*Little Nelson?*' Melrose was baffled.

'Her parrot.'

Melrose blinked. 'But you hate birds, Frederick.'

He smiled benignly. 'I know. She loves the little bastard, though. But I look at him and think fondly of the day he'll be stuffed and mounted in my office with all the others.'

Melrose decided to change the subject fast. Besides, he had to think very carefully. What was he going to reply to Daniel's enquiries? It was true that Grace Ellis was a good-looking, hard-working and ambitious woman, but she was no match for the Goodman empire. No suitable consort for the heir to The Lockgate.

He would have to be very careful how he handled the matter, Melrose thought. If he came down too heavily on Grace, Daniel would be all the more intrigued by her. And if his mother found out about her son's interest there would be hell to pay. He could imagine Lucy Goodman's reaction – a common working woman setting her sights on her son? She would without doubt set about destroying the relationship and offer to buy Grace off. When Daniel was ready to marry, *she* would choose the bride.

Rubbing his bearded chin, Melrose leaned back in his chair and then flinched as a manic screeching started outside.

'*Oh, you* wicked *boy to bite your mummy!*'

Frederick's expression was one of pure ecstasy as Melrose fought to regain his train of thought.

'Perhaps it's just a war romance?'

'Between my wife and Little Nelson?' Frederick asked wickedly.

'You know what I mean,' Melrose replied, his tone patient. 'This thing between Grace and Daniel – maybe it's just an infatuation which will blow over. Emotions run high amongst the young when the threat of death is ever present.'

Frederick sipped his drink. He was trying not to laugh at the sounds coming from beyond the room. 'Would it be so terrible if Daniel *did* fall in love with Grace Ellis? She has a good reputation and could certainly look out for herself.'

'But she's of a different class,' Melrose replied.

If he let it pass, he would be condoning it and what difficulties would follow later if he did that? Surely it was kinder in the long run to stop the situation developing now?

'I care about Daniel,' Melrose continued gruffly, his Edinburgh accent strong. 'Surely my reservations are reasonable? If David had been my own son I would feel the same.'

'Would you?' Frederick asked.

Melrose's temper flared. 'Of course I would! If Sandy had come to me and said he was interested in Grace Ellis I would have objected.'

'And your Sandy isn't the heir to the Goodman empire,' Frederick finished for him, filling up Melrose's glass and listening for sounds outside the door. 'Whoever Daniel chooses as his wife has to be his equal – *and* strong enough to stand up to his appalling mother. She should have breeding, background and money, because those are the weapons she'll need to defend herself. It wouldn't be fair on the girl otherwise.'

Melrose nodded. He had seen what wealth had done to Lucy Goodman, and she had been born into money. Her power and possessiveness had nearly broken her son's spirit. But Daniel had his father's inner courage and had survived. Would a woman – socially and financially inferior – find happiness in such an atmosphere? No, Melrose thought, and it would rest uneasily on his conscience to see an ordinary woman sacrificed.

Melrose sighed and emptied his glass. The dark panelling of the room looked prosperous, Frederick's handsome profile silhouetted against the firelight.

'Funny business, love.'

Frederick raised his eyebrows. 'Personally I never found it in the least amusing.'

Melrose was mellowing with the sherry.

'Why did you marry Emmeline?' His spoke Mrs Conrad's name with caution. *Everyone* treated her with caution.

'She had money and her father was desperate to find someone to marry her off to.' Frederick sighed. 'She was never a beauty, if you recall, Stephen.'

Melrose nodded, the sherry working on his senses. He could remember the first time he met the Conrads, Frederick urbane, his wife older than himself and – to put it mildly – homely.

'Did you love her?'

'Good Lord,' Frederick replied, 'don't be absurd! Emmeline wanted a handsome husband and I wanted a handsome legal practice.' He dropped his voice, dropping his guard as well, as his sherry intake rose. 'Emmeline is rather frightening, you know.'

Melrose knew. The Conrads had lost more staff than anyone else in those parts and he had personally witnessed one vicious exchange between them when Emmeline had caught her husband flirting with another solicitor's wife. No one was surprised that they had never had children. Emmeline would have been as easy to seduce as a rhino.

'Have you ever been in love yourself, Stephen?'

Melrose sunk further into his comfortable chair. This was the life.

'I loved my wife when I met her and I still love her.'

'Jolly good,' Frederick said, refilling their glasses. 'Your wife is a lovely woman. Lovely . . .' he drifted off, handsome and at ease. There was a silence between them, the fire crackling, shadows playing on the walls.

Suddenly the peace was shattered by a voice outside the door: '*Nelson! Nelson! Come down from there, this minute! I'm warning you.*'

Smiling, Frederick half opened his eyes and winked at Melrose.

'Poor Nelson, I rather think he's met his Trafalgar.'

It was mild up at St Anne's Church, the low building outlined against the darkening sky. A few birds wheeled overhead, the sun starting to slide behind warm cloud. What would she think of him, Daniel wondered, standing looking down the lane and waiting to hear Grace's footsteps. Would she like him? She had only seen his photograph and talked to him via letters, otherwise they were strangers.

He stared ahead nervously. Excitement like this he had never known before, and his mother's repeated references to Amy Thornton had been met with blank disinterest. Amy Thornton, Daniel mused, a whey-faced girl he had met only three times in his life, the girl his mother planned eventually to make her daughter-in-law. She hadn't said as much, but Daniel knew his mother well. It would be a good social and financial match; one people would expect. The right choice.

For Lucy Goodman, but not her son. Whistling under

his breath, Daniel paced the ground. Would Grace come? Had she got the time right? Had he? He stopped pacing, listened. Were those footsteps on the path?

The footsteps came closer. Closer and closer up the pathway and then, suddenly, Grace rounded the bend. He would have known her anywhere, her height, the way she carried herself. Then gradually her face came into full focus and she saw him. And stopped. He hesitated, moved towards her. His hand went out. She didn't respond.

'Grace,' he said simply.

Her eyes regarded him steadily.

'Daniel,' she answered, both of them locked into uncertainty. The moment shifted around them, neither sure of how to make the first move, their written familiarity suddenly mute in reality.

'Grace . . .'

She moved then, suddenly running towards him, her arms outstretched – and he took hold of her, burying his face in her hair, his mouth against her ear, whispering over and over, 'Thank God, Thank God, Thank God . . .'

The following day Melrose invited Daniel for a walk. First thing that morning Daniel had seen his mother and been told that the business was running smoothly – Lucy, cold with him, as ever. Her body stiff with unforgiveness, even after all these years.

Melrose was walking with the aid of a stick, his head covered, his coat collar turned up.

'Did you find out about Grace?' Daniel asked as they struck out towards the Heights over Lydgate. 'I suppose you looked into her background?'

A wind was blowing coldly, Melrose shivering.

'Daniel, do you really care about this woman?'

He stopped walking. 'Of course.'

'Then we have to talk seriously,' Melrose countered, sitting down on a worn stone bench, Daniel beside him. 'I have made some enquiries and she has a good reputation, albeit problems. Hers was a difficult background, and she still has a sick father to look after. Her mother is dead. Unfortunately Dora Ellis was not a respectable woman –'

'I know all of this,' Daniel replied hurriedly, 'but why should Grace's mother matter to me?'

'She was pregnant when she left her husband and child and ran off with another man.'

'What's that to do with Grace?'

'Everything,' Melrose replied. 'I don't want to upset you, Daniel, but I don't think this would be a good match.'

He winced. 'I suppose you'd rather it was Amy Thornton?'

Melrose blew his nose loudly. 'I have no interest in Amy Thornton –'

'Neither have I,' Daniel replied shortly. 'Anyway, who I marry is *my* decision.'

Stunned by Daniel's tone, Melrose turned to him. 'I was just offering my opinion.'

'Do you know Grace personally?'

'No.'

'Then how can you judge her?'

Melrose took in a deep breath. This was going to be harder than he'd thought. 'I don't have to know the lady to know of her background. Your mother –'

'Has nothing to do with this!' Daniel said, cutting him off. 'It's my decision who I marry. And when.'

'I understand. But you have to think of Grace too.

How would she cope with your way of life? How could she move in your circles?'

Daniel sighed and stretched out his legs before him. 'What circles?' he countered. 'We have no social life, you know that. My mother has no friends; her only interest is the business.'

'Which she would protect at all costs.'

'I say again – what threat would Grace pose to the business?'

Pulling his coat collar up further against the wind, Melrose held his ground. 'You need a wife who can cope with your way of life. Someone who knows how to behave.'

'As you already know, Grace runs her own business.'

'Some tuppenny-ha'penny cosmetic firm!' Melrose snorted. 'It's hardly in the same league as the Goodman interests, is it?'

'She set it up herself,' Daniel replied, his tone cold. 'I would have said that such determination showed a great deal of intelligence. Instead of seeing her as a disadvantage to me, you might well find that Grace could be an asset.'

'Not when people gossip about her mother – and they will, Daniel. There's nothing people like more than peddling dirt. And if they could peddle dirt about the Goodmans, so much the better. People are envious, Daniel. Haven't you thought that you might be doing Grace Ellis an unkindness to throw her into the deep end like this? Love fades all too quickly up against such odds.'

'Not if it's genuine.'

Melrose said abruptly, 'What do you know about love, Daniel? You've been shown precious little – how could you recognize it? Grace Ellis is the first woman you've really fallen for; you could change your mind. Don't rush into anything, please. Besides, what could she give you?'

Daniel stared at the old man angrily. He had expected Melrose, of all people, to understand.

'*What could she give me?* What would you like? Money? My mother had money – has it made her happy?'

Melrose was surprised by Daniel's stubbornness. Obviously the woman meant a great deal to him.

'You should marry someone of your own class.'

'No,' Daniel said simply. 'I know you're trying to help, Melrose, you always have. I've listened to you over the years and followed your advice because it was always sound. But not this time. I've found someone I love, someone who suits me. I don't want a woman my mother has picked. I have the right to make my own choice. And I want Grace.'

'It's all too sudden. You've hardly met the girl.'

'I've been writing to Grace for six months. I know her from her letters – *really* know her, I'm sure of it.'

'It's not enough!' Melrose replied, rubbing his leg fitfully. Marriage isn't romantic, Daniel. Living day in, day out with someone is very different from writing to them.' He paused, trying to keep the lid on his temper. 'This is wartime; people get carried away by their feelings. It's understandable – but this romance could turn out to be a mirage, Daniel. Think about it. If you marry Grace Ellis and later you realize how little you have in common, what kind of life would that be for either of you?'

Daniel stared at his old friend's outstretched leg. 'Is there something wrong with you?'

'Cramp,' Melrose replied testily, 'and don't change the subject. What are you going to do?'

'I'm going to marry Grace.'

'Your mother wants you to marry the Thornton girl.'

Daniel stared at him. 'Never.'

'Your mother and the Thorntons hoped that there was a chance that you two would marry and unite the businesses.'

'Why don't I just marry the bank?' Daniel responded sourly. 'Surely that would be even easier? We could have the ceremony in the vault.'

Melrose took in deep breath. 'I'm not saying marry her, but Amy Thornton is from a similar background to yours. She comes from money, her parents are land-owners.'

'And we *do* need more money, don't we?' Daniel replied, rising to his feet and looking down on the old man. 'The Goodmans always need more money. We need a bigger house, and more mines. Property, mills. We need to keep piling the money and acquisitions up and up – for what? Has one house, one mill, one millinery factory made anyone sleep better? How many times have you heard anyone laugh at The Lockgate?' His voice was hard with suppressed anger. 'You've watched us over the years, Melrose – don't I deserve happiness? How can you care so little for me that you'd wish on me a marriage of convenience?'

'Don't accuse me of not caring!' Melrose snapped, the pain in his leg making him more irritable. 'I've done my best for you, Daniel. It's unfair to suggest otherwise.'

'I know, you've been like a father to me. Which is why I can't understand you now. For years I've felt shut off from people, always looking over my shoulder, anxious, out of place. The women I've met before all wanted me for what I represented. For the money. I've been a fish on dry land all my life. I never believed that anyone else

264

felt like that. I thought the rest of the world knew exactly what it was doing and where it was going. Now I've met Grace. I feel secure with her. And she trusts me. Don't you understand, Melrose? We fit together, we make each other safe.'

The old man held Daniel's gaze steadily. 'And if you didn't have so much money, would she feel as safe?'

The words snapped at Daniel.

'Grace doesn't know about the money! I've told her nothing about the Goodman fortune. She has no idea who I am.'

'I thought you confided in her?' Melrose said craftily.

'I do!' Daniel retorted, 'but I had to test her first. I had to know if it was me she cared about, or what I had.'

Slowly, Melrose stood up. 'I'm glad that she doesn't know about the money, I really am. I'm glad you had the sense to think the situation out. Maybe I'm wrong, maybe Grace Ellis *would* be the perfect wife for you. But just think about one thing: what happens when you tell her who you really are, Daniel? Have you thought about that? Have you thought about what it will mean to her? Will she have the guts to stay with you then? To stand up to your mother and the gossip which will be sure to follow this match?' He could see that the thought had never occurred to Daniel and pushed his advantage. 'You're sure in *your* mind, and you tell me she is. But how *can* she be? She only knows what you've wanted to tell her – mostly in letters. Her feelings and decisions are based on half-truths. You tested her, Daniel – now maybe it's time you put yourself to the test.'

Having found her, Daniel was reluctant to risk losing Grace. He saw her every day of his leave but waited until the evening he was due to leave before confronting her. They were sitting in her kitchen, Arthur above, Don Clegg sitting with him. If the room seemed shabby to Daniel, he never showed it, and if the food was insubstantial he never once gave his feelings away. Instead he watched as Grace hung the washing over the clothes rack and winched it up to the ceiling over the range. He had never seen a woman perform such chores before; staff invisibly attended to himself and his mother, but he found the actions soothing.

Light-hearted, Grace had made them a meal and then sided away the dishes, sitting beside Daniel after making sure that the blackout curtains were securely in place. Beside them the radio was playing.

Daniel suddenly turned down the volume and took her hand.

'Grace, I want to talk to you.'

Her face was luminous, love in her eyes, her skin translucent. Over the past six months, in their correspondence, and now in the time they'd had together she had come to feel more for Daniel than she had ever done for anyone. The affection she had had for Tom Cox had been real, but nothing to the overwhelming love she felt now. She had managed to come to terms with the loss of Tom, but she couldn't have lived without Daniel.

'You know that I live in Lydgate,' he began. She nodded. 'Well, I live in The Lockgate.'

She stared into his face, not understanding.

'My family are very wealthy, we first made money in Farnsworth as milliners. Then the business was extended to property and mills.' She kept staring at him. 'When I became twenty-one I inherited the businesses and now run them with my mother.'

'I thought you . . .' She trailed off. What *did* she think?

Daniel had never told her what his job was, only that he was in business. Despite his well-modulated voice and obvious education she had presumed that he was the owner or manager of a local firm, not the heir to a local fortune. And she had never asked for details.

'What do you mean?'

'I'm rich,' he said, aware that the money had come down between them like a falling wall. 'I didn't want to tell you at first. I wanted you to get to like me – not who I was.'

'And who *are* you?' Grace asked, her tone cold. 'I thought I was in love with a man I could trust, a man who had been honest with me.' She folded her hands on her lap stiffly. 'Why didn't you tell me before, Daniel? Were you testing me? Checking out if I was after your money?'

Standing up, she walked to the sink and began to wash the dishes, her back rigid.

'I should have realized. *Lydgate*, of course! I should have put two and two together much quicker.' She slammed down a plate, chipping the edge. It never occurred to me to doubt anything you said.'

'I never lied to you.'

'You left a lot out!' she snapped back. 'What were you doing, Daniel? Checking to see if an ex-mill girl was worth courting?'

He was on his feet immediately, trying to take hold of her, but she would have none of it and backed away.

'We had a greengrocer's shop in Diggle – but I suppose you found that out too. We were evicted when my father had his stroke. I was only fourteen, I didn't know how to run a shop.' Her tone was bitter with disappointment. Daniel was no better than the rest, after all. 'My mother came from the slums and she died there. My father's senile – aren't you taking a risk with your fortune, Daniel? And what about your reputation? There's something else you should consider. Perhaps my father's mental illness is hereditary? Or my mother's morals? I could run off with some lout any day.'

'Grace, stop it –'

'Stop what?' she shouted. 'Don't think you're doing me any favours, Daniel Goodman. I don't need your family and I'm happy to keep my own name. I'll get by without you. I've always managed before.'

Daniel raised his hands to his head and sank down in his seat. Silence fell over the cramped room, the clock ticking relentlessly on the range. He was going to have to leave soon, Grace thought. This was to have been the perfect evening, a memory to treasure, but it had gone wrong, horribly wrong.

Daniel Goodman was out of her league. He had tested her like all the others, checking her out to see if she was a gold-digger. Hadn't she proved that she could make it on her own? It had all been a fantasy, Grace thought helplessly. Daniel Goodman was just a rich man fooling around with a working-class girl. There was nothing more to it.

Grace realized then that the words *I want to talk to you* meant that he was about to say goodbye. About to explain how unsuited they were. He would clear the air before he left, cutting any ties. *And she had believed that he loved her*. God, how could she have been so stupid?

'Grace,' he said at last, 'hear me out.'

'I've heard enough.'

Exasperated, Daniel slammed his hand down on the table between them, shaking the cups in their saucers. Surprised, Grace stared at him.

'I did check you out, and yes, I *did* test you. I shouldn't have done, Grace, but I did. I'm sorry, and I want you to let me make it up to you.'

'What with? A present? A cheque?'

'How about a marriage proposal?'

Shaken, Grace's legs gave way under her, and she sat down. Her mouth opened, but no words came out.

Daniel laughed and shook his head. 'You didn't expect it, did you?'

'No,' she said at last.

'So – what's your answer?'

What *was* her answer? She loved him but the news of his background made her anxious. Snippets of gossip came back to her: the old rich woman who lived in Lydgate who had inherited a fortune.

If she accepted his proposal she was committed to a life she knew nothing about. To a moneyed life, an existence without financial pressures. If she married him, her father would be well provided for, as would she. But in return for what? And besides, it was unlikely that Daniel's mother would be thrilled with the idea of an ex-mill girl as her daughter-in-law.

'Does your mother know about me?'

Daniel hesitated. 'No.'

'Because you know she wouldn't approve?'

'You're my choice, not hers.'

'But you're her son, Daniel. I don't want to cause bad feeling between the two of you.'

He laughed bitterly. 'Bad feeling? There never was anything *but* bad feeling.'

'So why add to it?'

'Because nothing would lessen it,' he replied, taking her hand. 'Come on, Grace, say yes. I love you, and I know you love me. We can make this work.'

She glanced away. 'I'm not the same class as you, Daniel.'

'That doesn't matter.'

'To you, maybe not. To me, it matters a lot . . .' she squeezed his hand. 'But I will marry you.'

'Thank God!'

'But not yet,' Grace said, trying to keep calm. 'I have to make something of myself first. I have to *be* someone, build up my own business. I don't want anyone pointing their finger and saying that I married you for your money. Wait and let me come to you a success in my own right. Please. I *will* marry you, Daniel. But as an equal – or not at all.'

Chapter Twenty-Seven

On 28 March 1942 aircraft of RAF Bomber Command attacked Lubeck, a vital industrial area of the Baltic. Fire bombs were dropped in their hundreds there and on the German arms factories in a raid which over-whelmed the fire-fighters on the ground. The RAF's new four-engined bombers were suddenly able to drop four-thousand-pound bombs, Spitfires backing up their heavy-weight companions in the fight.

Headlines at home read 'RAF Begins Terror Bombing Campaign'. Grace scanned the papers and listened to the radio. With news of every raid she thought of Daniel, wondering if it was his plane going over to Europe; every day she waited for news, miserable when his letters were delayed, ecstatic when they arrived.

She was in love completely, and knew that her feelings were shared. So deep was the understanding between them that Grace and Daniel formed a telepathic bond at times. She could *feel* it when he thought of her and late at night she lay on her bed and talked to him in her head.

Since she'd learned of his background, Grace had set about finding out all she could about the Goodman family: their businesses, their interests, their history. Old Grandfather Goodman's bench in the local park was still there, bearing his name, Grace running her fingers along it. Lucy Goodman was reclusive, Grace discovered, a cold woman who seldom left The Lockgate.

To her surprise, Grace felt in awe of her, and as she

uncovered more and more about the Goodman empire her nerves increased. A woman like Lucy Goodman wouldn't want her as a daughter-in-law. Not now, at least. But later, when Grace had really achieved something, later she would go to Lucy Goodman and *know* that she would be accepted. Then she would be someone, a woman on a par with her son. But not yet . . .

Loving Daniel was effortless. There was nothing she couldn't say to him, or write. He wouldn't let her down, wouldn't leave her. He had found her, and she had found him – they were never going to be apart. It was true that the war had separated them physically, but the war would end and Daniel would come home. In time they would marry.

If Daniel came home. . . Winded by the thought, Grace shook her head. Daniel would come home, of course he would. She had only to wait. In the meantime she would build up her business, become someone of value.

So she travelled to St Andrew's Place – patched up from the bomb and fire damage – and tried to concentrate every thought on her work. At times she found it impossible; wanting to go out on the street and shout out loud: *I'm in love, I love Daniel Goodman. Me, Grace Ellis. We're going to get married.*

But who would have believed her? She could hardly believe it herself. Daniel – who could have married anyone; Daniel – who had money, position, status; that same Daniel Goodman loved *her*.

'Grace.'

She spun round, surprised to find Aaron at the door of her office, watching her. It was quiet at the factory, the women having stopped for their midday break, sitting out in the early autumn sunshine.

'Hello there. I didn't expect to see you until later.'

'I thought I'd pop over in my lunch break,' he replied, sitting down and glancing at her quizzically. 'You look different.'

She wanted to say that she *was* different and tell him what had happened, but she couldn't. It would be too risky to tell anyone about Daniel before his mother knew. Grace had insisted on that. *We must keep it a secret for the time being. When the war's over we can tell people, but not now.*

But the secret tickled inside her, made her giddy, unlike herself.

'I'm fine. Just busy.'

He wasn't convinced. 'How's your father?'

'My father's about the same as he always is.'

'It must be hard, though, being on your own.'

No, it's not, she wanted to say, *because I'm not alone. Daniel's not here with me physically, but I take him with me everywhere. He walks down the street with me, unlocks the door to St Andrew's Place with me, sits with me at night in front of the fire. He's everywhere, his voice, his scent, the turn of his head.*

'I'm managing fine, Aaron. Don't worry about me.'

'I see there's still plenty of orders coming in,' he remarked, glancing over to Grace's desk and looking at the pile of invoices there. 'Maybe we should call the range War Paint.'

Grace laughed, grateful to have a reason to let off steam.

It wasn't that funny, Aaron thought.

'The news just came over the radio. They're evacuating more children from the cities, London first. I think that's due to the raids on Bath and Canterbury.'

273

'The RAF will strike back,' Grace replied. 'They'll beat them.'

Aaron nodded, then sat down, his head in his hands. 'What is it?'

'There more news, Grace, bad news. They say the Nazis have murdered a million Jews.'

'*A million Jews?*' she echoed, her skin chilling. 'How?'

'Shooting them. Gassing them. The Warsaw ghetto alone has over six hundred thousand people crammed into it, some living twenty to a room.'

'Oh God.'

'The Germans won't let old people and small children have medical supplies.'

Grace sat down heavily. 'How do you know? It could just be rumours.'

'News is smuggled out all the time,' he replied darkly. 'I *know*.'

His face was grey, dark purplish patches under his eyes. These weren't a result of a few nights' lost sleep, Grace thought, but months of insomnia, dread. Slowly Aaron rubbed his forehead, his hands shaking. He was an old man at thirty, the vein in his neck distended and throbbing.

'Aaron, what can I do to help?'

He said nothing, just shook his head, his mouth opening but no words coming out. Grace thought for a moment that he might faint, but although his body was shaking violently, he was fully alert, but in shock. He was thinking what she was – that Solomon might well be amongst the million dead.

'I have to get back to work in the factory,' Aaron said suddenly, rising to his feet.

Hurriedly Grace took his arm. 'You can't go back yet. Rest here for a while.'

'No, I want to work.'

'Aaron –'

He silenced her with a look. 'I know what I'm doing. I'll be back later.'

> My darling,
>
> Don't worry, I'm safe. I have you to come home to now – how could I let anything happen to me? I love you. I love you. I love you. Do you think of me? I see your face on my blanket, my locker, my control panel! I see your eyes in the landscape and hear your voice in the engine whirl. I am obsessed. Thank God.
>
> Daniel

Grace wrote back:

> Dearest Love,
>
> I went up to St Anne's today – where we first met – and I reached upwards.
>
> Silly, wasn't it? As though I thought I might just touch you as you flew over.
>
> We talk nonsense. Giddy, silly things. I don't know how I lived before I loved you. Or was that living? You are my heart and breath, nothing matters more to me than the future we will have.
>
> We are hearing desperate news – smuggled out – about the Jews. Aaron is sick with worry, no one has heard about his brother for so long. Solomon's letters have stopped. Maybe he can't smuggle them out any more, maybe something's happened to him ... Don't let anything happen to you, darling. Don't let anyone take you away from me.
>
> Fly high and keep your head low!
>
> Always,
>
> Grace

Curiosity had always been one of Stephen Melrose's vices, and age hadn't changed him. After his talk with Daniel he had become anxious and then inquisitive. Who *was* this Grace Ellis who had so fascinated Daniel? It was all right to see her details written down on paper, but what was she really like?

He brooded on the idea for months, not wanting to demean himself by spying, but eventually he could contain himself no longer. Dressing in light suit and carrying his stick, Melrose walked through the warm autumnal streets, passing the burned out Abbey Hills Road, and moving down to St Andrew's Place.

Well, it was a dump and no mistake, he thought, staring at the derelict church and the workshop down at the bottom of the alley. Had Daniel seen it? Or was love really that blind? Blowing out his cheeks, Melrose paced the street, his hat shading his eyes from the sun. Several passers-by – curious to see such a well-dressed man in this place – stared at him warily.

It wasn't even a proper factory, Melrose thought, not like the millinery workshops in Failsworth, or the Goodman mills. It looked amateur, run down. He could imagine only too well what Lucy Goodman would think of it. 'Is he mad?' she'd ask. 'How could my son even think of walking into such a place, never mind courting the owner?'

The owner was at that moment leaving the building. Turning, Grace locked the doors and then glanced up at the sky. Dipping back into an alleyway, Melrose watched her, feeling more than a little foolish. He was surprised, he had to admit: Grace Ellis had elegance and style. She walked erect, her clothes worn but smart, her hair shiny in the sunlight.

Still watching her, Melrose pressed himself against the

wall of the alleyway, putting his foot in some dog excreta at the same time. Swearing under his breath, he turned round again – and bumped straight into Grace.

'Oh, forgive me. I wasn't looking where I was going.'

'Think nothing of it,' Grace replied, walking off.

Flustered, Melrose called after her, 'I was looking for the park.'

'The park?'

'Yes, I hear it's lovely.'

Her grey eyes looked at him suspiciously. Melrose coloured. God, he thought, how humiliating. She thinks I'm trying to pick her up!

'It's over there.'

'But –'

Grace's voice was cutting, her distaste obvious. 'The park is that way. You can't miss it. Good day.'

Well, well, well, Melrose thought as he tried to scrape the dog muck off the sole of his shoe. She was quite imposing, was Miss Grace Ellis . . . Thoughtfully Melrose moved on, smiling to himself. Old Lucy Goodman might have met her match there, he thought, and not before time.

'Oh, Ivy . . .' Enid said when her friend came on the night shift. Ivy was holding a rag up to her mouth, blood speckling the cloth, her face white.

'It's m' teeth,' Ivy mumbled.

'Still troubling you?' Enid replied, pushing aside the boxes on the bench and leaning over.

'I had 'em out.'

Enid's round face flushed. 'Your teeth? All your bloody teeth? God, Ivy, whatever were you thinking of?'

'Just the top ones,' Ivy murmured, wiping her mouth,

277

her upper lip drooping. 'Oh, don't look at me like that, Enid! I was in such pain I was glad to be rid of them.'

'But couldn't you have had some treatment?'

'And how much would that have cost?' Ivy countered, dabbing at her mouth fitfully. 'I haven't got money to waste on things like that.'

Enid's plump hands pulled the half-filled box back to her. Ivy was only fifty but she looked like an old woman all of a sudden. Who'd have their top teeth out? Enid thought horrified. Ivy would never get a man looking like that.

Her own lip trembled. 'Oh, Ivy . . .'

'Pass me a box, Enid, and stop snivelling!' Ivy snapped firmly. 'What's done's done.'

Only minutes later, Grace came out of the office, looked round, and then called over to Enid, 'Have you seen Aaron?'

She shook her head. 'Nah. Not since yesterday.'

Surprised, Grace walked into the laboratory and moved over to his workbench. Aaron's notes were still on the worktop and his overall was hanging on the back of the door, but he hadn't arrived. Maybe he hadn't felt well enough to work after all.

Picking up some a rack of samples, Grace walked back to her office, treading on a note as she moved through the door.

'Damn!' she said, bending down to pick it up and recognizing Aaron's writing. Her mouth dried as she opened the envelope.

Dear Grace,

I'm sorry to let you down, but I've had to go away for a while. I can't seem to stop thinking about my brother. He made me come to England to be safe but he stayed in Germany. I can't come to terms with that. I keep thinking that he might still be alive and so I'm going to try and find him.

Oh God, Grace thought desperately. How could Aaron possibly find his brother? How could he leave the country and get back to Europe? Was he mad? There was a war on, no one could travel about as they used to. He would be stopped, worse . . . Shaking, Grace read the remainder of the letter.

You've been so kind to me, made me very welcome. But I can't live not knowing what's happened to Solomon. I can't stay safe when he's out there.
    Please understand, and I hope we meet again.
    Aaron

Chapter Twenty-Eight

On Daniel's next leave that autumn he brought a ring with him, slipping it onto Grace's finger and kissing her palm.

'We're engaged.'

Delighted, she nuzzled the back of his neck as he bent over her. 'Have you told your mother?'

'No,' he said, catching hold of Grace and kissing her, his lips hungry.

Laughing, she pulled away from him. 'How can I wear an engagement ring when no one knows about us?'

'Tomorrow they will.'

She stiffened in his arms. 'Why? What happens tomorrow?'

'You're going to meet my mother –'

'No, not yet! You promised me, Daniel, that you would wait until I was ready.'

'Which might take years. Oh come on, Grace, I love you for what you are. You don't have to prove yourself to me.'

'I know, but I have to prove myself to everyone else,' she replied, feeling him pull away from her.

His voice was suddenly cold. 'So other people's opinions are more important than mine, are they?'

'I didn't say that.'

'You implied it.' Incredulous, Daniel shook his head. 'You think like them, don't you?'

'Like *who*?'

'My mother, my class. You think that I should marry

someone more suitable. Perhaps I *should* court Amy Thornton? She's rich; it would be a good match.'

'Daniel, don't talk like this,' Grace said hurriedly. 'I want to marry you, you know I do –'

'But not yet.'

'No, not yet,' she agreed. 'I want a wedding when I'm ready to be your equal. After the war is over. I don't want to be scuttling around as though what we feel for each other is wrong. I want it out in the open –'

'So come and meet my mother.'

'No,' Grace said emphatically. 'I'm not ready for her. When she knows about us she'll have people out finding everything about me. You did, so she certainly will. Only your mother will want to know the worst, not the best. She'll be told about Miller Lane, my mother, my father, the shop. Then they'll tell her about my business. She'll think it's a joke. It would be, to her. But not to me. I built the Auden Line from nothing. Before war broke out we were busy, running two shifts. I had outlets all over the North and beyond. I was making a profit, Daniel.' She hurried on, 'You don't know how important it was for me to be able to report some success to my benefactors too. They've stuck with me for so long. Paid for my education, put up money even when they didn't agree with what I wanted to do. When I was really struggling, they were there for me. And they've *stayed* by me – I want to pay them back. I have to.'

But Daniel still didn't fully understand.

'I know what you're saying, Grace, but that doesn't matter any more. When we're married, you won't have to borrow money. You won't be beholden to anyone –'

'Except you.'

'I'll be your husband!' he replied, irritated. 'Grace,

what's mine will be yours. You won't have to go cap in hand to anyone.'

'Which is all the more reason why I want to come to you with something of *mine* to offer.' Grace pushed her hair away from her face and sighed. 'Money means little to you because you've always had it. But money is vital to me. When I was a child my mother took me down to the slums, to Miller Lane. She told me – *This is the place you run from.*

'The rich don't understand the poor; how poverty feels, how it beggars you. How daily you wonder how to make enough to eat, clothe, warm yourself. The poor know about shortage; and they mistrust abundance, mistrust people who offer too much. Because everything costs, Daniel, and for some that cost is beyond them.'

Subdued, he pulled her onto his lap and stroked her cheek.

'In your time then. We'll tell everyone when you're ready. But don't leave it too long, Grace. Don't leave it too long.'

Well really, Lucy Goodman thought, getting to her feet and staring out of the window. Her elegant fingers drummed against the wooden surround, her eyes fixed on the far-off glasshouses. He was always so devious, she thought. All his life Daniel had been secretive. Playing with that gardener's boy, for instance. Lying all that time about what he was doing.

And now lying again ... Well, maybe not lying directly, but certainly lying by omission. He was seeing some common tart from Oldham! A working-class woman with no breeding. No doubt a woman who thought she would end up taking over the Goodman fortune. Over my dead body, Lucy thought.

Grace Ellis was obviously some gold-digger on the make. It was all so ridiculous. How could Daniel be taken in by her? Lucy walked away from the window and sat down at her late husband's desk. Everything had been working out rather well, she thought. Daniel had David's facility for business and the future looked set. Then the war happened.

That was it, Lucy thought, it was the war which had confused her son. He had fallen in love like so many young men did, grabbing at happiness when he could. In peacetime, it would never have happened; he would have courted Amy Thornton and that would have been it. But he was confused, falling in love with the first tart who set his cap at him. They were obviously sleeping together. Cheap whore.

Her gaze moved back to the window, looking across the lawn and settling on an untidy flowerbed. The gardener wasn't keeping it up to the old standard, but then what could you expect? He was elderly, with a bad back. All the young men were away fighting. Like her son – who would have to be treated with kid gloves. Lucy wasn't about to come down hard on the relationship. No, that would only drive Daniel into this woman's arms more readily. She had to be subtle to get her own way.

There had to be something about Grace Ellis which would make Daniel turn against her. The woman had to have an Achilles heel. All Lucy had to do was to find it.

'MAKE DO AND MEND' said the sign, urging everyone to make their own clothes or make do with what they already had, no matter how shabby it was. Women had been inventive in their shortage; parachute silk had made a great many pairs of knickers and a woman on Waterloo Street had even got married in some of the bright yellow silk. *She looks like a sodding canary,* Mary Wells had commented at the time, *Her husband won't have to worry about the blackout, she'll glow in the bloody dark!*

The war ground on, shortages pandemic, rationing on clothes and food making life grim. It seemed that daily news came of some father, brother or son killed. Some bodies remained where they fell overseas, some were never found, but others were shipped home. Local burials were common sights, Leesfield sprouting an unhealthy crop of crosses. Money being tight, there were no big monuments or marble angels.

The lucky ones were invalided home sick – those who would recover. Others, mutilated and deformed beyond recognition, were never seen again.

'I heard about that hospital on the other side of Saddleworth Moor,' Don Clegg said, sitting beside Grace at the kitchen table. Arthur was asleep – or drifting – upstairs. 'Someone I knew had to go up there to do some emergency repairs after a bombing raid. The wards are like they always were, but he said there was some place at the back of the hospital which no one saw.'

'So how did he know about it then?' Grace countered.

'He got lost, wandered in by mistake. He said there were men in there who'd been sent back from the war, but no one knew about them. They'd no arms or legs and were hung up in canvas sacks along the wall.'

Grace stared at him: '*What?*'

'No one knows about them. They can't let them lie

down because they'd die, so they have to hang them up. He said the ward was dark, smelled foul.'

'Oh God . . .' Grace said, looking down at her cup, the tea weak, almost at the end of the ration.

What if something like that happened to Daniel, she thought. What if he ended up hidden away in some hospital, with no one knowing if he was dead or alive? What if she never saw him again . . . ? No, he would survive. He had survived this long, and everyone said that the war wouldn't – couldn't – go on much longer.

He was lucky, they all said. So many of the fighter pilots had been shot down. He had lasted so long, there were only a few of them who were that lucky. *Lucky* – that word again, Grace thought. She hated it, hated the way the two syllables tempted fate.

Daily the headlines screamed out the news of raids and casualties. Good news came like a blessing – 'TIDE BEGINS TO TURN IN THE U-BOAT WAR' – but that was the Navy, not the Air Force. The war was turning in the Allies' favour, everyone agreed, but still it went on and on.

The engagement ring which Daniel had given her two years earlier Grace still wore on a chain, laid against her heart. She wouldn't wear it on her hand until the war ended, she told him. But that had been a long time ago. Maybe she should now. Maybe it was time.

But announcing their engagement would mean meeting Lucy Goodman and Grace had dreaded that. Why? she asked herself repeatedly. She loved Daniel, Daniel loved her. Lucy Goodman had nothing to do with it really. After all, what could she do? Disinherit her son? Daniel had already talked to Grace about that. About how he wouldn't care about the money, if he had her.

But if Lucy Goodman *did* disinherit her son how

would they live? What was Daniel qualified to do? He had inherited a business, but how easy would it be for him to find a career in civvy street? Daniel had been born into privilege, Grace thought; would he grow to hate her if he lost that status?

Yet every time she had tried to talk to Daniel about it he'd just pressed her to marry him and confound everyone . . . There was no doubt in Grace's mind that she wanted Daniel. That was why she had thrown herself into her business. And she had done well, even in wartime. Women would scrimp for weeks to save up for some powder or a lipstick . . .

Don coughed, bringing Grace's thoughts back to the present. 'The papers also say –'

'No more!' Grace snapped suddenly. 'I can't hear any more.'

'He'll be OK,' Don replied, knowing that she was thinking of Daniel. 'He's coming home for some leave soon, isn't he?'

'Next week.'

'For how long?'

'Three days.'

'You should get wed.'

Grace stared at the old man beside her.

'Oh, come on, luv,' he joked, 'I've got eyes in my head. I can see what you two feel for each other. You want to get wed and give the lad someone to come home to.'

Grace fingered the ring on the chain round her neck. 'He *does* want to marry me.'

'That's grand. So what's stopping you?'

'He's well off, Don. I mean rich . . . His mother wouldn't take kindly to me.'

'But you're not marrying his mother.'

She nodded. 'I know. I've thought about it for a long

time. I've wondered if I shouldn't visit her and tell her how much I love her son. Make her see that I'm genuine, not some gold-digger.'

'So why don't you?'

There was a long pause. 'Because I'm scared,' Grace admitted at last.

'That's not like you.'

'Oh, yes it is, Don. I'm scared of a lot of things. The war, losing Daniel. I don't show how frightened I am, but I feel it. I try to look tough, but I'm not. Not really.' She stopped, embarrassed.

'Everyone's afraid at sometime in their life,' Don said kindly. 'You're not on your own.'

'I can't face Lucy Goodman,' she said her voice low. That's why I don't go to see her.'

'She's not a monster, Grace.'

'She's Daniel mother – and she won't want me as a daughter-in-law.'

'Oh come on, luv, it's his choice, not hers,' Don assured her.

At that moment Grace seemed vulnerable, slight in her dark dress, her eyes lowered. The capable woman who impressed everyone was suddenly unsure, sitting in front of the fire like a lost child.

'What if she hates me?'

'Grace, you can't hide away,' Don answered. 'You have to meet Lucy Goodman sometime. Good God, you've always faced up to everything before.'

She gazed into the firelight. 'I could go and see her, I suppose . . .'

'That would be a good idea.'

Grace shivered and pulled her cardigan around her tightly.

'It is very cold tonight?'

'No.'

'It feels cold . . .'

There was another long pause between them.

Then: 'Will you go, Grace?

'Where?'

'To see Mrs Goodman.'

She sighed, still looking into the flames. 'I'll go and see Lucy Goodman. Tomorrow.'

In the grate the flames flickered, the coals shifting against each other, sparks flying like comets into the dark well of the chimney.

Chapter Twenty-Nine

The pupils of Lucy Goodman's eyes were circled with a fine line of white. An arcus, her doctor told her. Nothing to worry about, just a sign of advancing years, or a possible heart weakness. Dr Mornald had hurried to reassure her, 'I have no cause for alarm, Mrs Goodman, and you mustn't worry either.'

She wondered how he had the right to tell her what to think. After all, she paid him to work for her, not dictate her thought process. So she might have a heart weakness, might she? How interesting, how very interesting. All the more reason to make sure that the future was settled. If anything happened to her Lucy wanted to make sure that the businesses were safe, all the hard-earned Goodman money wasn't going to go to solicitors or the Government.

Years earlier she had made a will in favour of Daniel, but things had changed radically during the war. The businesses had altered, some even changing direction – like the Shadow Factory in Delph, which now made electrical lamps for the services. Yes, it was time to reassess her assets, Lucy thought, time to make sure that every pound was protected for the next generation. Daniel's children.

'Mrs Goodman, you have a visitor.'

Surprised, Lucy looked up from her seat by the fire. Who on earth had come to see her? No one came to The Lockgate any more.

'Who is it?'

'A Miss Grace Ellis.'

The name registered like a bolt of lightning hitting a metal spike, Lucy taking a moment to catch her breath.

'Show her in.'

Timid sunlight heralded Grace's admission, the light filtering through the net curtains and scattering across the dark carpet. Dust motes flickered for a moment on the air between Lucy Goodman and Grace – then the sun went in again and the room became sombre. Heavy drapes at the windows, and a fire burning hotly, made the room stuffy. The dark silk dress Lucy Goodman was wearing gave her the look of a sleek and cunning jackdaw.

'Thank you for seeing me,' Grace said, walking over and putting out her hand.

Lucy took it, weighed it in her own.

'Sit down. I've heard a good deal about you.'

'From your son?'

'No,' Lucy replied curtly. 'My son *has* told me about you, but I don't think he's serious, my dear. Young men *will* have their little follies in wartime.'

Stung, Grace felt her face flush, and glanced down.

What a good-looking woman, Lucy thought, almost well bred. She stared at Grace's sombre clothes and smiled faintly. A little slum girl trying to look like a lady. Fine hair, though, and neat feet and hands. Could fool most people, but not her. Oh no, Lucy Goodman knew real class, and Grace Ellis didn't have it.

'I wanted to come and talk to you, Mrs Goodman. I care very dearly for your son.'

'Of course you do. He's attractive and rich.'

'I don't care about the money –'

Irritated, Lucy clicked her tongue. 'Oh really, don't

be so tiresome. We all care about money. Daniel cares about it, whatever he tells you in your moments of passion –'

'It's not like that!' Grace snapped, insulted. 'We love each other; there's nothing seedy about what we feel.'

'You can't fool me, I know your type.'

Grace's heart was pumping rapidly, a vein throbbing in her neck. She had never been so insulted in all her life. Even in a mill, she had been treated with more courtesy. Yet here was this rich, so-called well-bred woman, whose mind was like a sewer.

'I have nothing to be ashamed of –'

'I don't want to hear your confessions,' Lucy replied, patently bored. 'We should get this matter sorted out once and for all. Will you leave my son alone?'

'Daniel loves me –'

'That doesn't answer the question, Miss Ellis. Will you leave me son alone?'

Grace could feel the engagement ring pressing against her breast, could remember Daniel's face and suddenly wanted him more than she had ever done. They wouldn't wait any more, they would get married when he next came home.

'No, Mrs Goodman, I won't leave your son alone, because he doesn't want me to.'

'Perhaps I can persuade you another way?' Lucy paused, considering the deal. 'How much money would change your mind?'

'*Money!* What are you talking about? You think you can buy me off?'

'If you're anything like your mother you have few morals.'

The mention of her mother made Grace flinch.

'How dare you?'

'This is my house,' Lucy Goodman said coldly. 'I can say what I want here.'

She was supremely confident. Having now seen Grace Ellis, Lucy Goodman felt no threat. The woman was lovely, but third rate. Her worn clothes and desire to please were despicable. She might have his attention now, but Daniel would soon tire of her after the war. He would come round to his mother's way of thinking and marry Amy Thornton. Besides, Lucy was getting older, she had had a few palpitations. Her heart couldn't be strong. Which loving son would want to give his mother a heart attack by opposing her wishes?

'I repeat – how much do you want, Miss Ellis?'

'I don't want money,' Grace replied, her voice hoarse.

She had seen what Lucy Goodman thought of her and had nothing to lose any more. The woman despised her, thought she was pathetic. She was beneath contempt to her; just one more scrubber with no feelings. A lower-class whore who had obviously seduced her son and could be bought off.

'You can't buy me off, or bully me, Mrs Goodman.'

Surprised, Lucy's eyes flickered. 'I beg your pardon?'

'I said you can't buy me or bully me,' Grace repeated. 'I love your son and he loves me.'

'Daniel will never marry you.'

Grace's fear had evaporated. 'He *is* going to marry me.'

'Not if I have anything to do with it!'

'You can't stop it. He can make up his own mind.'

'Then I'll disinherit him,' Lucy retorted. 'You'll see how easy your life will be when you've no money.'

Grace smiled coldly. 'I've *never* had any money, Mrs Goodman, so it won't make any difference. As for Daniel, he's smart, and I'm smart, we'll succeed on our own.'

Lucy raised her eyes to heaven. 'Love in a cottage, how quaint. Just you, my son – and your mad old father.'

Grace stared her. 'I used to *defend* you. I was the one who wanted Daniel to get your permission for our marriage. I wanted you two to be friends; I wanted all of us to be friends.' She laughed bitterly. 'Well, now I see how I wrong I was. You're a selfish old woman. You live like a hermit up here and don't give a damn for your son's feelings –'

'That will do!'

'No, it won't!' Grace snapped back, seeing Lucy reach for the bell pull and tug it. 'You can throw me out of your house, but you can't throw me out of your son's heart. I won't let you win, Mrs Goodman. I wanted to make a friend of you, but that's impossible. You've insulted me and tried to make me feel like a common slut.' She stopped when a maid walked into the room.

'Miss Ellis is leaving,' Lucy said, her tone chilled, her own heart pumping. 'Show her out.'

Grace stood up and walked to the door, then paused.

'I'll leave now and I won't come back. But I'll never forgive you for what you said to me. No one can reason with you. It's your way, or nothing. Well, I love Daniel and I'll fight you for him. I won't take your insults, your money, or your contempt – but I *will* take the thing that matters most to you. Your son.'

Chapter Thirty

Grace clung to Daniel as she listened to a bomb falling many streets away. They could have run to a shelter, but they didn't. She had tried to confide several times then finally told Daniel everything his mother had said. Then she had wept, and he had kissed her and realized that he loved her even more than he had thought.

He had been white-faced, angry and determined that they would marry as soon as possible. He would get a special licence, he'd told her. They could get married this leave.

The siren had gone off then. Daniel had put his arm around Grace and hurried her towards the shelter down on Gladstone Street. Far away, the first bomb had hit near the River Irwell, the sky lighting up in the distance. Grace had looked over her shoulder.

'We can't make it. Hurry!' she'd said.

Daniel had suddenly pulling her into a empty building. In the semidark he had looked around urgently, then led her to the space under a staircase, the roof partially open to the sky.

'Let's get under here. It will give us some protection.'

In silence, she had clung to him.

'We should try to get to the main shelter,' he'd said, stroking her face. 'What would I do if anything happened to you?'

'I don't care what happens – if I'm with you,' she had replied, looking at him, her gaze resting on his mouth.

In that moment he had felt the need travel through her body as it had in his, his mouth roaming over hers, his hands running over her face, her neck, her breasts. She'd responded, unfastening his uniform jacket, her body moving against his. Her face, hidden in the darkness had been suddenly illuminated for an instant by the moonlight. In that instant he'd seen that her lips had parted, her eyes moist. Slowly she lay down and reached up for him.

They'd made love as the siren wailed overhead and the bombs rained down on Manchester and the industrial valley of the River Irwell. They'd joined and touched and lay with each other, and then finally they heard the all clear.

The sound echoed and rose like a note of triumph to the white stars over their heads.

PART FOUR

How few of his friends' houses would a man choose
to be at when he is sick.

BOSWELL, *The Life of Samuel Johnson*

Chapter Thirty-One

She couldn't remember what she was supposed to be doing, but knew it wasn't this. Hesitating, Joan stood outside St Andrew's Place. The building had survived the war and still stood next to the derelict church, as it had always done. She expected to hear the sound of the workers inside but there was silence, no lights burning.

Words would not come, either spoken or written, so in the end Joan had decided to visit Grace once again to see if, this time, she would let her in. Tom had urged her to go. Back safe from the war he had been magnanimous with relief. Go and see her, he had said, see if there is anything you can do. Or anything I can do. I'll sit with the kids for a while.

The war in Europe had just ended. It seemed incredible, unbelievable, after so long. Hitler had committed suicide, the Germans had surrendered and the full horror of the Nazi camps was being shown on the newsreels at the Roxy. Of Aaron there had been no word since one brief note sent many months earlier.

Having found the factory deserted, Joan climbed on to one of the infrequent buses and rode across Oldham and then up to Diggle. The village had hardly changed, even though it was years since she had spent time there, and when she reached the Ellis house she stood for a long time staring at the front door.

The argument she had had with Grace seemed so long ago, so trivial. Why had they fallen out? Because of Tom, that was why. But it didn't matter now, did it? Joan was married to Tom, and secure. The friend she had come to envy Joan now pitied. In the gamble that was living she had found a lucky table to play on, whereas Grace had lost everything.

She knocked twice and waited. There was no sound from upstairs. The curtains in Arthur's room were half drawn. Again, Joan knocked and was relieved to hear footsteps approaching.

Her first reaction on seeing Grace was shock. The weight had fallen off her, her eyes dull and vast in the white face. She was wearing a dark green dress and an apron with a cooking stain down the front, her hands ungroomed, the nails broken. No trace of the elegant Grace Ellis remained.

Joan felt her lip tremble, her eyes fill.

'Grace? How are you?'

She stared into Joan's face, but did not appear to recognize her and stood twisting the tea towel in her hands.

'Grace, it's me. Joan.'

Still no sign of recognition.

'You remember me, your old mate? We used to go to the Riviera together – tease that old pig of a manager.'

Grace's expression was blank as Joan led her back into the kitchen. Plates were piled high in the sink, a half-eaten loaf of stale bread on the top of a window ledge, the fire gone out and banked up high with long-accumulated ashes.

Settling an unresisting Grace into a seat, Joan began to tidy the room, filling the sink with water and washing the pots, then wiping the surfaces. Finally she cleaned out the ashes and relaid the fire. All the time she had been busy, Grace had merely watched her. Jesus, Joan thought, how long had she been this way? Another thought followed at once. What about her father?

Yet when she reached Arthur's bedroom Joan could see the old man on the bed, blankets piled high, and eiderdown laid on top even though the weather was mild. Quickly she crossed the landing and moved into Grace's room, standing, thunderstruck, in the doorway. There was only one sheet on Grace's bed. She would be cold at night, without comfort. The sheet was grubby, the room sour smelling, the furniture piled high with drawings.

Slowly Joan walked in and picked up the one nearest to her. It was a profile of Daniel Goodman. She recognized him from seeing pictures in the local newspaper. So was the next, and the next. Others showed him smiling, or turning his head, but every drawing was of him.

'Jesus,' Joan said simply, dropping the sketches onto the bed and sitting down.

She knew – as did everyone – that Daniel Goodman had been killed in action two months earlier. Grace and Daniel had announced their engagement only a week before. Rumour had it that Grace and he had married by special licence – but Joan didn't know if that was true. Certainly Grace wasn't wearing a wedding ring.

The body of Daniel Goodman had been brought home from France and buried at Leesfield Cemetery. Lucy Goodman hadn't told Grace when the funeral was, so she hadn't been able to pay her last respects to the man she had loved so completely. Instead she had overheard in the chemist that the funeral had already taken place, screaming and banging her head against the wall until someone called for help. The doctor sedated her, but she didn't sleep.

Grace fell off the world instead, ignored the knocks on the door and left letters unread. In the night the Coxes had heard her once or twice howl like a mad woman, but

Grace wouldn't talk. Instead she looked after her father behind the locked doors and cut bread and walked up and down the staircase like an automaton.

She dipped in and out of reality. *Daniel was coming home. No, Daniel wasn't*... It was all her fault. She had brought it on herself by defying his mother. She had said she would take him away – but someone else had. And now his mother had him for always.

Slowly, the weeks had staggered past after his death. Joan had called several times, but had never got an answer. Coral Higgins had visited too, but Grace wouldn't open the door. A letter from Frederick Conrad was the only one opened. In it he had written his condolences but was sorry to have to inform Grace that her benefactors would have to reduce their support. They would continue to back her, but for the moment the money was to be halved. The war had taken its toll on everyone.

Joan had heard the news. Rumours went round Oldham like bushfire. A secretary in Frederick Conrad's office told a friend, who told a friend, and before long everyone seemed to know. What a tragedy, everyone agreed, how would Grace manage, losing her man and now having her backers rein in their support? It was too much to bear, poor Grace.

How she would have hated people pitying her, Joan thought, returning to the kitchen where she left a pot of tea to brew and pushing a cup across the table to Grace. She didn't even seem to see it. Instead she stared blankly ahead.

'Grace,' Joan said, sitting beside her, 'please eat something.'

She ignored her.

'What can I do to help you? I'm so sorry about Daniel.

Please, talk to me, cry, do anything, Grace. But respond.
You can't stay like this or you'll go mad.'

Grace kept staring ahead of her.

'You have to get out of here,' Joan went on. 'Oh,
for God's sake, Grace, look at me! It's Joan, your Joan.
We were pals, we cared about each other. We laughed,
kidded each other. You used to come to my parents'
pub – my dad's as bone idle as he always was, and my
mum's feet have spread like dinner plates.' She paused,
frustrated by the lack of response. 'Look at me, Grace!
You were never a quitter, don't quit now.'

Grace blinked slowly. She saw Joan and frowned.

'*Joan?*' Her voice was hoarse, unused.

'Yes, it's me,' Joan replied. 'It's me, luv.'

As though waking from a coma Grace looked around
and ran her tongue over her lips.

'I have to get ready. Daniel's coming.'

Joan could feel the hairs stand up on the back of
her neck.

'Grace, no. No, he's not coming.'

But Grace had got to her feet, her cheeks flushed.
'I have to make some food. Good Lord, what was
I thinking of?' She began to take out some plates.
'I have to make something to eat. He'll be hungry.'
Hurriedly she pushed Joan aside. 'I need some more
bread –'

'Grace, stop it!' Joan said firmly. 'Stop it.'

'– and some butter. I should get some more butter –'

'STOP IT!' Joan shouted, her eyes full of tears as she
caught hold of Grace's hands again. 'Daniel's gone –'

'But he's coming back,' Grace said firmly. 'That's why
I have to be ready for him.'

'He's never coming back,' Joan said, her voice breaking.

At once, Grace tried to shake her off. 'Don't be stupid, of course he is!' Her voice rose shrilly. 'Daniel would never leave me. He would never leave me.'

'Daniel's dead, Grace.'

She stared at her old friend.

'No,' she whispered.

'Yes.'

Then suddenly Grace started to scream, her eyes widening, her head thrown back, Joan holding on to her and feeling her body go rigid.

'Grace, stop!' she said terrified. 'Please, luv. *Please*.'

But Grace couldn't, her nose running, her mouth wide open, her eyes frantic.

'Stop it! Stop it!' Joan shouted, shaking her.

Her body was stiff, the screams increasing as Joan stared at her. Then, without thinking, Joan slapped Grace as hard as she could. She saw her head jerk, the screaming turned off.

Exhausted, Grace's dropped her head down. Joan led her to a seat. Breathing deeply several times, Grace then looked up at her friend. Recognition came back uncertainly.

'*Joan?* Joan, is it you?'

She nodded. 'Come to my house for a while. I'll help you get back on your feet.'

'I don't want to get back on my feet,' Grace replied dully. 'I want to fall down and stay there. I want to die where I fall –'

'You don't. That's not like you, Grace. Come on, you can fight back. You always do.'

'Why?' she asked listlessly. 'Why should I?'

'Because you're special,' Joan told her. 'You always were and you still are. You've got ambition, a life to live.'

Grace turned her head away. 'I wanted Daniel; that was all I wanted.'

'No, you want more than that. You want to be someone.'

'I *was* someone! I was important to him,' Grace cried desperately. 'He loved me.'

'I know, I know that –'

'I've lost my man, I've lost him.'

Quickly Joan kneeled down in front of her. 'Listen to me, Grace, you have to go on. *You have to*. Daniel wouldn't want to see you like this.'

Her voice was a whisper. 'I can't go on.'

'You can and you will.'

'I *can't*,' Grace repeated. 'My benefactors are halving my income, Joan. I have to get back to work and make up the shortfall – but I can't. I don't want to leave the house any more. I don't want to live without Daniel . . .' She snatched her hands away from Joan and folded her arms, tears falling unnoticed. 'I should have married him when he first asked me. But I asked him to wait. I made him wait for years . . . I wanted to bring something to him, not come to the marriage like a poor relation. I went to see his mother, you know.' She stared blindly into Joan's face. 'She was a bitch; tried to buy me off. She thought I was a whore . . . We weren't lovers at first . . . we waited.' Grace's eyes fixed on the memory. 'When we did make love it was so natural, like it was right all along. I should have married him when he asked me . . .' Grace repeated. 'I would be Mrs Daniel Goodman now, not just Grace Ellis. I'm thirty, Joan, thirty years old, and what have I got to show for it? You've got a family, but what have I got?'

'Your work –'

'My work?' Grace said dully. 'What good is that? A

business doesn't hold you at night. A career doesn't listen to you. And what about that career, Joan? I'd have to work twice as hard as I did before the war to get it back on track.'

'But you can do it.'

'For how long?' Grace asked her and then fell silent.

Baffled, Joan looked at her and then frowned. It couldn't be what she suspected.

'You're not having a baby, are you?'

Grace nodded.

'Are you sure?'

'Yes.'

'How far gone?'

'Three months.'

Joan took in a breath. 'What d'you want to do about it?'

'What *can* I do?' Grace countered. 'Abort it? Never. This is Daniel's child, Daniel's and mine.'

'But you're on your own – how will you cope? You've got your father to look after and the money's going to be tight. Think about it, Grace. How could you manage to bring up a child?' She paused. Her voice grew emphatic as she continued.

'People will talk; they'll make your life hell. And what about your benefactors? Will they support you if they know you're an unmarried mother?'

'But I want Daniel's baby.'

'But you can't support it,' Joan replied pragmatically. 'Unless you go and see Daniel's mother again –'

'And ask for help? She wouldn't give it to me if she could. I can imagine her now – I bet she'd ask me if it was her son's child . . .' Grace chewed her thumb nail savagely. 'How long before I show?'

Joan stared at her.

'At about five months. Six, if you're lucky . . . You can't do it, Grace. A pregnancy's hard work, you have no idea what it takes out of you. Think about it, you'll be talked about, looked down on – an unmarried mother. People can't think of worse. Besides, if you go ahead with this, have you thought of the long-term consequences? If you have Daniel's child, he'll grow up without a name.'

'He'll be a bastard,' Grace said bluntly. 'Isn't that what you wanted to say?'

'All right, it's true. He'll be illegitimate. And what about you? What kind of man would take you like that?'

'I don't want another man! I only wanted Daniel,' Grace said, her hands agitated, fluttering uselessly. 'Why are you talking about some other man? What makes you think I'd want to ever get married now?'

'Because people change, and you will too. You think you'll never want anyone else, but you're only thirty, Grace. You've a long life to live alone.'

'I can do it. Anyway, I won't be alone, I'll have his child.'

'Children aren't companions!' Joan snapped, exasperated. 'They grow up and leave you. Unless you hang on to them and make them guilty for wanting to live their own lives.'

An image of Lucy Goodman rose up in front of Grace's eyes. She had clung to her son maniacally – every thought, every action centred round Daniel, and what his mother wanted from him. Grace had seen what it had done to the man she loved. Did she really want to inflict such unhappiness on an innocent child?

She didn't, but she also knew that she couldn't abort Daniel's baby. Having grown up with the stigma of her mother's behaviour, it even seemed poetic justice that Grace would follow in her footsteps. Oh, she had fought against her background, but in the end some shadow of Miller Lane had finally fallen over her life.

'I have to have this baby.'

'Twaddle!' Joan replied. 'You want to hold on to Daniel through his child. It's understandable – I'd probably feel the same myself – but you can't go ahead with it. You know how it is Grace: a woman who has a child out of wedlock is finished. You'll never be able to hold your head up again. People will point at you and gossip – and later they'll point at your child. You'll spend the rest of your life trying to live down the name they'll give you. And you won't manage it. Do you think you'll be able to run your business the same? Who would take you seriously? Your career, your dream, is *over* if you go ahead with this.'

Grace looked down at the cup of tea in front of her, growing cold. Everything that Joan said was true. She *would* be ostracized if she had the baby; she *would* have to go it alone from then on. But hadn't she always? Hadn't she managed to look after her father and herself since she was a child? Hadn't she started her business despite the episode with Elmer Shaw? Hadn't she found her own staff, her own customers, her own outlets?

Joan was wrong, Grace wouldn't be cut off – because she had never belonged. What punishment could people inflict on her? She belonged to no clubs, no cliques. Her world had been her home, her friendships had been with Joan and Geoffrey – and she had loved, and lost, Daniel. But not entirely. By having his child she would keep a part of him for ever.

His mother might think she had won, but she would be wrong. It was true that her son would never marry

Grace Ellis, but she would have his child. Grace would have the only living, breathing remembrance of Daniel Goodman.

She could do it, Grace thought. This child would be born and she would provide for it somehow.

'How long did you say it was before I would look pregnant?'

Joan sighed. 'Six months – well, three as you're already three months gone. But that's only if you're lucky. You could show a lot sooner.'

'Did you?'

'Nah,' Joan admitted, tapping her flat stomach. 'I nearly got to popping them out before I showed – and then I just looked like a snake who'd swallowed an orange.'

Grace took Joan's hand. 'I've not got long then – until August.'

Joan frowned. 'Not got long for what?'

'To get the business sorted. To get it up and running properly again before everyone knows I'm pregnant. My benefactors are still giving me half the money, that's a good start.'

Joan took in her breath. Grace never knew when she was beaten.

'Where are you going to find the rest of the money?'

'I don't know yet,' Grace admitted. 'I *can't* think about failing, Joan. I have to succeed. I've got responsibilities – my father and my child.'

'Don't make decisions now. You're grieving for Daniel, you can't think straight.'

'You're wrong! This is the time I know exactly what to do. I have to sort everything out before people find out about the baby. I can't give anyone an excuse not to help.' She paused, thinking ahead. 'We have to get the evening shift started up again. D'you think Geoffrey would want to come back to work for me?'

Joan grimaced. 'Need you ask?'

'Even when he knows about the baby?'

'Grace, you could murder everyone on Park Road and Geoffrey would say he'd done it.' Joan looked Grace in the eyes. 'I could do with a bit of work myself actually. Tom's not got himself back in a job yet and the kids cost money.'

'You want to work with me again?' Grace said incredulously.

'Well, only if you want me to.'

'I'm sorry.'

'What for? You're not going to offer me a job?'

'No! I'm sorry for the way I treated Tom,' Grace admitted. 'I didn't understand, Joan, and after our argument I missed you so much.'

'I missed you too, you silly cow.'

A moment opened its arms between them.

'An angel passing over.'

Joan frowned. 'What?'

'It's an expression Daniel told me about. They say that when a comfortable silence falls between friends an angel passes over.' She gripped Joan's hands tightly, her face flushed with colour. 'It'll be like it was before, I promise. Like it was before the war, before we quarrelled.'

'Yeah, like old times.' Joan replied, ''cept for the fact that you're knocked up and I'm skint.'

'Hey, we did OK then. But this time I'm going to take the Auden Line to the top. You watch me,' Grace said, the old ambition flaring up like a pilot light. 'Nothing will stop me; no one will stop me. I've got nothing to lose, have I? In fact, I might as well make a virtue out of being an outsider – because when people know about the baby, the outside is where I'm going to be. But I'm going to succeed, Joan – and God help anyone who stands in my way.'

Chapter Thirty-Two

It was harder than she had thought possible, to outlive her child. Now slightly stooped, Lucy Goodman walked into Daniel's old rooms and sat down heavily on the bed. All her years of planning had come to nothing; her son was dead. There would be no marriage to Amy Thornton, no grandchildren, no companions for her old age. She had lost him finally.

The business interests she had turned over to Daniel's second in command. A sound man, he would continue to follow her son's way of working – and, better, he would do whatever she said. The money would continue to pile up and she would continue to live at The Lockgate. On her own.

Her cruelty had been a direct reaction to his death. It would have cost her nothing to inform Grace Ellis of the date of the funeral, but she had never forgiven her for their argument. The woman had threatened to take her son away from her – but she too had lost him. Lucy had been so certain that she could have frightened or bought the woman off, but some force beyond both of them had dictated that neither woman would keep Daniel Goodman.

Unreasonably Lucy had blamed Grace. It wasn't her fault, but she wanted someone to carry the brunt of her rage and Grace was convenient. She hated Grace Ellis with every cell of her body, could remember how she looked, the cut of her clothes, the sound of her voice. Grace Ellis had loved her son; she had thought she was good enough for him; she had believed she could take Daniel away.

Days after her son's death Lucy had heard how badly Grace had taken the news. There was no feeling of pity. *She* was his mother – how dare the Ellis woman mourn for Daniel? She had loved him for only a little while, whilst his mother had loved him since the day he was born.

But that hadn't been enough, had it? Daniel had changed sides again, Lucy reasoned blindly, just as he had done when he was a child. He had picked another woman to love, just as he had picked a gardener's boy to spend time with instead of his mother.

She wanted to punish them both – Grace *and* her son. After all, hadn't Daniel left her just as his father had done before? ... Grief took shape inside Lucy Goodman and pushed out any remaining compassion. So when she heard about Grace's distress and then about her benefactors cutting back on her finance, she was triumphant. How could that upstart think she was someone? She was nothing, nothing. And before long Grace Ellis would have nothing.

Her loathing and spite growled inside her; she longed for gossip, to hear that her rival was ill, ruined. And for a while it seemed as though Lucy Goodman had her wish. Grace Ellis was brought to her knees. Then luck – in Lucy's eyes – dealt her a trump card.

She had been going through her son's belongings and giving away his clothes. It was too painful to see empty suits and unworn coats. After she had cleared Daniel's wardrobes, Lucy had finally turned to his paperwork, tackling a job the solicitors had urged her to undertake earlier.

It was then that she'd found Daniel's new will. It was all clearly stated so that there should be no mistake. Her son had left five thousand pounds of his own savings to

Grace Ellis. That, and his car – which still remained in one of the garages of The Lockgate.

The will was legal and witnessed, the solicitor from some firm in London. That was lucky, Lucy thought. If Daniel had used their local firm it would have been far more difficult to destroy it. If anyone saw it – especially her legal advisors – Lucy would have to honour her dead son's wishes – to pass over the money and the car to Grace Ellis. Lucy would see her rival triumph, see her business flourish – be forced to watch her dead son rescue his lover.

No, she wouldn't, Lucy thought. Memories of her husband came back for the first time in years – that, and the joy the birth of their son had brought them. Was she really still the same woman? Lucy thought incredulously. Was she the woman who had joked about having a baby at such a late age? *The old cat's kitten.*

She turned, catching sight of herself in a mirror on the wall. Her hair had greyed, her mouth turned down at the sides, glasses hardly disguising the calculating eyes. Once she had been plump, full-faced, a pretty woman with a light manner. Guests had come to The Lockgate and stayed for house parties. She had had food sent from Manchester and London, smoked salmon from Scotland. She had been alive. Once. A wife. Once. A mother. Once.

But now she was as dead as her husband and her son. And she had, in her hands, the means to destroy her rival once and for all. Grace Ellis wasn't going to profit from her son's death. Lucy wasn't going to stand by and see her spend Daniel's money. She couldn't bare to think of Grace touching Daniel's car or driving around Lydgate talking about how they had been planning to marry.

No, Lucy thought, if she destroyed this will no one

314

would ever know how much Daniel had felt for Grace Ellis. Without this written proof she might have been exaggerating, making something out of nothing. After all, who would know for sure? Grace Ellis might brag of their love, but who really knew if it was anything more than a wartime romance? Some idle flirtation until Daniel settled down with a woman from his own class.

But if people heard about his will they would know that he had loved her. They would look at Grace Ellis in a different light, even respect her. Had Daniel lived she would have been Mrs Goodman, the heir to The Lockgate. No! No one must know, Lucy decided. *No one.*

The papers were light in her hands and tore easily, scraps falling onto the carpet. When she had finished she bent down stiffly and picked up every dropped fragment, then tucked all the pieces into the pocket of her dress.

No one would ever better her. No one alive, or dead.

Three weeks after Joan went to see Grace the night shift was back functioning at St Andrew's Place. Tilly Sugden – recently widowed – Mary Wells, Enid Taylor and Ivy Morris were working full time again, Joan helping out in the office. The vacancy left by Aaron was filled by his second in command, Brian Lawley, who hired his own assistants, newly qualified, ambitious and fresh from college. Solar Giversky and Geoffrey were back in their old jobs, Solar looking over quality control, Geoffrey pressing the long-unused van back into service.

In the mornings Grace could hear the coughing of the engine and the sound of the choke, the occasional ominous sight of smoke coming from the exhaust. Postwar Oldham was grim, people unwilling to invest in such a town, the jobs Grace offered much in demand.

But her own funds were getting very low and she knew she needed money fast. Her benefactors cutbacks had hit Grace hard. Then news came that Violet Spencer had had a stroke.

'Out cold on the floor she were, dead to the world . . .' Mary Wells confided, Ivy watching her avidly.

'Were she dead?'

'Nah! Just paralysed.'

Joan overheard the conversation and walked over to the bench where the women were working. 'Was that Violet Spencer you were talking about?'

Mary nodded, her broad face triumphant. Mary loved gossip, the more gruesome the better.

'There were blood everywhere –'

'What about her sister?'

'She screamed when she saw her –'

Joan folded her arms and pulled a face. 'Hang on a minute. How the hell do you know what went on?'

Mary shifted her feet. 'Well, anyone would scream, finding someone smashed to death at the bottom of the stairs.'

'I thought you said she wasn't dead?'

'*Nearly* dead,' Mary replied, determined to regain the drama. 'Apparently her sister's looking after her now. With some nurse, called in from Manchester, they say. A huge woman with a moustache.'

Joan rolled her eyes. 'To go with her hump back, I suppose?'

Thoughtfully Joan relayed the information back to Grace. A full-time nurse would be very expensive for the Spencer sisters, she said. It would put a strain on anyone's finances, so perhaps it wasn't so surprising that Grace's *anonymous* benefactors had had to cut back on their generosity.

'That's why,' Joan said hurriedly. 'To pay for the medical bills.'

'Sounds more than likely,' Grace agreed. 'Poor Miss Spencer –'

'Poor nothing! She's got a nurse and you've got a problem. Money's tight, Grace, I don't have to tell you that. And it's getting tighter everyday.'

'I know!' Grace replied impatiently. 'I have to find another investor. I'm going to try London and Manchester. I'll try London first. That's where all the big make-up houses are.'

'But won't they be investing in Southern interests?'

'That I have to find out,' Grace replied, looking through the doorway as she heard voices, and starting in surprise.

She hadn't seen Elsa James for years and it took her an instant to recognize the glamorous befurred figure standing in front of her. The lovely Elsa had been in London, the rumour mill said. Holed up in some flat in Kensington. Certainly – beautifully dressed in a lilac suit and small hat perched on one side of her exquisite head – Elsa looked as though she had fallen on her feet.

Grace glanced over to Joan, who took the hint at once.

'I'll be off then,' she said, walking out reluctantly and closing the door behind her.

More than a little curious, Grace motioned Elsa to a seat. She smiled coolly, crossed her silk-clad legs and took out a cigarette, lighting it and inhaling the tobacco luxuriantly.

'I suppose you're wondering why I'm here.'

Grace didn't reply. The sight of Elsa James brought back the memory of Elmer Shaw and she felt wary, on her guard.

'I wanted to see you, Grace,' Elsa went on calmly. 'I have a proposition for you.'

Had Shaw sent her? Grace trusted neither of them, knowing that Elsa had been jealous of Shaw's interest and knowing that Elmer Shaw hated her for rejecting him. Yet Grace was no longer a gullible girl. She had seen and experienced a good deal in the years which had followed her encounter with the likes of Elmer Shaw.

'What kind of proposition?'

Elsa flicked the ash off her cigarette into the glass bowl on Grace's desk. She was – she had to admit – impressed by her. Who would have thought that the mill girl who had come to her for help so long ago would turn out to be a woman to be reckoned with? Elsa had expected to find Grace Ellis battered by the loss of her man and much of her finances – but here she was, looking grimly determined, not in the least cowed.

'The reassessment of your rent is coming up soon, isn't it?'

How did she know? Grace wondered. 'Yes, why?'

'Who owns St Andrew's Place?'

'The Lion Corporation.'

'Well, they *did*. But unfortunately the Lion Corporation has been bought out.'

Grace shrugged. 'By whom?'

'The Lion Corporation is now owned by our mutual friend Elmer Shaw.'

This was unwelcome news.

'So?' Grace asked, trying to sound calm although the information had shaken her.

'So Mr Shaw no longer wants to rent out St Andrew's Place. He doesn't want tenants any more.'

Grace could feel her mouth dry. Every time she thought she was getting back on her feet, something happened.

Property was difficult to find, rent soaring after the war. She couldn't afford any more strain on her finances. Jesus, Grace thought, what the hell was she going to do now?

'Did you come here just to rub my nose in it, Elsa?'

The woman blinked, surprised: 'I told you – I have a proposition to make.'

'Which is?'

'If you give me a cut of your business, I'll make certain that Elmer Shaw doesn't have the chance to throw you out of this place.'

'A cut of my business?' Grace repeated disbelievingly. 'No, I don't think so. I think I might just call Mr Shaw and talk to him myself. See how he likes his *girlfriend* doing business behind his back.'

'Don't try and bluff me!' Elsa replied impatiently. 'Shaw would do anything do carve you up. He wouldn't spit on you if you were on fire, and you know it.'

'So why are you trying to get one over on him? I thought you were on a good wicket there. He's been looking after you for years, set you up nice and comfy. Why kill the goose which lays the golden egg, Elsa?'

In response she stood up and then – to Grace's amazement – took off her jacket and silk blouse. Standing in the finest underwear. Elsa turned her back to Grace. The marks were deep and livid purple, obviously not made with the hand but some stick or bar. They had cut through the skin in places, blood caked in the weals, bruising darkening in livid blotches.

'Dear God.'

Elsa pulled her clothes back on and regained her seat.

'I've put up with that bastard for years. Ignored his other women, the way he treated me, the insults. I took his money and I made my choice. But lately he's been under a lot of pressure and the other night he struck out at me. Not just a slap, a real beating.' She lit another cigarette, her eyes flinty. 'It was one beating too many. I want my revenge on Elmer Shaw now – and I intend to get it.'

Grace didn't doubt it for an instant. But she *did* doubt that Elsa could be trusted.

'Where am I supposed to come into all this?'

'If I make sure that you can keep these premises, you can build up the business again. And you want to do that, don't you? You need to make money fast – if what I heard about your benefactors is true.'

'And in return,' Grace said carefully, 'you want a cut of my business?'

'It seems fair. Without my help you won't have a business to give me a cut of.'

Grace's voice was pure steel. 'How can I possibly trust you?'

'You've no choice.'

'Oh, I think I have.'

Elsa raised her eyebrows. 'Really?

'I don't need your help, Elsa,' Grace said coldly, getting to her feet and walking over to Elsa's chair. 'In fact, I'd like you to leave now.'

This was not what Elsa had expected and her eyes flickered. She had heard that Grace was struggling and had expected her to jump at the chance of help.

'You're making a mistake –'

'I would be, if I made a deal with you.'

It was Elsa's turn to bluster. 'I can ruin Elmer Shaw. I can bring that bastard to his knees.'

'You're bluffing.'

'You try me.'

'*How* could you ruin him?' Grace asked sharply.

'I'm telling you I could.'

'I don't believe you!' Grace snapped. 'How are you going to do it? And how are you going to make sure that I don't get thrown out of here on my ear?'

'I'm going to shop him to the police.'

Grace took in a breath, almost winded. 'The *police*?'

Elsa nodded. 'He's been up to a lot of things during the war which they would love to know about. Elmer should get ten years, if there's any justice.'

'But what about his property?'

'Oh, that'll be repossessed. But in the meantime, they'll want to keep things running the way they always have done. They'll go after Elmer and then sort out the details later.'

Grace stared at her: 'Which means that I could get thrown out of here later.'

'Not if you bought St Andrew's Place.'

'Bought it? How in God's name could I buy this place?'

Elsa looked up to Grace, her face bland. 'Oh, come on, this is a dump. No one would want it apart from you. It needs God knows how much spending on it. You want it for a factory, you *need* to keep your workrooms here. Anywhere else would be too expensive – the rental would cripple you, especially now. But why worry? You could buy this place for a song – when Elmer's out of picture.'

'How? They would freeze his assets. St Andrew's Place would still belong to him when he got out –'

'No, it wouldn't. Because it's mine.'

'You own St Andrew's Place?'

Elsa nodded triumphantly. 'Yes, I do. I said I wanted to get rid of you as a tenant – and he bought it. Hook, line and sinker.' She laughed throatily. 'He thought I was still jealous of you after all these years. He likes to think that I care about him. It tickles his vanity. Besides, he always wanted to see you broken.' Her eyes hardened. 'So Elmer signed over St Andrew's Place to me – little realizing that when he's banged up in gaol I'll sell it. I *could* sell it to anyone – but I thought I'd give you the first option. Now, isn't that worth paying me fifteen per cent of your business?'

Grace stared down at her. 'We haven't mentioned percentages.'

'So let's start,' Elsa responded coolly.

'You want fifteen per cent of my business, as well as the purchase price for this place?'

'Well, business is business,' Elsa said deftly.

'And blackmail is blackmail,' Grace retorted. 'What you're actually saying is that you'll let me have the chance to buy this place if I pay you a percentage of my business?'

'Look, I'm tipping you off in advance. If I hadn't come here you wouldn't have even known that Shaw bought out the Lion Corporation. I could have shopped him, then sold this place from under your feet. Fifteen per cent is letting you off cheap and you know it.'

Grace moved back to her seat and sat down, crossing her legs. She could sense that Elsa was beginning to sweat and pretended to scribble down some figures on the pad in front of her. A couple of minutes later, she looked up.

'Ten per cent plus what the premises are really worth, and it's a deal.'

'Too cheap!' Elsa said flatly. 'I want fifteen per cent.'

Grace tapped her fingernails on the top of the desk. The deal was fair, but she didn't want to give Elsa any more than ten per cent. Yet she didn't want to lose St Andrew's Place either. She had to secure it for herself, and her future. Yet how could she afford to give Elsa James even ten per cent of the business *and* the purchase price of St Andrew's Place?

Then she had an idea.

'Look, Elsa,' Grace said, leaning across the desk towards her. 'I have a score of my own to settle with Mr Shaw. What are you going to do after you've shopped him?'

She shrugged. 'I dunno. Try my luck elsewhere.'

'Another man?'

'What else?'

'I suppose you'd like someone rich, someone powerful?'

'Who wouldn't?' Elsa asked suspiciously.

'You're not likely to meet him in Oldham, though, are you?'

'You managed it,' Elsa replied. 'It was a pity about Daniel Goodman dying like that. You could have scooped a real prize there.'

It was no good trying to explain to Elsa James that she had loved Daniel. All Elsa thought about was money, the means to buy herself a ticket out of the North. Permanently.

Grace struggled to keep the loathing out of her voice. 'If I was to suggest a way by which your face would become famous all over the country, would you be interested?'

'What?'

'People would see you in magazines, on boardings. In Manchester, London – even abroad, in time. Think of the men who would see you, Elsa. You couldn't hope to reach so many on your own. You could be the woman everyone wants to know ... I can give you that.'

'Give me *what* exactly?' Elsa asked, her eyes burning with interest.

'I'll make you the face of the Auden Line,' Grace replied. 'You'll be my model, the image on my packaging. I'll give you ten per cent of the business, but no crazy purchase price for St Andrew's Place. Instead you'll have the chance to advertise your wares everywhere.'

Grace could see that the thought appealed to Elsa's vanity. Slowly, she ran her tongue over her bottom lip to moisten it before answering.

'I want a contract.'

'Fine.'

'For five years.'

'Two – and then we review the situation.' Grace's voice became brusque. 'Oh, think about it, Elsa! How else could you become famous? Your face everywhere – Elmer Shaw would see it and burn with anger. Who knows who else might see it? Photographers, film producers – they've discovered a lot of movie stars that way. And you're a beauty, Elsa. The sky's the limit for you.'

She stared at Grace fixedly. 'Ten per cent and a two-year contract?'

Grace nodded. The bait was on the hook; all she had to do now was to draw it in.

'Ten per cent of the business and a two-year contract as the Auden Line model.' She paused to allow Elsa time to consider. 'Two years might easily become five, Elsa – if you let me have St Andrew's Place for a song.'

Frowning, Elsa stood up, grinding out her cigarette and picking up her bag. Her beauty was mesmeric, hair white gold, skin perfectly, virginally clear. Grace could see that face bringing her a fortune. No one needed to know what the woman was like; the image was every-thing. Her customers would buy her make-up believing that it would make them look like Elsa James.

They would look into those unfathomable blue eyes and see heaven where there was nothing. They would copy her style and never realize that the brain behind the face was greedy and cold. But what did it matter? Her greed, her need for revenge would keep the Auden Line afloat; she would, indirectly, feed Grace, Arthur and, in time, Daniel's child.

So, without hesitation, Grace put out her hand.

'Do we have a deal?'

Elsa hesitated and then nodded, taking Grace's hand and shaking it firmly.

'It's a deal,' she agreed.

'When do you go to the police about Shaw?'

'Now. I just wanted to get our business sorted before I went.' She paused at the door. 'He hit you too, didn't he?'

Grace flinched. '*What?*'

'Elmer, he came home that night when he had called on you and told me about it. Bragged about it. He said you'd made a play for him – but I knew he was lying.' She pointed to Grace's left cheek. 'You didn't have that scar when you were at the mill. Looks like we both carry Shaw's mark.'

Instinctively Grace touched her face.

'Don't worry,' Elsa went on calmly, 'Shaw's finished. Wait until the police get him. Wait until his wife finds out what he's been up to. I'll take a lot from men; God knows, I don't expect that much. But when Elmer Shaw beat me he lost more than his temper – he lost everything.'

Chapter Thirty-Three

'God,' Joan said, sobbing, 'that was the saddest film I've ever seen.'

Sighing, Grace glanced over to her. They had just been to a matinée of *Brief Encounter*, the cinema filled with the sound of snuffles and suppressed sobs as the story came to its climax. Ever the romantic, Joan had loved the film and looked at it as a welcome relief from the grind of everyday life.

Tom hadn't found work yet and the two children were left with Joan's mother every morning before Joan went in to work at St Andrew's Place. Joan wondered if a childhood spent at the Bell and Monkey was what she really wanted for her two daughters, but knew there was no option. Until Tom found work, she was the only one bringing money in.

'Trevor Howard's so sensitive in the part. He loved her so much . . .'

'He was a married man,' Grace replied deftly. 'He wasn't that sensitive or he wouldn't have made a play for her in the first place.'

'Philistine,' Joan muttered, dropping into silence.

Surreptitiously, Grace touched her stomach. There *was* a small bump, but one she could still disguise with clever clothing. No one knew about the baby yet except Joan. But before long the secret would inevitably be out.

The idea of going to the film had been Joan's, in a vain attempt to stop Grace worrying about the business. Trips to London had been useless: no one wanted to invest and the last excursion to Manchester had met with complete failure. Time was moving on, Joan thought, sliding her arm through Grace's as they walked down Union Street. The business was going to fold unless Grace did something soon.

Joan had been in two minds about Elsa James's involvement, but when Grace explained the situation Joan had had to admit that their deal was a good one. Not that she trusted Elsa; she was too beautiful and cunning to be good – and her ruthless streak was dangerous.

However, she *was* true to her word in this instance. Elsa shopped Elmer Shaw to the police and had had the satisfaction of seeing him taken into custody. It would be a long haul before Elmer would come to trial, but Elsa wanted no slip-ups. Shaw couldn't be allowed to get off the hook. So she had taken the precaution of keeping copies of many damning documents and knew that – however good or expensive his solicitor was – Elmer Shaw didn't have a cat in hell's chance.

People disliked profiteers, the spivs who had made money during the war out of other people's hardship. Elsa was aware that Elmer would not get off lightly and if she ever regretted her action she didn't show it.

Instead she revelled in the idea of being the model for the Auden Line. It appealed to her vanity to have her photograph taken and she spent much time looking at the pristine images of her face. Otherwise, she had little interest in the business and kept out of the way, only badgering Grace to know who the next investor would be.

Grace would like to have known that too.

'I have to think of someone else to approach,' she said

to Joan now, stopping at the crossing and glancing down at her stomach. 'Does it show yet?'

'For the third time today, no.'

'I feel tired.'

'Well, at least you haven't been puking everywhere,' Joan replied cheerfully. 'When I was pregnant with the girls I couldn't stop throwing up.'

Grace changed the subject hurriedly. 'We need money fast.'

'Oh God, not again –'

'I *have* find an investor. And quick,' Grace continued, walking with Joan back to St Andrew's Place.

A letter was waiting, headed 'Simeon Grant, Ladies wear' – followed by an address in Manchester.

> Dear Miss Ellis,
>
> I believe you recently saw a colleague of mine, Mr Thomas Atkinson, who was unfortunately unable to help you. I have spoken at length to Mr Atkinson and would now like to have a meeting with you concerning your business.
>
> Please telephone the above number for an appointment.
>
> Yours sincerely,
> Simeon Grant

'Well, would you believe it!' Joan said when she had read the letter over Grace's shoulder. 'You've been running around looking for someone, and they've come to you. Your luck's turning, kiddo. This might be the break you've been looking for.'

Simeon Grant was struggling to hang a dress onto an already full rail in the warehouse off Davies Street,

Manchester. His stocky form pushed until the dress finally slid into place amongst its neighbours and then he stood back, re-counting the outfits on the rack. He had managed – through good bargaining and a handy network of gossips – to acquire some fine fabrics cheap and, working his staff long hours, he had turned out a mass of clothes which would sell from Kendal Milne to Tommy Fields market. Simeon was no snob; he wanted sales, not kudos.

He expected hard work from his army of staff and paid as well as anyone else in the rag trade area of Manchester. Long hours and attention to detail had paid off. Nothing escaped Simeon's eye and he had honed his instinct for cost-cutting; tissue paper – so treasured – was re-ironed after use to be put into service again. Dresses which had not sold were remodelled, the new fashions showing how much women craved for glamour after the hardships and shortages of the war.

Films had played their part too; every woman wanted to look like Joan Crawford or Constance Bennett, with the hard-edged elegance of lean lines and shoulder pads. After being forced into the uniform of the factory worker or the land girl, women wanted to look like women again. They wanted sex appeal, fantasy – and they wanted it *now*.

Never one to miss a trend, Simeon met the demand quicker than most, looking at the magazines and film posters and trying to recreate the look of the rich in London and Hollywood. He had even managed to find an outlet in Holland which supplied him with costume jewellery; the long strings of pearls so loved by Chanel, the faux flowers worn as brooches or hair ornaments.

He had always made money because he was successful at spotting trends and had an unerring instinct for what women wanted to wear – and how they wanted to look. This insight had come from his growing up surrounded by a widowed mother and five sisters – Simeon's comics mixing with film magazines, his *Flash Gordon* lying next to the shiny image of Jean Harlow.

Early on, his sisters had asked for his advice because they realized that their brother had an unusual gift: he knew how to make them look good. And why? Because Simeon adored women. He loved how they looked, talked, walked, acted; he admired their courage and their wit; their guile and goodness. In his personal harem of femininity he learned everything about the female psyche by absorption – and still retained his own masculinity.

The war had decided it didn't want him because of his poor hearing. Simeon – strongly built, with dark eyes, a hard jawline and a cleft in his chin – looked as though he could handle himself anywhere, but he was, in fact, almost deaf in his left ear. He compensated for the loss by turning his head slightly to the right to catch what people said, and he missed little. His natural intelligence and quick thinking masked the deficiency so well that on meeting him no one would have realized his handicap.

'Jesus!' he snapped suddenly, pushing the rack and finding one of its wheels sticking in a floorboard. 'Move this bloody thing!'

A couple of workers materialized at once and pushed the rack into the warehouse. Simeon walked back into his office and sitting down at his desk. The chaos was absolute; he mistrusted tidiness and only felt comfortable when he couldn't see the surface of anything in the room. Papers were cluttered with empty coffee cups, drawings smeared with cigarette ash, and two telephones covered in the chalk he used for marking out patterns on material.

'People who are tidy have no creativity,' he'd say bluntly. 'A tidy mind means a tight arse.'

Hurriedly rummaging through the stack nearest to him, Simeon drew out a magazine and looked at it for the third time that morning. His dark eyebrows drew together as he tapped his front tooth with one of his fingernails. Well, he knew about clothes and he'd made a lot of money from them, but he wanted a new challenge and this might be it. He read the page carefully. 'Make-up. How to Look Your Best on a Budget' it said, followed by a series of photographs of women in various outfits – each with a face to match. Make-up was altering – eyebrows arched, but less plucked, although the mouth was still full and sensual. Mascara now darkened the eyelashes to give a sultry look, and rouge enhanced the cheekbones in a obvious, stylized way.

Make-up ... Simeon thought again, remembering what his old friend Atkinson had told him about some woman in Oldham running a cosmetic business. She had gone to him for backing, but Atkinson hadn't wanted to know.

Stupid old bugger, Simeon thought affectionately, he would refuse a drink in the desert. Could never see a golden opportunity when it stood in front of him ... But *he* could. Which was why he had written to Grace Ellis and then spent the remainder of the afternoon finding out what he could about her. Which was interesting. She had had long-term backing, but that had been reduced. Now she wanted to carry on building on the profit she had made before the war. Apparently Grace Ellis was also ambitious and unmarried.

Not that the latter interested Simeon. He had a girl-friend – well, he had several – and no real interest in settling down at thirty-five, forty, fifty, or even sixty. He had had enough of family life as a child to be sure that he wanted no more of it. His sisters provided all the entertainment on that score; all married, most producing babies at regular intervals. Simeon was the adored uncle who brought presents, played around on all fours, and invested money for each of them in trust funds.

But have children himself? No, that wasn't what he wanted. No children, no wife. No, thanks. Just a vast extended family who offered affection, amusement and company – in measured doses. No one too close, for too long. And what he feared most Simeon had taken pains to assure he would never suffer. He would *never* be lonely.

'Miss Ellis is here,' Simeon's secretary announced.

'So show her in! Show her in!'

The first sight Grace had of Simeon Grant was of his backside as he bent down to retrieve something from under his desk. The office was a shambles, blinds half up, half down, grime thick as butter on the windows, the sounds of telephones ringing incessantly in the office outside.

Hearing the sound of Grace's approach, Simeon crawled out from under the desk.

'Hello there, sit down.'

She did so, crossing her legs. A pigeon eyed her beadily from the window ledge outside.

'You've done well, Miss Ellis, but you could do better. I like the sound of your business.'

'Thank you. I –'

'You need money – well, that's what any business needs if it's to make *more* money.' The phone rang next

332

to him. 'Not now!' he bellowed, turning back to Grace. 'My friend Atkinson said that you wanted someone to invest in you.'

She nodded. 'That's right. If you're interested, I've brought some accounts for you to see.'

'I don't go on figures, just hunches!' Simeon said shortly. He was hurrying, busy, busy, energy coming off him like a colour. Red as fire. 'I've had you checked out and what you're doing. I wanted to get into make-up myself. Well, not personally!' he said, laughing. 'As a business, you understand.'

She was finding it difficult to interrupt his flow.

'Mr Grant –'

'Simeon, call me Simeon, everyone does.'

'Simeon, I do need money, yes. I've worked out how much the business needs. I wouldn't expect someone to invest for no return.'

'You had benefactors for that.'

'They've helped me for years,' she agreed. 'But their support is now halved. I'm not complaining; without them I'd never have got this far. They always helped me.'

'Who are they?'

'I don't know. I've tried to find out from their solicitors and mine, but they want to stay anonymous. I have an idea who they are, but I'm not certain.'

'How romantic,' he said briskly. 'But now you need someone else. Someone with more cash to invest?'

She nodded again. 'I'd be willing – for the sum mentioned in those papers – to offer a twenty-five-per-cent interest in the Auden Line. I don't want to be beholden to anyone any more. I want to work *with* someone, not for them. I need a business partner, in fact.' She pointed to the envelope in front of him. 'Everything's set out in those papers, Mr Grant, if you would just take a look at them.'

All at once he seemed irritated. He didn't want to look at the bloody papers, his solicitor would do that. He just wanted to get a feel of the idea. Did it fire him up? Did she? Could he work with her, make money with her? Did he want to spend the time? Did he want her as a business partner?

'Pardon?' Simeon said suddenly, turning his head to the right to catch what Grace said.

'I said that I could make the Auden Line a real success.'

'Don't doubt it,' he replied, banging his hands down on the desk for emphasis.

'So will you look at the figures and tell me what you think?'

Getting to his feet, Simeon walked round the room and then tried to open the window, but it was stuck, the unseasonable autumn heat making the office clammy. His movements were rapid as though he had to keep active to burn off an energy which might otherwise consume him.

Intrigued, Grace watched him. He was, she realized, an attractive man, his dark colouring and strong features giving him a tough image. But his relentless activity, his staccato way of speaking, was exhausting. God, she prayed to herself, please let him say yes. Please. I've nowhere else to go.

'Just tell me,' Simeon said, leaning down over her, 'what is the most important thing in life?'

'What?'

'The most important thing in life – what is it?'

She frowned. What was he talking about? Was he mad?

334

'Fulfilment.'

'Fulfilment . . .' Simeon repeated softly, walking back to his desk.

She hadn't said love, money, fortune; she had said fulfilment. That was good, Simeon thought, he liked that, it was an answer which showed intelligent, level-headed sense.

'How old are you?'

'Thirty.'

'And you're single?'

She winced. 'I was engaged to Daniel Goodman, but he died before we could marry.'

This was news, Simeon thought: Grace Ellis had been about to marry into the mighty Goodmans. Interesting. And she was still suffering from her loss too, that much was obvious. He didn't like to think of death. His eldest sister had lost her husband in the war and had been nearly destroyed by it. But his sister had a family around her and monetary support from him. She had backup, no financial worries. Not like Grace Ellis.

'I'm sorry for your loss,' he said genuinely.

She nodded, her hands resting on her lap, only inches away from Daniel's unborn child. 'Many people lost their loved ones.'

'Which doesn't make it any easier,' Simeon replied. Then, changing the subject: 'I feel like a gamble, Miss Ellis.'

'You do?'

'I do. I feel like being reckless, rash and impulsive,' he grinned, his teeth large and white. 'Want to make a killing, Miss Ellis?'

'Need you ask, Mr Grant?'

Chapter Thirty-Four

It was done at the double, as was everything with Simeon. Within two weeks he had had his solicitor check the accounts of the Auden Line and then went over the books himself, just to make sure that nothing had been missed. He was glad that the deal could go ahead. He wanted a new challenge and was restless with the rag trade.

After the contract had been drawn up and signed, Simeon visited the workshop, for the first time, driving over early in the morning, arriving before eight to find Grace in the laboratory with Brian Lawley.

'Morning,' Simeon said briskly. 'Any food?'

Smiling Grace led him into the office and passed him a tin of biscuits. Simeon was immediately perturbed by the tidy space, although before long a scattering of crumbs on the floor marked out where he sat, and his morning newspaper, read and discarded, covered a side table.

St Andrew's Place was pretty much what he expected: a small factory/workshop with a laboratory off the main room, with storage space, two offices and a large garage – off which sealed boxes of cosmetics were piled up and labelled, ready for delivery.

'You've going to get a leak up in that roof any day now,' Simeon said, pointing up to the ceiling, 'and that van of yours is knackered.'

'Money's been short,' Grace replied evenly, 'I've had to buy the cosmetic ingredients with what there was available. And the packaging doesn't come cheap either.'

'Depends where you get it,' Simeon told her. 'I've a contact who can print up the labels for two-thirds the price you quoted on your accounts.'

'But is he any good?' Grace countered. 'It's all very well saving money, but if the stuff looks cheap no one will buy it. We want to give the expensive lines a run for their money. Anyone can do shoddy.'

Thoughtfully, Simeon kicked the van's back tyre.

'Get it fixed, we can afford it now,' he said. 'You need reliable transport. No good not being on time for deliveries.'

'What about the printing?'

He turned to look at her.

'You fix that,' he said simply. Her argument had been sound; cheap *wasn't* necessarily good. 'I want to meet the workers now.'

Tipped off, they were all waiting for him when Simeon got back to the workshop, some of the older women standing with folded arms, Solar watching the new arrival from the back of the room. On seeing Simeon enter with Grace, Ivy nudged Enid sharply with her elbow.

'Here comes the great white hope. Sodding men, who needs them? We were doing all right on our own.'

'We were about to lose the bloody place,' Joan hissed at her as she passed and walked over to Simeon.

Her expression veered between amusement and caution.

'So the cavalry's arrived at last.'

Simeon looked her up and down. 'So who are you? The Indian chief?'

'I'm Joan, Grace's oldest friend. I work here too – in fact I was here when the place opened.'

Simeon nodded abruptly, then turned to the rest of the workers.

337

'Miss Ellis and I are now partners in the Auden Line – she's not working for me and I'm not working for her. We're working together.'

His attention drifted suddenly as the swing door at the back opened. In walked Elsa, pausing for effect in the doorway. She was dressed in a cream summer suit, her hair piled on top of her head.

Raising her eyebrows, Grace glanced at Simeon.

'And this is Elsa James, the model for the Auden Line.'

Grace could see Elsa take in every aspect of Simeon Grant and work out, to the pound, what he was worth. His clothes, his watch, his cologne.

Not bad, Elsa thought, not bad at all. She had to hand it to Grace, she could sniff out money everywhere.

Enchanted, Simeon studied Elsa and then took her hand.

'With your face on our packaging, Miss James, I don't see how we could fail.'

Later, Enid couldn't stop sniggering about it.

'*With your face I don't see how we could fail . . .* Jesus!' she laughed, her plump cheeks shaking with mirth. 'What a bloody line! It was like watching two snakes eyeing each other up and wondering who'd be swallowed first.'

Mary Wells was laughing too, shaking her head at Ivy as the older woman jumped to her feet. With one hand on her hip Ivy struck a pose, fluttering her eyelashes, her top teeth missing, her voice a high falsetto.

'Ooh, Mr Grant, how could you . . . ? I'm not that sort of girl – and besides, five pounds isn't enough!'

In Grace's office Joan watched them, but she wasn't laughing, she was serious for once.

'Aren't you worried about Simeon and Elsa?'

Grace shrugged. 'Why? Because he's smitten? No, I'm not worried. Although I would have been if Elsa hadn't already sold me this place. No doubt she would have chucked me out and thrown in her lot with Simeon if she hadn't already committed herself.' She looked over to the lab where Ivy was dancing with a laughing Enid. 'If Simeon and Elsa want to have a fling, who cares? Elsa won't cross me. Remember, I still have the majority interest in the company and she likes the fame I've given her.'

'But what if she makes a play for Simeon?'

Grace raised her eyebrows. 'So what? Even if he becomes besotted with her it won't endanger my position.'

Moving over to the side table, Grace picked up the latest photographs taken of Elsa.

'These are really good. I want to see them on the new range. She has an incredible face.'

'It's your make-up,' Joan said peevishly. 'She'd look like a dog without it.'

'Oh, Joan!' Grace replied, laughing outright. 'Elsa's a beauty. That face could make our fortune. In fact, I'm going to Kendal Milne later in the week to see if they'll take our new line.' She stopped talking suddenly, her hands clenching her stomach. 'God . . . the pain.'

'Sit down,' Joan said hurriedly, settling Grace in her seat. 'You've got things organized now so you can afford to take it a bit easier. You've not got that long left before the baby's born.'

Grace's dark grey eyes fixed on Joan anxiously.

'I caught Ivy looking at my stomach this morning. She knows. Or suspects, at least.'

'Well, we knew you couldn't keep it a secret for ever.

You've only got eight weeks before it's due. God knows how you've managed to hide it so long.'

By clever dressing Grace thought, those useful swing coats. And the convenient weight loss she had suffered from worry . . . She breathed in deeply, tired with her pregnancy. Thank God the business had been organized in time.

'What's it like?'

Joan knew immediately what she meant. 'Painful. But when you hold your baby in your arms you don't remember what hell you went through.'

'I haven't picked a name,' Grace said wistfully.

'It comes with the kid,' Joan replied, sitting down next to her. 'They kind of name themselves.'

Grace nodded thoughtfully. 'You know, I've hardly thought about the baby until now.'

'You've had a lot on your mind.'

Grace nodded again, her hands moving over her stomach. Since she'd decided to get the business under way again there had been so little time to grieve for Daniel, or think of the coming child. Both had been pushed to the back of her mind. Harassed and anxious, Grace hadn't brooded on Daniel's death. But now – when she felt his child moving inside her – she thought of him.

And as she thought of him Grace remembered the first night they had made love. She had even revisited the ruined building in Manchester, but it had been boarded up, off limits. 'This Property is Condemned, Keep Out. Danger.' Danger, yes, there had been plenty of that. Danger which had killed Daniel, so soon before the war ended. If only he had managed to duck a little longer. He had been so lucky for so long, she had come to believe that he would be lucky for ever.

She would never want any other man, Grace thought. Who else *could* she want, apart from Daniel?

Why didn't I marry you when you first asked me? she thought helplessly. Dear God, *why*?

'Hey, Grace,' Joan asked anxiously, 'what's the matter?'

'I messed it all up, didn't I? God, I messed it all up so badly.'

'Ssshh,' Joan replied soothingly. 'We'll sort it out –'

Grace nodded, then straightened up in her seat, her voice firm again. 'Well, I can't go on ignoring it. I have to tell people about the baby. My father –'

'Your father doesn't understand anything. There's no point telling him.'

'I should tell Don.'

'Why? Everyone will know soon enough.'

Grace looked Joan in the face: 'Have you told any-one?'

She shook her head. 'You know me, compared to me the Sphinx is chatty.'

'Eight weeks,' Grace said, letting her hands run over the swell of her stomach again. 'In eight weeks I'm going to be a mother.' She took in another breath and then heaved herself to her feet. 'Well, there's no time to sit around. I need to get things ready. The baby will need a layette, a pram, nappies. We'll go shopping and get the back bedroom ready.' She glanced over to Joan and winked unexpectedly. 'It'll be OK, you know. I can do this.'

Pregnant! Lucy Goodman thought, horrified. That whore who had wanted to take her son away was pregnant. So she had tried the oldest trick in the book to catch Daniel, had she? Got herself in the family way. Lucy grimaced

341

at the expression. Grace Ellis was hardly going to have her child in a family environment, was she? She was on her own – and just look how long she'd tried to keep it a secret.

Still, you couldn't keep a child a secret for long. Many women had tried it and they had all failed. Grace Ellis was no better than a slut, Lucy thought. And sleeping with her son! Lucy stiffened. Maybe this bastard wasn't Daniel's, after all. Maybe Grace Ellis had tried to foist some other man's kid on to her son.

But much as she loathed Grace, Lucy Goodman knew better. Instinct told her that the child Grace was carrying was Daniel's. She didn't want to believe it, but she knew it was true. Her reactions were confusing; at first she could only think how common Grace Ellis was – then she realized she was going to be a grandmother. She would have a grandson, Daniel's child.

Excitement, unexpected and potent, flushed Lucy Goodman's cheeks. Her life wasn't over, not now. There was another member of the family to think of. But she would have to work it all out very carefully, talk to her solicitors and take advice. A bid of adoption would be made to Grace Ellis – how could she refuse when Lucy Goodman would be offering so much for the child's welfare? And a name. Of course Grace Ellis would be able to visit the infant, but the child had to be brought up at The Lockgate. It was the heir, after all.

Then another thought occurred to Lucy. She had been stupid. Yes, she had to admit it. If she had kept the will in which Daniel had left so much to Grace Ellis, it would have counted as proof, reinforced Lucy's claim on the baby. No man would benefit a woman in his will *unless* there was a firm commitment. And what had Lucy done? Destroyed the evidence.

Grace Ellis and she were enemies; there was only bad

342

blood between them. So how likely was it that Grace would willingly hand over her child? In fact, Grace could – and probably would – refuse to let her have anything to do with the infant. Angrily, Lucy rose to her feet, seeing her image reflected in the surfaces of the silver platters lined up along the sideboard.

She had lost her trump card by being reckless! If she had been magnanimous and let Grace Ellis have the money Daniel had left her, she could have kept an eye on the woman and found out about her coming grandchild. She should have made a friend of her – but she had been jealous and had cut off her own nose to spite her face. Now she was going to suffer for it. Her act of cruelty had managed to estrange Grace Ellis even further – and with her, the baby. Lucy's grandchild.

Frustrated, Lucy Goodman walked the floor, her image moving to and fro on the silver plates. She had to get her grandchild. There *had* to be a way . . . But how? Grace Ellis had gone into business with Simeon Grant; she had no money worries any longer. Incredibly, her business had survived and she no longer needed anyone to offer financial support.

But things might well change. When the baby was born Grace Ellis might start to feel the cold draught of people's disapproval; she might need a safe haven then. She wouldn't want the child to be thought of as a bastard – not if Lucy Goodman was around to acknowledge its parentage, give it a name and a background.

There was only one thing for it, Lucy thought, gritting her teeth. She would hate having to win over the woman she had seen for so long as her rival, but she would have to if hers was not to be a lonely old age. After all, she had a grandchild. And with that child came a future.

*   *   *

The labour was going on too long, Joan realized, waiting outside the hospital delivery room. Grace's waters had broken early at St Andrew's Place and now the baby was coming – three weeks before it was due. Dying for a cigarette, Joan jiggled her foot as she waited. She hated Boundary Park, thought it was a grim place since her father had come here years ago to get his leg put in plaster. He'd been tipsy and bad-tempered, her mother sitting in an apron and sandals, her face grim.

Funny, the things you remember at the worst times; like when next door's cat ate the laces of her mother's corsets ... God, what *was* she thinking about? Joan wondered, looking down the corridor for a nurse. Tom had been very good about it and stayed home with the kids. But he couldn't object really, could he? He was still out of work, odd jobbing when he could, but ashamed that his wife was the main breadwinner. It wasn't the life she had expected, Joan thought, and yet she wouldn't have swapped him for anyone.

Oh, come on! she urged, come on! What's happening? It was nearly fifteen hours now; it couldn't go on a lot longer.

She had called by at the house in Diggle to find Don Clegg sitting with Arthur. Without preamble, Joan had explained that Grace had gone into labour.

'She having a baby,' she'd said, waiting for the look of shock on Don's face.

'That's grand,' he had replied simply. 'I'll stay here with her father. No worries.'

It was only after she'd walked off that Joan realized he had obviously known all the time. Hurrying on to St Andrew's Place she had then told the night shift what had happened – but they already knew, the day shift

344

having filled them in. Then Joan hustled off quickly, not wanting to hear the comments which would follow. Or then again, maybe they wouldn't. The women were too wily to have been fooled.

Maybe there were a lot of people who had gone along with Grace's deception. Joan thought, wondering whether she should phone Simeon. But then she decided against it. After all, it wasn't his kid, so why should he worry?

Anxiously, Joan peered down the corridor again and then took out some chewing gum. Thoughtfully she put two pieces in her mouth and remembered how pale Grace had looked when she was brought into the hospital. Pale, but determined, even giving Joan instructions about the night shift as she was wheeled off on a trolley.

Joan could remember how she had felt put away in the delivery room, her legs in stirrups, the pain increasing until she thought that she was about to give birth to the town hall, not a baby. She had missed Tom then, but they hadn't allowed him in and it was only later that he had come and held her. But Grace didn't have a man around, no Daniel to bring flowers and argue with over names.

Suddenly she saw the doors open at the end of the corridor and swallowed her chewing gum noisily.

'How is she?' she asked the nurse.

'Who?'

'Grace Ellis, she came in earlier.'

'Oh, yes, Miss Grace Ellis,' she replied the emphasis resting firmly on the *Miss*. 'She's in the last stages of labour now. I suppose there's no man around?'

'He died,' Joan said coldly.

'Pity,' the nurse replied, her tone unconvincingly sympathetic. 'What relation are you?'

'Friend.'

'What about her parents?'

'Her mother's dead and her father's ill.' Joan paused. 'She hasn't got anyone but me.'

At that moment Grace was lying on the delivery table, breathing heavily every time the labour pain hit her. She couldn't have imagined the pain, couldn't have believed she could have borne it. The nurses who attended her were professional, but distant. She was an unmarried mother, hardly worth sympathy. A woman of loose morals in their eyes.

Grace thought about how much easier it would have been if Dora had been around. She would have looked after her, and put everyone in their place. Then she remembered that her mother had had Len Billings' child. That she had been in exactly the same situation Grace was in now.

Her eyes closed against the pain, her back arching. Oh God, she thought, let it be over soon. Let it be over. The fear welled up in her at once. Above her head the light was violently bright, her legs strung up in metal stirrups, the smell of the hospital nauseating. What if there was anything wrong with the baby? Grace wondered suddenly. Why was it taking so long? Surely something had gone wrong?

Biting down on her bottom lip, she fought the pain. Come on, she told herself, be calm, you have to get on with this. No one else can do it for you. Think of Daniel – this is his child. His baby ... She screamed suddenly at the pain and felt her vision cloud. I can do this, there's no one else who can, she told herself, *I can do it – and I will.*

Chapter Thirty-Five

'I have to get out of here,' Grace said quietly, holding her baby tightly to her later that night. 'I want to take him home.'

Joan leaned down and looked into the new-born's face. 'He's gorgeous.' Then she looked back to Grace. She was different, Joan thought smiling to herself. A mother. Good, now she had something to think about other than the business.

Grace was studying her child's face, the blond hair the same colour as Daniel's had been.

'I *have* to go home.'

'Oh yeah, and who's going to look after you there?' Joan replied. 'Stay here for a while, where you're looked after.'

'No,' Grace replied shortly. She remembered all too vividly the faces when the birth certificate was made out. *Do you know the name of the father?* they had asked.

'I want to go now.'

'OK,' Joan said patiently, 'if you insist on going home, I'll look after you for a few days.'

'You can't. What about your own children?'

'Tom's at home. You know, out of work again.' She rolled her eyes as though she didn't really care. 'He told me to send his best.'

There had been precious few congratulations from anyone else, or from the nursing staff. Instead Grace had been pushed to the end of the ward, a curtain around her bed most of the time. The sister said it was to shield her from the sight of all the happy fathers visiting their wives . . .

'He's a good baby,' Grace said, looking tenderly at her son. 'I'm going to call him Jonathan.'

'Good name,' Joan replied, putting the flowers she had brought into a vase.

It was the only gesture of congratulation. There were no other flowers or cards. This was the beginning, Joan thought. God, fancy having to face the criticism of the world just after the strain of giving birth.

'Oh, I forgot,' Joan said, 'Don was pleased to hear about the baby.'

'Did he know?'

'Oh yeah, he knew all right.'

Grace frowned. 'He never said anything.'

'Neither did you,' Joan countered, raising her eyebrows.

'What about everyone at St Andrew's Place?'

'They know.'

'And?'

'They wished you well. Tilly looked shocked, but I reckon all the others weren't surprised.'

'Did you tell Simeon?'

Joan nodded. 'I just spoke to him before I came in to see you.'

'And what did he say?'

'He burst out laughing.'

'He *what*?'

'Laughed,' Joan said. 'When I asked him why, he said that he had seen four sisters pregnant and thought he could spot a bun in the oven at ten paces.'

'That's comforting,' Grace replied drily. 'What else did he say?'

'He asked when you would be getting back to work.'

'As soon as I can. Next week.'

'Really? And who's going to look after the baby?'

'I'll take him with me.'

'Oh come on, Grace, give the kid a chance,' Joan snapped. 'He's going to need regular feeds, naps, changing – you can't do all of that. You need someone to help.'

'I don't need a nanny.'

'Who said anything about a nanny?' Joan replied. 'You just need another pair of hands. You can't seriously expect to look after your father *and* a new baby.'

'Don helps with Dad. As for the baby – actually I did talk to someone about giving me a hand.'

'Who?'

'A girl called Polly Rimmer.'

'That fat girl whose mother has the pot stall on the market?'

Grace winced. 'Apparently she's great with children.'

'If she doesn't fall on them.'

'Oh, come on! She's not *that* fat, Joan.'

'She's got a backside on her like a brick outhouse.'

'But she's calm and kind,' Grace retorted. 'I like her. I could ask her to help with Jonathan. If Polly came to help me I wouldn't have to rely on you so much. It's not fair, Joan, I ask too much of you already.'

'Well, I'm not sure about Polly Rimmer,' Joan replied, relieved, but also miffed that she was being usurped. 'Besides, I bet her mother would have something to say about it. Oh, don't look at me like that, Grace! Evie Rimmer is staunch Methodist, not into the ways of the flesh at all. I don't want to be mean, but I don't think she'd like her daughter working for you.'

Grace's expression was flinty. 'Evie Rimmer is poor; that makes everyone less choosy.'

*   *   *

Within a few days, Polly Rimmer was a regular at the house in Diggle.

Shy, and self-conscious about her size, Polly had been bullied all her life and only felt at home with children. They might be cruel at first, but when they had got used to her bulk they accepted her. Which none of her peers ever did.

She had been bullied at school, at home, and treated badly by the only boyfriend she had ever had. Cripplingly shy, Polly walked with her head down and avoided eye contact, shuffling around the town like an outcast. Her mother – the lean and sharp-tongued Evie – was ashamed of her daughter's appearance and nagged her, which ensured that Polly ate to console herself and compound the problem. 'No man will marry you,' Evie would say. 'You might as well get used to the idea of being a spinster.'

Polly never answered back, just kept quiet, but when she left school at fourteen she had found a job at Werneth Preparatory, a local school. It might only be helping to cook the children's dinners, but that hadn't mattered. Polly had found her métier. Soon she'd graduated to playground duties and the more she was with children, the more she relaxed.

She'd been articulate with them too, told stories, made faces, played games, even made fun of her weight – because they were children and they couldn't hurt her. They, in their turn, had adored Polly and called for her when she was on duty. But the pay at the school had been minimal and Evie had soon wanted Polly to work in a factory instead.

Terrified by the idea, Polly had lain awake worrying how to avoid the awful thrust out into a hostile world. Sweaty and afraid, she had pulled the sheets around her bulk and curled into a clumsy foetal position, praying repeatedly that something would happen, *anything* that would prevent her from having to work beside her hard-faced, confident, slim peers.

Then something *did* happen. Grace Ellis wanted help with her baby ... It had been difficult for Polly, wondering how she would tell her mother. Grace Ellis wasn't married, but she had a baby. That was wrong, wasn't it? Polly had been brought up to believe that sex was a sin. Only acceptable in marriage ... But Jonathan was adorable, and Miss Ellis was a lady. Well, she acted like one anyway.

The money had been the deciding factor. Evie might rail against loose morals, but she needed the rent and had no husband alive to help her get it. Only Polly. So her daughter had gone to work for Grace and had found that she was soon accepted by the various misfits who visited the Diggle household.

There was kind old Don, and shy Geoffrey, who came to play with the baby – and there was always the shadow of Mr Arthur Ellis lying upstairs in his room.

Timidly, Polly now stole a glance at Don. He arrived everyday and sat with the old man upstairs, only coming down to use the toilet or make food. He was short and bald, and wiggled his finger at the baby like a grandfather would, but he wasn't family, just a friend. Geoffrey wasn't family either. Apparently he worked in Miss Ellis's business, as did his sister, Joan. But he wasn't Miss Ellis's boyfriend, that Polly knew for sure.

The only person Polly wasn't sure about was Joan, because she teased her about her weight and gave her stern looks when she caught her eating biscuits.

'They'll make you fat.'

'I've got gland trouble,' Polly said shyly.

'You've got a problem with your throat, you mean,' Joan replied. 'You just keep swallowing.'

It was easy for her to say, Polly thought, she was stick thin, despite having had two children. Polly stared out of the window thoughtfully. Miss Ellis never mentioned her weight, Polly thought. Never even seemed to notice it. She felt comfortable with her employer, so at ease that she wasn't even clumsy when Miss Ellis was around.

Before long she would get the baby ready and push him over to St Andrew's Place as she always did. There, she would take him up to Miss Ellis's office. Then she would make up a feed – which his mother would give to him ... Jonathan had been a sickly baby at first, unable to get enough nourishment from the breast, but now he was on the bottle he was thriving. And Miss Ellis gave Polly full credit for that. Then the change in diet and all the long walks and the fresh air put colour into Jonathan's cheeks so that a bonny child was now being brought into St Andrew's Place.

The still grieving Tilly was ecstatic about the baby. She adored her own child and cooed repeatedly at Jonathan when he was brought round to the factory. As did Enid, maternal as ever.

Only Mary Wells was judgemental, her broad face hard. As ever, she loved the gossip – but this time it was a bit too close to home.

'We're working for an unwed mother –'

Ivy looked up sharply. 'You've room to talk! Your aunt had your cousin four months *premature*. She walked up that aisle bold as brass with a stomach on her like a landlord's beer belly.'

Mary flushed. 'I still say, who would have thought it about Grace Ellis? She's a dark horse, and no mistake.'

352

Roughly, Enid pushed a full box of lipsticks over to Mary. 'Take that out the back and stop your jammering.'

When Mary walked off, Enid turned back to Ivy. 'Daniel Goodman's the father, you know.'

Ivy raised her eyes heavenwards. 'I heard that. Is it true?'

Enid nodded. 'Oh yes. Well, what I say is this – if you're going to have a baby out of wedlock, you might as well pick the best man going.'

Ivy dropped her voice as she taped up the lid of the box in front of her.

'It's just a shame that she didn't manage to get him to marry her. She's a clever women – but in the end she got caught like all the rest.'

Yet before long the sight of Jonathan at St Andrew's Place sparked few comments. The employees had work and a good wage packet at the end of the week – what Grace Ellis got up to in her private life was no concern of theirs. So they kept their opinions to themselves.

The only person who really made her feelings known was Elsa. Looking at Jonathan in his pram in Grace's office she smiled archly.

'You slipped up there. I could have told you who to go and see.' She paused, preening. 'You won't see me getting caught like that.'

Grace's voice was cold. 'I wanted my child.'

'What as, leverage?'

'Don't judge people by your own standards, Elsa,' Grace retorted, pulling the pram over to her desk. 'When I look at Jonathan I remember his father.'

'Yes, well, memories are all you've got left, aren't they?'

For several weeks after Grace's return to work Simeon did not come to the workshop. Instead, he phoned to ask how the business was doing, and sounded as he always did. But Grace wondered if he was disappointed with her, or even shocked by the turn in events.

'Simeon,' she said when he called the next time, 'I want you to come over and look at the new lines Brian and I have been working on.'

'I'm sure they're fine.'

'But you're not interested?'

'Who said that?' he countered irritably. 'Jesus, Grace having a kid certainly hasn't improved your temper.'

She took in a breath. 'Does it make a difference?'

'What, your temper?'

'The baby, Simeon! I meant the *baby*.'

He laughed down the phone. 'Why should a baby make a difference – unless he's running the business?'

'I thought –'

'That I would judge you? Hell, Grace, you live your life your own way. What you do is no concern of mine. You're a smart woman, you obviously chose to have your son, so you must have wanted him.' He paused, his voice softer then. 'Is he like his father?'

'Same colouring.'

'My youngest sister's just had another baby, a girl. She's a spitting image of her husband, ears like a bat.'

Relief welled up in Grace. He was talking about the baby as though it was perfectly normal, in the same breath as he spoke of his sister's child. Simeon Grant had accepted Jonathan . . . Her estimation of him increased tenfold.

'So, are you coming over?'

'Tomorrow. See you then.'

He did as he had promised, and more. At two thirty Simeon walked into the workshop with a toy under his arm and then deposited the teddy and an envelope on Jonathan's pram.

'What's this?' Grace asked, pointing to the envelope.

'A gift for the baby.'

She opened it. Inside was a five-pound note.

'Simeon –'

'A child should start life with its own money.' he said, picking up Jonathan and staring at him. 'Good-looking kid. And quiet, thank God.'

He was tickling Jonathan under the chin, his dark brows drawn together. Obviously he was easy with children, the baby relaxed in his arms.

'Not many men feel comfortable holding a new baby.'

'If you not the father you can always give it back,' Simeon retorted, laying Jonathan back in his pram. 'How's things, Grace?'

'I'm managing. Polly helps me out.'

'I don't mean that. I mean, how are people reacting?'

She hadn't expected him to be the one to ask the question, and balked.

'Everyone's fine here.'

'But not outside? Hard thing for an unmarried woman to have a child on her own.'

'I wouldn't have been on my own if Daniel hadn't been killed.'

'It must be tough losing someone you care about so much,' Simeon replied, looking back to the baby. 'Still, you've got his son, haven't you?'

There was a sudden intimacy between them, so much so that Grace risked a personal question.

'Have you never thought of getting married. Simeon?'

'God, no! I don't want a family, I've got enough nieces and nephews to keep my paternal instincts satisfied.'

355

'Some woman will change your mind one day,' she teased him.

'No, not unless she's extraordinary. And let's face it, there aren't that many goddesses walking *these* streets.'

Smiling, Grace turned back to the papers on her desk. The moment of closeness had gone. He was, after all, just a business partner who was being kind. Because it served him. She wondered fleetingly if she would hear the same remarks repeated constantly over the years to come. Wondered if one day she would see Simeon marry his angel.

He was looking for the same woman all men looked for. An image of perfection, a morally perfect, physically beautiful paragon whose reputation was as unsullied as a child's. In fact he was talking about the woman she had been. *Once.*

But was no more.

Chapter Thirty-Six

Frederick Conrad was fascinated by the letter he had received. Grace Ellis's benefactors had heard that she had gone into partnership with Simeon Grant at the end of last summer and that the Auden Line was becoming more successful with every month that passed. They had seen the cosmetics on sale at Dudley and Proctors, many high-class chemists and in Kendal Milne, Manchester. Their faith in Grace Ellis, they wrote, had been amply rewarded.

They had also heard about the birth of her son ... Frederick had paused at this point, waiting to read the condemnation which was sure to follow. He had been astonished at the news himself, over six months ago now. No one would have expected such behaviour from Grace Ellis.

Emmeline had been blunt when she had heard. 'Blood will out,' she'd said, her gargoyle-like face not improving with age. 'Her mother's child, all right.'

Frederick had wanted to defend Grace, but challenging Emmeline was too exhausting. Now his thoughts turned back to the letter and he read on, Emmeline all ears.

'Grace's benefactors are offering to put away a small legacy for the child. Not a vast amount, but generous nevertheless.'

'A legacy!' Emmeline echoed, her voice hitting a high C. 'For her illegitimate child? The wrong people have children. *We* should have had children.'

Frederick had a sudden image of a miniature Emmeline in a bonnet and shuddered.

'Well, a legacy is a surprise and no mistake,' he went on. 'Most charitable institutions come down hard on unmarried mothers –'

'Who corrupt the morals of the young!'

'Quite,' Frederick said distantly. 'But these people obviously take charity to heart.'

'I'm a charitable woman myself,' Emmeline replied without a trace of irony. 'But I still say that damnation awaits Grace Ellis. Damnation and judgement.' She turned at the exit and paused. 'Breakfast in ten minutes.'

Frederick watched the door close behind his wife and then started to breathe again. He decided that he would write and tell Grace Ellis the good news. Then he wondered why Lucy Goodman had asked to see him that afternoon. She wasn't a regular client of his.

The Goodman fortune was impressive, he thought, and old Mrs Goodman was getting on in years. The factories, industry and property the woman owned were formidable assets, but even someone with the business acumen of Lucy Goodman needed advice at times.

Who better to offer it than he? Frederick thought, automatically increasing his charges to suit the prominence of his new client.

Over the past six months Simeon had seen a marked change in Grace: the old gentleness had been tempered and there was a new brusqueness in her manner. It was not entirely down to pressure of business, but of gossip. He had heard how Grace had been slighted in various shops, and recently the doctor who had attended her father for so long had been curt when he came out on a visit.

Grace had flown in the face of people's morals and

they resented her for it. Worse was the fact that, to outsiders, she didn't appear ashamed, but rather assured. Simeon knew it was a front to hide the hurt she was feeling, but others didn't, and merely regarded her as a tough piece.

Yet he was surprised to find Grace upset one evening when he'd stayed behind, hoping to have a discussion with her about his hopes for expansion. At first he wanted to leave and avoid unpleasantness, but he had come to like Grace. He didn't want to sleep with her – as he slept with Elsa – but she was like another sister to him and he'd felt suddenly protective. So he walked into the office and closed the door behind him.

Startled, Grace wiped her eyes and looked away. 'What is it?'

'I don't know. You tell me.'

'I had something in my eye.'

'The chip on your shoulder probably slipped.'

She turned on him. 'What the hell is that supposed to mean?'

'You've been crying; something has upset you. Why don't you tell me about it?'

'It was nothing.'

He put his head on one side, listening.

'I said *it was nothing*.'

'I'm not that deaf!' he replied good-naturedly, 'I just didn't believe what you said. Has someone made another moral judgement?'

'Don't they always? I thought they would have given it a rest by now.'

'It never finishes, Grace, so you'd better get used to the idea. Jonathan is the living proof of your fall from virtue.'

'It's not funny.'

'I never said it was,' he replied evenly. 'So who said what?'

She glanced down at her hands. 'A long time ago I had a teacher who believed in me. Coral Higgins. She gave me extra tuition – without asking for payment – because my parents couldn't afford to keep me on at school. She was my mentor; I cared what she thought. In fact she was the intermediary when my benefactors first started supporting me.'

'Go on.'

'She's married with a child, lives on Cheviot Avenue. Has the life I thought I would have.'

'You've got bigger ambitions than Cheviot Avenue.'

'You know what I mean, Simeon. She was someone to look up to. I admired her – an educated woman who had helped a young girl without asking for any reward.'

'But she got it. You turned out to be a success. In fact,' he said smoothly, 'before long we're expanding. You're a woman of some achievement.'

Grace shook her head. 'Coral didn't think so.'

'Did she say that?'

'She didn't say anything. I saw her on the street and waved to her. She saw me – and then walked on. I felt so cheap. *Coral*, of all people.'

Simeon took the seat opposite hers.

'Did you really expect her to react any other way? She's a normal woman with a normal life. You've never had that, Grace. You chose to act differently from the start. You chose a career, you chose to have a child. You chose to stand out from the crowd. You invite criticism and anger with everything you do, because you *dare*.'

'I don't really give a damn for myself,' Grace said defiantly, 'but I worry about Jonathan.'

Simeon looked at her blankly. 'I don't understand.'

'Jonathan will go to school and no matter how clever he is people will remember one thing and one thing only – he's illegitimate. I *chose* to be an outsider, but he didn't.'

'Are you sorry you had him?'

'Don't be crazy!' she snapped. 'I don't regret anything I've done. I've made my bed and I'll lie in it.' She paused. 'But I should have married Daniel when I had the chance.'

'You can't change the past.'

She gave Simeon a wry look. 'No . . . but I can do something about the future. Believe me, Jonathan is not going to suffer for what I did.' She blew her nose and composed herself, the businesswoman again. 'So, what did you want to talk about?'

'Expansion.'

Grace's eyebrows rose. 'Expansion? So soon?'

'We could open another factory in Salford – and you could use it as an excuse to move away from here. You could live in Cheshire, where people don't know you or your history, Where you could start again.'

'I'll be damned if I'm hiding away!'

'Think of your son. You could pass yourself off as a widow –'

'That would be a lie!'

'There are worse bloody things than lying!' he snapped back.

'Not to me.'

'So you're going to stick it out?'

'Yes, I bloody am,' Grace replied heatedly. 'Jonathan's a baby. He won't understand for a long time. It's my job to bring him up strong enough to withstand anything people say. He has to be tough, Simeon, resilient.' She stared into his face, formidable suddenly. 'He might not have a normal family, but he's surrounded by friends – Polly, Joan, Don, Geoffrey – and that's more than some children ever have. He might not have a father, but he won't lack for support.'

For a moment Simeon stared at her, then sighed. 'What about you? Who supports you?'

'I can take care of myself.'

'No one can keep that up for ever.'

'You want a bet, Mr Grant?' She smiled at him, then turned away, picking up some files. 'Now, what were you saying about expansion?'

Chapter Thirty-Seven

Joan was looking at her husband with affection, studying Tom's body, his hands, the way he picked up their younger child, Georgia. She longed for him suddenly, glancing towards her other daughter, Mary, asleep on the couch under the window.

They were struggling, but so what? Who wasn't at the moment? The kids didn't understand that they were poor; money didn't matter to children, Joan thought. After all, she hadn't grown up with money at the Bell and Monkey. She thought of her mother with her feet in a bowl of Epsom salts, her father lounging against the bar. Lazy sod . . .

Stretching, Joan glanced back to her husband. Tom would play with the kids for a while longer and then she would walk both of her daughters over to her mother's to give Tom time to go out and look for work. After she left them at the pub she would then go on to St Andrew's Place and work there for the rest of the day.

She missed the kids, but what could you do? Someone had to work. It didn't matter that it was she. When Tom got a job she would cut down her time at St Andrew's Place and take the girls out. Day trips – that would be good. Blackpool even . . .

Tom looked up suddenly, sensing that Joan was staring at him. Then she smiled and winked, eyes full of mischief.

What would she have done without him? Without the girls? What kind of a life would it have been? Oh, she might have pursued that crazy dream of hers and gone to Hollywood – like hell! She was happy enough. Leave the big ideas to others. Her man had come home safe from the war – what more could a woman want?

Resting her head against Tom's shoulder, Joan could feel his warmth and was comforted by it. They might have no money, but they had each other.

'I love you,' she said.

'What brought that on?'

'Lend me a fiver,' she joked, kissing his cheek. 'I just wanted to say it, that was all.'

'It's Friday; we could go for a walk when you get back later.'

That was a good idea. They could walk over to Alexandra Park with the kids and lift them up onto the stone lions on the steps. The thought of the weekend cheered Joan. She would have some time at home with Tom – even after she had done all the chores and shopping. They could go to bed early, and make love.

'Do you ever think of other women, Tom?'

He looked at her in surprise. 'All the time!'

She slapped him playfully on the shoulder. 'Do you ever wonder what life would have been like if you had married someone else?'

'Like Rita Hayworth?'

She nudged him in the ribs. 'Pig!'

'I'm happy,' he said sincerely, putting his arms around her. 'I'd like to rebuild the shed in the yard when we get a bob or two. And you could do with a washing machine.'

'You old romantic,' she teased him.

He smiled. 'Just think, Joan, one day we might own our own house.' his eyes shone with the thought. '*Our own house*. We could decorate it and let the kids pick wallpaper for their room . . .'

'And paint the front door red.'

'Red!' Tom said, aghast. 'That's a bit much, isn't it?'

'But it would be *our* house, so we could do what we liked. We could paint a Union Jack on the door and no one could say anything about it.' She nestled against him, savouring the dream. 'And a garden, Tom.'

'Yes. A garden,' he echoed.

'Not too big, with a bit of lawn.'

'And a swing for the girls.'

She sighed.

'Do you think we could ever get that lucky?' he asked.

'We found each other,' Joan replied contentedly. 'How lucky can you get?'

Lying with her hands behind her head, Elsa watched Simeon walk to the cabinet and pour them both a drink. The room was well furnished, if masculine in taste, and the house off Buile Park was worth real money. Elsa could see herself as the mistress here – well, not mistress. Wife.

She wondered what Simeon thought of her, apart from being fascinated and sexually hungry. After all, she wasn't a nobody. Her face was on billboards now, on packaging as far away as Manchester and Leeds. London soon. She smiled to herself. Grace Ellis had been right, her image *had* attracted someone. And she hadn't even had to go out for it; it had come to her. Simeon Grant, partner in the Auden Line, successful in the rag trade – *rich*.

They could join forces. It would be a good match. Elsa was a trophy and smart with it. As for Simeon, he would look good with a woman like her on his arm.

'Drink up and I'll take you home,' Simeon said calmly.

Elsa's blue eyes flickered with irritation. 'Home? It's only ten o'clock.'

'I have some work to do.'

'Work?' she echoed. 'Are you crazy? Who works at this time of night?'

'People who make money. Like me. Money to buy that sherry you're drinking, the meal you ate, and the dress you're wearing.'

'It was out of your stock.'

'It still cost money,' Simeon countered, smiling.

They were all the same, Elsa thought, suddenly bitter. Men got what they wanted and then they turned into bastards. Treating a woman like dirt. He was no better than Elmer Shaw. Not that she hadn't got her own back on *him*, Shaw now serving three years in Strangeways.

'Oh, come on, Simeon –'

'I have to work,' he said firmly, draining his glass.

'Here or at St Andrew's Place?' Elsa countered. 'Perhaps you need to work with Grace Ellis? The hands-on approach.'

He flinched at the implication. 'We're business partners.'

'Well, just keep that way! I've already had that bitch try and steal a man from me before.'

He turned at the words. 'What *are* you talking about?'

'Elmer Shaw,' Elsa said, wondering how to tell the tale so that she would come off best. 'I was a friend of his. He wanted to marry me –'

'He's already married,' Simeon replied, 'and in gaol. I can imagine what you were doing with Shaw, but what about Grace?'

She was jealous now, seeing her chance slipping out of her fingers. It was getting tiring, all this pleasing and trading favours. She wanted to be set up, protected –

and she wasn't going to let Simeon go easily. Especially not to Grace Ellis.

'She went to see Elmer Shaw to ask him to invest in her business.'

'Go on.'

'He took a fancy to her and she ... she played him along.'

Simeon crossed the room in an instant and stood over Elsa.

'I don't believe you and I suggest that you tell me the truth now, or we're finished.'

He meant it, she could see that.

'Oh, come on, Simeon,' she wriggled, 'it was a mis-understanding. Grace Ellis probably didn't mean to egg him on.'

'She gave you a cut in the business and uses you as her model. I've often wondered about that. Why she would keep an adder like you so close. Then I thought about the old saying – *Keep your friends close and your enemies closer*. I can see why she did it now.'

'Look here!' Elsa snapped, 'I used to own St Andrew's Place and I sold it to Grace Ellis for next to nothing. She owes *me*.'

Simeon was curious. 'Why did you sell it to her?'

'She wanted it.'

'So why did you sell it cheap, Elsa? You're no fool. It must have benefited you in some way to do it.'

'I wanted to get back at Shaw,' she admitted finally. 'We'd both suffered at the hands of that man.'

This was only part of the story, Simeon realized.

'Tell me the truth, Elsa, all of it,' he warned, 'or I'll never see you again.'

Outsmarted, she crossed her legs and toyed with the

hem of her skirt. It had no effect; Simeon wasn't about to be seduced into a good humour.

'Simeon –'

'Tell me the truth.'

'Oh, for God's sake!' she exploded. 'Shaw was keen on Grace and he went round to see her one night. He was supposed to be talking business but he was only after one thing.'

'What happened?'

'She rejected him.'

'Just like that? She blew her chances away so easily? No, there has to be more to it than that. Grace is no fool. She could handle a man's attentions without alienating him.'

'Not if he beat her up. You ask her where that scar on her cheek came from.'

The words were out of Elsa's mouth before she had time to check them, Simeon staring at her.

'He did *what*?'

'He beat me too!' she screeched. 'He nearly scarred me for life –'

'You probably deserved it. What happened to Grace afterwards?'

'She was all right,' Elsa said sullenly. 'She might have lost out with Elmer, but her benefactors soon coughed up the money for her business.' She softened her voice. 'She's not as innocent as she looks.'

'Which is more than can be said for you,' Simeon replied, snatching up Elsa coat and then marching her to the door. 'Go on, get out.'

'Get out?'

'Yes, get out. I never want to see you again.'

Elsa's perfect face was distorted with rage. 'I'll make you pay for this, Simeon Grant. God help me, but I will.'

'Now look,' he said, catching hold of her arm, 'don't threaten me. Elmer Shaw was tough, but I'm a lot tougher. You try and injure me – or Grace – and you'll live to regret it.'

Slamming the door behind her, Simeon could hear Elsa's footsteps hurrying away down the steps. They faded into the distance, her scent lifting from the room as he moved over to the sofa and sat down. Something about the story had altered his perception of Grace. Although he knew she wasn't the hard career woman she appeared, he had, nevertheless, thought her cold, a woman who had developed a carapace to protect herself.

Then he remembered her reaction when Coral Higgins had snubbed her. He also remembered the way she talked about Daniel, the way she looked when she held Jonathan, the banter between her and Joan. His feelings for her shifted and he realized with astonishment that he cared about her – and had done for a while.

She was different. Brave, resilient, responsible. The people who rebuffed her for having a child out of wedlock were hypocrites. They would have condoned an abortion. And such an act would have protected Grace's reputation. But Grace had not done what was easy, she had done what she believed was right.

He wondered why he hadn't thought about her before, why he hadn't allowed himself to notice that Grace was a beauty in her own right. Instead he had been entertained by the obvious Elsa. He had chosen the easy way, an easy lay.

It was obvious why. If he showed his feelings for Grace she would reject him. Her memory of Daniel was a obvious block to any other man. If he tried to court Grace how would he do it? He couldn't impress her – she had her own business. He couldn't buy her – she would refuse any emotional bribe, and besides, she was making money of her own now. Nor was Grace Ellis the kind of woman who would enter into an affair lightly. She would want commitment, and he had never offered that to anyone.

If he decided on her, Simeon realized that he chose a hard path. He would have to take on a woman with a reputation, along with another man's child and a sick parent. Simeon Grant – who had avoided responsibility like a hydrophobe avoids water – would have responsibility piled on him.

It would be difficult. Grace would never be a typical wife. But had he ever wanted a *typical* wife? Had he ever wanted a wife at all? Shaken, Simeon sat on the sofa and thought about Grace Ellis. He thought about the woman who had shown no interest in him emotionally, the woman who still loved another man, the woman who would be a match for him as no other woman had ever been.

And he wanted her.

That same evening Grace left St Andrew's Place to find a large Bentley waiting at the end of the ginnel. Frowning, she looked into the back seat and then flinched as she saw Lucy Goodman beckon her over. She nearly walked off but then her curiosity got the better of her.

'Mrs Goodman,' she said coldly through the open car window. 'I never thought I'd see you here.'

'Please, get in,' Lucy Goodman said, sliding over in her seat and closing the partition between her and the driver. 'I want to talk to you.'

Grace studied the silk dress, the grey hair fashionably styled. Money oozed from every pore. Money and malice.

'What do you want to talk about?'

'Your son.'

Immediately Grace moved to open the door, but Lucy Goodman put a hand on her arm.

'Please, hear me out.'

'My son is none of your concern.'

'Your son is my grandchild.'

Grace let go of the door handle and leaned back in the car seat.

'I'm surprised to hear you admit it.'

'It's the truth, isn't it? Your son *is* Daniel's child.'

'So?'

Lucy Goodman looked down at her hands, the oval nails newly buffed, the half-moons showing. Hands never used to hard work.

'People have been talking about you, Miss Ellis. Your reputation has been ruined.'

'Did you come to gloat?'

'On the contrary, I came to help,' Lucy replied, her tone even.

She wanted to slap Grace, to knock some respect into her head. After talking to Frederick Conrad, she had it all worked out. Yet here she was, in the backstreets of Oldham, about to offer her a chance in a million and the woman was talking to her like an equal.

'You must be struggling to support your father and your child.'

'The business is doing well. I manage.'

Lucy had heard about the business and was slightly annoyed. If Grace Ellis had been on her uppers the task would have been easier.

'But still, your situation isn't perfect by a long way. A child needs a proper home, a family environment. My son's child should have the best of everything.'

Grace let her continue without interrupting. She wanted to see what the old woman was getting at.

'It's not fair on a child to grow up with a stigma attached to its birth. Jonathan needs to be recognized as a Goodman. People need to know that he was Daniel's child.'

'The people who matter already do.'

'Society does *not*,' Lucy replied shortly. 'If you let him grow up as he is, he'll be the butt of cheap jokes. They will tease him at school, talk about his mother.'

'I've heard all this before, Mrs Goodman,' Grace said impatiently. 'Nothing you've said is any surprise to me. But I'll cope.'

'I'm not talking about *you*, I'm talking about Jonathan.'

Grace noticed how she kept referring to him as *Jonathan* – not your son – as though he was no relation to Grace at all.

'I can offer a good life for him. He could have the best education, the best home, everything. He could go to university and inherit the business when he came of age.' She paused, trying to read Grace's expression.

A clammy sensation of guilt washed over Lucy but she shrugged it off. Grace Ellis knew nothing about the will Daniel had left, suspected nothing of the money she been cheated out of. Or did she? She was acting very cool. Perhaps Daniel had told her what he had done and she had never forgiven Lucy Goodman.

'I want to make it up to you.'

'Make *what* up, Mrs Goodman?'

The old woman took in a deep breath, her cheeks colouring. 'The way I treated you before. I should have realized that my son loved you very much.'

'I told you he did. You knew that. Why apologize now?'

'We should be friends –'

'I don't think so,' Grace replied. 'We have nothing in common.'

'Except Jonathan.'

So that was it! She wanted to get close to her grand-child; she wanted to control the last of the Goodmans. The heir. Daniel was dead, but there was another male alive now, another life to order and govern. Over my dead body, Grace thought.

'I'll bring up my son the way I see fit.'

'Then you are a very selfish woman,' Lucy Goodman said flatly. 'I can give Jonathan everything you can't – a name, money, power. You can only pass on your own stigma.'

Grace had turned away, her heart beating. She hated Lucy Goodman for what she saying and yet she knew that there was some truth to it. A shadow would hang over Jonathan all his life because of the circumstances of his birth – but allow Lucy Goodman to be involved in his upbringing? Never.

'I want to adopt him –'

'You're mad!' Grace shouted. 'Do you think I would give my child to you, after what you did to your own son?'

'I loved my son!'

'You terrorized your son! You wanted Daniel to do everything you said, you wanted him as your lacky, your companion. You punished him as a child for acting like a child, so don't tell me how to bring up children when you made such a poor job of it yourself.'

Catching Grace's arm, Lucy leaned towards her. 'This is not about the past.'

'Oh, yes it is! It's about my past and your son's past, and all the rotten things that happened.'

'It would be different with Jonathan –'

Grace cut her off furiously. 'No, it wouldn't. You would want to rule him too. He's a child – what chance would he have?'

'And what chance has he got now? If you let me bring him up, give him the Goodman name, raise him at The Lockgate, he will be accepted. Jonathan will be respected; he could move in any circles then – go anywhere, do anything. Marry well. He could be someone – not just another bastard in a terraced house with no future.'

'How dare you?' Grace hissed. 'How dare you belittle me?'

Shattered by the anger in her voice, Lucy reared back in her seat. It wasn't going the way she had planned. She had expected that Grace Ellis would be grateful to her and would jump at the chance that was on offer. But she was arguing with her, rejecting everything put before her.

'You can't get on your high horse,' Lucy Goodman said acidly. 'Everyone knows where your mother came from. She had the morals of a rabbit and you're no better.'

Grace stared into her face and laughed softly. The old woman coloured.

'You can't insult me. Whatever I am doesn't matter. You know why, Mrs Goodman? *Because your son loved me*. Whatever my background Daniel loved me. Daniel Goodman – who could have had anyone – chose *me*.' She opened the car door and then turned back. 'I want to thank you for making me realize how strong I really am. I don't need your money, your name or your power. I have my own. I can teach my son what few other mothers can.'

374

'I doubt it.'

'Well, I don't,' Grace replied tersely. 'I don't doubt anything any more. You've taught me that. I look at you and I hate everything you represent. You want my son as you would want a possession, something else over which you could have total control. He would be crushed within twelve months.'

'And you think that he'll survive any better without the protection money can bring?' Lucy Goodman replied, her voice sour with spite. 'You understand nothing. Anything can be bought, Miss Ellis. Respect, position. Anything can be restored with the right amount of power. Even a woman's reputation.'

Grace got out of the car and looked back through the open window.

'Go home to The Lockgate, Mrs Goodman. And when you're there think about what you've said. You'll have plenty of time, with no interruptions. You can spend your old age counting your money. But as for my child – keep away. I lost Daniel, but I won't lose his son.'

'You're a fool!'

'And you're a ridiculous woman,' Grace countered contemptuously. 'Go home to your big empty house, Mrs Goodman – and I'll go home to my child.'

Chapter Thirty-Eight

Grace told Joan what had happened and Joan told Simeon. Lucy Goodman was an old bag, Joan said. She should be dead, not Daniel. Just think how perfectly everything would have worked out then. Grace and Daniel would be married and Jonathan would grow up in a normal environment. That was the way it should have been, shouldn't it?

Simeon glanced over to her. 'Oh, yes. Yes.'

Joan frowned. 'What's the matter? You look like you ate some bad fish.'

'How could I? I haven't been to dinner at your place lately,' he countered wryly. 'Where's Grace?'

'Out the back. She's checking some ingredients with Brian.'

At that precise moment, Grace was bending over the laboratory bench as she looked at the mixture Brian Lawley had created.

Carefully Grace slid her finger into the cream and rubbed it on the back of her hand. Then she smelled it. Brian, red-faced, red-haired, watched her with his pale amber eyes.

'What do you t-t-t-think?' he stuttered.

'It's effective but too sticky,' Grace replied. 'The questionnaires were right: women would hate that on their faces.'

Brian's ginger eyebrows rose. 'It's not possible, Miss Ellis. I've t-t-t-tried every which way, but I can't get the mixture any lighter.'

'Then make it less greasy, Brian. You can do it. I know

you can.' She looked over to the door, seeing Simeon walk in. 'Oh, hello there,' she said, taking hold of his hand. 'I want you to feel something.'

He already was, Simeon thought, as Grace smoothed some of the cream onto the back of his hand. Her fingers worked in the mixture gently, his mouth drying.

'How does that feel?'

'Good,' he croaked.

She frowned. 'Are you getting a cold?'

'No,' he said, clearing his throat. 'It's all the perfume around here. I never get used to it.'

She nodded, letting go of his hand. 'What's the matter with Elsa? She was in a foul mood this morning.'

'I thought she didn't come in on Mondays.'

'She doesn't usually. I think she came in to see you,' Grace teased him, surprised to see that Simeon seemed discomforted. Hurriedly she changed the subject. 'The new astringent is selling well. All it is basically is witch hazel and rose-water, but it works. An old wives' remedy.' She stared at him 'Are you *sure* you're all right?'

'I heard about the visit from Lucy Goodman.'

Grace shrugged. 'It's no secret.'

'Apparently you sent her off with a flea in her ear.'

'She wanted my child,' Grace said simply, putting her hands in the pockets of her laboratory coat. 'I couldn't have that, could I?'

'You couldn't even consider it.'

'She said I was a selfish mother, that I should think of my son.' She paused, controlling her temper. '*A bastard child*, she called him. Funny to hear that language coming from her lips – about her own grandson.'

377

Simeon was suddenly tongue-tied, wanting to continue the conversation and yet uncertain of how to do so.

'D'you want some lunch later?'

'No thanks,' Grace replied lightly. 'I have to get this cream sorted out.'

'Perhaps tomorrow?'

She nodded absent-mindedly. 'Yes, tomorrow's good.'

Thoughtfully, Simeon walked away, Ivy passing him with a tray of powder compacts. He stopped and picked one up, turning it over in his fingers. It was obvious he wasn't going to win Grace over by buying her lunch; he was going to have to come at her from an altogether different angle.

Distracted, he fingered the compact.

'Are you buying, or just bloody looking?' Ivy said, Simeon jumping and dropping the compact back onto her tray.

He would spend more time at St Andrew's Place and find a new workshop, somewhere neutral, with no memories of the past. His fashion business in Manchester was doing fine. He could afford to spend more time with the make-up side. Frowning, Simeon looked at the potions lined up along the workbenches, then wrinkled his nose against the sea of scent wafting across from the laboratory.

The radio was playing, the women talking and Solar packing boxes into the service lift. Downstairs, Simeon could hear the sound of Geoffrey revving up the new van, and through the glass partition he could see Joan sharing a joke with Grace.

He was jealous of Joan suddenly, stupidly jealous. *He* wanted to be the one in that office, laughing. But he would have to wait. Grace was not a woman to be hurried; she had to have time, time to see him as a partner – first in business, then in life.

Daniel Goodman's ghost had to be usurped; shunted into the sidings of Grace's life. But she couldn't stay tied to him for ever, just living for her son . . .

Her son, Simeon thought, of course! That was Grace's one weakness. Her emotional Achilles heel. What was the only thing Grace Ellis needed? She wasn't looking for a lover or a husband. But she needed a father for Jonathan.

However much she might reject it for herself, she needed a name for her child. *That* was the answer, Simeon thought, whistling to himself as he walked to the door. All he had to do now was to bide his time.

The boiler had broken down at St Andrew's Place, the cold making the women's hands stiff and clumsy. Tilly, still grieving for her dead husband, was silent. Mary Wells complaining loudly.

'My bloody fingers are numb.'

'Match your head,' Ivy said drily.

'It's too cold to work –'

'Oh, for God's sake, Mary, give it a rest,' Enid snapped, the sleeves of her jumper pulled down over her hands.

'It's all right for you,' Mary retorted meanly. 'You've enough blubber on your body to keep out any cold.'

Infuriated, Enid's eyes flashed, Ivy seeing the exchange and moving between the two women.

'Have you noticed anything about Polly?'

'Polly who?' Enid said, still staring at Mary.

'Polly, the girl who looks after Jonathan.' Ivy nudged Enid's plump flank. 'Well, have you seen a change in her?'

'Like what?'

'She's lost weight.'

'I thought she had,' Enid replied, suddenly forgetting Mary's jibe and turning to Ivy. 'I hope she's not sick.'

'Oh, she's sick all right,' Ivy said, winking. 'Love sick.'

'What! With who?'

'Polly's fallen for Joan's brother.'

'Geoffrey Cleaver!'

'Well, why not?'

'I didn't mean that there was anything wrong with Geoffrey. I was just surprised, that's all.' Enid dropped her voice. 'Her mother's not going to be best pleased.'

'That Evie was always jumped up,' Ivy replied scornfully. 'There's things about her that's been hidden well.'

Enid was musing to herself. 'Polly ... Polly and Geoffrey Cleaver. Wow.'

'She's wearing a bit of make-up too –'

'Never!'

Ivy nodded. 'Powder, a touch of rouge. Polly, of all people. I saw her looking at the new stuff that we'd just run off. I gave her a bit. You know, the rejects. She were right chuffed.'

Enid thought of the terrified girl who had come to look after Jonathan only nine months earlier. She had been agonizingly shy; turning away if anyone spoke to her. And now she was in love.

'I've never noticed how she behaves when Geoffrey's around,' she said to Ivy. 'Come to think of it, I don't think I've ever seen them together.'

Mary was leaning over the bench to try to catch the gossip. Ivy saw her.

'Little pigs have big ears!' she snapped, turning towards Enid again. 'I saw them on the street the other day. Polly's face went as red as a farmer's arse.'

'She's very kind. Geoffrey could do a lot worse.'

'He could marry a heifer,' Ivy replied bluntly. 'That would be worse.'

'Oh, come on!' Enid retorted. 'You've said yourself that Polly's losing weight. Anyway, Geoffrey might like a plump woman.'

'Not unless he's thinking of turning into a cannibal,' Ivy replied tartly.

The atmosphere chilled.

'It's all very well for you to talk about weight, Ivy Morris,' Enid said, her tone injured. 'But there's some of us who've always struggled with our size.'

Ivy pulled a face. 'Aye, I didn't mean you, our Enid. Anyway, your Patrick likes you fa – well rounded.'

Mollified, Enid relaxed. Patrick *had* always liked her plump. Not that he was up to slap and tickle any more. In fact, his health was like a game of snakes and ladders. At the moment he was up a ladder – ready to get bitten on the arse any day.

'Well, it's good to have some romance around the place,' Enid said kindly. 'Although, unless I miss my guess, it's not the only love affair on the cards.'

An hour later Joan came into Grace's office, pulled up a chair and sat down, her face only inches away from Grace's.

'Simeon's carrying a torch for you.'

Grace stared at her blankly. 'Simeon!'

'Yeah, it's true,' Joan insisted. 'He was acting all odd the other day when he saw you. And he's dumped Elsa.'

'What for?'

'I don't know. Maybe she bit his neck whist he was asleep,' Joan said dismissively. 'Anyway, he's got his eye on you, Grace. So what are you going to do about it?'

'Nothing.'

She didn't know what to think. Simeon Grant was interested in *her*? Never. It was ridiculous. They were business partners, that was all. And yet the thought didn't entirely repel her . . .

'He seemed very protective of you when I told him about what old Mrs Goodman had to say.'

'He likes Jonathan,' Grace replied. 'That's why he'd react to that. Simeon has four sisters and God knows how many nieces and nephews. He likes children.'

'That's useful.'

Grace stared into Joan's bright eyes. 'Why?'

'Because of Jonathan,' she replied deftly. 'Think about it, Grace. He would make a good husband.'

'Simeon isn't interested in marriage to anyone. He's always made that clear.'

'Oh, he *says* that, but the ones who shout the loudest fall the hardest,' Joan replied. 'You're the one who's never chased him, so he wants you.'

Grace glanced into the pram next to her desk. Jonathan stirred suddenly. Grace stroked his cheek as he fell back to sleep. She wanted to dismiss what Joan said, but she was intrigued. Was it true? Was Simeon Grant interested in her?

'I couldn't love anyone after Daniel, you know that.'

'I also know that life goes on, and that your son needs a father,' Joan replied emphatically. 'Grace, think about it. This isn't just about you, it's about Jonathan. I hate that old bag Goodman, but in a way she's right. Your son needs to have a male figure around, and you need a husband.'

'And marrying a man I don't love would be the answer?'

'Simeon loves you and could give you security,' Joan

382

replied practically, 'and he wants you because you're not interested in him. He wants someone different from all the women who've chased him and his money. Like Elsa James. He knows you're independent, that you don't need him financially or emotionally – but he's cute enough to know that he can offer you status.'

'And that's enough?' Grace asked surprised, 'Do you really think I could marry a man I didn't love?'

'I think,' Joan replied, 'that you could *come* to love Simeon. He has a lot of qualities, Grace. He's tough, no one's fool, a good businessman –'

'A womanizer.'

'In the past. Besides, he ran around because he *could*,' Joan countered. 'Why not? Any man would, if it was offered to him on a plate.'

Grace shook her head. 'No, Joan, it wouldn't work.'

'OK, so he's not Daniel. But Daniel was special. He had no side to him. He understood you and you understood him. But love like that only comes once in a lifetime, Grace. If you're lucky, you get to keep it. If you're not, you lose it. You lost . . . Oh, *do* think about Simeon,' Joan repeated. 'Life has a way of playing very funny tricks on people. It's uncertain – no one knows that more than you do. You're still young, Grace, but one day your father will die and you'll be left on your own with your son. Your life will narrow down to work – and more work. And when Jonathan grows up, you'll be alone. You're not the clinging type. I don't want to frighten you, Grace, but your work and whatever money you make won't make up for an empty bed and a lonely old age.'

Grace winced at the words. 'You never found it difficult to speak your mind, did you?'

'Someone has to,' Joan replied, squeezing Grace's arm

gently. 'I don't want to look at you years from now and wonder why I didn't speak up when I had the chance. I want to see you happy, safe. I want to see you married, Grace.'

'I don't know –'

'Well, I do! If Simeon asks you to marry him – snatch his bloody hand off.'

Chapter Thirty-Nine

1951

Frederick Conrad sneezed again, rain dripping off his black hat. Poor old Melrose, he thought, he'd been a good friend – in a distant kind of way. They had known each other for decades, qualified as solicitors at the same time, married within a year of each other. Later they had joined the same club, and Frederick had toasted the arrival of each of Melrose's children.

They had even shared the same clients – albeit at different times. Frederick thought of Lucy Goodman. Oh dear, how her little plot had failed. She had had it all worked out – but Grace Ellis hadn't fallen into line. Serve Lucy Goodman right, Frederick thought. He had never liked the old bitch. But she was still going strong – not like poor Melrose.

Frederick had known his friend was failing, but somehow the old Scotsman had always rallied before. Bluff, his beard as rough as a old dog's coat, his eyes sharp, missing nothing. Not so sharp any more, Frederick thought, sneezing again. He would get a cold, he knew it. He would get a cold and it would turn into pneumonia. Emmeline would nurse him. She would make him some of her poisonous soup with the unrecognizable bits floating in it.

God, Frederick thought, didn't some politician die after catching cold at another politician's funeral? . . .

He glanced at the people surrounding the grave. They were all in their seventies and eighties. As he was. Only he still looked good, Frederick thought with pride, still the handsome old devil . . .

Someone coughed behind him suddenly. That was it! He was bound to catch cold now; there were more germs in this graveyard than in a laboratory . . . Pulling up his coat collar, Frederick eyed the grave again. Melrose had been bad on his legs at the end, his walking slowing to an ungainly amble. Frederick didn't want that to happen to him. He was still quite sprightly really. Well, he was for his age.

They had all been young once, dashing, urbane. Naturally Frederick had been the most popular – but it all seemed so long ago. All that smug achievement, the getting of the sound houses, the legal practices, the good wine after dinner – what did it amount to, after all? The world saw them as old now. Old men, who had had their time. On the way down, not up.

Depressed, Frederick's gaze rested on Melrose's grave. *On the way down*, he thought. *All the way down.*

Then he sneezed again.

Satisfied, Grace stood back and looked at the dark blue door with the gold lettering. 'The Auden Line Salon' it read. Stairs led up to a first-floor room boasting five private cubicles, a hairdressing unit, two massage rooms and an exclusive shop selling Auden Line cosmetics. Grace Ellis had arrived in style.

She was someone now, and everyone knew it. Her make-up, kept reasonably priced for the average woman, was on sale everywhere, even as far away as London, where it competed with some of the biggest names in the market. Clever promotion and superb photographic advertising had propelled the Auden Line from a small concern to a large, flourishing company.

Elsa's face no longer graced the advertisements. She had lost interest after becoming the mistress of a brewery owner in Salford, but she still came to the Annual General Meeting and was very aware of her ten-per-cent interest in the company. Offers from Grace to buy her out had been met with a flat refusal. Elsa might have lost the contract as the Auden face, but she was smug to see her share increase yearly as the profits rose.

She hadn't been so smug to see Grace marry Simeon Grant. In fact, Elsa had raged when she'd heard and only Simeon's threat held her revenge in check. She would have loved to destroy them both, but she couldn't, and so when she had recovered from her envy, Elsa reckoned that they might as well work for her instead. Which is what, in effect, they were doing; their efforts putting money into Elsa's bank account. The more products sold, the more she earned. The better Grace Ellis did, the more she, Elsa, profited.

It was almost enough.

It had taken Simeon a year to win Grace over, but the more she resisted, the more he persisted, until he would have died rather than fail. Her reason for hesitancy was not to make him more keen, but rather that she hoped she might fall in love with him. She tried to see his actions, his jokes, his mannerisms as endearing. She tried to warm to his voice, his footstep, the sound of his car. But after a while she realized it would never happen. And told him.

'Simeon, I don't love you enough. You're a good man, you deserve someone who's crazy about you.' She had watched him play with Jonathan on the floor of the office. Did he want her, or her son? 'Simeon, listen to me.'

'I *am* listening,' he'd replied, 'I'm only deaf in one ear.' He had looked up at her. 'Don't be so serious, Grace. We can make this work. You'll grow to adore me, every woman does.'

She had laughed, because he always made her laugh and she'd wondered if he was right. But at night when she had come to bed Grace had always dreamed of Daniel and as Jonathan grew up she saw the ghost of his father in every smile or turn of the head.

In the end Grace had married Simeon because his determination had matched her own: he had seen what he wanted and got it – no matter how long it had taken. So finally they had had a small ceremony in the registry office in Oldham, inviting Joan, Tom, Polly and her fiancé, Geoffrey. And, of course, Jonathan.

Then something odd had happened to Grace. Within minutes – from the beginning of the ceremony to the end – she had felt her world adjust. Mrs Simeon Grant was a married woman, a mother, a businesswoman. She had her man, her place in the world. She had triumphed over the odds.

When she had thought back to Daniel during the ceremony, Grace had crushed the image at once. She *could* grow to love Simeon as a husband, she knew she could if she tried hard enough. After all, he was giving her so much for so little – what better love could a man hope to show a woman?

So when they had finally made love on their wedding night Grace had responded as though she had longed for him. As he'd touched her and stroked her, as he had entered her and licked her breasts she had thought of his kindness and willed herself to relax, to give herself

388

as completely as she had given herself to Daniel. When he had climaxed Simeon had smiled at her and held her in his arms. He had won her over.

And she had given the performance of a lifetime.

They had moved together into Lodge House, once owned by the Strattons, in Diggle, where Joan had previously worked as a maid. With money available Grace had redecorated every room in cool colours and Georgian furniture, her style as defined at home as it was at work. Proud of his wife, Simeon had invited business guests home for meetings and soon the previously reviled Grace Ellis was receiving invitations addressed to Mr and Mrs Simeon Grant.

An astonishing amnesia had settled on virtually everyone who had ever snubbed her. She was powerful in her own right – and more, she was married to a powerful man. The girl who had clawed her way up from poverty and humiliation was now the mistress of one of the finest properties in the county – on a par with The Lockgate.

Increasing frail and senile, Arthur had been moved into a part of the house which had been especially altered to accommodate him. At first Don had been nervous, expecting to be dismissed from the grand house. But he was soon reassured, Grace asking him if he would like to continue visiting her father, a nurse staying with Arthur round the clock so that Don was relieved from the sickroom chores he had shouldered for so long.

Grace could afford the best care now, but her father's condition never changed. He just held on, more a spirit than a man, the doctor repeatedly visiting and saying what had always said: that Arthur was barely alive, but still breathing. Once Simeon had suggested that it might be better for Arthur if he was put into a home, but Grace had rejected the idea out of hand.

'A *home*? What the hell are you talking about? This is my father –'

'I just thought that as we have the money now –'

'I've suddenly got so grand that I want to shunt off my inconvenient father?'

He sighed. 'I didn't mean it like that, Grace. Hear me out. I don't want to get rid of your father. After all, it's hardly as if we're stuck for space.'

It was true, everything was finally plentiful. Clothes, jewellery, cars, staff – everything was available to Grace. Together she and Simeon had increased their affluence month by month. They had also taken good advice, solicitors brought in to check out the business contracts at every stage as they had always done, but also to draw up the papers which had changed Jonathan's name from Ellis to Grant.

Grace's son was no longer a bastard. He had a name – and it wasn't one given to him by Lucy Goodman. For a long time Grace had expected to hear from the old woman, but when she married Simeon she knew she never would. Lucy Goodman had been bested – probably for the first and last time in her life.

At the end of their first year of marriage Grace realized that she had finally achieved what she had set out to do. She had a successful business, she was asked to lecture to other businesswomen at select lunches, and she had been accepted by society. It was a society she didn't want to belong to, but one which had had to bend its rigid neck to her. There was no little triumph in the thought.

She also had a husband and a stepfather for her child. And there was another child on the way – Simeon's. He had been ecstatic when she had told him, rushing to his club to spread the news and then throwing parties at St Andrew's Place, and Holly Walk, the romantic-sounding address of the dingy new factory in Salford. He had wanted everyone to know about the baby, just as he had wanted everyone to realize how much he loved his wife. He had it made, Simeon told them all, he finally had it made.

Yet although they had shared everything, there was one matter Grace had dealt with herself. Just before she had married Simeon she had gone to visit Frederick Conrad and told him that her circumstances had changed so much she felt uneasy taking money from her benefactors.

'I'm making so much profit from the business, and now I'm getting married I don't need to take any more from them,' she'd said.

Frederick had given her the benefit of his dazzling smile. Behind him Nelson sat stuffed on a perch.

'I hear what you're saying, but your benefactors wanted to continue with their support when you mentioned this before.'

'But that was a while ago, Mr Conrad. It seems greedy to take the money when I don't need it. The backing should go to someone else.'

'Then I suggest that *you* dispose of it as you wish.'

Grace had shaken her head. 'That doesn't seem right. I think my benefactors should decide who it goes to.'

'But I know what they'll say. They will ask *you* to decide. I'll talk to them, but I know what the answer will be. We've already spoken about this eventuality.'

Grace had looked down at her leather gloves on her lap, choosing her next words carefully.

'Mr Conrad, can't you tell me who they are? It wouldn't hurt for me to know now, would it? I want to thank them for what they did. For all the help they've given me.'

He had glanced down at the file in front of him as though momentarily tempted – and then he had sighed.

'I can't tell you, I'm sorry.'

'*Never?*'

He had closed the file and laid his hand on it protectively.

'I have to respect their wishes, Miss Ellis. I've been instructed from the first that your benefactors wish to remain anonymous. It is their wish and I must go along with it. These things happen all the time. It's no mystery.'

'Maybe not,' Grace had replied, 'unless it happens to you.'

It had seemed surprising to Grace how easy her life was that year following her marriage to Simeon. Why, she had asked herself repeatedly, had she been so afraid? Things were good at last. She was even growing to love Simeon, not as she had loved Daniel, but his generosity and humour buoyed her up. They had made, as Simeon had predicted, a good team.

And in the time they had been married Simeon had come fully to appreciate his wife. At first he had believed that he was the one who had the most to offer, but soon he had realized how wrong he was. Grace's elegance and style had hauled the business from Oldham and Salford up into the choice cloisters of St Ann's Square, Manchester. Her grace had made their home into a showplace, her honesty had made Jonathan well adjusted. Oh, he had given her his name, but hers was growing bigger than his would ever be and he had realized with amusement that in years to come it would be the name of Grace Ellis, not Grace Grant, which would live on.

It was a time of calm, a steady hiatus after all the years of struggle, poverty and humiliation. Simeon had lavished affection and money on his wife and she had repaid him by becoming pregnant with their child. It was, Simeon would say afterwards, a charmed time.

It was due to change.

Chapter Forty

Joan was standing with her hands in her pockets watching Grace as she sat on the edge of the bed. How she did it was anyone's guess – seven months pregnant and still running about the place like a kid. It was the doctor's fault, Joan had said to Simeon the night before. If he had told Grace that she had to rest she would have done. Who needed a doctor who said that she was a hundred per cent fit? Women needed to rest during pregnancy.

'White blouse or cream one?'

'Huh?'

'I said white or cream blouse?' Grace repeated, flicking her hair over her shoulder. 'I think the white one would look cooler.'

She was preparing to give a speech at the Midland Hotel, Manchester to a group of woman in the fashion trade. At the last count the audience had numbered four hundred. Bloody hell, Joan thought, she would rather disembowel herself than stand up in front of four hundred critical harpies.

'Ernie's ill.'

'Tom's dad?' Grace said, looking over her shoulder. 'Is it serious?'

'Only if he listens to his own diagnosis,' Joan replied shortly. 'He misses Sylvie.'

Tom's mother had died of flu the previous year. No one had expected it, least of all Ernie.

'Make me wonder how Tom would take it if I died.'

Grace flinched. 'Joan, what *are* you talking about?'

'I was just wondering . . . Put on the gold earrings with the pearls . . . if he would miss me.'

'He would die without you.'

'Nah,' Joan said, secretly delighted. 'I wouldn't want him to die – just be miserable, that's all.'

Grace was much bigger this pregnancy. Mind you, Joan thought, this time she didn't have to hide it. Instead she seemed to revel in her condition, taking all the opportunities denied to her before. She could now talk about the baby, discuss names, design a nursery. Not like before, in the little house in Diggle.

There had been no nursery there, just a cot by Grace's bed, every baby toy and all the baby clothes tidied away as though Grace was frightened to admit his existence and encourage comment.

But not this time, Joan thought. This time the nursery for the new baby was already painted with a mural, just next door to the master bedroom, Jonathan's room on the other side. The house was roomy, a garden the size of a park full of mature trees, Simeon's two Labradors playing with the five-year-old Jonathan outside.

Joan never once wondered if Simeon would favour his own child over Jonathan – it wasn't in his nature. He loved Jonathan as his own, and would continue to see him that way. Oh yes, she had dropped lucky, at last, Joan thought looking at Grace. And about bloody time.

'I'm late,' Grace said quickly. 'I'll be back around six.'

'I'll have gone home by then.'

'No, don't! Bring the girls back from school and they can have tea with Jonathan,' Grace said, snatching up her handbag and hurrying to the door. 'See you.'

When she arrived an hour later, the ballroom of

the Midland Hotel was very stuffy, the August heat building up relentlessly as the audience increased. Fans were brought in but as the women seated themselves and began to eat their lunch the heat crept up. High windows were opened, the summer sounds of pigeons and traffic coming in from the square outside as Grace looked down from the dais. The mayoress and several leading businesswomen were seated at the top table with her, the hotel manager fussing around his eminent guests.

Hot and slightly uncomfortable, Grace asked for some water. A few moments later they brought a carafe and a small fan was placed behind the table, the draft making a welcome breeze. Maybe she was pushing herself, Grace thought. She would – in all honesty – rather have been at home. She could have been sitting in the garden with Joan and the children, snoozing in a comfy chair. This would be the last engagement she took on before the baby was born, she promised herself. The very last.

'Are you ready?'

Grace's attention snapped back to reality. 'Yes, I'm ready when you are,' she said, rising to her feet and waiting for the chatter to die down. Professionally she tapped the microphone in front of her and placed her hands on the table for support and to stop her back aching. 'Good afternoon, ladies. I'm very pleased to be here today to talk about a business which interests every one of us . . .'

She was soon into her stride, as confident as always in her subject. For several minutes she spoke about her own struggles to launch the Auden Line and about her benefactors, explaining that their generous donation was now given to the local school to enable gifted pupils to continue their education.

It was strange, but the room felt suddenly a lot hotter,

Grace thought, a fly moving in front of her face as she flicked it away. The fan behind her seemed to be throwing out very little cool air and the sound of the insect's droning seemed to grow louder and louder in her ears.

God, she thought suddenly, she shouldn't have done this. She was too tired and too pregnant to give a speech ... But she went on never the less, making a joke and hearing the rewarding rush of laughter in response, a woman on the front table holding her hand over her mouth, her ring catching the light.

Then Grace suddenly felt sick. She wanted to sit down. Her breathing quickened. She swallowed and took in a deep breath before continuing. *Go on about the lanolin and the beeswax, then into the story about the Holly Walk factory and then you've finished* ... Her voice carried on evenly, but Grace was struggling, her eyes blurring, the fly droning on and on. She could see it out of the corner of her eye as it landed on her plate and sidled around the edge.

Oh God, don't let me be sick! she thought, then just as quickly as the nausea had come, it lifted and she relaxed. Her talk moved on, more laughter followed, then more stories, the women listening avidly. Even one of the hotel waitresses had stopped and was leaning against the door which lead into the kitchen, watching her.

Grace stared at the woman. Her skin went clammy. There was something about her. *There was something about her* ... Doggedly, Grace looked ahead, felt her hands press into the table, her legs weakening. The fan whirled behind her. The fly droned. The woman watched by the door. She wasn't a waitress, after all, Grace thought, she wasn't in uniform.

Her eyes blurred at the moment of realization, and

Grace felt her legs buckle and give way under her. She dropped where she stood, striking the side of the table and cutting her chin. She fell and whilst falling seemed to see white sheets and figures moving amongst them. A man and a woman. Len Billings and Dora. Her mother. The white sheets fluttered in the wind, making rushing sounds in her head as the manager and others bent over her.

Mrs Grant was pregnant, they said. Let her have some air. Call a doctor. Call for help. She was ill.

No, I'm not, Grace thought, I'm dreaming. I'm dreaming . . . But she knew she wasn't, knew that what she had seen was real. The woman who had been standing by the door she knew. She hadn't seen her for decades, but she recognized her through the passing of years and the greying hair.

It was Dora. It was her dead mother come back to life.

Chapter Forty-One

Grace woke to find herself in her own bed, and Simeon talking to Dr Leigh. They were whispering together, heads bent towards each other, Simeon's blue suit catching the rays of the summer sun coming through the window. Struggling to waken herself fully, Grace realized she was sedated and wondered at once if the medication would harm the baby. Her mouth was dry, her throat raw.

'Are you awake, darling?' Simeon asked suddenly, leaning over her. His dark eyes were fixed on her, the cleft in his chin like an ink mark. 'Darling, can you hear me?'

'Yes,' she said softly. Was that her voice, so far off, so faint? God, she had to pull herself together. What had happened? She remembered all at once, she had been giving a speech, the heat, the fly, the fall. *Her mother.*

'Simeon,' she said, catching hold of his arm, 'I have to talk to you.'

'Not now, Mrs Grant,' Dr Leigh said kindly, a tall man in a summer blazer, looking as though he had been called away from a game of cricket. 'You have to be quiet and rest yourself. Think of the baby.'

'Simeon,' Grace whispered again, 'I have to talk to you.'

'Later, darling,' he said, kissing her cheek. 'When you're stronger.'

She didn't have the strength to argue or raise her voice, and instead saw Simeon straighten up and talk to Dr Leigh anxiously. A moment later they left the room,

Grace staring helplessly up at the ceiling over her head. She *wouldn't* sleep, she told herself, not until she had talked to Simeon. Her eyelids drooped, fighting sleep, a bee humming drowsily against the curtain.

Her mother was alive. She had seen her. She had seen Dora. It was her, she recognized her. No one else stood like that, had the same features – even though they were now aged. Besides, why would just any stranger stand there listening? Who, but her mother, would come so secretively to the back of the hall to see her daughter give a speech?

Dora was alive . . . but if she was . . . Grace's eyes closed, her mind wandering. If she *was* alive, *how* was she alive? She had been killed in an road accident years before. She had been buried. Was she a ghost then? Grace suddenly opened her eyes and stared up at the ceiling. Had she seen her mother's ghost?

No, not unless ghosts wore summer dresses and blinked and moved, and watched. She was no ghost. She was solid. She was Dora . . . Oh, Mum, Grace thought helplessly, why didn't you stay? Why didn't you come home with me? But then how could she? Grace thought, she was dead. She was buried in Leesfield Cemetery.

The sedative was taking her down, way, way down into sleep. Frantically Grace fought it. She didn't want to go, wanted to think, wanted to talk to Simeon and get him to fetch her mother home. But Grace couldn't move, couldn't open her eyes, and instead she felt her body relax, sleep ringing over her like a peal of bells.

It had been reckless to have gone, but there was no point thinking about that now. The damage was done. Who would have thought that Grace would have seen her from so far away? She should have stuck to her

400

original plan and waited outside to catch a glimpse of her daughter arriving. That should have been enough.

She had been too careless. It was unbelievable, after so many years of caution. But it had been worth it to see Grace so handsome, so pregnant, so luminous. *Her child*, successful, courted, making a speech in front of hundreds of people. Her Grace, the girl she had known from the start would go to the top.

And now she had almost ruined everything. Grace had seen her and passed out. Was it shock or the heat? Either way it wasn't good for her or the baby she was carrying. Dora looked at her reflection in the mirror in the ladies room at Manchester Piccadilly station, and ran some cold water over her wrists to cool her down.

She had changed so much and yet her daughter had known her. Critically Dora looked at the lines around her eyes, the deep creases in her neck. She had kept her figure, but the fabulous eyes of her youth had become shadowed, the cheeks sunken. It was the face of a woman who had laboured. A dignified face, but one which bore the imprint of long hours and sustained worry.

Rinsing her hands, Dora kept staring at her face, her eyes fixing on the firm line of her mouth. That was what had changed most; no longer sensual, but controlled. A mouth which denied the fact that she had ever loved. Turning away, Dora dried her hands on the towel and tied on a headscarf. The evening was cool now. She could catch her train and be away from Manchester in an hour.

But what about her daughter? Was Grace all right? Was the baby all right? Slowly Dora moved out onto the concourse and looked at the timetable. The train for Liverpool was leaving at nine. From there she would pick up a ferry over to Ireland. Then she would be safe again.

Another thought struck Dora in the same instant. If her daughter had recognized her, had anyone else? She had been walking about Manchester and Oldham for the last two days. It had been a long time since she'd left, but maybe there were still a few people around who had known her once. Dora had thought that the changes in her were enough to keep her unrecognizable – but now she wasn't so sure. If anyone *had* recognized her, it would be a disaster. She had to get away as soon as she could.

Pacing the station platform, Dora kept her head down and avoided looking at anyone. Perhaps Grace would think she had imagined it. The heat, her pregnancy – surely they could be reasons for her to think she saw something? Yes, Dora decided, Grace would come to believe that she had imagined seeing her dead mother. A trick of the sunlight. A mirage on a sweltering August afternoon. Nothing more.

Her heels tip-tapped as she walked along, Dora only pausing when she reached the far end of the platform. There were no people there, no one to look at her. Damn it, she told herself, why had she given in to temptation – she, of all people, who could always control herself? Why had she gone to see her daughter that afternoon after so many afternoons and evenings she had spent thinking about Grace and longing to see her?

It was no good dwelling on it, Dora realized, breathing in and standing upright. It was done; it was over. Grace would never see her again, and to all intents and purposes she hadn't *really* seen her mother that day. A memory mother, nothing more. No, Dora thought, she would have to stay away for ever now. All the things she had wanted to say, all the words collected and collated over the years could never be expressed.

She could not hold her daughter, or her grandchildren. She could not meet her son-in-law, or visit the business Grace had built up. It was all off limits to her. For ever.

Because she didn't exist. Because she *couldn't* exist. The world believed that Dora Ellis was dead. She was lying in Leesfield Cemetery and had been for decades.

And now was no time to come back.

'I tell you, Simeon, I saw my mother,' Grace insisted, holding his hand tightly. 'Dora was standing there at the door when I was giving my speech.'

'It was hot, darling. You were overheated. I should never have let you go.'

'My mother is alive!' Grace shouted. 'Don't treat me like a child.'

'I have to make sure you don't exert yourself,' Simeon replied. 'You had a bad fall.'

'I had a shock which led to a bad fall.'

'Whatever, you need to rest.'

Grace heaved herself upright in the bed, the bump of her stomach swelling the sheet. 'Aren't you listening to what I'm saying? *I saw my mother.* My mother is alive.'

'You *thought* you saw her –'

'No, I did see her. I know my own mother,' Grace contradicted him. 'It was her.'

'She's dead, darling.'

'She isn't!'

He caught hold of Grace's hands. 'Your mother *is* dead. You saw someone who looked like her and you thought – in the heat and tension of giving a speech – that it was her.' He paused to let the idea sink in. 'Think about it, if it had been Dora, wouldn't she have stayed to talk to you? Stayed to see if you were all right?'

'How could she?' Grace countered. 'If people find out she's alive they'll want to know who the woman is who's buried in Leesfield Cemetery.' A chill settled between them. 'The only way my mother could see me was to sneak in, to catch a glimpse of me. She couldn't come out into the open, or she would have done. Oh, Simeon, think about it. If people found out she was alive the police would be called in, questions would be asked. She would be hounded.'

'With good cause,' Simeon said evenly. 'They would want to know why she let everyone think she'd been killed.' He stopped. 'What the hell am I talking about? Your mother *is* dead. Surely her body was identified?'

'Her face was mutilated,' Grace said softly, 'unrecognizable. My mother was only identified by her clothes and papers in her handbag.'

Simeon stared at his wife for a long moment, his curiosity aroused. Dear God, what if Dora Ellis *was* alive? What had she done to hide away for so long? Was the other woman murdered? He had been told, and believed, what everyone else did – that she had run off with some lout, leaving Grace and her father. Years later she had been killed in a road accident. But if she hadn't been the woman run down, she could have effectively 'died' without doing so in reality. She could then have lived her life in obscurity. But how, without papers, without someone else's identity?

'What are you thinking about?'

Simeon looked over to his wife. 'I was thinking that you have a very vivid imagination.' He kissed her cheek. 'I love you very much, Grace, and I think you imagined that you saw your mother today. Or you saw someone who looked like her. Either way, I don't want you to think about it. You have to rest and take care of yourself.'

Grace gazed at him patiently.

'Simeon, how can I? How could *you*, if the situation was reversed?'

'It'll never happen, I can't get pregnant.'

'You know what I mean,' she replied. 'You would have to find out what had happened. You would *have* to. So why am I any different? I have to know too. Whatever happened – whatever my mother did, or whatever was done to her, I have to know.'

'What if you find out that it was something you'd rather not know about? Something which you regret discovering? What if the knowledge turns out to be too terrible to live with? You have a family, Grace – are we worth risking?'

'She was my mother. I don't believe she did anything wicked.'

'People change, Grace. Life changes them. Who knows what happened to her? Who knows what she had to put up with? Your mother ran off, then let everyone believe she was dead for years. Why would anyone do that unless they had something to hide?'

'She's not a bad person.'

'She *wasn't* a bad person – but what if she's changed? Think about it very carefully, Grace. What trouble are you bringing to our family?'

'Why should it be trouble?'

'Why should a woman pass herself off as dead unless there *was* trouble?'

Gently, Grace rested her head on his shoulder, her breath against his neck. He could feel the swell of her stomach against his leg and ached for her.

'Grace, don't jeopardize our happiness for someone who didn't give a damn about you.'

'I won't,' she whispered. 'I just want to see her and talk to her once. No more. Just once . . . She's my mother, my blood. Somehow, I have to see her again, Simeon. I *have* to.'

Chapter Forty-Two

The morning came in sweet, the air high and clear over the garden. Sunlight lightened the roof tiles and flattered the trees with colour. On the grass, dew still remained before the heat began in earnest, and at the back of the house a swinging hammock rocked in a listless breeze.

Skirting the kitchen door, Dora paused by the window and looked in. There was no one around, as she had hoped at so early an hour. Her determination of the previous days had faltered and she found that she could not leave England again without knowing if Grace and the baby were well. The danger to her was secondary. So she had come over to Diggle at dawn and watched the house before finally walking up the drive, keeping close to the bushes.

Her daughter lived here, Dora thought with pride. Grace had a house which was grander than even she had imagined. Hearing a noise, Dora ducked back against the bushes, but it was only an early-morning cat, stiff-backed and challenging before it walked past.

What on earth was she going to do now? Dora wondered. She had got to the house, but how would she get to see her daughter without encountering anyone else? Her plans had not proceeded beyond this point. She had been driven by compulsion, not sense.

Suddenly warm, Dora opened the neck of her blouse and fanned her face with her hat. It was going to be another scalding day. She had seen photographs of Simeon in the newspaper so she knew she would recognize him. But she didn't want to meet him, to have to face the inevitable questions. He would be protective of his wife, naturally – would ask Dora what she wanted and how she was still alive. He would judge her, and then what?

Dora wasn't about to let that happen, so she decided that she would wait until she saw her daughter. Grace would look out of a window or walk into the garden. It was a warm day; she would be bound to come out sometime. All Dora had to do was to wait.

At the same moment that her mother was hovering outside, Grace woke and turned to see Simeon fast asleep beside her. Her head had cleared and the memory of the previous day came back with blistering clarity. Carefully she slid out of bed without waking him and walked downstairs. She opened the fridge door and drank a glass of cold milk. Thoughtfully, she rested the cold glass against her cheek and touched the swell of her stomach. The baby was still, only the occasional kick sending a flutter against the fine cotton of her nightdress.

Opening the back door, Grace looked out and then wandered into the garden. The heat surprised her and she kept to the cool shadow of the house, the glass still in her hand. She had been disturbed by a dream. Simeon had found her mother and told the police. Dora had been arrested without Grace ever knowing what had happened . . . Sweat clammy, Grace had woken to the realization that Simeon might *just* behave that way to protect her.

And how could he understand? Dora wasn't his mother. He had no memory of the handsome woman who had pressurized her daughter into expecting the best. The ambitious Dora had instilled in Grace the will to succeed and she knew that without her mother she would never have achieved so much.

Hiding behind the bushes, Dora was startled to hear Grace's footfall. Her eyes fixed on the woman in the white nightdress holding a glass of milk. She seemed like a child to her again, the serious little Grace she remembered. Without shoes, her hair messy from sleep, and no make-up, only the bulge of her pregnancy reminded Dora of the years which had passed.

Relieved that Grace seemed well, Dora decided that she could slip away again. She had done what she set out to do. But as she moved, she caught her leg against a twig, the snap of the dry wood sounding loud in the silence.

Startled, Grace turned, then stood rigid on the spot.

'Grace?' Dora said simply, walking out from the protection of the bushes.

Shaken, Grace lost her grip on the glass and it fell onto the grass, the milk making a white veil over the dewy green.

'Is that *you*? Is that you, Mother?'

Dora moved towards her quickly, then waited, only a foot away from her daughter. Timidly Grace reached out and touched her hand. She was real, her hand was flesh and blood.

'You're alive.'

'Yes,' Dora said, her voice as firm as it had ever been. 'I had to come and see that you were all right – you and the baby. I have to go now.'

'No! Don't go.' Grace gripped her mother's hand tightly. 'I want to talk to you.'

Dora looked round anxiously, Grace noting the action and drawing her mother towards the summerhouse at the end of the garden. From there no one in the house would be able to see them.

Heavily Grace sat down and looked at her mother.

'I thought I'd seen a ghost yesterday.'

'I'm sorry, I didn't want to frighten you,' Dora replied calmly. Above her head a spider's wed caught the light, the fibres shuddering in the breeze. 'I suppose I have to explain what happened. I owe it to you.'

'We heard you were killed in a road accident. You were buried in Leesfield Cemetery,' Grace said hurriedly, her hands resting on her stomach as though to protect her baby from the shock. 'If it's not you, who *is* buried there?'

'A woman I worked with, Moira Hughes,' Dora said, leaning against the guard rail of the porch. 'She was a lonely woman with no family. I lent her my coat that night, and so when she was knocked down someone recognized it as mine. I had left a letter in the pocket too, addressed to me. Her face was mutilated, so when they presumed it the body was mine there was no one who could say different. She had no family, no one to miss her . . . I heard what had happened almost immediately and knew then that I had a chance to get away. To lose myself.'

'But you were with Len Billings,' Grace said, frowning. 'I don't understand.'

'I was *never* with Len Billings. I had to get away and he provided the opportunity –'

'But we all thought that you had run off with him,' Grace replied, baffled. 'Why did you let us think that?'

'So that you would hate me,' Dora said simply. 'I wanted to you hate me so that you wouldn't miss me or look for me. If I had simply wandered off you would have searched for me.' Dora paused, glancing at the house. Her expression was unreadable. 'I was pregnant with Len Billings' child –'

'Was his baby more important than me?' Grace asked quietly.

Dora shook her head. 'You don't understand – how could you? I wanted to get out, Grace. I'd had enough of looking after your father and I wanted to feel alive again. Oh, it was madness, I know that now. But it happened . . . You can hate me, I deserve it, but Len Billings had come back into my life by then. At first I avoided him, but then I started to meet up with him. One thing led to another.' She hurried on, 'I don't make any excuses for what I did. But I was tired, Grace. I wanted to get away. Len Billings didn't make me go, the baby did.'

'Was that enough to leave us?'

'Think about it,' Dora said shortly. 'I couldn't stay and have you share my disgrace when people found out. You were better off without me. I knew how hard it would be for you, but I promised myself that I would help you as soon as I could.'

Grace's voice was distant, remote. 'What happened to the baby?'

Dora looked away. 'I was working as a cleaner almost until he was born. He was a sickly child.' She paused, struggling to keep her voice steady. 'He died of influenza when he was a year old.'

Grace winced. 'I'm sorry.'

'So was I,' Dora admitted. 'I thought it was a punishment.'

Grace touched her own stomach automatically to feel the child there.

'But you never thought of coming home?'

Dora shook her head. 'What for? I'd burned my boats. Oh, think about it, Grace. I would have held you back.

You didn't need to have your mother dragging on your coat-tails.' Dora turned away, choosing her words cautiously. 'I stopped feeling anything after the baby died. I just kept working as a cleaner wherever I could find work, and then there was the accident which killed Moira Hughes.

'I'd just heard about some old man who needed a housekeeper. So I went to work for him as Moira Hughes. But I wasn't his mistress, I was never that.' She paused for a moment, wondering if to continue, before adding, 'I had already made some money through hard graft – the first payments I sent to you – but soon after I was making substantial amounts. I arranged everything through Malcolm Seagrave.'

The hairs on Grace's arms rose. 'Malcolm Seagrave?'

'You know him, Grace. He was very efficient and after he died Frederick Conrad took over.' Grace could hear a rushing of blood in her ears. 'Virtually all the money I made I sent to you. I paid for your education, and I supported you and your father whilst you set up the business –'

'But I thought my benefactors were a charity, or the Spencer sisters,' Grace said dully. 'It was *you*?'

A smile passed over Dora's lips, then faded as quickly as it had appeared.

'It was me all along. Listen to me, Grace, I knew I could do better for you from a distance, when no one knew who was helping you. That way, you would presume it *was* a charity or someone like the Spencers.'

'But where did the money come from?' Grace asked, baffled. 'It was a lot of money, over a long time. How could you afford it?'

'Let's just say that I could,' Dora replied enigmatically.

'That's not enough,' Grace retorted. 'I want to know where the money came from.'

'Theodore Armstrong.'

Grace shrugged. '*Theodore Armstrong?* I've never heard of him.'

'He was the old man I worked for,' Dora explained. 'Theo was very rich. He had been investing in stocks and shares for a long time and had made a fortune.'

'Legally?' Grace asked, a note of caution in her voice.

'Oh yes, Theo was clever. He wasn't a crook when I knew him. That would have been too easy. He liked to use his brain, to work the markets. When he began, I don't think he was so particular, but when I was with him he was above board.'

Shocked, Grace stared at her mother. 'So how did *you* get wealthy?'

To her surprise, Dora laughed.

'I had been cleaning his house for only a week or so. I was surly, it was just after the baby died and I didn't give a damn what happened to me any more . . . I used to clean up, make his evening meal, then leave. Well, one night, I'd forgotten something and I doubled back. Theodore Armstrong was at the bottom of the stairs.'

'Dead?'

'No, but he would have died if I hadn't been there and got help.' Dora sighed and dabbed at her forehead with her scarf. 'He gave me a reward for saving his life. It seemed like poetic justice to pass the money on to you.' She paused, remembering, aware from her face that Grace was hardly able to take in what her mother was saying. 'Theo was a very superstitious man and after that he never wanted me far away from him. So I moved into his house and took care of him. He was lonely – no family – and he wanted to talk. Oh, how he liked to talk.

Gradually he taught me about his business, about stocks and shares. It was a game to him, and I was always a quick learner. I think it amused him to teach me what he knew, but before long he could see I was no fool.'

'*You* made the money?'

'Yes, I made it,' Dora said with pride. 'Every penny. Apart from the reward, none of the cash I sent to you was Theodore Armstrong's.' She put her head on one side as she looked at her daughter. 'You never have to worry about it – the money's clean.'

'But I don't understand,' Grace replied. 'My benefactors knew everything that happened to me. Private things, things no one knew.'

'Like the incident with Elmer Shaw?'

Grace rocked. 'You knew about that?'

'It's strange how life works out. How everything seems interwoven. Fated, if you like.' Dora stepped back out of the sunshine. 'After I had been with Theo for a while I knew a lot about his life. He was very generous with his money but I think he had a guilty conscience about his past. Maybe there were things he had done as a young man which he regretted, I'm not sure. I just know that he'd tried to make up for it. He wanted to make amends – we both did. Only he didn't know about my past, never knew where my money went.'

Grace frowned. 'I still don't understand how you knew about Elmer Shaw.'

'When Theo was younger he had been working in London. He was an important man, and important men have followers. One of his acolytes had been Elmer Shaw.'

'No!' Grace said hoarsely.

Dora nodded. 'It's true. Shaw admired Theo, looked up to him and was always hanging around in those days.

414

As for Theo, Elmer Shaw was the son he'd never had. But after a while Theo began to hear things he didn't like about Shaw. He was becoming corrupt. Theo didn't approve of his business methods and finally he wouldn't have anything to do with him any more.'

'But –'

'Hear me out,' Dora said. 'Theo was a very astute man. But he had no family and had always had a blind spot for Shaw. So, after a while, Shaw started coming round to see Theo again. I warned him to have nothing to do with Shaw, but he wanted to think the best of him. That was how I heard about you going to work at Shaw's mill. That was why I tried to stop it – and that was how I heard about what happened to you.'

Grace stared at her mother. 'How?'

'One night Shaw came to see Theo. He was drunk. He could never hold his booze. Well, Shaw was bragging about his business, Elsa James, and his other women. He kept drinking and talking – and then he told Theo what had happened with you.' Dora paused, swallowing. 'I was listening at the door. I heard every word. After that, I told Theo that I would leave him if he ever had Shaw in the house again. He never did.'

Grace's voice was hardly more than a whisper. 'What happened then?'

'I lived my life as Moira Hughes. I was very private and very careful that no one would get too close to ask any questions. Theo never knew that I was Dora Ellis, or that I had a family. He believed what I told him – and I was always very careful not to be found out. Can you imagine the scandal if I had been exposed for who I was? Everyone thought that Dora Ellis was dead. So let her rest in peace. I was doing much more for you as Moira Hughes.'

'Did Theodore Armstrong never find out?'

'Never. But when he died unexpectedly things got tough. I had money but I was sick and I had to pay for medical care for a long time . . . That's when I had to cut back on the money I was sending to you.'

'You were sick?' Grace repeated, shaken. '*How* sick?'

'It doesn't matter now. I recovered in time. It's the past, over and done with,' Dora said briskly. 'When I recovered, I bought a little place away from England – and that's where I've stayed.' She looked into Grace's eyes levelly. 'I *earned* the money I sent you.'

'I never thought –'

'You wondered about it,' Dora replied. 'I would have wondered the same. But I don't need your approval, Grace. I can live with what I've done and that's what matters to me. That money gave you an education, supported your father and started up your business.'

'I wondered why it was always there at the right time,' Grace said distantly. 'I wondered why my benefactors always knew what was going on in my life.'

'Money buys many things – possessions, power, the help of people just teetering on the right side of the law. I was born in Miller Lane, Grace, remember? I grew up with the feckless and the criminal. You learn about it because it's around you everyday. Street cunning, they call it. I always had that, that's why I've survived. That's why I could seize the opportunity to make a new life for myself.'

'Weren't you ever afraid?' Grace asked, her voice soft. 'Didn't you ever want to come home? I missed you so much.'

Dora seemed for an instant to soften and then straightened her back.

'I never stopped loving you, Grace. I never stopped

thinking about you and feeling guilty for what I'd done. But later I saw my chance to make amends.'

'You could help, but you couldn't come back?'

'To what?' Dora countered. 'To the police? Can you imagine the questions, Grace? Why hadn't I come forward and told them that it was a case of mistaken identity? That the woman buried in Leesfield Cemetery wasn't me? Where had I been since? What had I been doing?'

'But –'

'No, Grace, I couldn't come back; I couldn't face the questions then and I can't face them now. Far better that I'm believed dead.'

'But what about Frederick Conrad? He knows.'

'No, he doesn't. I arranged everything through an intermediary. No one knows.'

Grace hesitated. 'Except me.'

Grace felt the baby kick against her stomach. Wearily, she rested her head back against the wooden wall of the summerhouse. The sun had risen and begun to dry the dew, birds flocking into the high ash trees by the garden wall. The situation was like a dream from which she would wake. Her mother wasn't *really* here; she hadn't *really* worked and supported her for so long, had she?

Yes, she had. Because that would be typical of Dora Ellis. Slowly, Grace turned her head. Her mother was watching her, studying her as though making a mental image which would have to suffice when the real person was no longer there.

'Did he hate me for what I did?'

Grace knew at once what she meant. 'No, Dad never hated you. He missed you and then he became very ill.'

'Another stroke?'

'He's senile,' Grace admitted. 'He doesn't understand anything any more. He hasn't for years.'

Dora swallowed, her throat dry.

'I did love him, once. But he was a gentleman, and after a while I couldn't stay. I was drying up, getting old before I should have done. You were going to succeed, Arthur was just going to get older and older. I missed the life I had never had – I wanted to be rid of him.' Dora's eyes had dulled. 'You *should* hate me. I wanted things I never should have done. I wanted Len Billings once – you know that, Grace. You saw us once when I was putting out the washing.' She closed her eyes.

Grace could see the image too, the same image which had dogged her for years.

'But when I walked out I couldn't go to him. I had thought I was Miller Lane through and through, but I wasn't. I was better than that. Better than Len Billings, at least . . . Your father was too good for me, though. I should never have married him.'

'He never thought that. He never stopped loving you either.'

'He should have picked a better woman.'

'No one was better than you,' Grace replied. 'Your photograph was always by his bedside and your night-dress was always under the pillow, next to him.'

For an instant Dora seemed to rock, the words a body blow.

'Dear God, I never realized . . . I never knew . . .'

It was still early, no sign of life. Slowly Grace got to her feet and slid her arm round her mother. Without saying a word, Grace then led Dora across the lawn and into the house by the back door.

There was a warm stillness about the hall and stairs. Only a soft cooing of pigeons outside disturbed the silence. Gently Grace guided Dora up the stairs and then froze at a sudden noise. They both waited, then there was silence again. Slowly they moved on, Grace leading her mother into the separate part of the house where Arthur lived.

She knew that her father's nurse would be in the room next to his, her door left ajar so that she could hear any disturbance in the night. Sure enough, the door was open, Grace closing it as she passed and then guiding her mother across the darkened bedroom where her father lay.

Dora had gone with her in silence, not knowing what to expect – but certainly not expecting to see her husband lying still on a white-sheeted bed. Gingerly half opening the curtains, Grace saw the daylight fall across the sheet and across her father's profile. Dora walked towards him and kneeled down. He was immobile. Grace watched as her mother studied his face – the sunken cheeks, the fine hair hardly covering the skull.

Then she saw Dora's eyes settle on her photograph by the bedside. She stared at it for a long time. Then her hand slid under the pillow, her fingers closing on her old nightdress. It was then, for the first time in her life, that Grace saw her mother cry. It was noiseless, the tears slow as Dora rested her head on the bed beside her husband's hand.

Grace would say for the rest of her life that her father *sensed* that his wife was there. Arthur didn't move or speak, but something in the atmosphere of that room shifted. There was love there, an old love which he had remembered and which had kept him alive for years. A love which had been so strong that it had survived illness and madness. In his senility he forgot everything but the

419

one thing which had always mattered to him most – *his wife*.

Sick and confused, Arthur had refused to die before he saw Dora again. Whatever he had heard, whatever he had been told, he had never believed Dora was dead. That was why he had lived for so long, Grace realized. Because he had been waiting for his wife to come back to him.

And now, finally, he could let go.

Chapter Forty-Three

It seemed to Grace that she lost both her parents that morning. Deep in shock, she told Simeon that her father had died, then she told Jonathan. It was left to Simeon to tell a distraught Don the news. When he had done so, Simeon walked into the kitchen to find Grace silent and motionless.

'Are you OK? The baby's not on its way, is it?'

'No,' she said simply, wondering how to phrase the next words. 'My mother was here.'

'What?'

'My mother was here this morning before anyone was about. She's alive. I told you I hadn't imagined it.'

Disbelieving, Simeon sat down at the table next to her. Above them he could hear Polly calling for Jonathan. She would feed him and then walk him to school, doing the shopping afterwards. Despite her engagement to Geoffrey, there were no firm marriage plans. It seemed that she liked to be with Jonathan more than her fiancé.

'Jonathan's up and about.'

Grace stared at her husband. 'Did you hear what I said about Dora?'

'Yes, I heard,' he replied. 'I just didn't know what to say.'

'She was my benefactor. *She* provided the money.'

Grace saw him blink slowly. He seemed angry, she thought, but about what?

'I suppose she did that to salve her conscience.'

'Hey!' Grace snapped. 'She worked for that money.'

'Doing what?'

'My mother earned that money by hard graft,' Grace said coldly. 'There's nothing suspect about it.'

'Did she tell you that?'

'Yes.'

'And you believe her?'

'I know my mother!'

'You didn't know her well enough to know that she would have pretended to be dead. Or that she was the one providing you with money. Personally, I don't think you know your mother at all.'

Stung, Grace looked away. 'She's tried to make amends –'

'She had a lot to make amends for!' he retorted. 'Your mother got pregnant, left you and your father and cleared off with some lout –'

'But she didn't!' Grace interrupted him. 'She never went off with Len Billings. She just let us think she did –'

'A noble gesture.'

'Don't sound so snide, Simeon. It wasn't easy for her and she lost the baby,' Grace retorted hotly. 'She did her best; she's not perfect.'

'*Perfect!* Jesus!' he snapped, 'she's a long way from perfect. There aren't that many women who would let their families think they were dead and buried. Did she tell you *who* was buried instead?'

'A woman she knew. She was wearing Dora's coat and had some letters of Dora's on her when she was knocked down.'

'That was convenient.'

'What's that supposed to mean?'

'It means that it's all too pat. It means that no normal woman would be able to carry off such a cold-blooded deception and keep it up for decades.'

'My mother had her reasons.'

Simeon raised his eyebrows. He would never have allowed the woman near his family if he had known she was around. She was no good, everyone knew that.

'Why can't you realize that Dora Ellis is an opportunist? If she wasn't, why didn't she come forward until now, Grace? Now, when you're married and settled, with money and a big house.'

Grace shook her head to clear her thoughts. 'She didn't *mean* to come forward now. It was just an accident that I saw her the other day.'

'A well-planned accident, if you ask me,' Simeon replied. 'Look, darling, I don't want you getting upset. You've just lost your father and the baby's due any time –'

'I wasn't upset until you started saying all these things,' Grace responded sharply. 'I was pleased to see her, touched to know that she had been my benefactor all this time. It felt so good to know that she'd been watching over me. But now you've ruined it! You made it ugly, made my mother sound dirty. How dare you judge her? You never even knew her!'

Hurriedly Grace got to her feet, angry. He was making her defend Dora, making her choose sides. Either he was right – or Dora was. No compromise.

Simeon reached out to her. 'I didn't mean to hurt you –'

But Grace cut him off, moving away. 'You didn't think about it. You're annoyed because Dora came back, annoyed because she turned out to have been the one who helped me. You like to be number one in my life, Simeon, you always have done. You don't want to share me with anyone, do you?'

'Not with your bloody mother, no!'

'Well, you'd better get used to it!' Grace shouted, walking out of the kitchen and letting the door slam behind her.

Bloody hell, Joan thought when she saw Grace later, it was a day and a half, and no mistake. The news about Dora had come as a shock, especially followed by the death of Arthur and Grace's corrosive row with Simeon. Now Joan was sitting with a silent Grace in the drawing room, her brain reeling from what she had been told.

Arthur was dead. After so long, it seemed hardly credible. Joan thought back to the times in the old house, to the way she used to call up to Mr Ellis when she came visiting. She remembered him later, cursing and banging on the floor with his cane. Later still he was nothing but a shape in a bed, Cleggie talking incessantly to little more than a corpse. Arthur had seemed dead for years.

Like Dora . . .

'You should rest,' Joan said at last. 'You look terrible. All this shock can't be good for the baby.'

'My mother's back and my father's dead . . .' Grace trailed off. 'I can't believe any of this.'

'Why did you row with Simeon?'

'He was suggesting all kinds of things – like how my mother made the money.' The thought had gone through Joan's head too but she had had more sense than to voice it. 'I explained that she had earned it legitimately, but he said she was an opportunist. That the only reason she had turned up now was because I was successful.'

'Which you wouldn't have been without her,' Joan said succinctly. 'If your mother hadn't sent you the money you never would have made a success.'

Grace nodded eagerly. 'That's what I said! But Simeon

can't see it. He wants to think the worst of her, wants to keep us apart.'

'Why?'

'Because he's jealous,' Grace said flatly, getting up and drawing the curtains against the hot sun. 'He wants me on my own. Just the two of us. He wants me as his possession. He wants everything as his possession. He married me, therefore I am his. *His* wife. *His* children. He doesn't want me to love anyone else. He has to rule his world and everything in it. He sets the standards, at home and at work. I've given way to him when I wouldn't have given way to anyone else. It didn't matter before, but now it does. Simeon's a snob –'

'What?'

'Oh, he was man enough to marry an single woman with a child – but that's all forgotten. I'm respectable now. We're leading members of the community – a long way from Miller Lane. He doesn't want any of that to be threatened by Dora.'

'You can't blame him in a way,' Joan replied. 'He only wants the best for you.'

'He wants the best for himself more.' Grace said shortly. 'I can't think clearly any longer. I haven't even grieved for my father yet. What's the matter with me?'

'It's shock, everything happening at once,' Joan replied, getting up and walking over to her. 'You should rest.'

'Rest? How can I? I've lost my father, Joan. And now I've lost my mother all over again.'

Later that day Simeon came home from work to find Grace asleep in bed, Joan playing downstairs with Jonathan. Stern-faced and cold, Simeon was unlike himself, and Joan steered away from any mention of Dora. The funeral arrangements had been already been made, Arthur removed to a chapel of rest, the nurse paid up. An era was over.

Out of the corner of her eye, Joan watched Simeon and then phoned Tom to ask if he would pick up the girls from school. Something told her that she had to stay, but as the day lengthened and the evening came in she felt out of place and in the way. The atmosphere was strained. Something fundamental had shifted, and it was in the air, as pungent as an odour.

A couple of times Joan looked in on Grace, but she was sleeping, her dark hair over the pillow, her hands over her stomach. She slept deeply, as though exhausted, with that dead flat sleep of shock. Going down to the kitchen, Joan sat with Jonathan whilst he ate the dinner Polly had made for him.

The night had come down without anyone noticing. Lamps went on in the drawing room and in Simeon's study. Phones rang a long way off and a radio played up in Polly's room at the top of the house. Smoking a cigarette, Joan walked round the garden, deep in thought.

Simeon should be with Grace now. It was the time she needed him the most. But where was he? In his study, working. They should be holding each other, comforting each other as couples did in distress; as she had clung to Tom when her father died. This was not the time for either of them to be alone . . . Slowly Joan inhaled the smoke and narrowed her eyes as she watched the house. Trauma was what made or broke a marriage. Trouble made a couple closer or drove them apart.

Another minute passed and then she ground her cigarette out with the heel of her shoe. Dear God, she thought, just *what* had actually died? Grace's father? Or her marriage?

Chapter Forty-Four

February 1952

In the laboratory in St Andrew's Place, Brian Lawley was working on a new skin foundation. He had been talking to Simeon earlier and then gone in to see Grace, the latter contradicting her husband's instructions. It had been the same for months, since Grace had returned to work at the end of October the previous year, only weeks after the birth of her beloved Richard.

Congratulations had been met with subdued thanks, the atmosphere between husband and wife frosty. The staff were bewildered. Simeon and Grace had never argued before – in fact they had always laughed about things. Now Grace was distant with Simeon, at times almost curt. All the old touches, the winks of familiarity had gone. With Jonathan, Grace was as loving as ever, and she patently doted on the baby, but her love for her husband was in cold storage – and everyone sensed it.

After their argument Simeon had felt guilty but expected that the bad feeling would blow over. It was true that he distrusted Dora's motives, but he had good reason. She had been a poor mother and he wanted to protect his wife from any further hurt. But there was more to it than that, he admitted. Grace had been right, he *was* jealous of Dora, terrified of the possibility that he might have to share Grace with her. His possessiveness had never been obvious before – but then it had never been tested before.

When it had, he'd reacted badly. He wanted Dora Ellis out of their life. And he wanted her to stay out.

They had been so happy before – what was the point of letting some disruptive influence spoil everything? Besides, she was no credit to Grace. Everyone remembered Dora Ellis, how she had run off. What good could she bring them? How could she fit into their lives? Their social circle?

He hated her. Loathed her. And worse, Simeon didn't know whether or not his wife was in touch with her mother. Grace had never said. Her confidences had stopped that morning when she'd told him about Dora coming back. After that, she'd told him nothing. She'd never spoken her mother's name, or that of her father. It was as though she was holding on to her past alone, as though she had chosen memory over her present life with him.

It was obvious then to Simeon that she had never loved him. His insecurity rattled him; he should never have risked loving any woman so completely. It was true that Grace had told him she was not in love with him, but he had come to believe that she cared. Affection had been shared, certainly, and many laughs. They had made love and had had a baby – but it still wasn't enough. He'd even thought – meanly – that he would expose Dora. Tell the police and let them track her down. Get rid of her once and for all.

But Grace would know who had betrayed her mother. After all, who else knew about Dora apart from him and Joan? And Joan would never betray Grace. So instead Simeon waited for his wife to soften and formed numerous apologies in his head, which were never uttered because the time was never quite right.

Inch by inch Grace drew away from him. In her

428

distress she was distant; even at her father's funeral she had never once reached for his hand. Simeon knew that he should reach out to her but was afraid of being rejected. Dear God, he thought, so this was the pain of loving, was it? He had been right all along: he should never have married.

Christmas had come and gone, only baby Richard and Jonathan lifting the atmosphere. Polly having gone home for the holiday, and the staff off duty, the house had been left to the four of them. Snow had come down thick on Christmas Eve and made a postcard out of the garden, but the chill inside had been slower to thaw, the New Year coming in cold.

After a while the rift between them had grown so wide that no one had dared to bridge it. If one of them had tried earlier, it would have broken the spell, but neither had. Grace had been too hurt, and Simeon too afraid of rejection. Instead he'd let one malignant thought possess him: *Grace had never loved him.* It was obvious. She was like her mother in some ways, and certainly as ruthless. She had cut him out, isolated him in a space where he could move neither forwards nor backwards.

Grace felt marooned in the same place. She had expected Simeon to come to her, but he hadn't. That showed what he thought of her, didn't it? She had lost her father, there had been the re-emergence of her mother, all followed by the birth of their son. But it had *still* not been enough to force her husband's hand. After a while she'd become as afraid of rejection as he was; and so they shadow-boxed around each other in the big house, and at work. Together, and always apart.

'So give him a cuddle,' Joan had suggested hopefully. 'Men always come round after that.'

'I can't, we don't cuddle. We don't touch any more,' Grace had replied.

'No sex?'

'No, not for months,' Grace had admitted. 'He doesn't want me any more.'

'Do you want him?'

Do you want him? Joan had asked her and for a long time afterwards Grace had considered the question. The answer was damning, and had left her sick with emptiness. No, she *didn't* want Simeon, she never had. She had grown fond of him, but he had only ever been a poor second to Daniel. The driving, all-absorbing love she had felt for Daniel had been natural. They could never have argued for long, never have resisted touching each other. She would, Grace realized, have died for him.

Daniel Goodman had been the man of her life; no one could replace him. And she shouldn't have let anyone try. It wasn't Simeon's fault, it wasn't hers. Their quarrel had swelled and fed itself on their insecurities until it had gobbled up any vestige of love left.

'Mrs Grant?'

She turned back to Brian and then looked at the sample on the laboratory table. 'That's good. I want to see the finished product tomorrow.'

'I gave it to your husband,' Brian replied, frowning. 'He's had it since yesterday.'

Stiffly, Grace smiled and walked off, seething inside. Simeon had no right to do things behind her back! This was their joint business, not his alone. They *shared* it. Hurriedly Grace wrenched open the door of her office and dialled Simeon's number at Holly Walk.

'Hello?'

She paused, wrong-footed. 'Is Mr Grant there?'

'No,' came back the female voice. 'Who's this?'

Stupidly, Grace put down the phone without answering and then sat for a while staring blankly ahead. Simeon's secretary was a middle-aged lady called Mrs Dobbins – but the woman who had answered sounded young. Very young. She couldn't have been one of the workers – Simeon never allowed them near his office – so who was she?

Grace's heart rate increased rapidly, her fingernails tapping on the desk. It was her fault, Grace thought. She had spent too much time preoccupied, thinking about her parents, her children, and her marriage. For once she hadn't been able to concentrate on work and this was the result – *she didn't know what was going on.*

She could ask Simeon, of course. Just ask when they were at home tonight. But they hardly talked any more. Any question as loaded as this one would be sure to cause a further furore.

Maybe it was nothing, Grace assured herself, and then felt her imagination take over. If Simeon was having an affair, so what? He was married to her, she wasn't sleeping with him, so he had gone elsewhere. It was what some men did. She had always known that her husband was highly sexed. It didn't matter, did it?

But it did. If Simeon was having an affair it would humiliate her and wreck any chance of their marriage ever working. Besides, if he loved her, he couldn't be cheating on her . . . but maybe he didn't love her any more? But how could some other woman get her man?

Well, why not? Grace asked herself. If she didn't want him . . . It would have to be sorted out. Their marriage couldn't be allowed just to stagger on. Both of them had to talk.

So when Simeon came home that night he found

431

Grace waiting for him in the drawing room. When he walked in she turned off the television set and smiled uncertainly. He smiled half-heartedly back at her, and then sat down.

'What is it?'

'We have to talk, Simeon.'

'About what?'

'Our marriage.'

He sighed and leaned back in his seat.

'What's the matter with us?'

'You tell me, Grace.'

She struggled to hold her temper, feeling hot and embarrassed. This was her husband, for Christ's sake, and it was liking talking to an aggressive stranger.

'We're not getting on.'

'I know.'

'Why?'

'Enlighten me.'

'Simeon, don't do this. Talk to me.'

'Oh, you want to talk now, do you?' he said, his tone cold. 'You didn't want to talk for months, but now you do. For bloody months you've given me the bum's rush, walked away from me, moved away if I touched you! Why? Just because I told you what I thought of your mother?'

'It was more than that –'

'*Was it?* Well, was it the death of your father? The birth of Richard?' he queried. 'Just tell me, Grace, which particular event triggered all of this off? I don't know. You didn't turn to me in any of it. Not once! I wanted to help you when your father died, I wanted to hold you when you had our son. Richard is my child too!' He slammed his hand down on the coffee table between them. 'You never loved me, I know that now –'

432

'Stop it!' Grace shouted. 'That's enough! You're making it sound as though all of this is my fault. You could have come to me, Simeon. You were the one who said all those things about my mother – I never said a word about your family.'

'You had no need to!'

'And you had no right to criticize Dora! She did what she could to help. Besides, she's not in our lives any more, so don't use her as an excuse for all of this.'

'How do I know she's not around?' Simeon countered. 'After all, she was supposedly dead for years.'

'Leave her out of it!'

'Why should I?'

Grace was on her feet, shouting. 'Why are you so afraid that she would ruin our life? What life, Simeon? *This* life? *This* marriage?'

He was pale with fury. 'It was good enough for you before –'

'And I put as much into this marriage as you did.'

'I don't think so! Besides, you were lucky anyone would marry you with a bastard kid in tow.'

Without thinking, Grace lunged forward and struck him, catching the side of Simeon's head and sending him reeling into the coffee table.

'You bastard! You talk about class – what kind of man would say that to his wife?' She towered over him, her face chalky with anger. 'Get out! I never want to see you again!'

He staggered to his feet, humiliation making him bluster. He would show her! He would show her she couldn't play with his feelings.

'I'll ruin you!' he blustered, wondering where the words were coming from. She *should* have loved him, he thought blindly. 'I'll make sure you end up where you belong!' He was spluttering with resentment, hurt. 'I'll cripple you. I swear I will! You're like your mother, Grace. You're a peasant at heart – and you're way out of your league.'

Chapter Forty-Five

It was coming up to the first anniversary of Richard's birth. The house had seen a cool summer, the gardens heavy with leaf from incessant rain showers. Grace was sitting by the open French windows with Joan, Jonathan playing outside with Georgia and Mary, supervised by Polly, the baby asleep in his pram. At the age of six Jonathan was a stocky child, with his father's straight gaze and thick wavy hair – an attractive child, so unlike his half-brother, who was striking but in an entirely different way.

Richard had inherited his father's dark eyes and hair, and his mother's strength of character. Even as a baby he was determined and knew what he wanted. Jonathan, as the doting elder brother, gave into him constantly, as naturally loving as his father ... Grace watched them and thought of the letter she had received that morning. The one which Simeon had had sent via his solicitor; the letter which asked for a divorce.

In a way, she wasn't surprised. In fact she had heard rumours that Simeon was back with Elsa James and knew that Elsa would be pushing Simeon hard. Simeon felt rejected, scorned too – and was spiteful because of it. Grace confided to Joan how she couldn't understand the viciousness of the terms of the letter.

'Because he always swore he'd never get married and have kids,' Joan said, looking out at the garden. 'He can't understand how you couldn't want him.'

'I never said outright that I didn't want him,' Grace

435

replied. 'He was the one who pushed for marriage.'

'All the more reason to feel like a chump now then,' Joan responded. 'He'll be regretting that he ever let a woman get so close to him. I bet he was thinking that you'd try and win him over and get him back – and you didn't. You let him go. So now you're the villain of the piece.'

Grace shook her head. 'He wanted to settle down –'

'*His way,*' Joan countered. 'Otherwise, he doesn't like it. He's lost control now and he resents that, so he's going back to his old life – just to show you. Oh, you know what he was like, Grace: Simeon was the eternal bachelor.'

Grace's voice was cool. 'You pushed me to marry him.'

Joan nodded, discomforted. 'Yeah, I know. Sorry about that. But I thought he would change, settle down. He was crazy about you.'

'Not so crazy about me now,' Grace replied. 'He says he'll let me keep the house – because of the children – but he wants to buy me out of the business.'

'What?'

'Quite,' Grace replied, seething.

Her business, the Auden Line that *she* had built up from nothing! The backstreet dream that had netted a fortune. He wanted it – and it had now become apparent how much. Grace had always known that her husband could be unscrupulous, she had just never expected that he would turn that ruthlessness on to her. But now he had, and she was reeling from the shock. Her face showed traces of stress, her mouth tight and every movement of her body was stiff with tension.

Joan's voice was sharp with disbelief. 'He can't do that. It's your business.'

'He can,' Grace told her, 'and apparently he's been

planning his little coup for a while. Ever since that argument about Dora ... Funny to think of my own husband plotting behind my back.'

'I don't believe it.'

'Neither did I, but it seems that both of us underestimated Simeon's real character. I have to say one thing: he was very sly. Whilst I was grieving for my father and recovering from the birth of Richard, he was scheming.' Grace breathed out sharply. 'I trusted him, like a fool! Whilst I was so busy elsewhere, he was running the business and signing things on my behalf. What I didn't realize was that he was signing papers which effectively gave him control.'

'He can't have done! He's hasn't got a big enough share in the company to get you out.'

'He has now – with Elsa's ten per cent.' Joan stared at her incredulously. 'They've voted me off the board – saying I'm unpredictable and negligent. The way he's organized it they could make a good case too.'

Joan exhaled loudly. She could hear Jonathan and her girls playing in the garden. The three children were hooting with laughter and running, ducking behind the high trees, Polly following behind, pushing Richard in his pram.

'I don't believe it,' Joan repeated. 'Are you *sure* that Simeon's back with that slut James?'

'He has been for some time,' Grace replied, her voice wavering. 'They obviously plotted it together. Elsa was always trying to get back at me for marrying him in the first place.' She stood up, suddenly restless. 'I can't stand this, I'm going for a bath.'

Silently Joan followed her upstairs and watched as Grace drew the water, then slipped off her clothes and slid into the warmth. Slowly she lathered up some soap

437

and washed her face, long strands of hair lying against her damp collarbone. Her body bore little sign of the birth of two children. She was, Joan saw, quite beautiful. How in God's name could Simeon have chosen Elsa over her?

'What are you going to do, Grace? You can't let them get away with it.'

'I don't know what I'm going to do. Yet.' Her eyes closed, steam rising from the bath around her. 'I got a letter from Dora yesterday. I should tell her we're getting a divorce, but how can I? I don't even know where she is.' Slowly Grace's hands moved below the surface of the water, her fingers white as coral. 'I won't let him take the business, Joan. It's mine.'

'Then fight him!' she said hotly, surprised at Grace's calm acceptance. 'You can do that easily enough; you've got a good solicitor.'

'Frederick Conrad? Yes, he's good, but is he good with divorce cases?'

'Ask him. Anyway, what would the grounds be for a divorce?'

'Adultery,' Grace answered, the word rising up with the hot steam from the bath. 'I actually think that Simeon *wants* to be thought of as an adulterer. It makes the situation easier to bear for him. He couldn't stand the idea of people knowing that I had thrown him out.'

'You were a good wife –'

'I was adequate,' Grace corrected her. 'But then, how could you expect any man to keep loving a woman who was in love with someone else?'

Joan sat bolt upright; 'You're seeing someone else!'

Unexpectedly, Grace smiled. 'I meant Daniel. Simeon always knew I loved Daniel more than I ever loved him.

In a way it's a miracle that the marriage lasted this long. It was doomed from the start.'

'I don't see why,' Joan said shortly. 'You had a lot in common. You laughed together, you made a home, a family, a business –'

'Which he now wants.'

'Oh, come on, Grace! Does Simeon seriously expect you to give him the Auden Line on a plate?'

Grace nodded. 'Apparently I have to. I can't keep the name either.'

'But the business *is* the bloody name.'

'I know,' Grace replied quietly. 'By taking the name Simeon will make it all but impossible for me. I'll have to start under a different name and build it up with none of the reputation or customer loyalty I've worked for. The Auden Line will prosper – with or without me.'

'Christ, you've got to do something.'

What was the matter with her? Joan thought, bewildered. She was always such a fighter. Why wasn't she going mad? Swearing to take Simeon to court? Grace had never let anyone walk over her before – so why now? Why him?

'I was my own fault. I should never have trusted Simeon. I should never have let him have so much control.' Grace dipped her head under the water suddenly, then rose up her hair sleek as an otter's.

'But you're going to fight him, aren't you?'

Grace hesitated.

'Well, *aren't* you?'

'There's more, Joan.'

'What?'

'I told Simeon I would fight him tooth and nail when I talked to him the other day. He told me not to.'

'He was bound to say that! But he hasn't a leg to stand on if it went to court.'

'It can't go to court.'

Stunned, Joan leaned forward. 'What are you talking about! Of course it has to.'

'If I take it to court Simeon will use his trump card. He's already threatened to, and I believe he would do it.'

'What trump card?'

'Dora,' Grace said simply, getting out of the bath and wrapping a towelling robe around her. Her hands were shaking.

Joan was baffled. 'What about her?'

'Simeon told me that he would expose her, would tell everyone that she was still alive. Think what that would do, Joan. She would be hunted down and interrogated, God knows what else. She's getting old; I couldn't let that happen to her. I won't let that happen.'

'But –'

'Imagine the press, the gossip. Imagine how it would crucify her. She would be vilified. Again. Question on question would be asked – why had she pretended to be dead? Who was the woman in Leesfield Cemetery? Where had she been for so many years? Under what name? Doing what kind of work? You remember what I told you about Theodore Armstrong? He had a past, Joan, and although it had nothing to do with my mother, it would be dug up.' Grace paused, her voice shaking. 'It's Pandora's box. One which I can't let Simeon open.'

'So you're going to let him win instead? Take everything from you?'

'What choice is there!' she snapped. 'He's won. He's going to get the business and live with that slut Elsa

440

James. He's going to pull everything out from under my feet. Everything I've ever worked for – and I can't do a thing to stop him. He'll cover his back by letting me have the house. He'll do that to appear generous.'

'Oh yeah, and without the business how are you going to keep this place going?' Joan asked practically. 'It must cost a bomb to run and you have a housekeeper, gardener, Polly – they have to be paid.'

'I know, I know!' Grace said impatiently, walking over to her dressing table and sitting down. Slowly she looked into the mirror at Joan's reflection as she sat down behind her. 'I get to keep the children.'

'And to pay for their upbringing and education too,' Joan said bitterly. 'Oh, Simeon's really getting his revenge, isn't he? And what *about* the children, Grace? He loved Jonathan, accepted him as his own. And Richard is his own son. How could he walk away from them?'

'You've already told me the answer to that. Because I rejected him. That was the worst thing I could have done to Simeon. If I'd cheated on him, stolen from him, or been a lousy mother, it wouldn't have been so bad. But my crime was not to love him. And he's going to make me pay for it.'

Simeon expected Grace to relent, to come crawling back to him, to beg him to reconsider. The Auden Line was her business, after all; she would be bound to fight for it . . . But the days passed and he heard nothing. She wasn't seen at St Andrew's Place or at Holly Walk. Repeatedly he was asked where she was. Is she away? Is she ill? Brian Lawley wanted to show her some new colours and Geoffrey had a query about a delivery to Leeds. Questions piled up on questions and still she didn't show.

Exasperated, Simeon thought that he would call and see her at the house, but didn't dare. Elsa encouraged him to think that Grace's silence was a good sign, that she had given in. They were home free, she told him. They had the business and could make a fortune of their own . . . But when Simeon looked at Elsa he wondered how she could run The Auden Line. She'd become lazy, the work force didn't like her – she wasn't one to inspire respect.

Not after Grace . . . His brutality astounded him, but he couldn't relent. Cruelty hardened inside him. He wanted Grace to come back, to be the weaker one. But he had underestimated her. She had shown him that whatever he did, she still didn't want him. Even the threat of losing her precious business couldn't force her to act. She had, Simeon realized with fury, dismissed him from her life.

He had been right all along. He should never have married. God knows, he had enough girlfriends, enough nieces and nephews. An image of his son rose up before him, followed by one of Jonathan. He *did* love both the boys, but he had to admit that playing happy families had become harder and harder. A member of the golf club and the cricket club, he had taken Grace out for dinner and talked the talk – and gradually he'd felt middle-aged and had begun to long for his old freedom.

Grace had been the only thing strong enough to hold him. Somehow the tie to her had overridden his instincts; but now that had changed. By her actions she had thrown herself off the pedestal and there was a gap in his life so huge, so cold, that it threatened to cripple him. Hatred soon followed. He would divorce her and get the business from her and then see how she would manage.

So he set the ball rolling, thinking all the time that his sabre-rattling would shake his wife back into sense. But it didn't, and daily he brooded on Grace's rejection of him and allowed himself to be sucked down into his own malice. If he wasn't going to bring her to heel, he would ruin her. There was no middle way.

Polly was washing dishes in the kitchen when Grace came down the morning after she'd received Simeon's solicitor's letter. Looking up, Polly smiled at her employer.

'Morning, Mrs Grant.'

'Morning, Polly,' Grace replied, sitting down and picking up the morning paper.

'I was wondering,' Polly said nervously, twirling the tea towel in her hands, 'if I could have the afternoon off tomorrow.'

Grace laid down her paper. 'I don't see why not. Any special reason?'

'Geoffrey and I want to go and see the vicar,' Polly replied, her face flushing. She had lost some more weight and was becoming pretty.

A wedding, Grace thought, life goes on.

'About the banns?'

Polly nodded. 'Yes . . . we want to get married before Christmas. Is that all right?'

'Of course it's all right. You're a lucky girl. Geoffrey is a good man.'

'I know,' she said happily, her voice dropping as though she was afraid to be overheard. 'With the money I make here and the wage Geoffrey gets working for you we've managed to save up. We can afford to look for a little place of our own now. Oh, not that I'd leave you! I'll still look after the children. I love it here. But we want to get married now and we can. It's all due to you, though. We couldn't have got married if we hadn't both got good jobs.'

Grace stared at her dumbly. She had provided Polly and Geoffrey with work and wages to enable them to buy a home. Like all the other people who worked for her at St Andrew's Place and Holly Walk. She had kept them going for years – some of them she had employed even through the hungry thirties and the hard days of the war. They weren't just workers to her, they were an extended family, with all their different characters and problems. They were the people who had been with her from the start, when she had virtually nothing, when the Auden Line was just a dream. And now Simeon was going to take them from her? Employ them? Have them answer to him and his cheap tart?

Not bloody likely! Grace thought, suddenly galvanized. Her energy came back like a jolt of electricity through her body. He thought he could steal her business, did he? Well, there was more to running a business than employing staff and keeping books. There were things called respect, loyalty, shared history, pure bloody graft – and the workers Grace had employed had shared that with her. Not with him.

Simeon Grant had been an outsider, invited in. Did he really think they would just forget Grace and accept him as their boss? Was he that stupid?

Hurriedly, Grace ran upstairs and dressed, applying make-up and then checking her reflection. She was a handsome woman; her mother's child – with all her mother's courage.

Simeon wanted a fight, did he? Well, he was going to get the fight of his bloody life.

PART FIVE

From shadows and types to the reality

JOHN HENRY NEWMAN

Chapter Forty-Six

Feeling like a vagrant, Grace eyed St Andrew's Place and saw Simeon leave just after six. Elsa had called for him in his Jaguar, waiting outside, unaware of Grace watching her from the alley beyond. A few minutes later, they had driven off. Checking her watch, Grace waited until she saw the workers arriving from the other factory at Holly Walk. By seven fifteen, all the employees of the Auden Line were congregated at St Andrew's Place.

Go on, Grace thought to herself, *get in there. This is the time you'll find out where you stand.* Pushing open the heavy wooden door at the entrance, Grace smelled the old familiar scent of cosmetics. The odour made her skin tingle with pleasure. She had only been away for a matter of weeks but in that time she had come to long for the business. For the scents, the potions, the packaging. For the rows of boxes and tubes. For the photographs and sketches and the sure gold lettering on the van. Her baby, her creation. She felt as though she had come home again after a long trip away.

Confidently she walked into the workroom and saw the old familiar faces gathered round. They had all been asked to come by Joan, but warned not to mention the meeting to Simeon or Elsa James.

Elsa James? they'd all said. *Why the hell would they tell that cow anything? Anyway, what's it all about? What's the mystery? . . . Wait and see,* Joan had answered.

Grace looked round. There was Ivy and Enid, husband

447

sick again. Beside them was the fragile Tilly, and Mary Wells, bolshie as ever. On her right stood the red-haired Brian Lawley and his two assistants. Sitting apart from the others was Solar Giversky, Geoffrey by his side, reading a copy of the *Oldham Chronicle*. There were many other faces not so well known at St Andrew's Place, the people from Holly Walk – but Grace knew them all, had hired them all. Knew their histories, their tragedies, and every one of their names. Which was more than Simeon ever did.

She coughed behind them and they turned, several obviously surprised.

'Mrs Grant,' Tilly said happily, 'good to see you. How are you doing?'

'I'm fine, Tilly,' she replied, turning to the others and greeting them each by name. 'I wanted to see you all to explain what was going on.'

'What *is* . . . going on?' Brian asked, his stutter making him blush. 'We've not seen you for long enough.'

'I've been forced out of the business.'

'What!' several said in unison

Ivy sucked her remaining set of teeth. 'Forced out? I bet I can bloody guess by whom. That toerag husband of yours with that bint Elsa James. Don't tell me I'm wrong.'

Grace faced her. 'No, you're not. I'm going to lose the business and Simeon will be in charge. I presume he will try and bring his mistress in to help –'

'Bloody hell!' Enid exploded, her plump arms folding across her impressive breasts. 'What a flaming cheek!'

'Well, I'm not working for that cow,' Mary Wells added. This was a piece of gossip, and no mistake. 'I never could stand her from day one.'

Grace put up her hands to silence them: 'Look, that's

the way it is. I don't want it this way, but I can't do anything about it.'

'But it's *your* business; you set it up,' Ivy went on hotly. 'I can remember when we started here, long before the war. The place was a bloody mess but we got it up and running.' She paused, reminiscing. 'Aye, remember that powder which made all ours skins itch?'

A laugh went round the assembled workers.

'I couldn't go out to a dance that weekend. My family thought I had scarlet fever!' Enid laughed, shaking her head at the memory.

'And then there was that lipstick you couldn't get off,' Tilly added shyly. 'M' mother said I looked like I'd had a heart attack in the night!'

They all laughed again, Enid nudging Ivy in the ribs.

'Oh, stuff him!' Ivy said sharply. 'You can't let anyone take this place away from you, Mrs Grant, it wouldn't be right. What the Auden Line is is what *you* made it. Not some bloody fella.'

'Fight him!' Enid said forcibly. 'If our Patrick was on his feet, he'd topple the bugger.'

Grace couldn't help smiling. 'It's not that simple,' she said, glancing over to Joan. 'I'm back to square one.'

Geoffrey looked up. 'How's that?'

'I have to start up again –'

'WHAT?' a chorus went up.

'Where?' Geoffrey asked, turning to Joan at his side.

Don't look at me, she wanted to say, glancing back to Grace. God, just how can you afford to start again? she wondered. Grace had no premises, and now that she longer profited from the business, she would have limited funds to pay the wages. How could she afford to buy ingredients, pay for deliveries, advertising?

'Just how do you think you can do it, Mrs Grant?' Enid asked her.

'Because I have my experience and my knowledge.'

Ivy didn't like to say it, but she wondered just how long it would take for those qualities to get a business up and running again. She still had plenty of Alf's debts to pay off; now was not the time to start worrying about keeping up the repayments.

'Mr Grant,' Grace went on smoothly, 'will want to keep the Auden Line running here and at Holly Walk. I intend to start again elsewhere and want to offer a deal to those of you who want to join me.'

Mary Wells put her head on one side. 'What kind of deal? We need steady jobs, we all do. I don't want to work for Mr Grant if he's done the dirty on you, but I've rent to pay.'

Joan shot her a bleak look.

'I know that,' Grace replied calmly. 'That's why I'm making you all an offer you can accept or refuse. There will be no hard feelings either way.'

She leaned against the workbench, facing them. She was dressed in a simple woollen dress with a white collar and cuffs, her dark hair loose over her shoulders.

'I can't afford to buy or rent another workshop, so I'm going to set up the new premises at my own home.'

A murmur went round the room.

'My father had a separate part of the house when he was alive – we'll use that as the workshop and put a laboratory in the outhouse.' She turned to Brian Lawley. 'It's large, but cold at the moment, but it could be ideal with a bit of work. You'd be in control, as you always are.' He frowned but said nothing as Grace continued, 'I'll want to run two shifts, as I've always done, to produce the products fast. One day shift, one night shift. I'll need to employ the same number of workers – all of you, I hope.'

There was silence, everyone listening. Geoffrey was thinking about his coming marriage and the little house Polly and he wanted to buy. Would Grace have to fire Polly now? Jesus, if she did, how would they afford the house they wanted so much? His head slumped.

Beside him, Joan was wondering what on earth Grace was thinking of. A business in part of her house? What about planning permission? Equipment? Was it possible?

Yes, Joan realized, it would be possible, or Grace would never have put forward the idea. Well, it was worth a try, surely? Joan knew how much she had to keep her job, Tom still struggling with intermittent part-time work which barely covered the bills.

Sitting beside Joan, Enid was thinking about the doctor's fees for Patrick. Bloody hell, what a time to worry about keeping a job! she thought. And in the background, Solar was wondering what he would do with his life if his work for Grace ended.

In fact, every one of them was wondering what they would do. Would they stay on at St Andrew's Place and Holly Walk and keep their jobs with Simeon? Would he *want* to keep them on? Or would they be motivated by loyalty and go with Grace? Would there even be a business left to go to?

'There's more to it,' Grace continued. 'I'll be honest, I can't afford to pay your full wages.' A rush of voices sounded, all at once. Grace putting up her hands again. 'Hear me out!' she shouted. 'Hear me out!'

'We need our wages.'

'I know, Enid,' she replied. 'I intend to pay you all. But not the wages you have now. I can only afford to

451

pay you lower wages – but I am also offering you all a cut of the profits. When we all make a profit, we all get a cut. That goes for everyone.'

'What if we *don't* make a profit?' Tilly asked anxiously.

'Oh, Tilly,' Grace replied, 'how long have you known me? Since I had nothing, since we first came here all those years ago. You helped me sort this place out, and you, Geoffrey, you painted the ceiling and got the first van going. I remember you, Enid, helping Aaron to move the laboratory table in. And you, Mary – remember how you brought your sister's baby with you on the night shift?'

'That's all well and good,' Ivy answered curtly, 'but memories don't put food on the table.'

'No, they don't,' Grace agreed, 'but I do. I put food on every one of your tables.' She pointed at each of them in turn: 'You, and you, and you . . . I worked day and night to make this cosmetic business flourish. It was *me* who stayed on until midnight, *me* who tried out the colours with Aaron, *me* who made up the forms and chose the advertising. I made the Auden Line,' she said firmly. 'I don't care that the business has been taken away from me, because I'll do it again. I can make it from nothing, just as I did before. I'll use my own hands, my own time, and my own home – but build it again I will. And if you want to come with me, if you trust me as you did before, then I swear I'll make money for us all.'

They were all watching her, caught up in her enthusiasm. They too remembered how Grace had worked, the dogged determination, the grafting year in, year out. And during all that time she had never once faltered – even after all the scandals she had endured. Never once had she backed down or given up.

Shame-faced, Ivy looked away, remembering how it

was Grace who had loaned her money to cover her rent when her husband had gambled it away. How Grace had given her son a delivery job to keep him out of trouble. Tilly felt suddenly guilty too when she thought back and remembered how it was Grace who had helped her over the stillbirth of her second son and the death of her husband.

Silence fell over the workshop. It seemed that everyone remembered how big a part Grace had played in their lives. It was true, she *had* put food on their tables, and given many other kindnesses as well. Kindnesses not asked for, or done expecting repayment.

She had treated them as equals and now she was asking for help.

'How b-b-b-big a cut in wages?' Brian stammered. 'And for how long?'

'Twenty per cent,' Grace replied flatly. 'As for how long – that depends on you. The sooner we set up the business again, the sooner we make money.' She leaned towards them. 'No one has my contacts; no one knows the business as I do. If this had happened ten years ago, I wouldn't have been so confident, but now? I'm known, I'm respected. My name and the Auden Line name mean something.'

Enid raised her eyebrows. 'But you can't use the name any more.'

Grace's expression was chilling. 'Oh, my husband thinks he's beaten me by taking the name. Well, he hasn't. From here on in, our new cosmetics are called the Phoenix Line.'

Joan smiled. 'Nice – like the bird that was reborn out of the flames?'

'Just like that,' Grace agreed. 'We are all going to be reborn.'

There was a moment's silence. Then a deep voice came from the back of the workroom:

'What about your husband?'

Grace looked over the others' heads to answer him.

'*What* about him, Solar? He'll fail because he did what he did out of spite. And that's no way to succeed. He doesn't really care about the cosmetics – and as for Elsa James, she doesn't want to work hard any more.'

'Except on her back.' Ivy said, everyone laughing.

'So what about it?' Grace asked, looking round the familiar faces. 'The nub of the business is here. With you, with me. The Auden Line grew so big that we had to expand, bring in other people in other factories abroad – but I want you lot with me again, the ones who have *always* been with me. The ones who were there at the start, who know the history.' She looked at each of them in turn. 'If you trust me again, I won't fail you.'

There was a long pause, the women glancing at each other, Geoffrey turning to Joan, Solar silent. Grace wondered for a moment if she had miscalculated, if they would actually stay with Simeon – and her mouth dried. Even Joan was looking away from her.

Then a voice broke the spell.

'It sounds good to me,' Solar said quietly.

Grace smiling gratefully as Joan spoke up: 'Well, I'm certainly not working for that bastard husband of yours. I'm with you, Grace. Always will be.'

A chorus of voices followed: 'And me.' 'Count me in.'

'OK,' Ivy said, nodding, 'we'll have a go.'

The others agreed, only a couple of women slipping out of the back door. They would tell Simeon what had happened and he would now know that he had a rival. The one person who knew his weaknesses and had good reason to want revenge.

Good, Grace thought, I'm glad he'll know. He'll crow about it for a while and be sure I'll fail – but he'll be scared underneath.

He had played dirty, threatened her, tried to blackmail her. Used every trick in the book to ruin her. Oh yes, Grace thought, he had shown the kind of man he was – and she would never forget it.

Chapter Forty-Seven

That evening Grace asked Joan and Tom to come round, and invited Geoffrey too. Surprised, they arrived and then Grace called Polly in. She looked at her fiancé and seemed about to cry, terrified that she would be fired.

'I wanted to talk to you all,' Grace said calmly. 'Joan will have told you what went on at St Andrew's Place earlier – well, you know now that some changes have to be made around here. I've lost the business and with that, the income. So I'm going to set up again here for the time being, until I get the Phoenix Line on its feet.' She looked at Geoffrey. 'You've been with me from the start, and I want to make you an offer. I know you and Polly are saving up for a house and that you rely on the wages I pay you. Well, I have to reduce those wages – but I want to suggest that you two still get married and come here to live. There's room. That way you'll lose some money off your wages, but you won't have to pay board and lodging, so you could still save.'

Geoffrey stared at her, dumbstruck, then looked to Polly. 'What d'you think?'

She blushed, surprised at being asked for her opinion.

'I . . . I think we should do it,' Polly said, turning back to Grace. 'How long would we stay here?'

'As long as it takes to get the business up and running.'

'But I'll still be doing the deliveries?' Geoffrey asked.

'Of course.'

'Fine,' he replied. 'Living here? Wow . . .'

Smiling, Grace turned to Tom. He looked at her levelly and felt a rush of affection. Not love, that was reserved for Joan, but something like the warmth he had felt for Grace when she was younger, living next door to him in Diggle.

'Tom, you're struggling, aren't you?'

'Have been for a while,' he agreed. 'I can't seem to get settled in a good job.'

'And you have to find money for the rent and to look after the kids?' Grace went on, glancing over to Joan. 'As for you, you've worked like a dray horse for years, and yet you're still worried about money.'

Joan nodded. 'It's been tough – but we manage.'

'Which is your biggest outlay?'

'The rent,' Joan replied. 'That's always a worry to find.'

'So come here,' Grace said suddenly, 'I want to invite you and Tom and the kids to live here too.'

'Bloody hell!' Joan replied. 'It would be like one of those communes. People will think we're all into free love.'

'It would have to be free, no one has the money to pay for it,' Grace replied, laughing. 'Jokes apart, it's a serious offer. Both of you could work for me here, Tom as a book-keeper. As with Polly and Geoffrey, your wages would be cut but you could save on rent. If you're all careful, you *could* come out of this on the right side, with some savings. And a lot more, when we start making a profit.'

Tom studied her: 'What about you?'

'I save money by paying smaller wages.'

'But you still have to pay for the upkeep on the house.'

Joan studied him. 'There are gardens here – we could

grow food for the time being, Tom.' She nudged her husband playfully. 'Think about it. It would be an adventure. And anyway, it's the only bloody chance we'll ever have of living at an address like this.'

Grace felt her heart thumping. 'So, are you game for it?'

Joan nodded. 'Why not? The situation's bloody awful. If you don't start up the business again you'll sink and we'll sink with you. You have to make money to run this house, Grace, and to carry on paying for Jonathan's education and Richard's care. Mind you, you could get Simeon to pay for that –'

'No!' Grace replied shortly. 'Simeon might be his father, but I'm his mother. I know only too well that Simeon is going to punish everyone he can, and I'm not going to let my children suffer for our breakup.'

Grace looked round the opulent room, at the paintings, the walnut furniture, the damask drapes, the family pictures on a side table. If it took her longer than she thought to establish the business again she would be forced to sell her possessions, the paintings, the jewellery – but she wouldn't give up. Or ask Simeon for help he would relish refusing.

And there was a time limit. The Phoenix Line had to be set up and running within twelve months. It had to be making a profit to support her and her family or she would lose everything – the possessions *and* the house. If that happened she would be back to the start. Only this time she had two children in tow.

Stop it, Grace thought, stop thinking of failure. She *was* going to succeed, she *had* to. Besides, she had allies with her this time.

'I've set a deadline for us to look at the situation – a year from now. October the fourth 1953.'

'A *year*?' Joan said, aghast. 'We've only got a year to make this business work?'

Grace nodded. 'That's all I can afford. One year. Twelve months of hard work. And it *will* be hard on everyone. We'll have to pull together. No one can shirk, no one can moan. One lazy person will cost the others money.' She stared at their faces, each one close to her heart. 'We are a team. We live and work as a team.'

'We're also going to be the talk of the county,' Joan added. 'All living together under one roof – Jesus, Grace! If your reputation was shaky before it's going to topple now.'

'Why should I care what people think?' she countered. 'Society means nothing to me. It never really did. I came from the working class and it's the working class who've stood by me. My own people, no one else.'

There was a long moment of silence as each of them thought about the task ahead. Joan was thinking that it would be a lark, Tom was relieved to be actually working in a proper job again. Polly was simply overjoyed – to live here, with Geoffrey and have the children around! It was heaven. She would work as hard as she could, she told herself, or even *harder*.

The moment hung on, the silence warm as a blanket.

Looking up, Joan suddenly caught Grace's eye and nodded.

'There's an angel passing over . . .'

'I know. We can't fail.'

Within hours Tom and Joan and the two girls had moved into Grace's home, Joan putting the kids to bed and Tom falling asleep, exhausted, having carried all their belongings into the bedrooms.

Hearing his snores through the door, Grace knocked softly, Joan coming out onto the landing.

'He's buggered,' she said simply, 'but we're here!'

'You sure are,' Grace replied, taking out a bottle of brandy from behind her back. 'Do you know what this is?'

Joan stared at it.

'I was brought up in a pub, what the bloody hell do you think?'

Grace's expression was mischievous. 'Ah, but this is Simeon's most *expensive* bottle of brandy, which he left behind. We were saving it for a celebration –'

'Like now?'

Grace nodded. 'Like now.'

Quietly they crept downstairs and went into the drawing room, Grace turning on all the lamps and stoking up the fire. The room was glorious, rich, as she poured two large measures of brandy into crystal tumblers and passed one to Joan.

'To the future!'

Amused, Joan looked at her. Grace hardly ever drank, but tonight she was really lit up. Wicked.

'To the future!' she replied, as they clinked glasses.

The brandy had a soothing effect, Grace kicking off her shoes and curling up in a chair, Joan on the sofa beside her. They talked about the past, about the manager at the Riviera cinema and about Joan's mother's bunions.

Hours slid by, gradually merging into a dreamy boozy haze. The fire crackled in front of them, the shadows playing on the walls and on the photographs of Grace's children. Around them, there was silence. All the children and the other adults were asleep.

'I should never, *never*,' Grace said tipsily, 'have married

Simeon. It was all your bloody fault.'

'But he was very . . .' Joan tried to remember the word she wanted, '. . . sexy.'

'Nah!'

'He was!' Joan replied.

'Hey,' Grace said, changing the subject, 'd'you remember the Waxworks? Those Spencer sisters? I always thought they were my sponsors. You did too. I heard someone say that Violet Spencer was dead.'

'I wonder how they knew?'

Grace looked at her, shocked, then burst out laughing. 'What a horrible thing to say,' she said, her voice slightly slurred. 'They were very good teachers.'

'They were bitches,' Joan replied, changing tack. 'I'll tell you who I think is good-looking –'

Grace leaned forwards, her eyesight blurry. 'Who?'

'Frederick Conrad.'

'What! He's seventy odd!'

'Well,' Joan repented, 'he was handsome when he was younger. Mind you, his wife's another matter.'

'Face like a . . .' Grace frowned.

'. . . cow's arse.'

They both laughed uproariously, Grace then putting her finger to her lips.

'Ssssh! You want to wake everyone? There's not enough brandy to go round.' She leaned back in her seat drowsily, her hair dishevelled. 'You know what?'

'What?'

'We are going to be very ill in the morning.'

'With any luck.'

Grace nodded, then topped up Joan's drink and her own.

'To us,'

'Yeah. Us to.'

'No,' Grace said dreamily, '*to us.*'

'That's what I said,' Joan replied. 'You don't listen.'

Sighing happily to herself, Grace rested the brandy glass on her chest, the firelight making the liquid golden.

'I think,' she said at last, 'that we have just drunk about ten poundsworth.'

Joan nodded, Grace's face coming in and out of focus.

'Very extravagant,'

'Yes,' Grace agreed. 'very . . . Are you asleep?'

Joan shifted position on the sofa. 'Nearly . . .'

'If I live through the night,' Grace said dopily, 'I swear, I'm going to give that bastard a run for his money.' Her eyes closed, her hand relaxing round the glass.

Sleep, like an angel, settled its wings over them.

Chapter Forty-Eight

It was a bad winter, the outhouse freezing soon after December as the new year winds came biting from over Saddleworth Moor. Having installed an electric fire inside the laboratory, Grace watched Brian Lawley work on the batch of cosmetics they were due to put on sale in the spring.

The ingredients had been costly, not everything could be hand made, and soon the money Grace had put away in savings was virtually gone. She said nothing, though, kept paying the small wages and kept selling the jewellery Simeon had bought her during their marriage. The first to go was a watch, which paid the wages for a month, then she sold her engagement ring, which paid the house bills and for one term of Jonathan's schooling.

The figures she had costed out were exact, but even Grace hadn't anticipated just how fast the money would run out. She banked all her hopes on the launch of the new range, spoke to old friends in the press to ensure coverage, and accepted offers to speak. Her reputation as a businesswoman had been shaken at first, but when the rumours went round that Simeon had left her to live with Elsa James, the tide turned in her favour.

He has taken over her business, people said. *What a nerve, what a bastard! Does he really expect it to flourish without Grace Ellis at the helm? She made the Auden Line what it is. Without her it was only a shadow ...* Mentions in the gossip columns fuelled curiosity and indignation. Simeon Grant had cheated on Grace Ellis and then cheated her out of her business. What kind of a man would do that?

Naturally, people took sides. Simeon's friends and family sided with him because he told them lies about Grace's tempers and how bad a wife and mother she had been. His sisters – who had always remained remote from Grace – were protective of what they saw as their wronged brother. And his widowed mother did what she had always done, believed him. But the working women, the women who had bought the Auden Line cosmetics and admired Grace Ellis's success – they had no truck with Simeon's version of events.

They saw in Grace a version of themselves. A girl who had worked as a mill hand, who had struggled to support a sick father, whose mother had run off and left them both. They also remembered that she had had a child out of wedlock, but somehow that crime was assuaged by the enormity of Simeon's betrayal. Grace Ellis – for she had reverted to her maiden name – was one of them. She was a victim of male arrogance. After triumphing and proving that a woman could get to the top, she had been stopped in her tracks.

By whom? By a *man*, and worse, a man from a wealthy family. A man who had never understood just what it took to climb up from the gutter. So whilst glossy photographs of Simeon and Elsa popped up in the papers, Grace emerged as a serious woman intent on success. Her pictures appeared after she had given a talk, or spoken at an event about her coming launch. She was sombre, professional, determined.

In short, she became an icon. After all, they said, would the workers stick with her unless she was a bloody good boss? And when they were on lower wages too? Grace Ellis had promised them a cut of the profits too. No boss has done that round these parts before . . . They talked about the arrangements at the house as well. Joan and Tom Cox, Geoffrey and Polly, now married, and Grace – all under one roof! With four children to boot!

It was incredible. What the hell did they get to up there? . . . But soon the gossip died down when stories started to be spread about the real nature of their life. About the hours – six in the morning to six at night, and longer for Grace. They heard about the shifts too, the women coming in cold to hot soup and bread. They would eat and then start work, all of them working hard, for themselves. If they succeeded, they showed the world what they could do – and they put bread on their own tables.

Trouble came in the form of men. Mary Wells's husband didn't like the fact that she withheld her wages now, and struck her one Friday night. Geoffrey called round with Tom to have a word with him. It was strange how the two had reacted instinctively. If any of the women had problems with their husbands and sons, it was down to Tom and Geoffrey to apply pressure.

Brian Lawley was another matter. Always the shy outsider, he worked on his own. Stammering orders to his two assistants, he sent Solar on endless trips to find ingredients which were obscure, or cheaper than he had used before. The trick, Brian knew, was to repeat the cosmetics cheaply without impairing the quality. It was a challenge he relished at first, but after a while he became irascible. Leaving him to his own devices was the only way to treat him, but when he started to produce the first lipsticks and powders of the new line he was flushed with triumph.

'These are wonderful,' Grace told him, Joan trying

on a lipstick and staring into the polished surface of the worktable to see her reflection.

'Good colour,' she said approvingly, Brian taking the box away from her.

'You can only t-t-t-take one. I haven't got enough to spare,' Brian stammered, then turning back to Grace. 'It's too cold in here for some of the p-p-p-products. They don't set right. We need more heat.'

Rubbing her hands together, Grace nodded. The laboratory was chilled, even with the electric fire turned full on. The house was like a morgue too, now the bitter weather was settling in. Coal was expensive and still rationed, the big Aga making a focus in the kitchen, the kids hanging round it until it was time for bed. But in the early hours the temperature in the workshop dropped viciously, the mean little electric fires hardly making an impression on the overall chill.

Ever frugal, Joan turned them off when she came in.

'Hey, it's bloody freezing –'

She gave Mary a stern look. 'Electricity costs money that none of us can afford.'

'Well, my arse is numb,' Ivy replied. 'Surely we could have them on for a bit longer?'

Joan's reply was to make them all some tea.

Grace came out of her office to get her just as Enid dropped a bottle of rose-water.

Grace jumped. 'Be careful, that costs money.'

'I *was* careful,' Enid replied, chastened. 'It's just that my flaming hands are so cold I can't grip anything.'

In silence Grace took her tea and walked back to her office. She picked up the papers on her desk. She had refused to phone back the bank manager to listen to another lecture about her finances. It was something she didn't need to hear. Pulling her cardigan around her she looked out at the working women, Ivy talking to Tilly, and Mary Wells counting the lipsticks as she packed them in a box.

Would it work? Would the Phoenix Line sell? Would people buy it? Her confidence dipped suddenly and she shivered. There were so many people depending on her. What if she failed? What if there was no profit for them to share? They would be out of work – and she would lose everything. There would be no house, no business, no money for the children's education . . .

Preoccupied, Grace picked up the papers in front of her and tried to read them. She had to think about advertising for the new line, but how could she possibly afford that? She had no model now and no money to pay for the hire of one. Or the hire of a photographer. But without publicity no one would know that the Phoenix Line was in production – and no one would buy the stocks which were slowly beginning to mount up in the garage – parcels of cosmetics, bottles, tubes all getting dusty and cold.

The children were relying on her too, Jonathan, coming home from school and asking his mother about the other children's taunts, one day. Was Daddy going to divorce her? What did that mean?

'Doesn't he love us any more?' he asked sadly.

Grace held him to her tightly. 'Of course he does. He just doesn't love Mummy any more.'

Jonathan looked up at her, stunned. 'But he *must*.'

'It's all right,' she assured him, sounding for all the world as though she meant it. 'Things will work out for us. You're happy here, aren't you, sweetheart? With everyone round?'

He stared into her face, Grace's heart turning.

'It's OK . . .'

'But?'

'I liked it better before.'

So did I, Grace thought, so did I . . . But they couldn't go back, and suddenly Grace realized the enormity of what she had done. Endangered her children's welfare and taken on responsibility for the workers. Carrying everyone's hopes, and promising them some Utopia just round the next bend. And the next, and the next. Whereas in reality, bills were piling up, credit refused, Grace's ambition seeming suddenly wilful and selfish.

Panic was sudden and intense. The house was freezing and unwelcoming. The rooms had been half emptied, spaces now where paintings had once hung, unoccupied patches on the carpet where pieces of furniture had once stood.

There was a feeling of discomfort about the house – as though it was a place that no one longer belonged to anyone, employees coming and going giving the place an impersonal feel. Richard was only a baby, Grace thought – he wouldn't understand – but Jonathan. What memories of his childhood would he look back on? What little griefs would he carry? The taunts, the gossip, the threat of struggle which was coming closer every day.

Choked, Grace held her son to her and rocked him. She rubbed his hands and stroked his head and wondered how she – and all those who relied on her – would survive.

Joan was struggling to tie her hair back when the phone rang in the kitchen. Hurriedly she picked up it.

'Hello?'

Silence on the line.

'Hello? Hello?'

'Who is that?'

She knew the voice at once and was about to answer when she heard Grace pick up the receiver upstairs. Reluctantly, Joan put the phone down.

'Mother, is that you?'

Dora's voice was curt. 'Who was that?'

'Joan – you remember? Joan Cleaver. Well, she's Joan Cox now. Are you all right?'

'Are you?' Dora asked, as though she knew instinctively there were problems.

'No. I'm in trouble.'

Dora's voice never wavered. 'What kind of trouble?'

'Money. Simeon's divorcing me and he's cut me out of the business. I'm trying to get a new range going.' She had started talking and couldn't stop. 'I'm struggling with lack of money and the kids. It's so bloody cold here.'

'I'll come back to England.'

'No!' Grace said sharply. 'No, you must never do that.'

'But you need help –'

'That's true,' Grace said bitterly.

'I hope you've stopped giving that money away to the school?' Dora said firmly. 'You need it now.'

'I couldn't withdraw it, could I?'

'Why not?'

'It would look bad, that's why,' Grace countered. 'You can't give something and then take it away again.'

Dora took in a breath: 'I can raise some money –'

'No, you've helped me enough.'

'Oh, come on, Grace, I owe it to you,' Dora replied. 'I can't raise as much as I used to, but you'll have a bit of something coming to you.'

'I don't want the money –'

'And I don't want to see my daughter fail,' Dora

replied. 'Don't kid yourself, Grace. I want you to succeed as much for myself as for you. I was a bad mother in some ways, but I taught you to survive. Don't tell me that it was all a waste of time. Don't tell me that you can't take help when you need it most.'

'But I feel guilty taking money from you.'

'You didn't feel guilty when you thought it was coming from strangers,' Dora answered coolly. 'Then you just set out to prove yourself and show them they had done the right thing by investing in you. Why is it any different now? *I'm* investing in you and I never invest in losers. I didn't put my money on a lame horse, I put it on a thoroughbred.'

'But –'

'No buts!' Dora said sharply. 'There'll be money coming. Not much, but enough to tide you over for a while. When that runs out, we think again, but we'll manage. I won't let you down.'

True to her word, Dora sent money. The letters dropped onto the mat weekly and Grace opened them in secret, paying the money into the bank to keep the manager sweet. It was almost enough and her confidence rose. The Phoenix Line would save them, Grace thought. All she had to do was to finish the range, get it in the shops, and they were out of trouble.

Then suddenly the weather hardened. The house, already cold, was painfully chilled, draughts down the chimneys and the locks freezing on the outer doors. Extra coal had to be brought in and more food provided for the children, and often the workers. Sometimes the snow came down so hard and fast that the night shift were snowed in, Geoffrey and Tom clearing the paths in the morning. Tired women, pinched-faced and silent, walked home down the icy driveway.

Petrol for the van was saved, the vehicle only used for precious pick-ups and deliveries. Otherwise, it stayed in the garage. Grace's own car had long since been sold. Despair settled on the employees, the radio no longer playing in the workroom, Brian Lawley keeping to himself as he slogged away. His temper rendered him distant, abrupt, and when the next fall of snow came, he slept in the laboratory on an old couch, mittens on his fingers.

No one said what they were all thinking. They had gambled and lost. So, silent, they watched Grace and she refused to let any of them see her own distress. All that mattered to her now was the make-up line which had to be ready for spring. And spring was coming fast. The weather might deny it, but in the shops the buyers had already decided what to purchase, Grace coming in late with her new line.

Action was needed and there was no one else to do it. So, dressed smartly, Grace foot-slogged round Oldham and Manchester, then caught trains over to Huddersfield, Liverpool and Leeds. The trains were often late in the bad weather, and many times she came home after midnight. Exhaustion was always just one step away. But she went on, day after day, only stopping briefly for a cup of tea and some toast. The cheapest thing on the menu.

She was driven by adrenaline and guts, refusing to leave until she'd seen her old buyers and the managers in the make-up halls; giving away free samples in the hope that they would try them and buy the Phoenix Line.

'You know how good my make-up is, you always bought from me before,' Grace cajoled them. 'This is just as good quality, but the colours are even better.'

'We heard you were back in business, at your own home.'

'It's only temporary,' Grace replied, smiling. 'Before long the Phoenix Line will be the top seller around here.'

She persuaded some, but not others. But the ones Grace *did* reach, she moved. Grace Ellis was down on her luck, but she was fighting back. The female buyers admired her for that, and felt anger towards Simeon. So they bought the spring line from Grace and Grace dutifully entered their orders in her notebook.

But it still wasn't enough ... Snow stopped falling at the beginning of March and everywhere there were premature photographs of spring make-up in the shops. Models and actresses appeared in *Woman* and *Picture Post*, and clothes inspired by Dior's New Look were now everywhere. It seemed that the long lean years of the war were over and people were flourishing again – but not Grace.

She had failed. Worn out by constant travelling and sales pitching, she came back to the house on 3 March and knew that she had lost. All her efforts hadn't been enough. It was too big a mountain to climb a second time. Simeon had continued to sell to their suppliers and deliberately confused everyone. *Were they buying from him, or Grace?* The people she hadn't been able to reach had favoured him, and it was too late to reorder with her. Besides, they said, hers was a cottage industry and the cosmetic business had changed. It was no place for tyros.

Sitting down at her dressing table, Grace let her head slump and slipped her feet out of her shoes. The lining was bloody around the left heel. She would have to sell the house and face the workers to tell them it was over.

They had worked like dogs for nothing; they had trusted the wrong woman. Grace Ellis had done it once, but she couldn't do it again.

It was over for her. And for everyone else.

Her heart seemed to beat sluggishly in her ears, exhaustion overwhelming her. She was nearly forty years old and felt used up. Her beauty was fading with worry, her hair showing the first signs of grey. Small aches in her bones and muscles had begun to plague her, and the poor diet she had been on had shaved inches off her body. She might go without, but the children never did. Grace was not slim any more, but thin.

All her spark, her sensuality, her drive, were dimmed. She was running on instinct, no more . . . Grace's eyes closed, her mind wandering back to a night so long ago when she had met Daniel on his last leave. She could still feel his skin and his breath on her neck, still hear his voice. He was, in that instant, more real to her than reality.

If only he had lived, Grace thought, if only . . . Silence came down over her slumped figure. The daylight had faded away. Outside the final snow was melting and the children were all safely asleep. In the distance Grace could hear the murmured talk of the workers and the noise of Geoffrey revving the van for a delivery that evening.

Getting to her feet, Grace staggered over to the bed and lay down. She would just rest for a while and then go to the workshop and help the night shift. She would just rest for a little while . . . Her eyes closed, her body aching with exhaustion. And she thought of Daniel again; felt that he was *around* her. That he was watching over her. Comforted, Grace slid under the eiderdown. And comforted, she slept.

*　　*　　*

473

Joan woke her an hour later.

'You'll never guess what – Old Ma Goodman's popped her clogs.'

Grace struggled to wake up. 'Lucy Goodman's dead?'

'I just heard. She died this morning.' Joan pulled a face. 'Imagine that, the old cow dead. I bet she's trying to sneak in her money past the Pearly Gates even now . . . God, Grace, you look awful.'

'Thanks.'

'But you *do*,' Joan said, frowning. 'What's the matter?'

Grace swung her legs over the bed and stood up. 'I'm fine, I'm just tired, that's all.'

'Then stay in bed –'

'I can't do that when everyone else is working!' Grace said shortly. 'Were there any calls whilst I was out?'

Joan shook her head, she too had noticed how quiet things had become – no new orders for a while – at the time when they should have been their busiest. She knew why they were falling behind. There was no money to promote the Phoenix Line, to buy advertising space and paste posters up. The other brands were seen all over the place, all the time – and so people knew to ask for them. They increased their business whilst the Phoenix Line was running behind – and there was no solution because there was no more cash.

Simeon was doing all right – not flourishing, but then he wasn't that interested in cosmetics any more. He had had his fingers burned in that area and was looking for a new venture. But his remaining at the helm of the Auden Line had caused confusion and Joan suspected that the end was close for all of them.

'Come down into the kitchen,' she said. 'I've made

some cheese on toast. You look like you could do with a meal.'

Grace took her hand. 'Thanks.'

'For what? Cheese on toast?'

'You know what I mean. Thanks for everything.'

'We're friends, you and me,' Joan replied. 'We'll survive, whatever happens. And besides, it was great living here – even if this house is bloody freezing.'

Grace bit her lip. 'I don't think the business is going to work . . .'

'I know,' Joan said, her tone resigned. 'But you did your best, Grace. We all did.'

'But if it does fail, I've let so many people down. You, the workers, my mother.'

'Your mother won't see it that way.'

'She's still sending money.'

'Personally I think she's robbing banks,' Joan said drily. 'Although I wouldn't breathe a word of it outside these walls.'

'I really thought I could do it. I *still* could, you know,' Grace said defiantly. 'I just need a break.'

'That's the spirit. Never give up.'

'After all I said,' Grace replied, suddenly angry. 'I made it all sound so great for us all to be living here and building up the business. We were all going to be rich – what a joke!'

Joan shrugged. 'I wasn't interested in the bloody money. I would have done it for nothing. It was a lark, Grace, a good laugh. We had a try. No one died. We're all alive, the kids are well. You've found out what people think of you *and* seen how they've stuck by you when you were in trouble. God, if you hadn't earned a penny out of this you would have learned how much you were loved.'

Touched, Grace glanced away.

'You think about Lucy Goodman,' Joan went on. 'Think about that miserable old sow. Some people have a million pounds – and no one cares if they live or die. You're richer than you know, Grace. And personally I'd rather die poor and loved, than rich and loathed.'

Chapter Forty-Nine

Tom was lying awake next to Joan, blankets pulled up around both of them to keep out the cold. The large bedroom was chilled, the fire in the grate unlit to save coal. On the other side of the house Tom could just make out the sounds of the night shift, although how much longer they would be working was anyone's guess.

Shivering, he blew on his hands and rubbed them together, the rough skin making a rasping sound. He had worked as hard as everyone else; seen things he never thought he would, and heard tales which had shaken him. He would never before have thought himself naïve, but watching the women work and struggle with their men and their children, seeing Enid falling asleep on her feet and Mary Wells still coming to work although she had twisted her ankle and could hardly walk, had been a revelation to him. His admiration for them went deep, as it did for his wife who had never once complained about the work, and doing without, just carried on cheerfully.

To his surprise, Tom could suddenly hear Joan laugh beside him and turned over, taking her in his arms.

'What's so funny?'

'Living here,' she said, 'all of us freezing our backsides off and working like navvies. I was just lying here imagining Old Ma Stratton's face if she could see me now, in one of her precious guest rooms.' She laughed again. 'I used to dust this place, clean out the grate, run errands for her. I never thought I'd end up living here.'

Tom clung on to her tightly. 'Will it work?'

'The business? Nah, Grace has run out of money and she can't compete with the big names in the market. She gave it her best shot – we all did – but there wasn't enough cash in the end.' She rubbed her cold feet against Tom's, hearing his teeth chatter. 'I know for a fact that Grace has sold all her jewellery – and I notice that the paintings keep disappearing off the walls.'

Tom sighed against her. 'So what will happen?'

'We'll survive,' she assured him. 'We'll get by, we always do. *Somehow*. I feel sorry for Grace, though; I think her luck's finally run out.'

Shivering again, Tom snuggled up her. 'God, that bad, hey?'

'Unless a miracle happens, yes.'

Frederick Conrad stood up when Grace walked in. Behind him the same stuffed eagle loomed from its perch, the other stationary wildlife looking down from their domed cabinets, Nelson beady-eyed, his beak half open as though caught mid-bite. Nothing had changed since the first time Grace had come to the office and little had changed about Frederick Conrad either. He was as perfectly handsome and well preserved as one of his own birds of prey, his white hair rising up from his head like the feathering on a crested owl.

'Welcome,' he said charmingly. 'Do sit down.'

Grace took a chair, and gratefully accepted the coffee he offered. The taste was good; it had been a long time since she'd been able to afford to buy real coffee.

'I have some interesting news.' He paused for effect. 'You know that Mrs Lucy Goodman died the other day?' Grace nodded. 'Well, a while ago I was called in to draw up her will – and it is now my duty to tell you what it says.'

'Why me? Lucy Goodman never wished me well.'

'I admit that she was a strange woman,' Frederick agreed, 'but she changed as she got older. When Mrs Goodman knew she was dying she was afraid. Nothing seemed to matter to her any more – not her money nor the Goodman fortune. She had no relatives, no children. She never got over the death of her son.'

'Neither of us did,' Grace said quietly.

'I can tell you now that Mrs Goodman confessed something to me which will come as a shock to you, so be prepared. Before Daniel Goodman died he drew up a will in which he left you his car and a considerable amount of money.'

Grace stared at Frederick Conrad uncomprehendingly.

'Lucy Goodman destroyed that will –'

'She did *what*?' Grace could feel her temper rise, her face flushing. 'So why tell me now, Mr Conrad? Did she instruct you to inform me so that she could have the last laugh, even after she was dead?'

'Mrs Goodman genuinely regretted her actions.'

'I bet she did!' Grace snapped. 'But not enough to own up and make things right.'

'But that's the point. At the end she *did* want to make amends.' He stared at Lucy Goodman's will lying in front of him. 'She had no family left – so she left her fortune to you and your son – her grandson.' Shaken, Grace said nothing as he continued. 'Mrs Goodman has left you The Lockgate and put the businesses into your hands until your son Jonathan comes of age. She then asks that he will inherit the Goodman empire.'

Grace was still staring at him.

'She asks only one thing of you – that Jonathan will

479

take on the name of Goodman and be recognized as Daniel's son, the rightful and legal heir . . . Are you all right?'

Grace had slumped forward in her seat. 'I'm fine . . .' she said at last, taking a sip of the coffee and pushing her hair away from her face. Her palms felt moist, her hands shaking. 'Go on.'

'You've been left a fortune, Mrs Grant –'

'Miss Ellis,' she corrected him.

'Miss Ellis, you're wealthy now, and your son will be too when he reaches twenty-one. Congratulations.'

Grace blinked slowly, her mind clearing. She had known the other night that Daniel was around, she had felt him watching over her. And this was proof. At her lowest ebb, with everything against her, the man who had loved her so deeply had saved her.

He had always loved her and still did.

When Grace returned to her house it was lunchtime, the women in the workshop snatching a quick break, Joan in the office on the telephone. She saw Grace's ashen face and put down the receiver, hurrying over to her.

'God, what is it?'

'We're rich,' Grace said dumbly, 'we're rich.'

'Have you been drinking?'

'No!' she said, laughing. 'I've just been to see Frederick Conrad. Lucy Goodman cheated me. Daniel had made a will leaving some money to me, but she'd destroyed it. I never knew. And she never said a word about it. All the time she was pressurizing me to let her have Jonathan she thought that she had boxed me into a corner. I was in disgrace, worried about his future. And there was no need. If she had followed Daniel's wishes I would have had enough money to sail through. I would never have had to struggle. But she watched me stagger on. She knew what she had done, but she didn't help. God, how could she?'

'I don't understand . . .' Joan said, her eyes blank.

'Lucy Goodman cheated me,' Grace replied, 'but when she was dying she couldn't live with what she'd done. So she left me the money Daniel always wanted me to have, *and everything else.*'

Joan's lips felt parched. 'Like what?'

'The Lockgate is mine now –'

'Jesus!'

'– and the businesses.'

'Christ!'

'. . . I'll run them until Jonathan's old enough to take them over. He'll be a wealthy man, Joan. He'll have his father's name and his father's fortune. It's justice, after so long.'

Joan was finding it hard to breathe; '*Lucy Goodman left you everything?*'

'Everything,' Grace repeated, laughing. 'Oh, and I can imagine how hard it was. Her conscience would be troubling her and she'd have to make amends. She was dying and scared. And besides, she had no one to leave the fortune to. All her plotting had gone wrong. She was alone. She had no family, only her grandson, and me – Grace Ellis, the woman she had hated for so long. But what was her choice? If she didn't leave it to us, the Government would have got it, and she would have hated that even more than she must have resented giving it to me.'

Joan was feeling faint. 'So what happens now?'

'We don't lose, we win.' Grace replied eagerly. 'I have the money to make the Phoenix Line the best, enough funds to wipe the others out of the running. I've got the money to pay for advertising, promotions, to buy a proper factory. Of course, I'll sell this place –'

'Sell *this*?'

Grace nodded. 'Yes, I'm going to live at The Lockgate.'

'But you hate that place!'

'I did when Lucy Goodman was alive, but remember Daniel was born there. It was his home. And it'll be like going home for me now.' She caught hold of Joan's hands. 'We'll make the biggest profit this town has ever seen, this bloody country! You'll all make money, everyone of you. You can get a new house now, Joan, everything you ever wanted. So can Geoffrey. You stuck by me when I needed you, and, my God, I'll reward you all for that.'

'I still can't see you living at The Lockgate,' Joan replied warily. 'It's a tomb.'

'Not when I've finished with it,' Grace said triumphantly, looking round. 'I never liked it here much. This place reminds me of too much heartache. I'm going to sell it and buy a factory with the money –'

'But there are other Goodman factories,' Joan interrupted. 'Why don't you use one of those?'

'Because they're not mine,' Grace replied, 'Those will continue as they are. But the Phoenix Line is mine and it always will be.' Grace's voice was hurried, enthusiastic. 'There will be jobs, Joan. Good jobs. A proper job for Tom, a job for Geoffrey. I want to keep the people around me that I can trust. There will be a job for you too – whatever you want.'

'I'd like more coal,' Joan replied drily. 'It's bloody freezing here.'

Chapter Fifty

By the time the month was out Grace had bought a factory on the outskirts of Delph and had settled all her workers in it. Money was put to good use and there were many innovations. A crèche was established, and proper facilities for the women, and she brought in another chemist to help out Brian Lawley. Together with every possible piece of equipment needed. Everyone's wages had been raised and the scheme of profit-sharing looked set to bring its first rewards at the end of the summer.

The news of the legacy struck the North like a thunderbolt. Newspapers jostled with one another to interview the woman who had been left a fortune. Grace Ellis, the cosmetic entrepreneur who had had a child out of wedlock – why had she inherited the Goodman empire? What connection had she had with the Goodmans?

The answer stunned everyone. The illegitimate child of Grace Ellis was none other than Daniel Goodman's son. And no one could argue with the announcement – it was stated clearly in Lucy Goodman's will. Jonathan was the rightful heir, due to inherit a fortune. People who had shunned Grace before were now suddenly trying to court her. The scandal and gossip which dogged her life was no longer important: she had money and the Goodman empire. She had arrived.

She also had a long memory.

On hearing the news Simeon reeled. His spite had been such that he had been pleased to see Grace struggling and certain that she would never regain her status. But the tide had turned and now he found himself beached with Elsa James, his money a relatively small amount in comparison to the Goodman fortune.

He even tried to attempt a reconciliation, but although Grace allowed him to see his son, she stayed remote. There had never been enough love between them, so there was nothing to rekindle. All Simeon's posturings meant nothing. She knew only too well that he would have seen her ruined, would have seen his own child suffer to get his own back – and she wanted none of him.

It was a clear May morning when Grace finally collected the keys from Frederick Conrad and drove up the long steep drive to The Lockgate. Climbing out of the car she stood for a long time looking at the shuttered windows and the unkempt gardens. There was no cheer about the place; so much of Lucy Goodman's misery had permeated it that it seemed gloomy, without heart. Slowly Grace walked round the back and then moved on to the glasshouses. She pushed open a door and walked in.

The old vines were dying from lack of water, orchids dried in their pots. She could imagine Daniel playing with the gardener's boy there and – in her mind – saw the glass cleaned, the flowers green and scented. Her man, her beloved Daniel, had been here, she thought, he had breathed here.

Walking back to the house Grace's hands trembled as she unlocked the double entrance doors and walked in. The hall was shaded, still, without life, a stair-case winding upwards to the floor above. Dust sheets covered the furniture and paintings, the marble floor echoing eerily with her footsteps. In the library there were rows of untouched books; in the study a pair of reading glasses left on a window ledge. Thoughtfully, Grace picked them up and opened the nearest shutter.

The light came in fierce and threw her long shadow behind her. Sadness was everywhere, and for a moment Grace could sense the loneliness which had stalked Lucy Goodman for so many years. She even felt a brief pity for the old woman, but it was fleeting. The misery she had endured, she had brought upon herself. Whilst she had had so much, she had seen Grace and her grandson struggle.

Having opened the other shutters, Grace moved out of the library and up the staircase towards the bedrooms. There were four on the first landing, one larger than the others. It had not been decorated for many years, the furniture heavy and Edwardian, the wardrobe still full of Lucy Goodman's clothes. Beside the bed, there was a book, with a marker in it to keep her place, and on the bedside table was a telephone.

But who had she rung? Grace wondered. Apart from business contacts, managers, solicitors, who had she talked to? Laughed with? Shared her days with? No one. She had cut herself off so successfully that there had been no visitors, only professionals running her fortune and making their own. No one had *cared* about her . . . Grace picked up the book knowing that the last hand which had touched it was Lucy Goodman's. Why did you do it? she wondered suddenly. You could have had a family around you, you could have died loved. But you couldn't give an inch, could you? It had to be your way, or nothing.

So it had turned out to be nothing . . . Putting down the book Grace then opened the drawer of the bedside table. Her hand closed around a photograph frame.

Taking in a breath, Grace looked at the picture of Daniel as a child – and it was like looking at a mirror image of Jonathan.

It's all so right, she thought. I'm bringing my son home, *Our son*. She was speaking to Daniel in her head. I'm bringing your son to his rightful place. Oh God, if you'd lived, Daniel, we could have been here together. We could have watched Jonathan grow up here and we could have grown old in this house.

A sudden noise behind her made Grace jump.

'I beg your pardon,' a woman said, appearing at the door. 'I didn't realize anyone was here.'

She was old, well into her eighties, a little woman dressed in an old-fashioned housekeeper's uniform.

'Nor did I,' Grace said moving towards her. 'I'm Grace Ellis.'

The woman nodded, 'Welcome, madam. I was expecting you.'

Her voice was polite, but wary. She had been in service for many years and seemed like someone from another time, someone who had lived a subservient life between the wars. In the streets, posters of Marilyn Monroe were pasted outside the cinemas and two Cambridge scientists, Crick and Watson, had discovered the secret of hereditary characteristics in DNA – but at The Lockgate this old woman was untouched by change and unmoved by progress.

'Who are you?'

'Miss Sargeant. I've been with – rather, I *was* with Mrs Goodman for many years.'

'Did you know her son?'

The woman watched Grace, took in the smart waisted suit, the white-rimmed sunglasses and the high-heeled shoes. She had read about her in the papers and wondered how she herself had managed to work for Lucy Goodman for so long without knowing anything of her grandson.

She nodded. 'Yes, madam, I knew Master Daniel from his birth.'

'I was his fiancée.'

'I know, madam. I read about you in the newspaper. I also read that you had inherited the Goodman business and this house.'

'You would be welcome to stay on here. If you wish,' Grace offered, knowing automatically that she would refuse.

'I don't think I can, madam. I wouldn't be much use any more. I'm too old now.'

'But you've always lived here, where would you go?'

'I have a sister in Wales. I'll go there now.' She seemed anxious to be gone. 'I've left written details about the house — where things are, who Mrs Goodman used to use for repairs — that kind of thing. It's all on the kitchen table, if you want it. I was just waiting to see you, before I left.'

'Do you want to take something with you,' Grace asked hurriedly, 'something of Mrs Goodman's? To remember her by?'

The old woman paused, then shook her head. 'No, thank you, madam. There's nothing I want.'

Then she left quietly, the door closing behind her. Grace was glad that there would be no one around who had served Lucy Goodman. The Lockgate was hers now, to change as she wished. She wanted no reminders of the past — except memories of Daniel. Nothing else.

The man walked up the steep road, stopping several times to catch his breath. He was slightly stooped, but not old, just someone worn out with struggle. Wiping the sweat off his forehead, he then replaced his hat and walked on. Would Grace have changed? he wondered. Would she remember him?

He sighed, stopped again and stared at the house at the top of the hill. The Lockgate. It looked forbidding, he thought, and for a moment he was tempted to turn and walk away. But he had come so far, it would be foolish to fail at the last.

Slowly he moved up the drive and then walked to the front door. He could hear voices, a laugh he recognized, and then saw Joan come out into the daylight. Seeing him, she put her hand up to shield her eyes from the sun just as Grace walked out behind her.

'Oh, hello,' Joan said, her head on one side.

He couldn't speak.

'Have you come to see Grace?' Joan continued, with no trace of recognition in her voice.

But Grace recognized him at once. Stepping out of the shadow of the house, she studied the man. She noted the beard and the stooped back, the sallow skin.

'Aaron?' she said, her voice hardly above a whisper. 'Is that you?'

She moved towards him. He had taken off his hat and was turning it round and round in his hands nervously.

'Aaron?' she repeated.

He looked at her then and nodded. Moved, Grace took his hat from him and slipped her arm through his.

'I'm so glad you came back,' she said simply. 'I'm so glad you came home.'

As soon as sufficient rooms of The Lockgate were redecorated, Grace moved in with her sons. She had invited Joan and Tom to come with her, but they had found a new place to rent, and later buy. Polly and Geoffrey had moved on too, Polly coming to The Lockgate every morning and leaving every evening at six.

As for Aaron, he had found rooms nearby. He was sick, weakened by deprivation and the old long search. Having lived on his wits for years to avoid capture, he had finally found news of his family. His brother and sister-in-law had died in one of the concentration camps. Of them, nothing remained.

Afterwards, he had tried to make a home for himself in Germany, but couldn't settle. Years passed and Aaron grew older and more ill and finally decided that he would return to England. To the North where he had worked with Grace Ellis. He had made no other friends and couldn't face dying alone. So he returned to England and discovered immediately that Grace had become phenomenally wealthy. On hearing the news, he had nearly gone away again. She would have so many people pressurizing her now. People begging for help. And he didn't want her to think of him like that. After all, he didn't want anything.

Except a family. Which was precisely what he got.

At first The Lockgate seemed to Grace – after living so long with others – to be vast and empty. But when the old wallpapers were removed and the Edwardian furniture taken out, the rooms came into their own. Ceilings and wood panellings were restored to pristine perfection, the kitchen gutted and remodelled with all the latest equipment. A couple were hired as house-keeper and gardener, and they lived in the basement. Grace renovated the upper floor as a playroom for the children. Soon The Lockgate clattered with the sounds of hammers and saws, and reeked of sawdust. And outside, the garden was hacked and teased back into order, the atmosphere and scent of old Lucy Goodman fading as the paint dried.

'God Almighty!' Joan said, calling round to find five men working in the drawing room on the first floor. 'What a transformation.'

'Not like it was, is it?'

'It used to be a gloomy hellhole, so no, it's not like it was,' Joan replied, looking round. 'You going to have parties here?'

'Maybe,' Grace replied, knowing that it was unlikely. The Lockgate was being restored and repaired for herself, her children, and her memories. She would invite friends over – but ultimately this was to be her haven, the place where Daniel had lived, the place where both of them would have lived, had he survived.

Simeon had been a mistake. That much was obvious, especially after the details of the divorce had come out. He had been unfaithful not once, but several times. But it no longer mattered to Grace. She didn't want her ex husband – she had Daniel. And that would be enough for the rest of her life. She needed nothing else apart from the Phoenix Line, her work, and her children. She didn't need romance, which was sure to bring heartache – and besides, to allow any other man into The Lockgate would seem like a betrayal.

'The *Manchester Guardian* rang this morning,' Joan said, picking up a small package and weighing it in her hands. 'They want to do a piece on you and your new factory.'

'When?'

'Soon as you like,' she replied. 'They want to please you now. Funny, they wouldn't give you the time of day before.'

'That's what money does.'

'They want to know about this scheme you're setting up to apprentice girls in the industry. Oh, and they want to know about the donations you're giving to the local schools.'

'Anything else?'

Joan grinned. 'They wondered if you would comment on the legacy and Jonathan's inheritance. They wanted to take pictures of him and print them next to photographs of Daniel.'

'To see if there was a likeness?' Grace said exasperated. 'No chance.'

'They also wanted you to comment on the divorce.'

'Anything else? Like my weight? Or if I dye my hair?'

Joan smiled. 'Well, you're famous now. People want to know all about the notorious Grace Ellis. The woman who flew in the face of convention and came out a winner.'

'They want to set me up, you mean. Trade on the gossip. The divorce made a good story and scandal sells papers.'

'Speaking of which, I saw Elsa James on the front page yesterday. She's putting on weight, I'm glad to say. Now that you and Simeon are divorced, d'you think he'll marry her?'

'Not if he's any bloody sense,' Grace replied. 'That reminds me – we need a new model for the Phoenix Line. I'm not that keen on the girl we're using. We need someone with more class.'

'Why don't you do it?'

'Oh come on, Joan. I'm pushing forty, a bit long in the tooth to be a cover girl.'

'I don't agree.' she replied flatly. 'The Phoenix Line is your baby. You made it, so who better to represent it? Besides, it would set an example to the women who buy the make-up – show them they can look good even if they aren't eighteen any more.' She stared at Grace. 'You're looking great again, less strained. You could do it.' She pulled a face. 'Oh, come on, think about it! After all, you might as well cash in on your notoriety; make a virtue out of a scandal. You'll never be unknown again, you can't hide away. So instead of trying to fight your fame, why not use it?'

It was a sound idea, Grace realized. Perhaps the women who bought her make-up might identify with her more readily than some unknown model. After all, they had heard and read about Grace Ellis for years. The London cosmetic houses might hire expensive, perfect models – but their products were gauged at a different market. The Phoenix Line *was* Grace Ellis; the two things were inseparable. The image of Grace would be a reminder of someone who had succeeded despite everything; a figurehead, not some remote idol with no history.

'It's not a bad idea,' Grace said at last. 'It would depend on the photographs, though. I don't want to look like an old hag.'

'Put a bag over your head then,' Joan replied, rolling her eyes. 'Look, all you need is a good photographer. Someone who could get the image over.'

'I don't know,' Grace said doubtfully. 'I'm not sure I could live with my face looking out at me from shop windows and hoardings.'

'You lived with it looking out at you from newspapers long enough,' Joan replied deftly. 'You might as well use it to your own advantage this time.'

Dora read the letter twice and then put it back in the envelope. As ever, Grace had written to the box

492

number Dora supplied, her mother's address withheld. Dora didn't want her daughter to know where she was in Ireland. Some things should remain secret.

Thoughtfully, Dora stared at the table in front of her and then began to clear away the dishes. Her daughter had triumphed, above anyone's expectations – even hers. Her beautiful, elegant Grace had made a mark in the world which could never be removed. Her grandson would be the heir to the Goodman fortune, and to the Phoenix Line. When he married, his children would carry on the business. It was all very good, very good indeed.

She was glad she had lived to see it, Dora thought. She was also glad she had lived long enough to repay her child for the past. Every pound Dora had sent to Grace had been recompense for the days her daughter had striven to learn whilst working in the greengrocer's shop. Every cheque was a salve to Dora's conscience for leaving her child to struggle as a mill hand and support her father. All the gossip and innuendo Grace had endured about her mother could never be fully expunged, though. Money had helped her, but the emotional scars went too deep to heal entirely.

Dora knew that she should never have left her daughter to shoulder her responsibilities. For that, there was no recompense. It had made Grace what she was – but at a price. Her upbringing had made her survive hardship, betrayal, and heartache, but the disadvantage was yet to be fully recognized.

Wiping a plate with a cloth, Dora thought about what she had just read. Grace had renovated The Lockgate, the best house in Lydgate – one of the finest in the county. It sounded extraordinary, Grace promising photographs. Dora knew she would never see it in reality – she dare not visit England again and risk her luck – but she could guess what kind of a house it would become.

A fabulous, comfortable, welcoming tomb. Dora sighed, put the plate in the drying rack and dried her hands. Her daughter was making a mausoleum for Daniel. A place she could keep as a shrine. She would work and expand the Phoenix Line – it was already being sold in Europe – and Grace would protect the Goodman interests until Jonathan came of age. But that was work, what about love?

Grace was not yet forty years old. That was no age to give up. She needed a man, not a shadow. Not Daniel, but a living person to share her life with. Otherwise what would happen when the boys grew up? Grace would be alone. They would go out, have girlfriends, get married and raise their own families. And then Grace would be *what* exactly? The matriarch, sitting alone in The Lockgate – and indirectly following the example of the woman she had hated for so long – Lucy Goodman.

It was no life for her child, Dora thought. Grace might know how to fight for her business and her children, but she was a coward when it came to love. Real women risked their emotions and their hearts. Real women tried and failed and tried again. Real women never settled for ghosts.

She knew that Grace had been hurt; knew how humiliated she must have felt to see her love life picked over in the press. The divorce dinner-table gossip all over the country. But to give in was too easy, too commonplace. And Grace was never commonplace.

A life was meant to be whole, to carry triumphs, losses, humiliations, disappointments and joy. No one who lived fully, lived without guilt or without the few

494

snatches of insanity. *She* had known that, Dora thought. And until her daughter did, her life would be only half lived.

Chapter Fifty-One

Mickey Kennet was sitting in a taxi jam at Hyde Park, his foot jiggling with impatience. By his feet he had a portfolio of his photographs and was on his way to see an editor for *Lifestyle* magazine. They had phoned him the previous week about an article they were doing on Grace Ellis, sending him some press cuttings and photographs about her to whet his appetite.

Not that it needed whetting. Mickey had already heard of Grace Ellis and had followed the scandalous divorce case in the papers a couple of years ago. He had to admire a woman who divorced her husband on the grounds of adultery and allowed every sordid detail of his affairs to come out in court. The Phoenix Line – and the story of Grace Ellis's life and struggles – had made her into a local heroine, her fame gradually spreading from the North down to the South. Just as her cosmetic empire had done.

Yet it was the astonishing inheritance of the Goodman fortune which had pulled Grace into the national limelight overnight. Her story was the subject of much magazine rivalry. Everyone wanted to be the first to get the big profile. Sighing, Mickey drew the papers out of his bag and looked at the questions the magazine intended to ask Grace Ellis.

What did it feel like to inherit a fortune? And then have enough money to regain your own power in the industry? Would she expand The Phoenix Line now? What was it like to be a woman in business in the 1950s?

And what about her son? Her child out of wedlock, her love child? Did she still think of Jonathan's father? And what about Simeon Grant? Did she know how often he had been unfaithful to her? What did it feel like when her husband betrayed her with another woman, and tried to ruin her in business?

How did they *expect* it to feel? Mickey wondered, exasperated, staring out of the taxi window and watching a group of tourists taking photographs. He had been born in the East End, a London lad through and through – an advantage, if the truth be known because the magazines were starting to look for new options, growing tired of the elegant formality of Cecil Beaton and his ilk. The times were changing, fashion was changing – and so were people's lives. It was a new world and it needed to be represented in a new way.

So Mickey Kennet had begun to tout his wares and now he was a thirty-one-year-old success, slim, fashionable, his fair hair floppy over his forehead. With an engaging shyness about him which put people at their ease. The stilted glamour of the old ways was not to his liking; Mickey liked to see his subjects react – smiling, talking, moving around. Nothing too formal, too set. Women in particular were different now, he argued. They worked, they drove cars, competed with the men, they weren't tied into corsets any more. The old world had gone. Look at the movie stars now, he said to the magazine editors, sex is news. Marilyn Monroe is news, people are glossy, fast, greedy for life. I want to show that in my photographs, he told them. I want to show what new living is all about.

To that end Mickey had taken and exhibited photos with his own trademark informality, his montage of Ruth Ellis, the murderess, drawing much comment.

He went abroad too; to the USA and Europe, charting the difference in the cities after the war. He photographed Tito and Khrushchev and then Annigoni, who was having a massive success with his portrait of the Queen. Mickey had even infiltrated Hollywood because he wasn't brash, and the stars had let this charming self-effacing photographer into their lives.

His portfolio was unlike anyone else's because Mickey Kennet didn't specialize. People had told him – *Don't be a jack of all trades and master of none*. But he wouldn't hear of it. *How about being the master of all trades?* Mickey answered, and set about proving that it could be done. He took pictures of children, war zones, heroes, villains and the famous – and every picture that he took told the sitter *and* the viewer something about the subject they had never known before. That was his skill.

If he had followed his father or uncle, Mickey would have ended up a joiner or a plumber. No shame in that, he thought, but his father had brought him a box Brownie when he was seven and that was it. It turned the world into a manageable size; made people fit into his square of lens. Looking through a camera, Mickey could move people about and make them smaller, less formidable. The box Brownie suddenly gave a shy seven-year-old control of a world which had previously terrified him.

He and the camera went everywhere together from then on. It was a joke in his neighbourhood, and people were pleased to sit for Mickey. His father made a darkroom in the garden shed and learned how to develop the kid's pictures. Mickey learned too, and by the time he was eleven the house, the shed and the garage were stacked with photographs.

For a family who was not well off, it was an expensive

hobby, but Mickey was an only child and his talent was indulged. After all, how many people had a kid so gifted? Mickey's mother, a square-jawed Yorkshire woman, was curtly impressed, but his father, the allotment king of the East End, lived vicariously through his son. *Mickey Kennet*, he'd brag in the pub, *you watch that name, it'll be famous one day . . . Yeah, but for what? Thieving?* someone replied, laughing.

But Mickey didn't need to thieve. His was a smooth ride to the top. Opportunities and luck had graced his career and although another man might have become complacent, he didn't. Some of the sweet shyness of his childhood stayed with him, a gentleness of spirit which encouraged confidences.

His shyness extended to women too. He could, in all honesty, have charmed most, but Mickey wasn't one for a quick seduction. The models and actresses he photographed he found fascinating, but there was a hardness about them, a metallic glamour which appealed to his intellect but not his heart.

'How much longer?' he asked the taxi driver, the man shrugging and staying sullenly silent as Mickey slumped back in his seat.

He would accept the job to photograph Grace Ellis because he had never been up to the North, and besides, he was intrigued by her. Was she the driving business-woman she appeared? The handsome effigy who had been photographed arriving and leaving court during the divorce, saying nothing, her eyes shielded by sunglasses, her head always turned away from the cameras?

Or was she more than she appeared? Certainly a woman who had defied convention needed to be two things – hard and honest. She had come from the industrial heartland of Lancashire, what did that make her, a tough piece? Or a down-to-earth woman who refused to court publicity? Either way, Mickey was curious to know.

When he finally arrived at his destination, the editor of *Lifestyle* told him that the magazine wanted photographs of Grace Ellis which would fit into the image of her as a beautiful rebel. If she's tough, they said, so much the better. We want strong shots, and try to get some pictures of her two sons.

The shoot was arranged for the following week. Mickey travelled up to the North and was hit by the dark gloom of Manchester when he arrived. Rain was falling – he had been warned of that – and the streets were full of depressed shops and waste spaces. It was even worse in Oldham, Mickey thought, driving through and only stopping briefly to take a look at the new factory.

The red-brick building was forbidding. Yet the huge gold Phoenix sculpture on the wall outside – the emblem of the comestic line – caught what there was of the daylight and made a powerful image. As Mickey walked round outside he could hear the sounds of the workers within. Their voices seemed curiously amiable amongst the bleak surroundings, and when he looked up a woman waved at him from a fire escape.

Memorizing the site as a place to take pictures, Mickey then drove out to Lydgate and was stunned by the solemn beauty of the place. The moors rose up autocratically behind The Lockgate, the long drive winding up to the house, regal at the top. Mature trees and bushes stood guard around the building, and only the sight of a child's bike gave a clue to the family who lived there.

Mickey was admitted and shown into the drawing room, the pale yellow walls and silk curtains as opulent as anything he had seen in London. If Grace Ellis had

come from nothing she had got her style from somewhere – unless she had called in an interior designer.
But something told Mickey that everything had been personally chosen. There were just too many photographs
of children, too many cushions and books to please a
professional's uncluttered taste. He was just looking at
a marble head of a man when he caught sight of a group
in the garden outside.

The rain had stopped and a woman was running with
her children, hooting with laughter, the bottom of her
trouser legs wet from where the grass brushed them.
The elder boy ran past her and she stopped, clapping,
then turned and picked up the smaller child, holding him
high up in the air. She was laughing, casually dressed,
her hair damp. This couldn't be Grace Ellis, could it?
Mickey thought, bewildered.

In that instant she saw him at the window, frowned,
then waved and ran in. A few minutes later she walked
into the drawing room. His first impression was one of
surprise. She had changed entirely, both in her clothes
and her demeanour. Fascinated, Mickey studied the
fine-boned face, the dark hair long to the shoulders.
In a pale blue suit and high-heeled shoes Grace seemed
utterly composed, her voice welcoming but wary.

'Hello. I'm sorry to have kept you waiting, Mr
Kennet –'

'Call me Mickey, everyone does.'

She smiled. 'Hello, Mickey. Have you been offered
something to drink?'

He nodded, pointing to the tray on the coffee table.
'I've been well looked after.'

'Good,' she said simply, glancing at her watch. 'I
suppose we should get started? Have you decided which
room you want to use?'

He hesitated, looking round and then glancing back to Grace. Her eyes were darkened with make-up, the look smoky. By her left eye was a small scar – what was that? he wondered. He would like to incorporate it into one of the photographs, the mark making the rest of Grace's face more perfect, not less.

'I was wondering about taking some shots at the factory.'

'Fine,' she replied, her gaze moving to his bag where he had tucked a copy of the morning paper.

If he asked about the divorce, she would dodge the issue, Grace had already decided. The same about Jonathan. In fact she would talk about her work – and nothing else.

'We could start in here,' Mickey went on, aware that he had somehow spooked her and anxious to make her comfortable again. 'This is a lovely room.'

Grace nodded, and then watched as Mickey took out his cameras and light meter. Then he took out a reflector and began to assemble them around the sofa. He was aware that she was studying him and felt self-conscious, clumsily knocking over a vase as he moved around.

'God!' he said. 'I'm so sorry.'

'It's nothing,' Grace replied, picking up the broken pieces.

'I'll pay for it,' Mickey said, hot with embarrassment.

'There's no need. I never liked it anyway,' she said sweetly, moving over to the sofa and sitting down.

Relieved, Mickey continued to set up the equipment and tried the light meter against Grace's face. The flash made her blink.

'It takes a bit longer, but I like to work alone,' he explained. 'I can't stand people doing things for me.'

'Problem delegating?'

'Something like that,' he agreed, relaxing a little and looking at Grace's face through the lens.

She looked back without fear or any vanity. As though she was looking at a person, not an object which would take an image for thousands of people to see and scrutinize. Surprised by her lack of ego, Mickey looked over the top of the camera.

'Do you want to check your make-up?'

'Do I need to?' Grace replied, frowning.

'No, No . . . I just thought that . . . most women like to check before I take their pictures.'

'I'm pushed for time,' Grace told him. 'Besides, I've seen your work and I like it. In fact, if these photographs come out as well as I think they will, I want to consider using your work to promote my range of make-up. I've been convinced,' she paused and smiled, 'that I should continue to be the model for my own products.'

'I think you should,' Mickey replied. 'Women like to see someone who looks real. Besides, with the story of your life and the background to the Phoenix Line it would be a selling point.' He paused, seeing her stiffen. God, what *had* he done? Why had he mentioned her life story? 'Look,' Mickey said, straightening up. 'I don't want to know anything, or try and trip you up. So relax. I just want to take a beautiful photograph of a beautiful woman.'

Diffidently, Grace smiled. 'I'm not beautiful.'

'Oh, yes you are. All truly beautiful women have the same quality you have – distance.'

'Distance is a useful quality for anyone.'

Her head was tilted slightly to one side, her eyes lowered as though she was thinking, totally oblivious to the camera. In a way, she *was*, Mickey realized. She had presented her face and kept herself remote.

He could have her eyes, her nose, her mouth, but nothing of her.

Only the previous day Mickey had spoken to the journalist who had done the interview and was amused to hear that Grace Ellis had answered none of the prepared questions. She had been charming and very forthcoming about the Phoenix Line, and her struggle to set it up and then recover it, but on her private life she had been silent.

Probing had got the journalist nowhere. Provoking Grace had done no good either. She was not prepared to talk about Simeon, Jonathan, or her inheritance of the Goodman fortune. Exasperated, the journalist had finally told her that it might not be enough for an interview. 'I'm sorry,' Grace had told her simply, 'but that's all there is.'

The session took a lot longer than Mickey intended because he was seeing something through his camera that he seldom saw. Vulnerability. This clever, handsome woman was scared of being hurt. He could identify with that, and after a while, Grace seemed to sense the empathy between them, relaxing and letting the camera take a little more than she would normally offer. She laughed, then looked ahead, then turned, the scar by her left eye showing white against the darker hue of her skin.

Mickey didn't try to charm her, just talked about his childhood and the box Brownie, knowing instinctively that she would be interested and not sneering. Childhood confidences passed between them like two children swapping sweets, Mickey only stopping when – to his amazement – he realized he had used up all his film.

'That's it,' he said, disappointed.

She stretched and stood up. 'You made it very easy, thank you.'

He didn't want to leave, to drive back to London. He wanted to stay and get to know her.

'I wondered if you would like to have dinner?'

The question caught Grace off guard.

'I don't think so.'

'I mean . . .' he stammered. 'I mean to talk . . . not . . . Oh God,' he said, flustered, 'I'm not what you think, not just some jack the lad. I really enjoyed this afternoon and I'd like to get to know you better. As a friend, nothing else.'

Grace studied his open face, the fine unruly hair, the kindness of manner. He was tall but slight in build, not at all the kind of man she had ever been interested in. He was also a lot younger than she, and she had no wish to make herself look ridiculous.

What would the papers say if they saw them having dinner somewhere? Even something so innocent would be blown up out of all proportion. *Look at that, Grace Ellis with a man so much younger than herself. Is she looking for more scandal?* Grace could imagine the gossip and yet she was sorry to refuse. She too had enjoyed the conversation, the friendship which had sprung up between them.

'I don't think so.'

Mickey was flustered, but not about to give up. 'We could go somewhere quiet.'

'That would make it look worse!' Grace laughed. 'My name is in the papers enough.'

'But, what about –'

'Mickey,' she said gently, 'I like you, but you're a lot younger than I am. Besides, I'm not looking for an affair.'

'Neither am I!' he replied, blushing, to his horror.

Grace saw the reaction and realized that she had misunderstood him. Maybe he wasn't thinking of her like that, after all. Confused and embarrassed, she stared at the floor like a school girl.

'I really want to see you again,' Mickey persisted. 'Could I come back later to talk to you?'

'Thank you for asking me, Mickey, but it wouldn't be a good idea,' she said, walking to the door. 'I really did enjoy meeting you, though, and I'm looking forward to seeing the pictures. Thank you for making it so pleasant.'

He stood in the doorway, stammering. 'But –'

'I have to go now. Bye, Mickey.'

Chapter Fifty-Two

No one believed it was platonic. Not even Joan, at first. Two days after Mickey had taken the photographs, he was back in the North, calling on Grace at the factory. She was surprised to see him and even more surprised to note that she was pleased.

Aware that they were being watched by everyone on the factory floor, Grace ushered Mickey into her office.

'You could have posted these to me,' she said, taking the photographs out of his hand.

'I know. But I wanted to see you again.'

Her hands shaking slightly, Grace looked through the pictures, aware of the buzz of speculation outside on the work floor. Why couldn't she have a photographer come and see her? she thought. Why did they immediately presume that there was something in it?

Taking in a deep breath, Grace pointed to one picture. 'It's beautiful.'

'They're all beautiful, because you are.'

She put up her hands in a quick gesture of dismissal.

'Oh, come on, Mickey. I'm too old and too wily to fall for a line like that.'

'It's not a line –'

'You shouldn't have brought these up here, you should have sent them.'

'We're already been through that,' he said patiently.

'All right,' Grace replied, confused by his attention and wanting to clear the air, 'I'll make it clear. I may appear to be something I'm not. I have a reputation, I know.' She paused, flustered. 'I might seem like I've been around, but I haven't. I don't have affairs, Mickey. I loved Jonathan's father and I still do. I don't want to have a fling.'

'Neither do I,' he said evenly. 'What happened to friendship? I don't need anything from you. I haven't come up here to try and get a notch on my belt. I'm not that type of man. I came back because I *like* you. It's as simple as that.'

She stopped short. 'Are you really offering me friendship?'

He frowned. 'Wasn't that what I said before? Look, tell me you don't need a friend now, a man on your side – without any hidden motives – and I'll go.'

Grace hesitated, still wary. She *did* want a man around, that was true. Aaron visited often, but he carried his sadness with him and it affected Grace. She had watched Joan with Tom, and Polly with Geoffrey, and she had longed for someone to come home to, to talk to. Sex was not important to her, but affection was, and though Grace had once believed she could give over the rest of her life to Daniel's memory she had come to doubt it.

'Yes,' Grace said at last, 'I could do with a friend. But people will talk, they always do.'

Amused, Mickey raised his eyebrows. 'Like you can't deal with the publicity?'

It was all over the factory by the end of the week.

'Having a fling with a younger man!' Ivy said, sucking on her upper set of dentures. They clicked as she talked. 'She never did care what people thought, did she?'

Fatter than ever, Enid jerked her head towards the office.

'I say good luck to her. It'll get back at her ex-husband, and no mistake.'

Even Joan didn't believe it was platonic.

'He's a friend to me.'

'You're kidding.'

Grace shrugged her shoulders. 'It's true.'

'Well, he's human and he's male,' Joan retorted. 'He'll want more one day.'

'Then again, he might not.'

'But if everyone thinks you two are having an affair, it seems as bit of a waste – I mean, all that gossip for nothing?'

Grace laughed, shook her head. 'I learned a long time ago that you can't put your hands over people's mouths. If they want to talk, they will.'

'And you don't care?'

'You were the one who was telling me I should find someone else! "Stop hanging on to the memory of Daniel," you said.'

Joan pulled a face. 'OK, OK, I did. But is Mickey Kennet the right one for you? He's young, from London, and you know so little about him.'

'And that,' Grace replied deftly, 'is why he's a friend and not a lover.'

There was a moment's pause before Joan spoke again.

'Of course, he might not fancy you.'

Grace looked up, stung. 'Huh?'

'Well, he might be being completely honest. He *might* just see you as a friend. An older woman –'

Outraged, Grace was on her feet in an instant. 'Who said he didn't find me attractive?'

Joan chortled to herself as she continued, 'But it

doesn't matter anyway, does it? Because you're not interested in him. Except as a *friend*.' She paused, mischievously to assess the effect of her words. 'It's nothing to be embarrassed about. It happens all the time. Older women are always finding young companions.'

'Have you quite finished?' Grace asked, her hands on her hips.

Joan nodded, walked to the door and then turned.

'I think you're being very wise, Grace,' she said with mock admiration. 'After all, there's no point looking for trouble, is there?'

Simeon entered the drive of The Lockgate and stopped the car. In the back seat Jonathan was talking to Richard, his head bent towards his half-brother. Simeon studied them through the rear-view mirror and felt an ache, a pinch to his heart.

It had all gone so bloody wrong, he thought sadly, as he leaned back in his seat. Why had he let go of Grace? She was three times the woman Elsa was, and now she was rich. Had the money to buy and sell him ten times over.

In fact, Grace was a remarkable woman, Simeon thought bitterly. So bloody remarkable that she had triumphed over him good and proper. First she had thrown him out, then she had managed to inherit a fortune and now – if the gossips were right – she had a new man in her life. A young man, a Londoner with all his hair, and no doubt very active in the bedroom.

It was enough to make any man choke! Simeon thought self-pitying. And now Elsa had given him the elbow – *Elsa James*, a tart who had obviously just used him to get back at Grace. And she had for a while –

until another man had come along. She had left a note for him, *a note*!

It was fun whilst it lasted, bye for now.
'See you on top of a bus,' she meant.

So now he was alone and hating it. In the space of a year he had floundered: the cosmetic business was teetering on the brink of collapse, his extramarital affairs had cast him as the villain in the divorce, and now Elsa had left him . . .

Simeon fingered the cleft in his chin and looked back to the children in the back seat.

'Jonathan.'

The boy looked up. 'Yes, Dad?'

Dad, Simeon thought. He *had* been a dad to this child. And he was a real father to Richard. He could never have believed how much he would miss them; how much he would think about them, yearn to hear their voices. How could he have walked away from them so easily?

'D'you want to go home?'

Jonathan put his head on one side: 'We are home.'

'I mean, do you want to stay with me for a bit longer?'

Jonathan considered the question carefully. 'Mummy's waiting for us.'

'I just thought we could go somewhere else. You know, do something else . . .' Simeon blundered.

Yet there were only so many things a divorced man could do with his children. Go to the circus, the zoo, the park. That afternoon he had taken them to the boating lake, but Richard had been fractious, out of sorts, wriggling out of his father's grasp. He was becoming a stranger to them, Simeon thought dully, and it was no one's fault but his own.

Through the rear-view mirror, he saw Richard yawn.

'We could go on holiday, the three of us,' Simeon said hopefully, turning round in his seat to look at them. 'In the summer. Would you like that?'

'OK, Dad,' Jonathan said simply, opening the car door and taking Richard's hand as he led him up the drive.

'Jonathan!' Simeon called after him, getting out and running over to the two boys. Suddenly emotional, he kneeled down, putting his arms round both of them. 'I love you.'

'Love you too,' Jonathan said easily, Richard rubbing his eyes sleepily.

'I'll come and see you again at the weekend,' Simeon went on. 'On Saturday.'

Jonathan nodded, then smiled. 'Have to go now, Dad. Bye.'

With a numb feeling in his chest, Simeon watched the boys walk to the front door and knock. A moment later they were let in, the door closing behind them. Clumsily he got to his feet and moved back to the car. He would *have* to get back with Grace. Back to his children. His family.

He stared at the house, self-pity and emptiness welling up inside him. He should have been a more attentive father, he thought regretfully. But he had been too consumed with bitterness to want to go near his family. He had wanted to punish Grace for not loving him and indirectly he had punished the children.

Now he was trying, belatedly, to make amends. *Because he missed them.* Being a bachelor again was hard, lonely work. He couldn't undo what was done, but he loved his son and his stepson and he had been mad to jeopardize that bond. Surely no one could just wipe that out as though it had never existed. Certainly not some London snapper trying to take his place.

Simeon looked at The Lockgate and felt depression overwhelm him. This was not his home. And never would be – unless he did something about it now.

Briskly, Simeon walked up to the front door and rang the bell, pushing past the housekeeper when she answered.

Alarmed, the woman called up to Grace, 'Miss Ellis! Your ex-husband's here.'

Jonathan had gone out to the garden but, seeing his stepfather come back to the house, had crept towards the library window. There he watched his mother walk in, her hands clenched behind her back as she faced Simeon. Jonathan couldn't hear what they said, but could see from his mother's face that she was angry.

It was certain that there was going to be trouble. There always was with his stepfather. In fact when Simeon had kept away for so long Jonathan had half hoped he would never come back, even though he had missed him at first. Besides, Simeon wasn't his father. His mother had told him about Daniel, and he had his real father's photograph in his room. Daniel Goodman had been fair, handsome, a man of importance – not this dark stocky man with his showy manner.

Straining to listen at the window, Jonathan leaned over the flowerbed.

'What d'you want?' Grace asked, facing Simeon with cold hostility.

'We were fools –'

'*You* were the fool,' she corrected him, walking over to the fireplace and putting one arm along the mantelpiece.

'Nice house,' Simeon said, trying to keep the bitterness out of his voice.

'Even nicer when you're not in it.'

'Hey, Grace!' he said pitifully. 'Don't let's fight. I've missed you. I wanted to see you.'

'Funny how you never wanted to see me when you left and set up home with Elsa James. When I was poor – in that house you so kindly left me. I couldn't afford the coal, Simeon. No coal to keep the family warm. It got so bad that I couldn't pass a cheque. I sold the jewellery and the paintings to keep bread on the table.' She paused to let her words sink in. '*You* did that. *You* pulled the rug out from under my feet by taking the business away. If the workers hadn't rallied round me I would have sunk.'

'I was wrong.'

'Wrong!' she shouted. 'You were a bastard! You were a pig to do what you did to me – but to do it to your children as well – that showed what kind of man you were.'

'I want to make it up to you,' Simeon said pathetically. 'I want us to try again.'

He thought for a moment that she was going to hit him, but then she laughed.

'*Try again!* I was mad to try it once with you, let alone a second time. Do you really think I'm so stupid? I know why you're here, Simeon. People talk; I hear all the gossip. Elsa dumped you and you're struggling with the business.' She waved her arm around the room. 'And I inherited all this. God, how that must stick in your craw! You thought you'd punished me and here I am, at the top of the midden.'

He had grown pale, the cleft in his chin a dark mark against the white skin.

514

'You can stop crowing!'

'You crowed long and hard enough over me,' she snapped. 'You and your bloody mistress had a high time watching me struggle. Well, it feels good to be on the winning side for a change, Simeon – and I intend to enjoy every minute of it.'

'With your lover?'

Her eyes fixed on his. 'Yes, *with my lover*,' she lied, watching Simeon wince. 'It hurts, doesn't it? Well, now you know what I went through when I found out you'd been sleeping around.'

'I haven't treated you well, I know,' he said helplessly, 'but I miss you all so much.' He took a step towards her, but Grace moved back. 'Let's try and talk this out.'

'Talk what out?'

'Us.'

'There is no us,' Grace replied, aghast. 'We're divorced now. You and me are over.'

'We don't have to be,' Simeon said, pleading. 'Grace, we could start again, build up the business –'

'Good idea, then you could steal it from me again,' she said sarcastically.

'But –'

Her patience snapped, Jonathan watching outside the window as his mother walked towards his stepfather.

'Just get out, Simeon! I don't want to see you again.'

'We have a son,' he said, his voice wavering.

'It took you a long time to remember that. I'm just glad that Richard was too young to know that you walked off without giving him a second's thought.'

He was desperate to convince her, to get things back to where they had been. 'I want to change now. Can't I come and see you when I see the boys?'

'You saw me for years, Simeon. You saw me day

in, day out. You saw me – and all the time you were seeing someone else. I know about three women, were there more?'

'It's the past.'

'It's *your* past,' she countered, 'and you have to live with it. But not me. I don't have to see you, or think of you for another minute.'

Thwarted, Simeon caught hold of her arm. Seeing Grace wince, Jonathan moved away from his spying place and ran round to the front door.

'You listen to me!' Simeon snapped, suddenly aggressive. 'You think you've got it made, well, maybe you have. But when two people get married they share more than a bed. They share secrets too – like your mother doing her Lazarus turn.'

'Leave her out of this!' Grace shouted, trying to shake him off.

He held on grimly, past reason.

'It would make a good story, Grace, another one to add to your press cuttings. "Grace Ellis's dead mother resurrected. Corpse in Leesfield Cemetery – who is it?"'

She stared at him, speechless. 'You wouldn't!'

'I would!' he snapped back. 'I would be doing a duty to society, exposing a fraud.'

'Dora's an old woman,' Grace replied helplessly. 'What possible reason would you have to hurt her?'

'Because it would hurt you.'

At that moment the door opened, slamming back on its hinges, Jonathan running in. Shouting, he threw himself against Simeon and slammed his fists into his stomach, Grace frantically trying to pull him off.

'Get out!' Jonathan screamed at the top of his voice. 'Leave my mother alone and get out!'

Angrily, Simeon pushed the boy away and then turned back to Grace.

'I mean what I say. You think about what I've said or I'll tell everyone your secret. The choice is yours.'

Chapter Fifty-Three

He hadn't needed asking twice. Only minutes after Grace
had phoned him, Mickey was in his car and heading for
the North. She had sounded distressed, almost incoher-
ent. God, he thought, was she all right? All she could
say with any clarity was that her ex-husband had been
round to see her.

'Will you come up?' she had asked Mickey.

'I'll be there as soon as I can. It's OK, I'm on my way.'

All the lights were lit on the ground floor of The
Lockgate, the house glowing from a distance at the
top of the incline of Lydgate. Driving quickly up to the
entrance, Mickey could see the outline of two women at
the drawing-room window, one holding a child.

'Are you all right?' he said, hurrying in to see Grace
holding Richard, Joan beside her. 'What happened?'

'Simeon came here this afternoon,' Joan said without
preamble. 'He threatened her.'

'With *what*?'

Slowly Grace came to her senses. Why had she called
Mickey? She had asked for Joan to come round, but
that made sense; Joan knew about Dora. But Mickey?
He was a virtual stranger.

'I don't know why I called you –'

Immediately, Joan chipped in, taking Richard from
Grace's arms.

'This little one needs to be in bed, asleep like his brother.
And when I've done that, I'll make us all a drink.'

Grace waited for the door to close and then stood, stupidly silent, in the middle of the room. Her face was drained of colour, her eyes flat. Alarmed, Mickey wondered if she was in shock.

'Is someone ill?'

'No,' Grace replied, wrapping her arms around her body.

'Then what is it?'

Without answering, she moved around the room, touching surfaces, and curtains. Moving, moving, restless. Her mind replayed every word Simeon had said, and all she could focus on was his threat to expose Dora. But how could she tell Mickey about it? She didn't really know him. He could be anyone, could rush away with the news and betray her. But she didn't think so, and besides, she was suddenly tired. Hours spent discussing the matter with Joan had been useless; neither of them could think of how to stop Simeon – but they knew they had to find a way or he would go ahead with his threat.

'Grace, talk to me,' Mickey repeated, instinctively knowing that she was having second thoughts about calling him. 'Don't you know that you can trust me?'

'No, actually I don't,' she said honestly.

He took the words full force, but didn't flinch.

'I suppose you're right. Why should you trust me? But when you were in trouble you called me. You can tell me anything and I won't repeat it. I'll just want to help you.'

'It's so complicated,' Grace said, sitting down and then getting up again, '. . . so complicated.'

He took her hand and led her over to the sofa. 'Talk.'

Quickly and concisely she told him the story of her mother's life, and supposed death.

When she had finished, Mickey took in a deep breath. 'Does your ex-husband know about your mother?'

'Of course he does. He was my husband. I confided in him.' Grace ran her tongue over her dry lips. 'He came back to see me this morning. Wanted us to get back together again. He's lonely, regretting what he did. When I told him there was no chance, he was furious. Then he threatened to expose my mother.'

'Oh Jesus,' Mickey said softly.

'Think about it. Dora's old now. The scandal would kill her. People would want to know *who* was buried in Leesfield Cemetery, under her headstone.'

'But she just assumed another woman's identity. She didn't kill her.'

Grace nodded. 'I know that. But she wanted to escape Dora Ellis for ever. She wanted to hide. *And I don't want her found.*'

'Maybe your ex-husband was just bluffing –'

Grace shook her head. 'Simeon wasn't bluffing. He meant what he said. A man who could repeatedly cheat on his wife, then try to ruin her by stealing her business is a man without any scruples. Oh, come on, Mickey, he would do anything.'

'But does he know where your mother is?'

'Just that she's in Ireland,' Grace replied, rubbing her forehead with her fingertips. 'But if he goes to the police, they would find her. The scandal would be all over the press. "Grace Ellis – the latest. Mother back from the Dead."'

Despite himself, Mickey smiled.

'What's so funny?'

'I don't think that even the press would guess that your dead mother had resurrected herself.' He paused, thoughtful. 'It would be a field day for the media.'

She winced, Mickey immediately shaking his head.

'That didn't mean that I was about to run off and sell your story. I meant that the press must never find out.'

'But they will when Simeon goes to the police.'

'*If* he goes.'

'He will.'

'Not if we stop him.'

Grace stared blankly at Mickey. 'How?'

'I don't know,' he admitted. 'but there's always a solution. We just have to find it, that's all.'

Grace didn't sleep that night, getting up repeatedly to check on the children and standing for a long time at the door of Richard's bedroom. He was very like his father, she thought, similar in looks and hyperactive . . . Her mind wandered. Mickey had gone off in a hurry and it was only after he had left that the doubts set in. What if he let her down? What if he was selling her story now?

No, she thought, he is a good man.

Softly, she closed the door of Richard's bedroom, glanced in on a sleeping Jonathan, and then moved back to her own room. Chilled, she sat on the bed, pulled the eiderdown around her and drew her knees up to her chest. If Daniel had been alive he would have known what to do, she thought. But Daniel was dead.

She wondered suddenly if Daniel had sent Mickey. God, she never let him rest, did she? Always calling Daniel back to help her. It wasn't right, she thought, glancing at his photograph. She should let him be. She had his son, his house, she had had the best of him. But she missed him.

A more practical thought followed. There had to be a way for Simeon's threat to be circumvented. But how? And why had she confided in a London photographer who was virtually a stranger? God, Grace thought, shivering under the eiderdown, she had been reckless. She would call Mickey in the morning and say that Simeon had retracted his threat. She would put him off the scent and then draw back gradually. Their friendship would never work anyway; he was too young and she was too vulnerable. A man of his age would make a fool of her if she – God forbid – fell in love with him.

Then all the demons closed in on her. They flickered against the ceiling, turning in and amongst all the memories. The night staggered on, passing the witching hours, the cold making Grace's limbs stiff. But she couldn't sleep.

She wanted to close her eyes and shut out everything. Life – which had seemed so very sweet at last – was bitter again. It was all Dora's fault. It had been Dora who had indirectly caused the rift between her and Simeon; and now here Dora was again, forcing her daughter's life into chaos.

But from a distance, always from a distance. Where are you? Grace wondered. Where are you? I can't phone you and I don't have an address. I can't reach you and unless I'm very lucky, this time I can't save you . . . God, Grace thought in desperation, if you *had* died it would be simple. No one could get at you, or at me. But she knew her mother was alive. And so did Simeon.

Chapter Fifty-Four

It was a chance for him to prove himself, Mickey thought. If he could help Grace now he would go up in her estimation. The problem was, how could he help her? He had thought about going to see Simeon Grant, and then realized that it would be a wasted mission. Grace's ex-husband wasn't going to listen to him – in fact, the visit might have the opposite effect and force him to act.

But how long was Simeon going to wait before he exposed Dora Ellis?

On returning to London very late the previous night, Mickey had called Grace and suggested that she phone Simeon.

'What!'

'Listen to me,' Mickey said firmly. 'We have to stall him, to play for time. If you do nothing, he'll carry out his threat, but if you look as though you might be thinking of letting him back into your life and the business –'

'The hell I will!'

'Grace, calm down,' Mickey said evenly. 'You have to play a game with him for a short while. We need time. And you have to get that by stringing Simeon along.'

'I don't like this.'

'Neither do I, but it's the only way. You keep Simeon Grant sweet – and I'll find some way to stop him.' What the hell was he promising? He had no idea how to stop Simeon. 'Talk to him, Grace. Ask him to give you a couple of days to think about your relationship.'

'Are you certain this is the right thing to do?' she asked. 'I don't want to let that man back into my house and my life –'

'It would only be for a short time.'

'Are you sure?'

Mickey swallowed, but kept his voice steady as he answered. 'Yes, I'm sure.'

In the world of dahlia exhibiting, Bert Jessop was a man to be reckoned with. Since he had retired three years earlier, he had turned his back on journalism and now spent his days at his bungalow in Southend with his wife, who disliked him, and two snappy Jack Russells, who didn't like him either. It was a shame about the dogs, but Bert didn't care whether his wife liked him or not, because he saw very little of her. His life – which had once been a rush from London to Paris, to Monte Carlo and back to Rome – was now tiny, petal-cushioned. He was a dahlia man and had cups to prove it.

He was also a retired tabloid journalist who had dealt in numerous murky scandals over the past four decades. At twenty-one Bert had been lucky enough to hear about some visiting actor who had bedded a transvestite. A scandal ensued and so did a contract – for Bert. From then on he wheezed his way through the scandals and grubbed for stories. His memory was prodigious; he could remember who had slept with, cheated, injured or left who – and had, in the past, put his recall to tremendous use.

Like most people who worked with journalists, Mickey had heard about Bert Jessop and remembered something the old pro had once said: 'Never make a threat, unless you have nothing to hide. And *who* has nothing to hide?'

It was a sound thought, Mickey realized, asking the picture editor of *Lifestyle* if he knew Bert Jessop's number.

Luckily the journalist had Jessop's number and address, and Mickey, instead of calling first, drove over to Southend on a long shot. What had he got to lose? Nothing. So he pushed open the low front gate and leaped back as two Jack Russells came careering out of the porch.

'Who the bloody hell is that?' came a deep voice, as Bert Jessop walked out to the front. He was wearing outsize flannel shorts and a battered Panama, which was dog chewed around the edges. 'What d'you want?'

Mickey kept to the other side of the gate as the Jack Russells barked furiously up at him.

'I wanted to have a word with you, Mr Jessop.'

'I've got my dahlias to see to,' he said, turning his bulk away. 'Bugger off.'

Determined, Mickey opened the gate, the dogs rushing at his ankles. Wincing as one made contact with the bone, Mickey hurried round to the back of the house. He was hot and flustered, his hair falling over his forehead, his shirt sleeves rolled up, his jacket over his arm as he tried to shake off the attached dog.

Grinning broadly, Bert watched him from inside his greenhouse.

'You really do want to see me, don't you? Dogs – SHUT UP!' he roared. The animals slunk away to lie in the shade. 'I bet that bite hurts.'

'Actually, it does.'

'Yes, bites do,' Bert replied, turning to his dahlias as Mickey limped to the doorway of the greenhouse.

'Mr Jessop, I've driven from London to Manchester, then from Manchester back to London, then from

London to here.' Mickey paused to rein in his temper. 'I'm tired and I need a break.'

'What do I look like? A travel agent?'

Still struggling to keep his patience, Mickey stared at Bert Jessop's belly overhanging his shorts.

'I came to see you because you've covered more scandals than anyone. Everyone knows that you heard all the gossip, all the things people wanted to hide. You were told things that other people never heard about.'

'So?'

'So what do you know about the Grace Ellis divorce?'

'She divorced that Simeon Grant bloke. I read about it in the papers.'

'What *else* do you know about her?'

'What everyone else does. All the scandal about Grace Ellis is on record. There's nothing else, or I would have heard about it.'

Mickey rubbed his ankle gingerly. 'What about her husband's mistress?'

'Elsa James? Just a two-bit whore. Ran around with Elmer Shaw for a while, but that was a long time ago.'

'Elmer Shaw?' Mickey asked, surprised.

Shaw was a known crook, had been in gaol, and then suddenly he was back in the money and running a hotel in Kensington. Rumour had it that Elmer Shaw was also into beating up women.

'He's a bit rough, isn't he?'

'Sure is,' Bert replied, pushing his bulk past Mickey and filling a bucket with water. 'I bet that dog bite's really beginning to hurt now.'

Mickey was getting to hate Bert Jessop.

'Is Elsa James back with Elmer Shaw?' he asked patiently, looking for any information he could use.

526

'Nah, she's too old for Shaw now. He's with some Chinese bit, and a few others. Shaw always likes to have plenty of women on the go.' Bert poured the water onto the nearest dahlia. 'Now I think about it, Grace Ellis worked for Elmer Shaw a long time ago.'

'What?'

'Yes, at his mill. I'm sure I read about it,' Bert replied, 'but Grace Ellis had her sights on bigger things – like Daniel Goodman. She goes and inherits the Goodman fortune because she had his bastard!' Jessop laughed harshly, 'Jesus, *that* is one lucky woman.'

Mickey was finding it hard not to punch Bert Jessop in his fat head. No wonder he had made a living by grubbing about in the muck. It was his natural habitat.

'Is it bleeding yet?'

'Look, just forget my bloody leg, will you?' Mickey snapped. 'I don't want to talk about it.'

'So what *do* you want to talk about?' Bert asked him, snipping the dead heads off one of his dahlias. 'What d'you want to know, Mr . . . ?'

'Kennet, Mickey Kennet.'

'OK, Mr Kennet – what do you want to know?' He paused, making mental calculations. 'It'll cost you.'

'I don't know if you've got the information I want yet.'

Bert smiled, showing his overlarge teeth. 'I'll have it. If it was scandalous, I'll know about it.'

'I want to know if . . .' *what* did he want to know? Mickey wondered, struggling, then rushing on, '. . . if you have anything on Simeon Grant.'

'Apart from all his affairs, you mean?'

'Everyone knows about those,' Mickey replied shortly. 'They were in the papers at the time of the divorce. Anything else?'

527

'He can be ruthless – but then Grace Ellis would know all about that, wouldn't she?'

Mickey was disappointed. 'Was none of Simeon's women suspect?'

'None of them was a murderer, no,' Bert replied drily. 'Now, if you were asking about Elmer Shaw –'

'But I'm not,' Mickey said wearily.

'No, but it's interesting that you're asking me about Grant, because Shaw and Simeon Grant had a connection a long while ago.'

'What?'

Bert wiped his sweating face with a handkerchief.

'Let me see, oh, this is years and years ago, when I was at the *Scope*.'

Mickey could feel his heart rate speeding up. 'What kind of connection did they have?'

'Give me a chance!' Bert replied, adding slyly, 'If I do remember, I'll want paying for this. Good fertilizer doesn't come cheap.'

And you should know about shit, Mickey thought.

'Ah, yes, it's coming back,' Bert said suddenly, sitting down on a rusty stool, the sun beating through the glass panes of the cramped greenhouse. 'Elmer Shaw – oh, this is in the late thirties – had a mistress. Well, he had a stable of mistresses, in fact. But he had one he liked real well.'

'What's this to do with Simeon Grant?'

Jessop shifted his bulk on the stool.

'Simeon Grant had come down to London from the North. You know, he was little more than a kid, believed all that stuff about how London streets are paved with gold, blah, blah . . . Well, he fell in with Elmer Shaw, acting as a gofer really. At that time Shaw was working for Theodore Armstrong in the rag trade. Amongst other things. Well, Armstrong was a bit iffy in the old days, but even he was wary of Shaw. Kept him on a short leash. Anyway, Armstrong hears that Simeon Grant – who's only a kid then, like I say – has gone all gooey over this girlfriend of Shaw's.'

Mickey frowned. 'Who was she?'

'Oh, she was *somebody*,' Bert said, smiling insidiously, 'It'll cost you fifty quid.'

'Fifty quid!' Mickey replied. 'That's steep.'

'That's my going rate, take it or leave it.'

Irritated, Mickey scrambled in his pocket and passed Bert Jessop the money.

'Now tell me.'

'Lilian Holmes.'

The name rang a bell in Mickey's head, but he couldn't quite place it.

'Lilian Holmes was a beauty in her day,' Bert explained, 'but she's in the back end of her fifties now. She's married to Charlie Holmes – I see that name means something to you.'

Mickey nodded. Charlie Holmes was a London crook, the sort who mixed with the likes of Elmer Shaw. But did he know that Shaw had had a thing going with his wife? Or that Shaw had shared the affections of Lilian with Simeon Grant?

'Now, Charlie Holmes is a very jealous man,' Bert went on, 'he always has been. He was crazy about his wife when he married her and he's never looked at another women. Trouble is, he thinks that his wife never looked at another man. But she did – *when she was engaged to him*. She looked at Elmer Shaw *and* Simeon Grant.'

Mickey stared into Jessop's sweaty face: 'Simeon Grant had an affair with Lilian Holmes?'

'Nah, he was just love-struck, innocent stuff. But Charlie Holmes wouldn't have understood that.'

'Did Holmes ever find out?'

'Grant's alive, isn't he?' Bert asked wryly. 'No, Holmes never found out, because Theodore Armstrong intervened; got Grant out of London and back up to his family in Manchester. Out of trouble fast . . . I remember Theodore Armstrong well,' Jessop said thoughtfully, 'a really hard man. No one could ever pin a thing on him, but Armstrong was up to some tricks when he was younger. Turned over a new leaf when he got old, so they say. But he always had a decent streak.'

'Can't you remember anything else about Simeon Grant?' Mickey said, pulling Jessop's thoughts back to the present.

He smiled slyly. 'Only that he wasn't known as *Simeon* Grant then.'

'What?'

'It'll cost you.'

Mickey shrugged. 'Naturally.'

'Simeon Grant was called Lawrence Grant then. But when he was shunted home to Manchester, Theodore Armstrong thought it would be a good idea for the lad to use his middle name from then on. God, this is years ago . . .' Bert said, wheezing and wiping his forehead with a handkerchief. 'So as Simeon Grant, he went back home and settled down to being a good boy –'

'But he was once Lilian Holmes's lover?'

'I've just told you that.'

'He wouldn't like that to be made public, would he?' Mickey said eagerly. 'I mean, Charlie Holmes wouldn't like it one bit. And people would wonder why the respectable *Simeon* Grant used to be *Lawrence* Grant and why he used to mix with some very suspect types.'

'It would look even worse if it came out that Grant had been sharing Lilian Holmes's affections with Elmer Shaw,' Bert laughed. 'Oh yes, that would finish Grant off. His business reputation would be in tatters – and Charlie Holmes would want to have a word with him too.'

Mickey frowned. 'So how come Grant's affair with Lilian Holmes stayed a secret for so long?'

'It just did,' Jessop replied, tapping the side of his nose. 'People *forgot* what they'd heard and Lilian got all respectable, the loving wife. Remember, both Shaw and Grant went up North, so they were out of the way. And there were only a few of us who knew about it when it happened. There was nothing to be gained by exposing them.'

'I suppose you were rewarded for keeping it quiet?'

Jessop shrugged. 'They were in business, I was in business. You work it out.'

Triumphant with what had heard, Mickey handed another twenty pounds over to Bert Jessop and watched him count it. It was a lot of money, but the information was worth every penny.

A few hours later, Simeon was watching the man in front of him. He tried to brush him off, but when he heard what Mickey had to say he hurriedly walked to the door and shut it. The mere mention of the name Lilian Holmes had been enough. How the hell did Mickey Kennet know about her? It had been years ago, when he was nineteen. Another lifetime. One he had no intention of revisiting.

'I suppose denying it would do no good?'

Mickey shook his head. 'No.'

Pouring himself a glass of water and sipping at it to wet his dry mouth, Simeon sat down behind his desk.

'You're Grace's little boyfriend, aren't you? A bit young for her, I would have thought.'

Mickey stood his ground.

'If you say a word about Dora Ellis, I'll tell every journalist I know about you and Lilian Holmes. Charlie was powerful then, but nothing like he is now. And besides, it wasn't just you and Lilian, was it?'

Simeon's face coloured,

'There was Elmer Shaw too. *Elmer Shaw*, of all people. You were a bit indiscreet weren't you, Mr *Lawrence* Grant? When you were young, that is.'

Simeon's dark eyes flickered. He was beaten and he knew it. News of the affair with Lilian Holmes and his connection with Elmer Shaw would ruin him. He might think himself hard done by now, but after that came out, he would be finished.

So who had told this *boy*? Simeon thought bitterly. This young man with all his hair, without a belly and so bloody chivalrous. A right little Lancelot, riding to the rescue of his Guinevere . . . Simeon sipped at the water. It was strange, but it wasn't the fact that he had been beaten that burned him so much, it was the fact that he had been beaten by a *child*.

He was getting older and slower, Simeon realized. You could kid yourself for only so long, and then there it was – slap in front of you. He had been smart, but Mickey Kennet had been smarter. The King was dead, long live the King. And now the new victor would get his prize – Grace. *Grace*, Simeon thought rancorously, who had been so cunning, so clever, who had lulled him into a false feeling of security.

Give me time, she had said on the phone. *I have to think it out, Simeon. About us, about our future . . .*

And he had fallen for it!

Smiling, Simeon drained his glass and then lifted it to Mickey in a mock toast.

'To the victor, go the spoils,' he said, letting the glass drop from his hand and shatter on the floor at his feet.

Chapter Fifty-Five

Weary and aching from the long drive, Mickey got out of the car at The Lockgate and rang the bell. Grace answered at once and led him into the drawing room. There he slumped into a chair, Grace sitting down and staring at him anxiously.

'I was waiting for you to ring me all day. They said that you were out when I called the *Lifestyle* office. What's been going on?'

He took the drink she offered him and smiled wearily.

'Your mother's safe.'

'What?'

'It's all over.'

Nonplussed, Grace kept staring. 'What have you done?'

'I've got Simeon Grant off your back for ever.'

'How?'

'I found out something about him which he wouldn't want known. Then I went to see him and confronted him. He realized that if he exposed your mother, I would expose him and he would be ruined. He knew he'd lost . . .' Mickey trailed off, triumph turning to dust in his mouth as he looked into Grace's face.

She was staring at him with disbelief. 'What did you do?' she said coldly. 'You went behind my back?'

'I thought –'

'You thought what?' she snapped, getting to her feet and looking down on him. 'That I had confided in you so that you could take over my life? So that you could ride out into the sunset and play the hero?'

He was shaken, embarrassed. 'Hey, I've sorted it all out, Grace.'

'You blackmailed him!'

'Christ, he was blackmailing you!' Mickey shouted back. 'Why did you ask for my help if you didn't want it? I did what I thought was right, what would please you.'

'You did what *you* wanted to do,' she replied. 'You did what you thought would make you look good in my eyes.'

'What if I did?' Mickey countered bluntly. 'It worked.'

'No,' she said, 'it didn't. You don't look good, Mickey, you look like a typical man. The one thing I didn't think you were. *You sorted it out for me* . . . Poor little me, the struggling, defenceless woman on her own. Did it ever occur to you that I wanted to sort this out *with you*? I thought that was what friendship was about?'

He was confused and angry.

'This is ridiculous! I can't please you whatever I do! I just wanted to help you. But you're not a real woman, Grace. The most important thing in your life is that you keep control. You mistrust men, because you won't let them act like men.' He stood up, facing her. 'I wanted to help you, and not just because I wanted to be a hero in your eyes. Yes, there was some of that in it, but it wasn't all. You *are* on your own, that's true, but you don't have to be alone. You accuse me of taking things out of your hands, but wasn't that what you wanted really? I acted like a man, because I *am* a man. I thought you were woman enough to understand that.'

'But I didn't want you to take over,' Grace said, her tone softening. 'That doesn't mean that I'm not grateful to you for what you've done.'

535

His voice was flat when he answered her. 'I don't want gratitude . . . You just don't understand, do you?'

'Mickey, I –'

He rose to his feet. 'You're not ready for friendship,' he said bitterly. 'Don't worry, I'll close the door on my way out.'

Chapter Fifty-Six

A month passed. Grace carried on with her life as she had done before, visiting the factories and making engagements in her diary to give talks. Charities were asking her for help, the newspapers for articles, and the local mayor requested the use of the garden at The Lockgate for the late summer fête.

It was a high warm day, all the worthies of Oldham invited, Frederick Conrad arriving with Emmeline in a wheelchair, the remaining Spencer sister being pushed in another wheelchair by her nurse. Every notable gathered in the grounds, mixing with Grace's workers and friends, the children mingling with the adults. Delicacies of all sorts were laid out on tables in the garden, Aaron talking animatedly with the local MP.

Jonathan had been invited to a friend's house in London the previous week. The holiday with Simeon had never materialized. It's good to let him go, Grace thought. He has to have friends his own age. But with Jonathan away, there was just her and Richard, and after she put him to sleep in the early evenings the hours dragged.

So Grace had intensified her work load to fill the loneliness. And soon she was at the factory more than she was at home, Polly attending to Richard in the day. Joan watched Grace with exasperation. Only rarely did she take days off – like today, the day of the summer fête.

Frederick Conrad had taken the day off too and was now pushing the arthritic Emmeline towards one of the serving tables. She was clutching a plate of food and was dressed in a summer outfit. Funny, Frederick thought, he had never thought of paisley as being sinister before.

'Mr Conrad,' the vicar said happily, walking over to Frederick and glancing down the gardens, 'isn't this a perfect day?'

'I want beef, not fish!' Emmeline said from her wheelchair. Irritated, she lifted her stick and jammed the end at a tray of nearby sandwiches.

'Just a moment, my sweet,' Frederick said patiently.

The vicar continued unperturbed: 'Wonderful weather, don't you think –'

'I want *beef*!' Emmeline repeated, an impaled sandwich now dangling from the end of her walking stick.

Frederick realized then that he had only to release the brake on the wheelchair and Emmeline would sail down the green lawn and into the lake beyond. He would miss her, but he could always have her stuffed like all the other old fossils in his office.

'I think that Miss Ellis has done us proud,' the vicar went on cheerily. 'Such lovely food –'

'I want some cake!' Emmeline snorted from her chair. 'Frederick! I want some cake.'

Both men looked down at her, the vicar's expression strained.

'You seem well, Emmeline. I said, you seem well.'

She gave him a bleak look, waving her stick in exasperation, the sandwich flying off the end and landing at the feet of a local JP.

In another part of the garden, Joan had been sitting under the oak tree in the shade. Relieved to have the kids off her hands for a while, she was watching the guests from a distance, smiling to herself as she noted Frederick Conrad rapidly alter the direction of his wife's wheelchair as Miss Spencer's approached. There had been an argument many years ago, about scones . . .

'What are you doing, hiding away?' Grace said, dipping into the shade beside Joan.

'Watching this lot,' she replied. 'And thinking . . . Are you *ever* going to contact him?'

'Who?'

'Don't bugger about! Mickey, that's who.'

'No, I'm not. What would be the point? It wouldn't work out.'

'You never gave it a chance,' Joan replied, turning away.

She couldn't believe what had happened. Taking into account all of Grace's troubles with men, to treat Mickey Kennet in such a way was a bit harsh. Grace had overreacted, slapped down a man who had helped her. It was downright cruel.

'I think you should call him and apologize –'

'Joan, no, I can't.'

'But Mickey got rid of Simeon for you. You should be grateful for that at least.' Joan smiled as Frederick Conrad doffed his hat to her. Reluctantly she turned back to Grace. 'That wife of his is frightening . . .' She changed back the subject: 'Simeon's not been round for weeks, thanks to Mickey. Not even to see the boys.'

'But –'

'The way you treated Mickey wasn't right!' Joan persisted. 'He deserved better.'

Smiling stiffly as the local doctor's wife passed by, Grace then gripped Joan's arm and led her behind the nearby marquee.

'Look,' she said furiously, 'I'm not having an argument in public.'

'Who said anything about an argument?'

'There's going to be one if you're determined to hammer on and on about Mickey Kennet. He tried to take over my life.'

'You let him into your life,' Joan retorted. 'Don't blame him for responding to a damsel in distress. Besides, it was incredible what he did. You should be grateful to him – and so should your mother.' She paused, gathering her courage. 'In fact, I've been thinking about Dora. You know, the real rift between Simeon and you started because of your mother.'

'Miss Ellis,' a voice said suddenly, the vicar materializing by Grace's side. 'I was just saying what a wonderful spread you've put on for us. To open your lovely home and gardens like this – so generous.'

Joan was about to move away, but Grace tightened her grip on her arm.

'It's a pleasure, Vicar. I'm glad to see you enjoying yourself,' she said blithely, waiting for him to walk off before she turned back to Joan. 'Now, *what* were you saying?'

Joan shook off Grace's grip on her arm. 'It was an argument about Dora which started the rot. Then, indirectly, she caused Mickey and you to split up.'

'That's not fair!' Grace snapped, then lowered her voice as she looked round. 'How did she know anything about what was going on? Did she know that she was in danger of exposure? Did she hell!'

'She never knows, does she?' Joan retorted sharply. 'Unless it happens to be one of those few times she chooses to come out of hiding.'

'Hey, watch it, Joan.'

But Joan was past the point of no return. 'Why? Dora has been hanging over your life like the Sword of Damocles. She left home. She was killed. Then she wasn't dead after all. She risked her safety to come and watch you that day in Manchester – but you saw her. Why, Grace? *Because she wanted you to.* Because she had picked her time.'

'Miss Ellis,' a woman said suddenly, walking over to Grace, 'I wanted to ask you about your azaleas –'

'What?' Grace croaked, then composed herself. 'Just give me a minute, will you? Then we'll have a chat.'

As the woman walked off, Joan continued heatedly, 'Dora always picks the time. *Her* time to leave, *her* time to confess, *her* time to come forward,'

'She wants to be in control of her life.'

'Sounds like someone else I know,' Joan muttered. 'Your mother will never realize what it cost you to protect her. Unless you tell her.'

'Really?' Grace countered. 'Maybe I'll write a letter and post it to her box number – *You were a lousy mother and I've messed up two relationships because of you. Love, Grace.*'

Joan pulled a face. 'But Mickey was a good friend. And he proved that.'

Grace threw up her hands in exasperation. 'I know.'

'So why don't you get in touch with him?'

'I can't,' Grace said quietly. 'I just *can't.*'

'Well, it's your choice! But your mother wouldn't have wanted any of this to happen.'

'I know she wouldn't,' Grace admitted, looking round at the people massing about. 'When I first came here I thought I wanted to be alone with Daniel's memory. But it was a fantasy. I loved him but he's dead – and I'm still alive.'

'Only just.'

A cloud passed over the sun momentarily and chilled them both.

'I want to live again, Joan. I want to stop going in and out of factories, filling my time, giving speeches. I'm sick to death of the smell of perfume and the sight of rouge. It's all show. I see those posters of my face and look at them as though I was looking at a stranger.'

'You're exhausted, that's why.'

'No, I'm *empty*,' Grace replied. 'I want to slow down, to go to sleep in a man's arms and make love. I want to be a woman again.'

Joan shrugged. 'So ring Mickey.'

'It's too late. I blew it.' Grace glanced away, looking down the lawns of The Lockgate. 'Anyway I never knew what he thought about me really. Whether it was just a friendship, or something else.'

'Have you ever wondered,' Joan said pragmatically, 'if he was thinking the same?'

Shaken by what had happened, Mickey had taken a couple of days off, and then extended it to a fortnight, cancelling his assignments. He hadn't understood what went wrong and was amazed that he had misjudged everything so badly. Was it arrogance that had made him act as he had? Or simply wanting to help?

He knew it was the latter, but somehow knowing it didn't make anything better. Packing up his cameras, he went to France and took some pictures, but there was no excitement in them. They were flat images, as deflated as himself. There were many young women who were willing to pose for him, but there was always something lacking in their faces. Experience, sadness, longing.

Yes, he thought, *that* was it. He had seen longing in Grace's face. So he was in love then? But how could he be? She was older than he, out of his league. He didn't feel that way about her. Or maybe he did. He didn't know.

Slowly, Mickey started to walk along the dusty track back to the village where he was staying in Brittany. Birds were flying low in a heavy summer sky, crickets chirruping eerily in the hedges. He had not phoned Grace – what would be the point? He had offended her, their friendship was over. *Their friendship* . . . He stopped by a hedge and lit a cigarette.

He was missing her – but that wasn't conclusive evidence. People missed their friends all the time. It didn't mean they were in love with them. She was a divorced woman, with children. She was famous, for God's sake. So what? Mickey had been mixing with well-known people for years. But this missing feeling was different. He felt compelled by her, intimidated, affected – and absorbed by her.

Oh God, he thought, I *am* in love . . . He walked on hurriedly, then remembered an old story about a woman who had cared for a man very much. Certain of him, she had asked if – when they died – he would want to go to heaven with her. No, he had replied, that would mean eternity.

Well, Grace, Mickey realized with astonishment, I would spend eternity with you. I would be puzzled and irritated and angry with you, but never bored. Yours would be the face I would want to wake up to; the body I would want to make love to; the heart I would offer my heart to.

He stopped walking suddenly, and sat down at the side of the road. *It was love.* There was no doubt in his mind any more. Nothing else hurt so much. Emptiness, deep and terrifying, clawed at his soul.

* * *

It had been a surprise, Dora had to admit. Of all the people in the world she had never expected to get a letter from Joan Cleaver. Or Joan Cox, as she now was. She had never liked the girl, had thought her common, but she had had to change her opinion. Joan had stuck by Grace for years, the friendship providing sustained stability, something she had never offered her child.

Ever resourceful, Joan had confessed in her letter that she had looked in Grace's diary for Dora's box number. Then she had written and asked Dora to phone her. Which she did the day she received the note.

'So,' Dora asked her brusquely, 'what do you want of me?'

'Just hear me out, will you?'

It took Joan nearly ten minutes to say everything. At the end she paused, then took in a deep breath. Dora had never known about the rift she had caused between Simeon and Grace, or that he had threatened to expose her. She hadn't known that Grace had broken up with Mickey Kennet because of her either. In fact, she didn't know anything about Mickey Kennet – except what Joan told her.

And she liked the sound of him. He was exactly what her daughter needed to oust the memory of Daniel once and for all, Dora thought. You love the living, not the dead.

'I didn't know anything about any of this.'

'I know,' Joan replied, 'but I thought that maybe it was time you did. You see, I know you've helped Grace out with money, but you owe her, Mrs Ellis –'

'Don't call me that!'

Joan flushed. 'Sorry . . . I was saying that you owed Grace something she's never had. Security.'

'You're blunt, I'll give you that.'

'Grace doesn't need you with her now, she needs a man. And this was just one too many romance which didn't work out.'

There was a long pause on the line.

'Leave it with me,' Dora said evenly, then rang off.

Seven o'clock, a soft evening, Grace lying down on the bed and dozing for a while. She had filled her days up entirely for the next four weeks, giving herself no time to think. Downstairs, Polly was making dinner for Richard. She would just doze, Grace told herself, and then she would get ready for the function she was attending that night.

The new range of powder was a *sensation*, the press reported, light on the skin and giving a natural glow. Grace thought of the photographs which had accompanied the launch, her face remote, the perfect image. Not real, not breathing, just promoting itself relentlessly. Looking out of windows, off the sides of buildings and buses. Saying – *look at me, I'm working, always working. My face is out there so that even whilst I sleep I'm working . . .*

Restless, Grace turned over, kicking off her shoes. She hadn't got to be bitter, she had a wonderful life. She had her children, her home, her business and her friends. That was enough for anyone, surely? But try as she might, sleep wouldn't come and, frustrated, Grace flung her arm across her eyes.

When the phone rang it came as a relief. Grace picked it up, expecting to hear Brian Lawley's voice. 'Hello?'

'This is Dora.'

Grace sat bolt upright at the words. 'Dora – how are you?'

'Angry.'

'What?'

'What did I teach you all your life, Grace? To be the best, to make the most of yourself. You could go to the top, I told you.'

'I did, I made it.'

'No, you didn't.'

Surprised by the unforeseen attack, Grace bridled. 'What do you know about it? You're never here. You only ring occasionally. You know next to nothing about my life.'

Dora smiled to herself; this was more like it.

'I meant for you to have a whole life, Grace. Not to become some working machine. You need someone around, a man to love you.'

'I *did* have a man!' Grace snapped. 'I had him and I lost him – because of you.'

'I heard all about it from Joan,' Dora replied evenly, 'and as for losing him, that was your choice. Don't you try to put the blame on me, Grace. I'm not taking on that guilt. I've got enough to carry. Did you care about him?'

'Yes.' Grace said sullenly. 'I think I did.'

'Did you love him?'

'Yes . . . But he's angry with me and he's gone now.'

'Then go after him,' Dora replied. 'Don't give up. You never do in your business. This man fought for you, Grace – and for me, if it comes to that. You have to return the compliment now and fight for him. I didn't raise a weakling. You weren't a puny child, and you're not throwing in the towel now. Get him, Grace – before some other woman does.'

Chapter Fifty-Seven

He was still abroad, they said at the *Lifestyle* office. Not due back for a while. Grace held on to the receiver tightly, fighting the shake in her voice.

'Do you know where he's gone?'

'No, just that he's in France somewhere.'

Grace sighed. 'When he gets back, will you tell him that I called? It's Grace Ellis, from the Phoenix Line.'

'I know who you are, Miss Ellis, I'll get Mickey to call just as soon as he returns.'

The day wore on and then the week. There was no call. Grace thought about telephoning again, but was certain that Mickey would have rung her if he had returned to England. He *would*, she told herself, he would. Then the doubts set in. Maybe she had overplayed her hand? Maybe he wasn't interested in her any more? Or maybe he was simply playing games, making her wait until he chose to ring? If he ever did.

It was unbearable! Grace thought, getting up from her desk and picking up some colour charts. She had to think of something else or she would drive herself mad. Slowly she studied the charts. She would have to talk to Brian Lawley and hire a couple more women for the night shift. The factory was so busy now.

The people who had stuck by her had been rewarded. Polly and Geoffrey had their own house, and Joan and Tom had bought a car. He was happy in his work in the accounts office of the Goodman's Failsworth business, and Grace had already tipped him for promotion at the last board meeting.

Her watch must have stopped, she thought suddenly, tapping the dial. No, it was working, it was just that time had obviously stalled ... Restlessly, she paced the office floor. She had never suffered like this before, never been so much in love since Daniel. And she had been sure of Daniel.

But she wasn't sure of Mickey. It had been days since she'd tried to call him and he hadn't called back. She would leave it another week and then presume that he wasn't interested in her any more ... Oh, but she couldn't do that, Grace thought, laying down the colour charts and pacing again. She *would* phone again. He might not have got the message. Yes, that was it, he had never got the message.

Of course he had! she told herself. Just relax. Get on with your work and he'll call. He's a friend, he'll call. Just relax ...

Breathing deeply, Grace walked out onto the corridor which looked over the factory floor below. Seeing Enid come on shift, she waved.

'Like the new packaging, Miss Ellis,' Enid shouted over the blaring radio. 'Our Kate's got some of that powder for the Co-Op dance.'

Beside her, Tilly was smiling shyly, her hair freshly permed. She had met a new man and was courting.

'Our Tilly's fella's coming to meet her off work tonight,' Ivy said, walking past with a tray of tissues, her dentures clicking. 'Unless I'm much mistaken, I feel a wedding coming on.'

And surrounding them all, Grace could hear the steady *hush, hush*, of the packing machine.

It seemed suddenly that she went back in time to those

long years ago at St Andrew's Place. Those had been the days when her father was still alive, and Don Clegg, both now dead and buried in Leesfield. Those had been the days before war broke out. Grace thought of Aaron, now writing about his wartime experiences. And thinking, always thinking.

Solar had had to retire, finally too stiff with rheumatism to work. Grace had seen to it that he was looked after and his share of the profits went into the Oldham Bank monthly and paid for his nursing. So many people, Grace thought, so many lives. Like Geoffrey's . . . Suddenly she thought of him the night before he'd gone to war, how he had slept in her arms and how she had accompanied him to the train station to wave him off.

It had just been a kindness, that was all, but if she hadn't gone that morning Daniel would never have seen her; he would never have taken Geoffrey under his wing and started to write to a girl back home. A girl he came to love, a girl who bore his child and who cried for him when he died.

And then there was Joan . . . The packaging machine continued its soothing, rhythmic beat as Grace looked down at the factory floor and saw Joan. Joan, who had fallen in love with the boy next door. But not *her* next door, *Grace's* . . . The memory was as clear as yesterday. Tom coming home and Ernie Cox smoking his pipe. Ernie Cox, who could diagnose everyone's illness but his own.

'Must have felt bloody cheated,' Joan had said when he died. 'Fancy missing out on your own pneumonia.'

All in all, it had been a good run, Grace thought . . . She leaned on the guard rail, glancing round slowly, remembering. Elmer Shaw and Elsa James. Elsa James, with the face of a statue and the heart of a stone. Elsa James, always trying to get one over on Grace, running after the men her rival never really wanted.

Like Simeon. The father of Richard, stepfather of Jonathan . . . The packaging machine juddered, then restarted itself. A dance band tune was playing loudly on the radio, Enid throwing back her head and laughing . . . And then Grace remembered Lucy Goodman. She had been beaten in the end, forced to give over the business empire to Grace, an empire which would be passed on to Jonathan, Daniel's child . . .

The dance tune was coming to a climax, Mary Wells scowling as she struggled to tape up a box, Ivy washing her hands at the sink, Enid still laughing fit to burst. And at the end of the factory, high on the wall, the gold emblem of the Phoenix caught the late summer light . . . It had been worth all the heartache, Grace thought suddenly. I wouldn't have changed a thing. In the end, it didn't *really* matter if Mickey called her or not. She would like to hear from him, but if he didn't phone, she'd survive.

Moving back into her office, Grace picked up her coat and walked to the exit.

'Part-timer!' Joan called after her. 'Where are you off to?'

'I'm going for a walk. I want to stretch my legs for a while.'

'Yeah, well, don't forget you have a meeting at six with the accountant,' Joan reminded her. 'And it's Georgia's birthday on Saturday, so we all expect you at the house.'

As she left the factory the sun felt warm on Grace's face, although the real heat had gone out of it. It would be folding down to autumn soon, soft days and those misty mornings up at The Lockgate. She would think about taking a holiday, Grace thought, somewhere with just her and the children. It would do them all good. She would finish off her engagements next month and they would go abroad. The boys would like that at Jonathan's half term; it would be a novelty for them. Yes, Grace thought, pushing her hands deep into her pockets, they would all enjoy a change.

Then a sudden camera flash made Grace flinch, her hand automatically going over her face, her eyes blurred with the light.

'What the hell . . . ?' she snapped, trying to focus. 'Who's that?'

'I needed some new shots, Miss Ellis. The others didn't do you justice.'

Slowly Grace's eyes cleared – and then she saw him: Mickey standing on the pavement in front of her, a camera in his hands.

'Go on,' he teased her. 'Smile for the camera.'

She ran towards him, Mickey backing away, taking pictures all the time, both of them laughing.

'Mickey!' she shouted. 'Mickey, you came back!'

'Hold it right there,' he told her, moving towards her and staring into her face through the lens. 'Miss Ellis, you are quite beautiful.'

She could hardly speak. 'Only because you take such good photographs, Mr Kennet.'

'Did you miss me?'

She nodded.

'Miss your old friend?'

She nodded again. He kept taking pictures.

'Did you miss me, Mickey?'

'Well, I came back.'

Her heart was hammering, flashbulbs going off around her.

'As what? What did you come back *as*?'

He put aside the camera momentarily, kissing her softly on the lips, then drawing away again.

'Smile.'

'Aren't you supposed to say *cheese* or something?' she said, looking at him through the camera lens. 'You're supposed to *coax* a smile out of your subject.'

'Really?' Mickey said, clicking away. 'What should I say?'

She shrugged, grinning like a child. 'I don't know. Say anything. Say what you want, Mickey.'

'I love you,' he replied.

Then the last flashbulb burst around them and caught the moment forever.